A SONG OF COURAGE

RACHEL WESSON

Storm
PUBLISHING

Copyright © Rachel Wesson, 2024

The moral right of the author has been asserted.

Ebook ISBN: 978-1-80508-225-5
Paperback ISBN: 978-1-80508-227-9

Cover design: Debbie Clement
Cover images: Shutterstock

Published by Storm Publishing.
For further information, visit:
www.stormpublishing.co

ALSO BY RACHEL WESSON

The Resistance Sisters

Darkness Falls

Light Rises

Hearts at War (WWII)

When's Mummy Coming?

A Mother's Promise

WWII Irish Standalone

Stolen from Her Mother

Orphans of Hope House

Home for Unloved Orphans (Orphans of Hope House 1)

Baby on the Doorstep (Orphans of Hope House 2)

Women and War

Gracie Under Fire

Penny's Secret Mission

Molly's Flight

Hearts on the Rails

Orphan Train Escape

Orphan Train Trials

Orphan Train Christmas

Orphan Train Tragedy

Orphan Train Strike

Orphan Train Disaster

Trail of Hearts – Oregon Trail Series

Oregon Bound (Book 1)

Oregon Dreams (Book 2)

Oregon Destiny (Book 3)

Oregon Discovery (Book 4)

Oregon Disaster (Book 5)

12 Days of Christmas Coauthored Series

The Maid (Book 8)

Clover Springs Mail Order Brides

Katie (Book 1)

Mary (Book 2)

Sorcha (Book 3)

Emer (Book 4)

Laura (Book 5)

Ellen (Book 6)

Thanksgiving in Clover Springs (Book 7)

Christmas in Clover Springs (Book 8)

Erin (Book 9)

Eleanor (Book 10)

Cathy (Book 11)

Mrs. Grey (Book 12)

Clover Springs East

New York Bound (Book 1)

New York Storm (Book 2)

New York Hope (Book 3)

*Dedicated to Ida and Louise Cook,
who showed the world ordinary women
can do extraordinary things.*

'You never know what you can do until you refuse to take no for an answer.'

Ida Cook

ONE

LONDON, FEBRUARY 1933

Constance Fitzwalter poked the fire, sending sparks and the scent of burning firewood – a combination of earthy pine and aged oak – into the air. She watched the wood crackling and popping, the brilliant orange and crimson flames roaring up in the blackened hearth. At a tut of annoyance from her mother, she reluctantly returned the poker to its place and settled back into the comfy worn leather armchair. Glancing at the clock, she saw the hands had barely moved. Time seemed to stand still: there was still an hour to go before they had to leave for the opera.

The Tiffany lamp cast the room in a soft flickering light allowing her mother to work, hunched over a wooden embroidery hoop that cradled a delicate piece of linen stretched taut. Connie watched her mother with affection as, with an air of quiet concentration, she meticulously embroidered one of a set of chairbacks.

Connie rubbed the tops of her fingers, feeling every needle prick from the days she'd spent trying but failing to master the skill her mother made look so easy. She hadn't been gifted with any creative abilities; they had passed to Dottie, who was not only a skilled dressmaker but also an accomplished writer.

Connie closed her eyes. Mother said everyone had a gift but Connie was still waiting to discover hers. She got on with her job at the Civil Service, living for those evenings when she could indulge her true passion: opera. She thought of the last time they'd seen the amazing Elana Bernardi. Her incredible portrayal of the innocent and vulnerable Gilda, Rigoletto's daughter, had captivated both her and Dottie. Connie brushed her cheek, remembering the tears that had fallen as Elana's crystal-clear soprano voice had carried them away, especially during her rendition of 'Caro Nome'. Dottie had gripped her fingers so tightly Connie had bruises for a week, but she hadn't cared. They'd returned to the opera night after night.

She became aware that her mother was chatting away to her. 'I like the way you've styled your hair. I was worried you would cut it too short, but shoulder length suits you, and the fringe highlights your green eyes. Constance, are you listening to me? What are you thinking about?'

Her mother's voice dragged Connie back to the reality of the sitting room. She opened her eyes to see Mama looking at her questioningly. 'Sorry, I was miles away, reliving Elana's performance of Gilda. Mama, it is so easy to say someone has stage presence, but you must see her performance to believe it! She had us all believing she was the young, innocent daughter of the clown, Rigoletto. I completely believed she was in love with the duke, her acting is that good.' She sighed. 'I wish we'd insisted on you accompanying us to the performance, then you would understand what I mean.'

But Connie knew that if their mother had been with them, they wouldn't have waited at the stage door to ask for a photograph. Miss Bernardi and her husband, Mr Sterling, had been so kind, not only posing for photographs but telling them they recognized her and Dottie from their attendance at so many performances. For someone so talented, the famous soprano had treated them as if they were her closest friends, chatting to them for several minutes. And when her husband had chided her gently, saying they would be late for their supper, the look of love the couple had exchanged had Connie wondering if she would ever find someone like that in her life?

Feeling her mother's gaze, she glanced at her. Her mother couldn't hide her bemused expression.

Connie leaned forward in her chair, unable to contain her enthusiasm. 'You know opera isn't just about the music – it's the whole story, the acting, the chemistry that exists on stage between amazing singers. I simply can't wait to see her play the part again when—' She stopped herself just in time. Her mother didn't know about their plans to go to America, and this wasn't the right time to tell her. Connie knew she wouldn't be happy that her daughters were going abroad for the first time, and to New York, of all places.

Dottie had been just as surprised when Connie had told her that they would go to see Elana on Broadway. They'd been distraught after reading in the newspaper that their favourite soprano would no longer travel abroad but had decided to only perform in America. Connie had declared: 'Well, if she can't come to London, we will just have to go to New York.'

Dottie, shocked for a couple of seconds, had nodded and then grabbed her hands and they'd danced around the sitting room. It might take them years to save the money to get there but they were both determined, and between her job at the Civil Service and Dottie's earnings from writing, they already had half the money saved.

But now wasn't the time to tell their mother.

Connie's foot tapped on the wooden floor, her excitement bubbling like a recently poured glass of champagne. Her eyes darted to the door but it remained closed. She fancied she could hear the *tap tap* of her sister's typewriter on the other side. If

Dottie was caught up in a scene, Connie could be waiting all evening. Her fingers drummed a rhythm on the armrest before she jumped to her feet, startling her mother.

'Constance, what *is* the matter with you?'

Her mother pierced her with her deep blue, almost violet eyes, a look that had sent Connie and her siblings running for their bedrooms when they were children.

'Sorry, Mother, I didn't mean to startle you. I'm just worried we are going to be late.'

Connie walked over to the door, opening it and called to her sister, who was busy writing in the poky little room Dottie called her study. 'Dottie, are you ready yet? We'll miss the best seats if you don't hurry up.'

Dottie didn't look up, frowning intently at her typewriter as she tapped the keys feverishly. 'Coming. I must finish this last paragraph.'

Reluctantly closing the door once more, to save her mother from a draught, Connie returned to her seat, throwing herself down into it and staring into the fire to distract herself from her restlessness. Her mother said it was her red hair that caused her lack of patience, but her mother didn't seem to be similarly afflicted.

'What are you going to see tonight, Constance?' Her mother put the sewing hoop to one side, her wedding ring glinting as she ran her hand over her auburn hair, now lightly streaked with traces of silver, smoothing back the wisps that had escaped from the neatly coifed bun at the nape of her neck. 'Is it *Rigoletto* again?'

Connie shook her head. 'No, Mama, tonight we are going to see *La Traviata*. Would you like to come with us? There are sure to be seats.'

'No, thank you, darling. My opera days are over.' Mama glanced at the fire before muttering, 'I wish we could afford to send you in style.' She stared into the fire, and Connie knew her mother was thinking of a time when she'd once enjoyed going out to the opera or to dine with old friends. Connie could remember the thrill of seeing her mother dressed for a night out in long satin gowns and white gloves, discreet diamonds adorning her earlobes; the look of adoration as she gazed up at the tall figure of her husband.

Connie blinked at the familiar dart of pain memories of Papa evoked. The times of bright satin dresses and diamonds were only memories now. Her gaze travelled over her mother's tailored skirt and blouse in a muted shade of purple, the only adornment a simple brooch gracing the lapel of her blouse.

'Don't fret, Mama. I would sit on the roof so long as I got to watch. I don't mind. Neither does Dottie.'

Her mother turned to stare at her. 'Dorothea, dear. It is quite common to call your sister by that name.'

'Sorry, Mama.' Connie apologized automatically. She loved her mother, who had a heart of gold, but she lived in a bygone age and could never understand her daughters' modern ways.

The Great War had destroyed her father's health. He had returned, but he was never the same. He had died an old man at the age of fifty in 1931, a year or so after the financial crash that had taken away his last hopes for the future.

Still, Connie considered themselves lucky. They had the London townhouse, left to Connie and Dottie by their maternal grandmother. As it wasn't an asset of the estate, it therefore hadn't fallen into the bailiffs' hands. In addition to the house, they had a small annual allowance. It wasn't much, but they muddled through with the help of a part time cook and maid. They were rich in comparison to the many servicemen who had returned from the war to find there were no jobs for them. Even now, fourteen years after it had ended, you could still see ex-servicemen begging on the streets, an empty sleeve or a wooden leg highlighting the enormous price they had paid for everyone's freedom.

She sensed her mother's sadness and tried to bolster her mood. 'Mama, would you like to listen to some music? I bought a new phonograph. I think you would like it.'

'No, thank you, dear. I shall have an early night. I didn't sleep well and am feeling my age. Have a good time.'

'Thank you, Mama.'

The door to the sitting room opened as Dottie walked in looking ready to go, her blonde hair arranged in a tidy bun, carrying a brown envelope in her hand, an expression of relief on her face. 'I can drop this manuscript in on our way.' She laid it on the table before turning to look in the mirror. She buttoned her coat and adjusted her hat. 'Alicia said she would have a read first, before I submit it to the agent.'

Thank goodness for Dottie's old schoolfriend, Alicia. Connie didn't think she could read the story again. Not after reading it four or five times already. Romance wasn't even her genre. She much preferred to read tales of espionage – give her a John Buchan or a Leslie Charteris any day of the week. Or even an Agatha Christie.

Connie jumped up and put her coat and scarf on, then hurriedly kissed her mother goodbye. Taking Dottie's arm in hers, they left the house and started walking towards Covent Garden. She pulled her scarf tighter around her neck, shivering at the difference in temperature. Briefly tempted to get a cab, Connie pushed that thought away. It wasn't a long walk, and they needed to save their money for America.

The sisters had agreed to save half of what each of them earned straight away into their American fund. They took every opportunity to save money, taking packed lunches to work rather than splurging on a café. Tea and a currant bun in Lyons' Corner House became a luxury, a treat every month instead of every week. But all the sacrifice would be worth it.

Connie tucked her hand further under her sister's arm.

'The smog's bad tonight, isn't it?' They hurried along, taking care to avoid other pedestrians, as well as lampposts.

'Shall we wait for the bus? It might be safer.' Dottie looked around as if the bus might appear any minute.

Connie shook her head. 'It won't take long if we walk, and we can save the bus fares. I almost told Mama about us going to America just now.'

Dottie glanced at her, her hazel eyes full of concern. 'I thought we agreed to wait until we had most of the fare saved, to show her we are serious. She doesn't like us taking the train to Brighton alone, never mind going overseas.'

'We did. I was telling her about seeing Elana in *Rigoletto* and it almost slipped out. I nearly told her about writing to Elana too, to tell her about our visit. I wish she'd reply.' Connie hesitated before adding, 'But we will go anyway, won't we? I mean, even if she doesn't answer us?'

Dottie didn't answer, her gaze focused on the path ahead.

Connie's stomach churned. Had her sister changed her mind? She couldn't go alone to New York. And, anyway, it wouldn't be the same without Dottie.

'What is it?' Connie asked, taking care while crossing the road. It wasn't unheard of for pedestrians to be knocked over in the smog.

'Don't be angry, but I'm a bit scared by the thought of crossing the ocean. After what happened to the Armstrongs and everything.'

Connie squeezed her sister's arm. Trust her to think about their parents' friends, who had gone down with the *Titanic* in 1912. 'Cross-Atlantic travelling is much safer now, thanks in part to what happened. It's just as safe as negotiating London in this smog.'

Dottie grimaced as the first drops of rain fell. 'Hurry up before we get soaked.'

The sisters walked faster.

'Do you have the camera?' Dottie asked, after a moment.

'Of course.' There was no point in expecting Dottie to remember to bring it. Her sister spent too much time with her head in stories, dreaming of true love. Connie considered herself much more practical-minded.

Before they had purchased the camera, they had waited in line for autographs from famous singers. Now they asked the stars for their photographs, and most obliged.

'Don't we have the best lives?' Dottie huddled closer to Connie's side as they made their way to Covent Garden.

Connie didn't respond. She was grateful for the life they led, which allowed them the luxury of going to the opera. But, of late, she was aware of suffering from a lack of contentment. She realized she was bored with her work, and if it wasn't for the plan to visit America, there didn't seem to be much point to her life. Somewhere deep within her she felt a longing for excitement. For adventure. To travel and see something of the world. They had only been as far as the coast.

She caught the anxious look on Dottie's face. Her sister worried about everything. She quickly sought to allay her concerns. 'I will like our life even better when we reach New York.' She gave a little cry. 'Look at that queue! We better get a move on.'

TWO

Connie pushed Dottie ahead of her as they stepped into the foyer. The queue had moved fast. She passed over the coins and, taking the tickets, handed one to her sister. Leaving their coats in the cloakroom, they entered the auditorium, Connie's heart quickening with excitement. The lights were about to dim, and the orchestra was tuning up, sending a shiver of anticipation through her body as they settled into their seats. She glanced around, wondering if any of their friends were in attendance tonight.

She noticed Dottie was rather quiet again. 'You're not still worrying about the crossing, are you?' Connie whispered.

'No.' Dottie flushed. 'Not really. But what if we're not able to go? We haven't made great progress on our savings.'

Connie frowned. 'Dorothea Fitzwalter, that's quite enough of that. We are going. You can be sure of it.' She settled herself in her seat. 'When you sell your book, we are going to put that money straight into the savings account. I have been saving as much as I can out of my salary. Why don't they pay female civil servants as much as men?' But even as she made the comment, Connie knew it was pointless to talk about the unfairness of her pay. It was accepted: men earned more than women. Nothing was going to change that.

As the audience took their seats, Connie looked up at the occupants of the boxes, the women in their finest evening gowns, jewels sparkling like stars at their ears, necks and wrists, accompanied by sophisticated-looking men dressed in black tie. Although she wasn't sitting among them or wearing fancy clothes, she felt part of their world. *Our world*, she corrected herself. Because it was a shared world, one only a true opera lover could appreciate.

She listened to the buzz of conversation, the rustling of programs, her stomach bubbling away again in the knowledge that soon, in seconds, they would be transported to another century.

As the music started, the melody sent chills through Connie's arms. She inhaled sharply as the curtain rose, transporting them to a world of glamour and intrigue among the sumptuous ballrooms, the ladies wearing elegant gowns with daring décolletage, their blushes spared by elaborate ruffles or lace. The men looking just as dandified in their black tailcoats, vividly embroidered waistcoats, black trousers and pointed shoes. Connie sighed in appreciation as the soprano, playing the TB-stricken heroine, Violetta, carried the audience away into the story. She leaned forward in her seat, eager not to miss a second of the love story between Violetta and Alfredo playing out as if it were real life. She wiped away tears as the tragic Violetta risked everything for love, ending up betrayed by both her lover and society.

Dottie gripped her arm as the music rose to a crescendo, and when Connie glanced at her, she could see her sister's eyes glistening with tears. They both held their breath, focusing on nothing but the soprano on stage as Violetta begged for forgiveness and redemption. Connie's heart beat faster, her breath forcing its way from her chest despite the fact she had seen the opera many times before, and knew the story.

The whole audience appeared to feel the same as, when the last note died away, the opera hall erupted with thunderous applause. Connie joined in, jumping to her feet, clapping till her hands hurt, feeling bruised but emotionally satisfied.

'Wasn't that just wonderful?' Dottie turned and beamed at her. 'I so wanted Violetta to survive.'

Connie smiled. 'I did too. It was as if I was seeing the story for the first time!' It was still miraculous to her that music could give her the experiences she longed for; she could be transported to other worlds, from ordinary London life to Paris. She sank back into her seat, content to watch as the audience moved toward the exits. This was her world; this gave her existence its meaning.

THREE

LONDON, JULY 1933

Connie closed the front door behind her as she dashed out. She was late for the office.

'Morning, Miss Fitzwalter. I have a letter for you, from America, and the usual ones for your mother.'

Connie tried to curb her excitement, waiting patiently on the doorstep as the postman rooted in his bag, resisting the urge to snatch the letters from him. He handed over a couple of envelopes before tipping his cap and heading back to his route.

Connie turned back, opened the door and placed her mother's post on the hall table before she opened her envelope very carefully, not wanting to spoil its appearance.

Yes! Inside was a letter from Elana Bernardi. She put a hand over her mouth so she didn't scream and wake their mother. Not caring now that she would be even later for work, she tiptoed back up the stairs, and woke Dottie.

'Elana wrote to us! She's promised us tickets for all her appearances in America! That means we don't need as much money as we thought.' Connie pinched herself to see she wasn't dreaming. 'She really wants us to go and see her.'

Dottie took the letter and, as she read it for herself, her eyes widened with excitement. 'She sounds almost as excited as we are. Isn't this just marvellous? To think she wrote! To us.'

Connie glanced at her watch. She was really late now. 'I have to run, but when I get back we must tell Mother. The postman may mention a letter from America and we really should tell her our plans before he does that.'

'I hope she won't be too upset.' Dottie twisted a length of her hair in her fingers. She always played with the same curls when she was nervous.

'We aren't children anymore, Dottie, but grown women. When your agent sells your new book, we will have the money to go.'

Dottie frowned. 'Don't be irritable. I know that, but I hate the thought of leaving Mama worrying about us.'

Connie moderated her tone. 'I will telephone Stephen on the way to the office, to invite him for dinner. You know how much Mama loves him, and she takes notice of what he says – him being a man.' Connie ignored the look her comment elicited and added, more firmly: 'Mama needs to accept we are going and we have to tell her tonight. Now I must dash. You hide the letter.'

Stephen wasn't at his office when she rang, so Connie left a message asking him to meet her after work. As she came out of her office building, he was standing waiting for her. His dark chestnut hair, although neatly combed, had a hint of unruliness at the edges, while his charcoal-grey tailored suit emphasized his broad shoulders, drawing more than one female gaze of admiration.

Stephen appeared oblivious to all this, a warm expression in his hazel eyes as he leaned in to kiss her cheek. 'What are you looking so pleased about? I can't imagine work was all that exciting.'

Connie grinned. 'Miss Bernardi answered our letter. She's going to give us tickets to all her American performances. It is going to happen, Stephen.'

He smiled back at her. 'I had no doubt it would. What does your mama say?' Connie flushed guiltily, making him laugh. 'I take it that's why I received the dinner invite.'

She poked him in the arm. 'Don't be silly, you're always welcome in our house. It's practically your home from home.'

And it was. Her parents had offered him a home as soon as they heard about the loss of his parents, his mother and hers having been best friends since nursery. He hadn't been allowed to take them up on it, instead being packed off to boarding school and then to Oxford. But he had spent almost every holiday with them and thus had a relationship with her mother as that of a favoured nephew. Mama valued his opinion, and he had a way of smoothing the occasional rough waters that arose between mother and daughters.

As they walked to the tube station, he asked what she thought her mother's objections might be. 'I'd better have my argument prepared.'

'She is worried about the neighbours, about what people will say. But what do they care what Dottie and I do? We are not children anymore.'

'No, but you are single women. Maybe your mama is worried you'll meet two Americans and settle over there.'

'Never. England is our home, and we have no interest in finding husbands. We just want to see the operas.'

Stephen didn't persist with teasing her. Instead, he took her arm. 'I'll speak to your mama, of course. Maybe she will listen to me.'

'Thank you, Stephen. You're such a darling.' Connie squeezed Stephen's arm as they walked into the station, bought their tickets and headed down the stairs to the underground.

'I hope you always consider me so. I would hate to fall from your good graces.'

Something in his tone made Connie glance up at his face. He looked tired, exhausted even, yet there was a funny expression in his eyes. One she didn't recognize – or didn't want to. She pushed the thought away.

'You could never do that, Stephen. You are the brother I always wanted. Come on, let's run and catch the tube, I can hear it arriving.'

'Stephen, what a pleasant surprise. How are you? Burning the candle at both ends by the look of you. I hope you aren't spending all your evenings in those nightclubs I keep hearing about?'

Stephen kissed Mama on her cheek. 'Nothing as adventurous as all that, Aunt Margaret. It's just busy at the office. I'm hoping for a promotion so am chained to my desk. You look fantastic – I like what you've done with your hair.'

'Oh, you smooth-tongued rogue.' As her mother lifted a hand to her hair, Connie saw she was pleased with the compliment.

When everyone had eaten and had retired to the sitting room, sitting opposite the fire, Connie glanced at Stephen for reassurance, gathered her courage and brought up the subject of the trip.

Her mother's eyes bulged as she looked at each of them before turning her gaze back to Connie. 'America? You cannot go there alone. What will people think?'

'I do not care what people think, Mama. And I am not going alone. Dottie is coming with me. This is our dream.'

'How can you afford to travel to America? We don't have the money for such things. How long will you be gone for? Who will meet you in New York?' She looked from Dottie to Connie and back, rubbing her hands together in agitation. 'I have a cousin over there, it's been a while since we corresponded but...'

'Mama, everything will work out.' Connie pushed down on the guilt of seeing her mother distressed. 'We are only going for a month. We have been saving and we have more than half the money in the bank already. Elana has offered us free tickets for all shows so the September trip will not be as expensive as we had envisioned. We will continue saving and that, together with the money Dottie will receive for her book manuscript, will be enough.'

Mama rolled her eyes to heaven, but Connie straightened her shoulders, determined to pay no heed.

Stephen sat forward and gave Mama a kind but firm smile. 'Aunt Margaret, I know you are upset and you have every right to be concerned, but I believe the girls will be quite safe. I have a good friend living in New York, and I'll arrange for him to meet them off the ship. He'll make sure their hotel is respectable and keep an eye on them.' At Connie's glare, he added, 'Not that they will need it, of course.'

Mama's shoulders fell. 'I can't argue with all three of you. It's not fair when you gang up on me like this.'

'Don't see it like that. You should be proud of them. They have saved for the trip, and you know how often Connie complains about her salary. I think they are to be commended.'

Her mother raised an eyebrow. 'You would.'

Stephen took a sip of his tea, not quite hiding his smile of triumph.

'I can't say I'm pleased but yes, of course I am proud of you, girls, for your commitment to your goal. But America? Why couldn't you have chosen Europe for your first trip abroad? It's closer.'

'They speak English in America, Mama. It is also the only place Miss Bernardi sings now, and she is the best. We simply must go.'

Silence lingered after Dottie's exclamation.

Stephen cleverly changed the subject. 'According to the news, the signing of the four-nation pact has just averted another war, although I wonder if anyone believes that.'

Connie nodded in agreement, but before she got a chance to say anything, her mother intervened.

'Stephen Armstrong, that is enough of that talk. You know I forbid you to speak about those rumours in this house. Let Germany get on with their own problems. We have enough issues of our own.'

'I apologize, Aunt Margaret. I won't forget again.'

'See that you don't, you rotten boy.'

But even as her mama reprimanded Stephen, Connie could see the smile behind her eyes.

Mama adored Stephen – they all did.

* * *

The weeks flew past in a flurry of sewing dresses, getting travel paperwork and letters back and forth across the ocean confirming their plans.

The day that Connie and Dottie were due to travel, a telegram arrived from Stephen just as they were double checking their packing lists and giving their last-minute reassurances to their mother.

'Isn't he lovely? He arranged for a friend of his to meet us off the boat just like he promised.' Connie glanced at her sister. 'He says we're to have lots of fun.'

Mama sighed. 'He should have told you to stay in London and not go gallivanting across the sea.'

'Mama, this is the chance of a lifetime.' Dottie leaned in and kissed her mother on the cheek. 'We will be quite safe, you know.'

'You'd be safer listening to her sing on the gramophone.'

Mama waved a hanky delicately around her face. 'I don't know how I will face the worry of not knowing where you are and who you are with.'

'Mama, you can trust us.' Connie checked their passports and tickets again before tucking them into her handbag. 'We would never do anything dangerous. Please give us your blessing. We need to be on our way.'

With a wave and a muttered prayer, their mother stood on the doorstep as they set off on their adventure.

FOUR

NEW YORK, SEPTEMBER 1933

Connie and Dottie stood side by side at the ship's railing, eager to see their first view of New York.

Despite the sunshine Connie shivered, her lips stinging from the salt-laden wind, as she stared at the iconic statue that had welcomed hundreds of thousands of travellers to America.

'The Statue of Liberty, Dottie. We are here.'

'I thought it would look white, but it's kind of green, isn't it?'

'I guess that's the effect of the weather.' Connie leaned forward, out over the railing, but Dottie pulled her back.

'I don't want to have to fish you out of the water.'

They both jumped as the ship's horn blasted, sending seagulls flocking to the skies. Connie laughed, her eyes bright with excitement.

Other passengers gathered around the railings as the ship sailed into port guided by smaller boats. Connie saw the fear in Dottie's eyes as the large ship neared the docks and squeezed her sister's hand, confident they wouldn't crash. The ship's captain had completed this manoeuvre several times already – he had told them so himself during the voyage. Waves splashed against the ship, sending a light spray over them but they didn't move, too eager to see the city they'd read all about in the Rand McNally guide.

The New York skyline became clearer. 'Look, that's the Empire State Building – it only opened two years ago. I can't imagine working at those heights, can you?' Dottie said. 'Are you listening to me?'

'I prefer the Chrysler Building. Look at its gleaming stainless-steel crown reflecting the early morning sun. You can just make out the eagle gargoyles and triangular windows.' Connie looked up from the guidebook to stare at yet another fabulous building. 'And there's the Woolworth Building. That was once the tallest in the world.'

Connie shaded her eyes as she took in her first view of Manhattan. 'I wonder how far it is to Washington Square, to our hotel? I can't wait to see it; the accommodation here is supposed to be much bigger than in London.'

Dottie shook her head. 'I hope our hotel isn't half as tall as those skyscrapers. You know I don't like heights.' Connie changed the subject to distract her. 'Thank goodness you made us new clothes.'

She looked down at her skirt, one shorter than she had ever worn before. She knew it was the height of fashion, thanks to Dottie's fascination with the periodical *Mabs Fashion*. Although they were travelling third class on the ocean liner, she knew they looked richer than they were. She sent up a prayer of thanks for her sister's skill as a seamstress.

For a few more minutes they watched the crowds on the dock. Some of them were workers waiting to unload the cargo, while others waved at the ship, obviously waiting for friends or family to disembark.

· · ·

As luck would have it, they saw their escort was waiting for them before they passed through Immigration. Connie was the first to spot the raven-haired young man of average height, with a well-built, muscular frame and a slightly misshapen nose – perhaps testament to having played rugby in his youth – who gave them a small wave as he walked towards them. She guessed his age to be in his late twenties. He dressed in a stylish yet understated fashion: polished black shoes, a tailored grey suit, and hair that had been brilliantined to sweep neatly to the side. He exuded elegance and confidence, and she immediately sensed that they were in capable hands.

They shook hands, and Connie asked him how he could meet them this side of Customs.

'Perk of the job, you know. Did you have a comfortable trip?'

They both nodded, neither wishing to tell the attractive stranger of their bouts of seasickness and the cramped quarters on-board. They were glad to be leaving the ship behind.

Mr Reynolds helped them progress through Passport Control very quickly, and they found themselves outside in the middle of what could only be described as organized chaos. It was completely overwhelming. Connie closed her eyes, silently thanking Stephen for insisting that his friend meet them. She didn't think they would have negotiated their exit if they had been alone.

Throngs of people moved this way and that, their shouting competing with blaring car horns. Heavy traffic dominated the streets. The aromas from food vans competed with the smell of rubbish on the pavements.

Mr Reynolds motioned for the driver of a sleek, glossy black car to park at the kerb. It reminded Connie of the cars they had seen in London ferrying the royal family around, only this one appeared to be bigger. The driver stepped out, tipping his cap in acknowledgment before holding the door open so they could step in. A polished wooden running board extended along the side of the car. The interior was a blend of luxury and functionality. Connie sank into the plush, leather-upholstered seats as Dottie took a seat beside her.

Tom helped the driver load their bags into the boot before he sat up front. Connie was about to ask him why he was driving before she realized that everything was on the opposite side to that used in Britain. She blushed, thankful she had not said anything to make herself look stupid.

As they made their way to their hotel, Tom pointed out various landmarks. 'If you ladies have time, we could take a trip up the Empire State. The views are unbelievable.'

'Thank you, Mr Reynolds. I prefer to keep my feet on the ground.' Dottie glanced at Connie as she said this, but Connie wasn't about to argue. She'd love to see the view, but for now she was content to look out of the window, fascinated by the sheer number of people moving around the city. Everything was so vibrant and fast-paced.

'Call me Tom, please. Stephen said you were here to see an opera. Seems a long way to travel just to see someone sing.'

Dottie frowned at his words, but Connie just smiled. 'Have you ever been to the opera, Tom?'

'Once. My parents dragged me to one a few years back. I much prefer to go to the movies.'

Connie opened her mouth to reply, but Dottie got there first. She leaned forward in her seat, eyes sparkling, her voice full of passion. 'You cannot possibly compare a moving picture to an opera. A movie is a form of entertainment, but opera, well, it transports your soul.'

Tom turned to stare at Dottie, who continued, her hands moving as she spoke. 'There are no retakes in an opera. The artists have to perform to the best of their ability, right there, on stage, in front of our very eyes. They pour out their emotions, becoming the characters they play, and their voices soar to the rooftops.' Dottie clasped her hands to her chest. 'It is simply the most powerful connection built with the audience.' She blushed as if realizing she was being too passionate. In a lower tone, she concluded, 'You just can't get the same experience from a movie.'

Tom seemed unable to take his eyes off Dottie. He continued staring as the silence grew longer. Dottie's cheeks were flushed and she seemed incapable of saying anything else, so Connie added, 'It depends a lot on the location and the quality of the artists. We've heard the Metropolitan has wonderful acoustics and an incredibly talented orchestra. The music tells a story as much as the acting does.' Connie hesitated a second, waiting for a response, but Tom was still looking at Dottie. Hiding a smile, she continued. 'Miss Bernardi is a world-leading soprano, singing in her favourite venue. That's why we had to come. When she hits a high note, the music resonates inside you.' Connie paused. 'It takes your breath away.'

Tom smiled. 'You both make a compelling case. Perhaps I could accompany you one evening?' He pulled at his tie, his tone sounding a little nervous, his eyes flickering back to Dottie.

'Of course. We'd be delighted.' Dottie's reply sounded slightly stilted to Connie's ears but Tom grinned.

'Wonderful. Now, we are just pulling onto Washington Square. As you can see, there are lots of small cafés around if you need sustenance. The subway station entrance is over there' – he pointed to his left – 'and right here is your hotel. George, park here, please.'

'Yes, sir, Mr Reynolds.' George ably manoeuvred the car into a parking space that had looked far too small. He got out to get their luggage as Tom jumped out to open their doors. Offering his hand to Dottie, he helped her out of the car before doing the same for Connie.

'Despite being a modest hotel, it has a wonderful reputation. You will be safe here. Stephen told me your mother is inclined to worry.'

'She is, but she won't now, knowing we are not alone in New York. Thank you very much, Tom.' Connie nudged Dottie, who was staring open-mouthed at their surroundings.

George passed their luggage to a waiting bellboy. Connie wondered if they should give George a tip. The guidebook had said tipping was expected but he appeared to work for Tom. She hesitated a second too long as George tipped his hat once more before retaking his seat behind the wheel.

'I shall walk you ladies inside and see you get situated.' Tom offered Dottie his arm and led them inside.

Connie glanced at Dottie, who had turned pink – but not from the heat. Her sister struggled to make conversation with men who appeared to find her attractive.

When they were inside the foyer, Connie stepped forward and held out her hand. 'Thank you again, Tom. Please don't keep George waiting any longer.'

He didn't quite manage to hide the look of disappointment on his face. 'My pleasure. It is nice to catch up with people from back home. I was hoping I could take you both for luncheon.'

'That would be lovely, but another day perhaps. We are both exhausted from our travels.'

He blushed, running a hand through his hair. 'Of course. Perhaps when you are rested.' He turned to leave but changed his mind. 'My mother is hosting a party tonight and although she understands it is very short notice, she wished me to issue you both with an invitation. You may be too tired, but I hope you will consider attending. It would give you a chance to meet some more of the British community. I could pick you up at 7 p.m.'

'Lovely, thank you.' Connie smiled as she accepted. Dottie stayed silent. Connie knew she wasn't too keen on meeting new people, but it would be rude to refuse.

After they had checked in, they followed the bellboy into the lift, and then to their room. The bellboy deposited their bags and then stood there expectantly. Connie opened her purse and slipped the boy a dollar bill. His face lit up in surprise, and she realized she had probably been overly generous.

'Connie,' Dottie exclaimed, opening her arms wide to take in the bedroom. 'It's enormous.' And it was. Floral-patterned wallpaper in muted shades of blue and cream adorned the walls, with matching covers on the twin beds, which were larger than their beds at home. Dottie sat on the side of one as if afraid she would dirty it. 'This is so pretty, isn't it?'

Connie nodded and walked over to the other bed, her hand touching the pristine, neatly tucked-in white linens and plump pillows. Between the beds stood a small wooden nightstand with a porcelain lamp, a simple alarm clock, and a couple of books. Light flooded into the room from a large window framed with lace curtains, heavy drapes hanging by the side. She walked over to see what their view was like, while Dottie jumped up and headed towards the other door, which led to their private bathroom.

'Connie, come and look at this,' Dottie called out.

Connie went to the bathroom to see Dottie gazing at a clawfoot bathtub with a showerhead, a stack of white fluffy towels to one side.

'Why is everything so much bigger than at home? This could be a small swimming pool. I can't wait to try it, but maybe later,' Dottie said, her yawn not quite concealed.

'Let's unpack and then take a nap.' Connie walked over to the wardrobe, noticing how her feet sank luxuriantly into the woollen rug covering most of the wooden floors.

They worked quickly and efficiently, not having too many garments to unpack and hang in the wardrobe or leave folded in the drawers.

'We have a desk. What lovely flowers. Isn't that a nice

touch?' Dottie walked over to the vase, bending her head to inhale their fragrance. 'Oh, there's a card.' She opened it and turned back, smiling. 'They're from Stephen. He said he hopes we have a fantastic time.'

'He is so thoughtful.' Connie smiled, but then struggled to suppress a yawn. She stripped off her clothes and got into bed, the luxury of lying in a bed that didn't roll from side to side not lost on her. She was soon fast asleep.

After a long nap, the sisters got up and had a bath before getting dressed and going out to explore their new surroundings.

They walked, not daring to take any form of transport as they didn't know how much it would cost. They had memorized the route, having read all the guidebooks to New York they could get their hands on over the last two years, and Connie had a paper map in her handbag as backup.

Connie glanced up at the street name. 'This is Fifth Avenue, so we have to walk up to Thirty-Ninth Street and then along to Broadway.'

They walked and walked, immersing themselves in the sights and sounds of New York, until Dottie came to a standstill, an expression of awe on her face as she clutched Connie's arm. 'That's it. The Met.'

They stared at the Metropolitan Opera House for several minutes, earning some grunts of disapproval from passers-by who shoved past them, although one or two people smiled, assuming rightly they were tourists.

'Now we have to find the offices of Evans & Salter. In her letter Miss Bernardi said they'd ring her to tell her of our arrival.'

They consulted the map, found the office relatively easily and were soon there.

All bravado disappeared as the sisters exchanged glances. Now they were there, it seemed rather a lot to ask for the telephone number of a star. Dottie stepped up to the challenge, clutching Elana's letter as proof of their connection.

'Excuse me, please could you telephone Signora Bernardi? We have just arrived from England and...'

'Hello?' The voice came from an inner office. 'Is that Miss Fitzwalter?'

As they peered around the doorway, Connie recognized Octavian Sterling, Elana's husband, his dark wavy hair only a little greyer than it had been when they met him at Covent Garden.

He stepped forward, the welcoming expression in his eyes matching his warm smile. 'How are you gals doing? Did you have a good trip?' Before they could answer, Octavian turned to the desk clerk. 'We met these lovely ladies in Covent Garden, that's in London, England. Despite the fact they look totally different, they are sisters – Connie and Dottie Fitzwalter. They said they would travel the ocean to see my Elana sing, and now here they are, right here in New York. Can you believe that?'

The young man didn't get a chance to respond.

'How are you finding New York?' Octavian rummaged around the desk, producing tickets. 'Tomorrow evening. *Traviata*, one of my favourites. We are up to our tonsils in rehearsals but as soon as all that dies down, you two must come to dinner with us in our apartment. You will, won't you?'

Connie and Dottie, caught up in his enthusiasm, grinned back. 'Of course, we will. Thank you.'

He took a breath and then the questions started again, and the two women were barely able to keep up as he rattled them off, ending with: 'Where is your hotel?'

'Washington Square,' Connie replied.

'Did you take a cab?'

'No, we walked.'

That made him pause. 'You *walked*? Nobody walks in New York, at least not that distance.' He escorted them out of the office and whistled loudly. A cab pulled up. 'Take these lovely ladies to Washington Square.' He handed the driver a bunch of dollars and with a quick hug to each of them, bundled them into the cab.

'I love America!' Dottie exclaimed, as they returned to their hotel room once more.

Tom arrived promptly at 7 p.m. to collect them. 'How are you feeling? A little better after your rest, I hope. I took the liberty of buying you these.' He handed Connie a small bouquet of white roses, with red for Dottie. 'They go well with your colouring,' he stuttered, his eyes on Dottie.

Connie waited for Dottie to reply but when the silence lasted more than a couple of seconds, she said, 'Thank you. The flowers are beautiful. We appreciate you collecting us.'

His eyes darted to her and then back to Dottie as he replied, 'My pleasure. I have a car waiting outside.'

Connie kept up the conversation, as Dottie seemed to have lost her voice. She had never seen her sister so tongue-tied.

After a short trip, Tom pulled up outside a grand residence.

'Oh, my,' Dottie exclaimed. 'We should have dressed up.'

Connie stared at the brownstone, adorned with tasteful decorations that paid homage to both American and British culture. Strings of soft, glowing lights hung in the trees in the front garden, creating a warm, inviting atmosphere in the dusk evening.

'You both look stunning. Allow me?' Tom offered them both an arm as he escorted them inside.

The house buzzed with vibrant energy as guests – a mix of diplomats, expatriates and local dignitaries – mingled. Gentle laughter and the hum of conversation filled the air, against the backdrop of a jazz quartet. Connie's feet tapped along with the music. It was invigorating.

A couple stood near them, discussing the prohibition laws.

'I must say, it's a refreshing change to attend a gathering where the wine flows as freely as the conversation,' remarked a well-dressed gentleman, his British accent distinct as he sipped from a glass of red wine.

A beautiful woman in an elegant, scarlet, halter-neck silk evening gown chimed in with a playful tone: 'It's quite the novelty to enjoy a proper drink without the need for secrecy. Your British hospitality, in defiance of our peculiar American laws, is most appreciated.'

Connie and Dottie exchanged a smile; neither were big drinkers, but they could imagine not being able to drink in public was an issue for a lot of people.

'They say the prohibition will be repealed later this year, or early next.' Tom glanced around, then added in a whisper, 'But as you can see, the rules don't apply here. Would you like a glass of champagne?'

Connie answered, 'No, thank you, Tom, but some water would be lovely.'

'I'll have the same.' Dottie didn't look up from the floor until Tom walked away.

She reached for Connie's hand. 'Don't leave me alone with him, will you?'

'Why? Are you worried he will behave improperly?' Connie teased, but seeing the extent of her sister's blushes, she stopped. 'Aren't you pleased he likes you?'

'No. I don't have time for all that now and he is at least five years younger than I am.' Dottie smoothed her hair and glanced around the packed room. 'Look at this place, these people. Imagine what Mother would make of this; she'd love to be here, wouldn't she?'

'I think she would really like Tom; he's well-mannered and has potential.'

'Stop it,' Dottie pleaded. 'Please.'

Connie grinned. 'What would your readers think? Surely your heroines don't run away from the first glance of their heroes.'

FIVE

Connie came out of the bathroom rubbing cream into her face after brushing her teeth. 'That party was an eye-opener, wasn't it? I got the impression the English were quite homesick, didn't you, Dottie?'

'I suppose travelling here to see an opera is quite different to living here.' Dottie plumped her pillow, her lips pursed.

Connie walked over and sat on her sister's bed. 'What's upset you? You know I was only teasing you about Tom.'

Dottie flushed. 'I know.' She glanced up, meeting Connie's gaze for a second before looking down again. 'I feel guilty.'

Surprised, Connie took a second, waiting for Dottie to explain but she didn't speak. 'Why? Are you worried about Mother being alone?'

'No. I don't think she will enjoy it, but she will be fine.' She looked at Connie. 'Did you see those men in the street earlier? The lines and lines of people? I thought they were just queuing up for something, but Tom's mother explained that they were waiting for food. Connie, the depression over here is so bad. There are people going hungry as the men have been out of work for months. I know things are a little tough in London but it's much worse here. She said about a quarter of the labour force is out of work.' A tear trickled down her cheek.

'Come here.' Connie pulled her sister into a hug. 'You have nothing to feel guilty about. We saved up to come on this trip – my feet still remember all that walking instead of taking the bus.' Connie squeezed her sister's hand. 'We deserve to enjoy it.'

Dottie didn't look convinced, but she pulled her covers up. 'Sorry, all the travelling's caught up with me. I'm just being silly.'

Connie kissed her cheek. 'You have a huge heart. Try to sleep. Tomorrow is a big day for us. We'll see an opera at the Met for the first time!'

Dottie fell asleep long before Connie did. Despite her words to her sister, Connie had been upset too at the sight of the lines of men standing around, their faces a mask of despair. But they shouldn't feel guilty about their trip – they had saved so hard to get to New York, and gave to charity. But should they have stayed home? No, that wouldn't have achieved anything. If people stopped going to the opera, those employees would end up in the unemployment lines too.

* * *

As they entered the opera house, Connie and Dottie felt like they had been transported to another era. The building was filled with beautiful chandeliers, detailed mouldings and luxurious curtains that gave the place an air of timelessness. Despite being surrounded by women wearing luxurious furs and glittering diamonds, Connie felt a familiar sense of belonging among the diverse group of opera fans, all ready to be taken away by music's power.

Seated in the auditorium, Connie's heart raced as the lights lowered and the conductor lifted his baton. The overture began its recognisable melody, and a hush descended over the audience as they awaited what was to come.

At last, the renowned Elana Bernardi stepped onto the stage. Dottie gripped her hand painfully and gave her a grin of triumph. 'We did it.'

Several people surrounding them shushed them as Elana began to sing. Connie's breath was taken away by the mesmerizing power of that ethereal voice, which filled the room, captivating all who were listening. As Violetta, Bernardi effortlessly conveyed every emotion, her voice soaring to unimaginable heights, leaving the audience spellbound.

Throughout the performance, Connie was transported into the heart of the story, feeling every joy and sorrow that Violetta experienced. The sets were opulent, the costumes exquisite, and the supporting cast exceptional, but it was Rossi's voice that truly stole the show. Connie brushed tears from her eyes as the final act unfolded, and Violetta's heart-wrenching demise left a profound impact on her soul.

As the last note resonated in the theatre, the crowd erupted into thunderous applause, showering Bernardi and the entire cast with appreciation. Connie and Dottie joined in. Connie turned to her sister. 'This made all the scrimping and saving worth it. I'm so glad we came, aren't you? Her voice is just tremendous.' She looked around. 'This whole place, it just made it so special, don't you think?'

Connie couldn't agree more. The lights came on and they stood up and began to move with the rest of the crowd toward the exits. But another surprise awaited them.

'Ladies, where are you going?' They turned to see Octavian gesturing to them. 'You can't leave yet. My darling Elana wants to see you at the after-show party. Follow me. Watch your step, now.' He led them past the press photographers and once more

put them in a car, but this time it was with his own private
driver.

'Charles, take these lovely ladies over to the party and then
come back for me. Look after them – they are our very special
guests, all the way from London.'

'Yes, sir, Mr Sterling.'

The man drove them a couple of blocks. Pulling up, he got
out and held the pavement-side door open for them. 'Right
through that black door over there, ladies.'

'I wish we had some furs and a few diamonds. I feel rather
underdressed,' Dottie murmured, as they followed the small
crowd into the private room.

Connie shook her head; she was far too excited to care what
she was wearing.

'Nonsense, you look just beautiful as you are with your
blonde hair and blue eyes.'

Dottie blushed at the stranger's comment, even though he
had walked on.

Connie took her sister's arm, teasing her: 'First Tom and
now that man. You are really putting your mark on America.'

'Connie, don't. I'm mortified. I didn't think anyone would
hear me.'

They spent a little while people-watching until they spotted
Mr Sterling coming towards them.

He took Connie's arm. 'Tell me, what did you think of it?
Did it live up to your expectations?'

Connie smiled up at him. 'It was amazing. De Luca just
swept me away with his voice. I heard it described as having the
quality and colour of dark honey with sunshine but until
tonight I didn't really know what that meant. And, of course,
Elana was incredible, as always.'

'I see you're picking up New York habits already, Miss
Connie, not taking a breath between sentences.'

Connie put a hand to her mouth. 'Oh gosh, I have, haven't

I? Forgive me. Thank you for inviting us to your party, that was very kind of you.'

'I think it is you who has been kind.' With these words, Octavian tapped the top of his glass, bringing the collection of artists and writers, politicians, and prominent members of society surrounding them to silence.

'Ladies and gentlemen, let me introduce two very special women. These English ladies, Constance and Dorothea Fitzwalter, have travelled from Britain solely to hear my Elana sing.' He waited for the clapping to die down before he presented them with tickets for all her performances and insisted they attend a party at her mansion on Millionaires' Row on their second to last night.

All evening, Connie kept pinching herself to make sure she wasn't dreaming. If this was what America was like, maybe her mama had been right to worry that they might not go back.

The next morning, the sisters had coffee sitting in their hotel lounge watching the world go by. To Connie's amusement, Dottie was scribbling away, filling her notebook with notes on plot ideas, descriptions and scenery to share with her readers.

'So will Mr Reynolds feature as the hero in one of your novels?' Connie teased her sister, who blushed a becoming shade of pink.

'No, and that is the way it is to stay. Some things are just for us, Connie. Promise?'

'I promise. But I'm curious as to why you didn't flirt with him, even just a little bit. I don't think it would be hard to land him.'

Dottie raised her eyebrows. 'You make it sound like I am fishing. I am not interested in getting married. I just like him as a friend. Anyway, he is much too young for me.'

'I don't believe that for one second,' Connie replied, grinning.

'Good morning, ladies.'

Connie saw Dottie cringe in disbelief as they recognized the male voice that interrupted them.

She turned to greet him. 'Tom, when did you arrive? I didn't see you come in.'

His eyes twinkled with amusement. 'No, you were too engrossed in your conversation.'

Dottie looked like she'd prefer to be anywhere but there at the moment.

'Do you mind if I join you?' He ran a finger around the collar of his shirt as if expecting to be refused.

'Of course not, where are my manners? Would you like tea or coffee?'

'Coffee. The Americans still haven't managed to produce a cup of tea like us British are used to. I gather the Germans haven't, either.'

As they waited for Tom's coffee to arrive, Connie kept the conversation going as Dottie was completely tongue-tied.

'Are you going to stay in America or return to Britain, Tom?'

'Actually I'm being posted to Germany. I got a job with the American Embassy, courtesy of my American father. I have dual nationality.'

Connie glanced at Dottie but she still refused to join in the conversation. 'When do you go to Berlin?'

'I think I'll be there by the new year. I wonder if I'll meet Stephen over there?'

'Stephen? In Berlin? But why would he go there?' Connie frowned. Why hadn't he said anything to her about going overseas. Was he keeping it a secret? She couldn't imagine having Sunday dinner without him. He was part of their family. Did Mama know?

'For the same reason I am going. You know he works for the Foreign Office.'

Connie discreetly nudged Dottie as Tom was looking at her, but her sister remained silent. Connie replied, 'Well, no, we didn't. He just said the government, but we got the impression it was secret, so we didn't ask questions.'

'Well, he's not a spy or anything. Just a civil servant, like me. I guess he may be playing up his part to impress such beautiful ladies.'

Connie struggled to keep her face straight as poor Dottie turned pink at Tom's teasing. But was he teasing? Moving in diplomatic circles, Tom was used to talking to everyone and putting them at their ease.

'What are your plans for Thursday evening?' he asked.

'We are going to the Metropolitan. We will have been twice already, but we will never grow tired of *La Traviata*,' Connie replied. Dottie still seemed to be struck dumb.

'I haven't seen it.' He waited, an expectant expression on his face.

Connie looked to Dottie but her sister remained silent. She wanted to roll her eyes and give her a swift kick under the table but Tom might have noticed.

'Why don't you come with us, then?' Connie asked. 'We can make it a night to remember. Can't we, Dottie?'

At the lack of response, Connie discreetly pinched her sister's arm.

'Of course,' Dottie stuttered, her tone not exactly warm.

'I would love that, thank you.'

Thursday night was amazing, and not just due to the incredible production of *La Traviata*. At the end of their performance, the cast stood back as the prima donna pointed out Connie and Dottie to the crowd.

'These sisters travelled all the way from England just to watch this performance. Please give my English friends a round of applause.'

They got a standing ovation from the crowd. Connie glanced at her sister to see her tears mirrored on her sister's cheeks. This was the moment that made the last two years of scrimping and saving worth it.

Outside, the press were waiting, and they took their pictures.

Some instinct told Connie to ask for copies of the pictures for their mother.

She was not to know these pictures would one day save the sisters' lives.

SIX

VIENNA, FEBRUARY 1934

Sarah Liberman tried to push down the horrible churning in her stomach as she reread the contents of her cousin's letter. She didn't notice her husband come in until he kissed the top of her head. She brushed aside her tears, putting the letter on the bedside table.

'What are you doing home? You only just left,' she said. Embarrassed at being caught crying, Sarah pushed the covers aside to get up.

The mattress creaked as her husband sat down beside her, taking her hand in his. His thumb gently caressed her palm. 'Sarah? What is it? You're crying.'

'It's nothing. I'm just being silly.'

'Tell me.' His coaxing tone made her look at him. She saw concern mixed with sadness in his eyes. 'Is it the baby?'

She shook her head. 'No, darling. I knew the chances I was with child were small. Who becomes a mother at my age?'

He bent over and kissed her hand. 'You are the best mother our children could ever have. You've given me two boys and our beautiful Leah. God has been good to us, Sarah.'

She knew he didn't mean to chide her but still his words

made her bristle. Yes, she was lucky to have her children but did that mean she should ignore her body's yearning for another baby?

He nodded towards the notepaper. 'Who wrote to you?'

'My cousin's daughter, Helga. You remember, she married Paul Müller and moved to Berlin. She wants to come back.'

'To Vienna?'

Sarah glanced at her husband; she knew he didn't like her worrying about anything, especially politics. It irked her sometimes: she was a grown woman, a mother of three. She wasn't a fragile piece of glass who would shatter at the first hint of trouble. 'Ben, it's horrible. She wrote that Paul's shop was involved in the boycott last April. They had stormtroopers standing outside warning people not to shop there. Since then, Paul has been arrested a few times, yet he hasn't done anything. She's scared. She's six months pregnant with her first child.' At her husband's silence, she kept talking. 'I want to invite them to come here. Paul can help Papa in the store. You're too busy with your patients. We have plenty of room...'

'You want to invite a man known to the police to our home?' Ben dropped her hand.

'He isn't a criminal. They're targeting him because he's Jewish. Helga has written of other Jewish men being arrested for doing nothing wrong. They are taken away in the night – some do not return.'

'Nonsense, Sarah. Müller is too outspoken, political. He is bringing trouble to his own front door. I won't have him bring it here.'

'Ben...'

'Enough.' He kissed her on the cheek. 'I must go now. Write back to your cousin and tell her to stay where she is. Travelling during her pregnancy could be dangerous.'

Sarah waited until the door shut behind him before picking up her writing pad. Was Ben correct? She pushed the voice saying he was wrong to the back of her mind. Her husband worked with policemen every day. If there was a real threat to Jews he would know. The people under threat in Austria were the political opponents of Dollfuss and his Fatherland Front party. Since he had suspended the parliament last year, social democrats and members of the communist party had been targeted. Papa ranted about the suspension of civil liberties and the arrest of politicians, but at least nobody disappeared, like in Berlin. Sarah sighed and started writing her letter. Maybe her cousin would be better off staying where she was.

Less than a week after Sarah's conversation with Ben, civil war broke out in Austria, with rioters marching through the streets.

'Mama, Mama!'

Sarah rushed into her daughter's small bedroom, thankful the bed was pushed against the wall opposite the one with the window. Her sweet thirteen-year-old daughter usually protested she wasn't a child, yet now cowered in her bed, eyes wide with tears, the tracks on her cheeks glistening in the light of the bedside lamp, her limbs shaking.

'Darling, don't be scared. We're safe here. Those people aren't going to come in. It's just a march outside.'

Sarah's grip on Leah tightened as the door to the bedroom burst open, her heart racing faster than her daughter's as icy tendrils of dread wound through her veins as Samuel and Daniel stormed in. She froze, eyes widening at the sight of a gun glinting in Samuel's hands – a reminder that Ben had failed to keep it locked away.

'Samuel, put down that gun. At once.'

'Mama, you can hear the fighting. Papa said the mobs are dangerous, they act like pack animals. It's my job to protect you.'

The sound of crashing glass filled the air as an army of boots stomped over the cobbled streets, accompanied by the sporadic sound of gunfire.

Samuel silently walked to the bedroom window, his hands trembling. With one finger he lifted the curtain a fraction, revealing a mass of people gathering outside. Closing the curtain again, he faced his mother with a determined look in his eyes. 'Don't worry, Mama,' he said firmly. 'I'll keep you safe.'

No sooner had the words left his lips than a rock flew through the window, narrowly missing Samuel's head. Leah's horrified scream pierced the silence as Sarah threw her arms around her, trembling and fighting back tears. Her gaze met her eldest son's, the gun still shaking in his hands.

'Put that gun down before it goes off,' she demanded. 'We will be safe here on the bed away from the window. Come and tell us a story. Daniel loves it when you do that.' She forced a smile onto her face, trying to be brave for her younger son, who was watching them with wide terror-filled eyes.

In that moment, Sarah wanted nothing more than to crawl under the bedcovers and disappear.

Where was Ben? Knowing her doctor husband, she could imagine him out there in the raging chaos amongst the desperate and broken, doing whatever he could to help his patients. She wished, not for the first time, he'd chosen a private practice and not a hospital.

Outside, the chanting rose to an ear-piercing cacophony while police whistles shrilled and explosions rocked the night air. She trembled in fear at the thought of all the violence raging in the streets outside and hoped her father had stayed in his apartment upstairs. *Should she go up to check?* But even as she had that thought, she dismissed it. Her place was with her children. Clutching Leah and Daniel's hands, she prayed desperately that the terror would stay far away from her doorstep and not enter her home.

. . .

The next two nights passed the same way but the children slept in Sarah's room instead of Leah's. There was still no sign of her husband. She pushed her fears aside – she'd have heard if he'd been hurt, or worse.

Trying but failing to stop yawning after three sleepless nights, Sarah checked to see if the gas was working before putting the water on to boil. Hearing the door to the apartment open, she rushed out hoping it was Ben. Instead, her father shuffled inside, a brown paper bag in his hands.

Isaac greeted Sarah with a kiss on both cheeks and a brief hug. Opening the bag, he placed some bread and milk on the table, tucking his tobacco into his pocket. 'The federal army has taken up position outside the state opera house. I couldn't find Benjamin, but I met some men who had seen him last night. They said the doctors are kept busy, with several victims on both sides.'

Sarah clasped her hands together. 'I never thought it would come to this. A civil war in Austria. What do they hope to achieve?'

Isaac's eyes, normally clear as day, clouded over. 'Dollfuss ordered the army to shell the Karl-Marx-Hof. That will bring things to an end, for now at least.'

Sarah closed her eyes, saying a quick prayer for the people living in those apartment buildings. 'What happens now?'

Isaac shrugged. 'The streets will return to normal. The curfews and shortages will be removed and hopefully your husband will return to his family. Austria as we knew it will cease to exist. Dollfuss has plans to bring in a state like that of Mussolini in Italy. After he has finished murdering all the social democrats.'

Sarah had heard enough. She hated politics. She turned away. 'I must get back to preparing dinner. Excuse me.' She walked to the kitchen and only when the door was closed, and she was alone, did she let the tears fall.

She prayed like never before her husband would be spared and return to her.

A week later, her bedraggled husband stumbled through the door. Ben's weary face was etched with fatigue, his clothing caked with filth and smeared with blood.

'It's over,' he croaked. He leaned heavily against the door-frame, unable to hold himself up any longer. 'Samuel, come help me,' he begged weakly.

With Sarah and her son at his side, they guided him to the bedroom where he collapsed onto the bed before Sarah could so much as remove his filthy garments. His breathing became heavier and deeper as his eyes slowly shut, surrendering to a deep sleep.

Torn between letting him rest and wanting to burn his clothes, she reached over and kissed him tenderly on the forehead. Even after all these years, she loved every inch of this man. How close had she come to losing him?

Hearing a noise, she turned to see Leah at the doorway, holding a glass of water.

'Thank you, darling. Put it there on the bedside table. Papa will be thirsty when he wakes up.'

Leah moved closer, her nose wrinkling. 'He smells bad.'

Sarah smiled. 'Yes, he does, but at least he is safe. He can have a bath later. Come, let him sleep.'

Sarah followed her daughter out of the bedroom. With a last look at her husband, she closed the door behind her.

Ben slept for almost twenty hours. They were alone in the apartment when he woke up, the children upstairs visiting

Isaac. She ran a bath for him and helped scrub the layers of dirt from his hair. While he rinsed off, she changed the bed linen.

She sat on the freshly made bed waiting for him to finish in the bathroom. He came out wiping soap from his chin, freshly shaven and looking more like her husband.

'Ben, I was so worried when you didn't come back. I thought you... you might have been killed.'

'I'm sorry, it must have been awful for you. Waiting here, not knowing anything. Time flew for us. We were kept so busy, one patient after the other arriving, like a tidal wave with no end in sight.'

Sarah twisted the bedcovers in her hands.

'What is it, Sarah?'

'People are saying that the Nazis are coming. This was a warm-up for Hitler and his friends. A test to see if Vienna is prepared to fight.'

'Who are these people? They must be blind, deaf and dumb. Both sides of the fight claim to be Austrians. Even if Hitler took over, which he won't, Austrians aren't going to let him introduce his policies here. Almost three per cent of the population is Jewish, my darling, compared to about one per cent in Germany. People here don't fear us, they don't believe those stupid rumours about us killing children to make bread.' Ben patted the bed, smiling at Sarah. 'Why don't you join me? It's rare we have the place to ourselves. Let's not waste it by talking about that madman.'

SEVEN

FRANKFURT, MARCH 1934

Connie let out a gasp as they stepped off the train at Frankfurt station. 'Just look at those windows... and the chandeliers! It feels more like a luxurious hotel than a train station. It's simply beautiful,' she exclaimed.

Dottie nodded in agreement, her eyes scanning the platform while she held on to her travel bag tightly. 'Not quite up to par with Paris, though. The French certainly have a more refined taste, don't you think? And Italy, oh, it was breathtaking as well!' She chuckled softly. 'Sometimes I catch myself talking as if I've been travelling all my life, not just this past year.'

'Feeling tired after the journey?' Connie shivered with the chill in the air as they walked down the platform.

'I'm excited! It was very kind of Stephen to invite us to Frankfurt for your birthday.'

'It was, but I wonder why he chose here rather than Berlin. That's where he works.'

'I wanted to get away from work for a few days, and I also managed to persuade someone to come with me.'

Connie whirled around at the sound of Stephen's voice, and

put a hand over her mouth when she saw Tom standing next to him. She glanced at Dottie who stood open-mouthed, not able to cover her shock.

'I trust I'm a nice surprise.' Tom's voice hitched slightly, his eyes darting to Dottie, who remained silent for a second too long. He ran a hand through his hair, discomfort radiating from him.

'Of course. It is so nice to see you again. How are you liking Germany? Do you see much of each other?' Dottie looked from him to Stephen and back. 'You being in a similar line of work, I mean... um...'

Connie cringed for her sister. She sent an appealing look at Stephen, who gallantly offered to carry Dottie's case and took her arm. Connie and Tom watched as they walked ahead of them.

'I'm sorry, maybe I shouldn't have come along.' Tom's morose tone told Connie to tell him the truth.

She turned to him and smiled kindly. 'My sister likes you, Tom, we both do, but she isn't looking for anything more than friendship.' At his downcast expression, Connie added, 'Nobody could change her mind, not even the Prince of Wales, and everyone knows how popular he is with the ladies.'

He smiled as she'd hoped. 'You have a kind heart, Miss Fitzwalter.'

'Connie,' she corrected, taking his proffered arm as he took her bag. 'Now tell me, how are you finding Berlin?'

'It's very different to New York but I like it. At least I do some of the time.' He glanced around before dropping his voice. 'I'm not a fan of the current regime or their antics, but I try to keep out of it. My boss said he doesn't want me to cause a diplomatic incident.'

Connie kept her voice low too. 'I'm sure you are an asset to the embassy. You have such delightful manners and a good nature. Look how well you looked after us in New York. I don't think you have anything to worry about.'

'Perhaps you are right.' His tone wasn't confident as he stared at a group of uniformed men marching toward them.

Connie waited until they had passed before asking, 'Is there some event on in Frankfurt? I saw quite a few men in that uniform on the train.'

'That's just normal life here in Germany, now. Lots of men pretending to be soldiers.' He grimaced but then seemed to regret his comment. 'I believe you are here to see another opera. Will it be as good as the ones in New York, do you think?'

She took her cue from him, realizing he didn't want to talk about Germany. 'Why, Tom, I believe we may have turned you into an opera fan after all.'

He laughed. 'I wouldn't go that far, Connie. But I am looking forward to spending time with friends, having real conversations and some laughs. I've missed that.'

The opera, *Prinz Eugen, der edle Ritter*, wasn't the best they had seen. Afterwards, they walked to a restaurant Stephen had booked. Connie shivered, pulling her coat tighter around her. There was a chill in the air but it was nice to walk and see the fantastic old buildings.

'I can't understand why they put that opera on. There are so many better ones to choose from.' Dottie looked to Stephen as she spoke, but it was Tom who answered.

'I assume it was chosen for the story. It's based on a popular German folksong about the triumph of German military prowess, something the current government is keen to remind people of.'

Dottie shook her head. 'Why do they need to be reminded of some battle hundreds of years ago? I hate wars.'

Connie studied Stephen as Dottie and Tom chatted. He was quieter than usual. 'What did you think, Stephen?'

He looked at her, holding her gaze before whispering, 'I think the current conductor of the Frankfurt opera is hoping to curry favour with the regime. He only got the position after they sacked all the Jewish staff.'

Connie stared at him in disbelief. 'Sacked them? Why?'

'They are Jews,' he said, his expression regretful. 'In the eyes of the Nazis, that is a good enough reason.'

'But...'

He cut off her words by taking her arm, his tone slightly strained. 'Let's not discuss that now. The walls have ears.' He nodded to the restaurant door, which was just ahead of them. 'Let's just enjoy a meal as old friends can and leave all talk of religion or politics out here.'

Connie was about to argue but Stephen silenced her with a keen look. She watched him carefully; she could read his expression. It wasn't that he didn't want to talk about things – he didn't feel like he could. She wasn't going to put him on the spot, but how she wished they were back in London sitting in the sitting room in front of the fire, where he might be able to talk more freely.

In the restaurant, Tom kept them entertained with funny stories. He spoke about a woman he wanted to ask out but that first he had to find a way to convince her father he wasn't going to tie her up and ship her to America. Connie knew the story was for Dottie's benefit and it worked, with her sister relaxing as the evening progressed.

She took a sip of wine, taking note of the other people eating dinner. Aside from the language difference, they could have been sitting in a restaurant in London. Everyone looked normal, no uniforms in sight, just men and women enjoying a night out. Her eyes caught Stephen's. He smiled as he raised his glass, but she couldn't stop feeling that he wasn't as comfortable as he was trying to appear to be. What was he really doing in Germany? Why choose to work in a country where people lost their jobs because of their beliefs and where conversation had to be watched for fear of being overheard?

EIGHT

LONDON, APRIL 1934

'Mama, are you coming with us to Covent Garden?' Connie cleared the table as her mother finished her cigarette. Cook had left for the evening and Nellie, their daily maid, had the day off.

'No, thank you, darling.'

'Please, Mama, you need to get out of the house. Keep your mind off things.'

Her mother ground out her cigarette, her blue eyes turning purple with irritation. 'Constance, the prince being involved with that awful Simpson woman is not "things". The man, God bless his soul, is bewitched.' Her mother stood – for a second, the light highlighting the grey in her once auburn hair – picked up her glasses and a newspaper and said, 'I'm going to go sit by fire.'

Connie didn't reply. She believed the prince would do his duty as was expected. The rumoured dalliance with Mrs Simpson could only be gossip.

'Do you mind us going out and leaving you alone this evening, Mama?'

'No, of course not, darling. You and Dorothea will have a

wonderful time. I know you enjoy Mr Krauss, so hopefully the opera will be better than the one you saw last month in Frankfurt.' She paused a moment. 'Is Mr Krauss German?'

'No, Mama. Austrian. His wife... oh, Mama, you should hear her voice! She sings like an angel.'

'Well, go and enjoy yourself, darling. Come home safe. Is Stephen escorting you, tonight?'

'Yes. He is back from Berlin on embassy business. He returns on Monday.'

'Good, that boy needs some respite – he is working far too hard for someone so young. You three have fun.'

'Thank you, Mama.' Connie kissed her mother on the cheek and walked quickly out of the room.

As the final thunderous applause for the opera rang in their ears, Connie, Dottie and Stephen made their way into the private salon reserved by Clemens Krauss for his party.

Connie's heart fluttered with excitement, not just because of their opulent surroundings but because she could soon congratulate Viorica and the other artists on their performance.

The salon was bathed in the soft glow of the huge crystal chandeliers, their light reflecting off the polished wooden floors. Rich drapes adorned the numerous windows. A small ensemble of musicians provided soft melodies against which the murmur of conversation filled the room. Waiting staff passed through the crowd with silver platters of filled champagne glasses and delicious-looking canapés.

Mr Krauss, looking very distinguished in black tie, waved them over. He bent in to kiss Connie on the cheek, his moustache tickling her skin. 'Darlings, you came. Did you enjoy the performance? Wasn't Viorica wonderful?'

Connie smiled as Clemens Krauss blew a kiss at his wife,

who was looking as regal as she did on stage dressed in a flowing white gown with a diamond-studded neckline, a matching tiara adorning her dark upswept hair. 'Yes, Mr. Krauss, enchanting as always. You both were. You are so talented.'

Viorica leaned in and kissed her on each cheek in the European style, enveloping her in the heady scent of her perfume. 'Excuse me, my dear Connie, I must mingle.'

Mr Krauss's adoring gaze followed his wife for a second before he remembered where he was. He bowed in apology. 'Please, call me Clemens.' He turned slightly to reveal an elegantly dressed young couple standing to his right. 'This is my nephew, Ernst, and with him, his fiancée, Sonja.' Ernst, blond-haired and blue-eyed with a sharp jawline, clicked his heels and bowed as Sonja, a very pretty brunette wearing a beautiful rose-coloured gown, her subtle make-up accentuating her eyes and lips, blushed.

Connie held out her hand as the introductions were made. 'Congratulations. How do you do? This is Stephen Armstrong, a very close friend of ours. He lives in Berlin now.'

Clemens shook Stephen's hand, engaging him in conversation. Connie turned to Ernst. 'Did you enjoy the opera?'

'Yes, my uncle is very talented, Miss—?' The young man, who spoke English with a heavy German accent, looked to his uncle for help, but Clemens was talking to Stephen in rapid German.

Connie rescued him. 'Fitzwalter, but my friends call me Connie, and this is my sister, Dorothea – Dottie to her friends.'

'I love your hair, Miss—I mean, Connie.' Sonja gave her a small smile.

Self-consciously, Connie reached up to touch her curls. 'Thank you. I wasn't sure the new style would suit me, but I wanted a change. Are you enjoying London?'

'Yes, very much. I feel free here.'

Connie thought it an odd comment to make but she didn't get a chance to quiz the young girl as she glanced over at Stephen, and spotted that he was now standing alone at a small table. She was concerned about him, his air of distraction and worry making her wonder what was wrong. His once dark chestnut hair was now streaked with grey, she realized, his hazel eyes were surrounded by dark circles and he'd lost weight. She was about to walk over to him, but Clemens turned his attention back to them just at that moment.

'You and Dottie should come and see us in Salzburg for your summer holidays. You would be in for a treat.'

Dottie clasped her program to her chest. 'We would love to go, Clemens! To see *Don Giovanni* and *Die Ägyptische Helena* would be everything we dreamed of, wouldn't it, Connie?'

'Of course we would. Thank you very much.' Connie caught her sister's glance of concern but just smiled. Now was not the moment to mention her worries about Stephen. He had sat through the whole opera as if he was at a news conference. There had been no emotion on his face, not even during the final moments. She sensed he was very worried, and she wanted to know why.

She made small talk for a few more minutes before a lapse in the conversation allowed her to excuse herself and make her way over to his table.

'So, what is on your mind, Stephen? A girl?' She tried to sound casual so he wouldn't pick up on her concern.

He avoided her gaze, his voice flat. 'Nothing at all, Connie. I am just tired.'

She wasn't at all convinced. She put a hand on his arm. 'That excuse might work with Mama, but I know you. There is something worrying you. I want to know what it is.'

Stephen looked at her and sighed. 'I can't tell you.'

Was he trying to protect her? But from what? Frustration bubbled over. 'Don't give me the excuse that it's top secret. I'm sure some of your work is, but you can give me a hint. Is it over that madman, Hitler? He won't last forever.'

His eyes darkened, their expression sending a chill down her spine. 'I do not think that is true, Connie.'

'What?' Despite her best efforts, her voice trembled. 'Stephen, how can you say that? German people are not naïve. They can see a monster like Hitler for what he is. Can't they?'

He stared into the distance, and for a few seconds, she thought he was going to ignore her question. But: 'Oh, Connie, how I wish it were so. If you could only see the things I have seen, heard the things I have heard. You wouldn't be so confident. The world...' Stephen stopped abruptly and took a large drink as if trying to drown his sorrows. 'So, did you enjoy the opera?'

She leaned in nearer to him, wanting to understand why he was worried. 'Stephen Armstrong, don't you try to change the subject. I want to know more. Tell me, please.' She was determined to help him.

Stephen took her hand in his, squeezing it gently. 'I forgot how you are when you get the bit between your teeth. We can't talk here. I will meet you for lunch tomorrow. I promise to tell you then. For now, let's just enjoy the evening.'

She wasn't usually put off so easily, but something in his gaze made her change the subject. 'Did you hear Mr Krauss has invited both Dottie and me to be his guests in Salzburg?'

'How lovely! But perhaps you should reconsider going.'

'Why? Don't you like our friends?'

'What? No, it's not that. There was some trouble in Vienna earlier in the year. It's over now, but there is...' He glanced around before lowering his voice. 'Some believe trouble could spread any moment. There is a large contingent of Nazi supporters in Austria.'

Connie looked at Stephen. What had that to do with going to the opera? 'I'm sure we will be fine. And Mama won't mind.

She knows we're experienced travellers now.' She patted Stephen's arm. 'Let's rejoin the others. I'd like to hear more about Sonja and Ernst's plans while they are in London.'

As Connie took Stephen's elbow she noticed how he smiled his relief at her compliance.

He might be smiling now, but tomorrow she wasn't going to let him make excuses. She cared too much about him to let him suffer in silence.

Connie watched the office clock, the minutes ticking by slowly until finally it showed 1 p.m. She stood up, put on her coat and scarf, picked up her handbag and strode out of the door.

Stephen was waiting at the bottom of the steps, a large black umbrella sheltering him somewhat from the rain.

'I should have met you at the restaurant. You're soaked.'

'A bit of rain never hurt anyone, Connie. I hope you are hungry. I'm ravenous for fish and chips.'

She took his arm as he held the umbrella over them. They made their way past Charing Cross Station, stopping at the Clarence Restaurant. Connie held the door while Stephen shook the worst of the rain from the umbrella before he followed her inside.

It was crowded as usual, but they were able to find a table for two. Stephen ordered a pint for himself and a gin and tonic for her. The waiter returned with their drinks.

Connie waited until the man left before asking, 'What's the occasion?'

He clinked his pint glass against hers. 'Two friends enjoying a quiet lunch.'

She laughed as she looked around them. 'Hardly quiet, but thank you.'

They both ordered fish and chips and chatted about this and that until their meals arrived. When they were finished,

Connie decided it was time to get serious. She pushed her plate aside and sat forward, leaning her arms on the table.

'Stephen, talk to me. We, Mama, Dottie and I... we're all worried about you. You've aged about ten years since your posting to Berlin.'

Stephen sat back and ran a hand through his hair. 'Flattery isn't your strong point, Connie.'

'Stop trying to avoid the subject. You know I won't let it go until you tell me what is bothering you. What's wrong.'

Stephen sighed. 'I need another drink. Want one?'

She shook her head. She had to return to the office, and drinking during the day didn't suit her.

'Things are difficult in Berlin, Connie. I'm not sure how much you know...'

'About Hitler and the Nazis? Only a little. I've read the newspapers.'

Stephen rolled his eyes. 'They don't print the truth, well, not much of it. There are things happening in Berlin that shouldn't happen in any so-called civilized city. People are being arrested for no reason.'

'By the police?'

'Occasionally but mainly by the SA – the so-called Brownshirts – and Himmler's SS.'

'What have these people done?'

'In many cases nothing at all. The Nazis say they are cleaning up Berlin. They have imprisoned communists, homosexuals, Jehovah Witnesses...'

Connie shifted in her seat, her cheeks heating. 'Being a homosexual is a crime here too, Stephen. And communists aren't liked either.' She glanced around, hoping nobody had heard her.

'Yes, but here nobody disappears. If they are suspected of committing a crime, they are arrested and if the evidence is enough, there is a trial.' He looked around and leaned forwards, lowering his voice. 'In February 1933, the Nazis introduced a new law that goes by the nickname of the "Reichstag Fire Decree", named after the fire that damaged the Reichstag. This law removed several rights us British deem sacrosanct, including the right to privacy, the right to due legal process – that sort of thing. In Berlin now, anyone the Nazis or their followers deem to be a criminal can be bundled into a truck and driven to special camps. There they are subject to beatings and worse.'

Connie clasped her hands together. 'Worse?'

'There are rumours people are being tortured. Anyone who opposes the Nazis is seen as fair game. Especially if they are Jewish, like Wilfrid Israel.'

Connie didn't know who that was.

'His father owns one of the biggest department stores in Berlin, called N Israel. Wilfrid manages the personnel department.'

'He is one of your friends?'

'Yes. A finer man you couldn't meet.' He looked up and held her gaze, his hazel eyes dark with frustration. 'Wilfrid is extremely worried. Hindenburg appointed Hitler as chancellor in January '33 and by June, Wilfrid had been arrested three times.' Stephen clenched his hand on the table. 'Until the Nazis came to power, the man had never had any issues with the police. He is a law-abiding, stand-up citizen.'

'I'm sorry your friend is having such a difficult time... and don't take this the wrong way, Stephen, but you can't just be worried about that.'

Stephen gave her a knowing look as if to say *I knew I couldn't fool you for long*. 'The Nazis have brought in new rules, Connie. They keep changing things.' His nostrils flared as he continued, in a clipped tone. 'First there was a boycott on Jewish shops, then they brought in the law for the so-called restoration of the professional civil service. That was only an

excuse to sack anyone Jewish. Lots of good men lost their jobs.'
Stephen took another sip of his drink, his voice cracking with
emotion. 'Our office has become so busy. People are desperate
to leave Germany, they queue up outside asking for British
visas. Tom has the same over at the American embassy. Berlin
used to be a wonderful city. Now, there is a feeling of fear and
intimidation in the air.' He leaned in, whispering, 'German citizens are encouraged to inform on their neighbours. People
mutter about the Gestapo, a new police force, but there are
probably fewer than one officer for every ten thousand people.
They don't need many when ordinary citizens are such
wonderful informants.'

Connie hated hearing him be so cynical. Stephen believed
in people, in their inherent goodness and honesty. He was not a
cynic. Or, at least, he had never been before.

'Maybe things will settle down. From what I have been
reading, Hitler has created many new jobs. People can find
work and feed their families. Some, here in London, would say
he could help us recover from the effects of the depression.'

Stephen looked up at her in despair. 'That's part of the
problem. He *is* creating jobs, he *is* building up the so-called
German national pride. But the cost, Connie... it is too high. I
have read his book – if you could call it that. They now read it to
German children. It's an incoherent jumble of nonsense with
one evil message.'

'Which is?'

'He won't be satisfied until Germany rules the world and
every person he considers undesirable, be they Jewish, communist, Slavs or Jehovah Witnesses, are dead. I'll spare you the
gruesome details, but he outlines his plan for the annihilation of
men like my friend, Wilfrid.'

Connie didn't want to believe what she was hearing.
'Stephen, the German people won't stand for that. They are
cultured and educated. And, like us, they don't want another

war. They know the cost, just like we do. Their fathers, brothers, friends died in the war to end all wars. Nobody wants to go back to those days.' She glanced at her watch and finished her drink. 'I must get back to the office or I will be in trouble. Again.' She saw the joke roll off him and sighed. 'Maybe you could persuade Mr Israel to come over here for a holiday, or a longer visit. Then when the real German people find out what Hitler and his cronies are up to, they will stop him. And if they don't, Britain, America and France will. I don't pretend to understand everything, but I do know that there were rules put in place at the end of the last war to stop Germany becoming a threat again. Everything will work out just fine. Now you, my friend, need to get some decent food, sleep and relaxation. That's an order.'

Stephen raised an eyebrow and smiled before standing when she did and leaning in to kiss her on the cheek. 'Well, I admire your positivity. I hope the governments of these countries live up to your expectations. At the moment, the focus is on the threat of communism. They are more concerned about that than anything Hitler has planned, and, of course, he is playing into their hands by telling the Allies he is anti-communist.'

'Yes, you said he was arresting communists.'

'He is, but there is also a very strong rumour that German troops are being trained on Russian soil. I think Mr Hitler has a foot in both camps.'

Connie didn't pretend to understand. Politics was confusing at the best of times.

Stephen sighed. 'I see I'm not going to stop you from travelling. Would you like me to walk you back to the office?'

She looked out of the window to see the rain had cleared. 'No, thank you. It's stopped raining now and it's only a quick walk back. You enjoy the rest of your pint.'

Despite her efforts to cheer him up, Connie had been

listening to what Stephen had to say, and walked back to the office deep in thought over what he had said. The Russians had revolted against the czar and horrible things had happened over there, but Germany wasn't like Russia. They were more like England, and that sort of behaviour wouldn't last.

NINE

LONDON, JULY 1934

Carrying the newspaper, Connie hurried into Dottie's study where she was working on her book. 'The borders have been closed. We won't be able to go to Salzburg. Someone shot the Austrian chancellor.'

Dottie stood up, grabbed the newspaper and quickly scanned the headlines. 'It says here it was Hitler's supporters who killed Dollfuss. Why can't that little man just crawl back under whatever stone he came out of? There have been Nazi marches all over Austria.'

'Yes, but the police have put a stop to them. They haven't taken over. What did they hope to achieve?' Connie rubbed the side of her temple to try to rid herself of a headache. Stephen's warning about the trouble last February reverberated through her mind.

'Don't fret, Connie, dear. Everything will work out just fine. We will telephone the man at Cook's travel agents tomorrow and see what they say.' Dottie smiled before she gestured to her typewriter. 'I had best get this finished.'

. . .

Despite the reassurance from Cook's that the border closure was a temporary response to the assassination, Connie felt worried about the trip and couldn't quite hide her annoyance. 'We should be excited about travelling to Salzburg, having read how beautiful it is and the plans we made for the sights we wanted to see, but...'

Dottie placed the empty suitcase on the bed. 'But what? Don't you want to go anymore? Are you scared? Maybe we're being reckless?'

'Not scared exactly, just... oh, *drat* those Nazis. They shouldn't be allowed to make us change our plans. Let's pack our brightest clothes and go. We are seasoned travellers, after all.' Despite her attempt to project confidence, Connie couldn't suppress the trembling in her voice.

Dottie reassured her. 'As you said, we managed the trip to America on our own and have travelled to the Continent several times now. We can handle this,' she said with conviction, as she began packing some clothes into her suitcase. 'As for Mother, we'll simply tell her that we'll return home at the slightest sign of trouble. We'll have a chat with her after dinner tonight.'

Once their meal was over Connie glanced at her sister, prompting her to start the conversation. Of the two of them, Mother felt Dottie was more risk-averse, so if she said it was safe to travel, Mama was more likely to believe her.

'Mama, we spoke to the travel agency and they have assured us it is perfectly safe to go ahead with our trip.'

As Dottie spoke in her calm, collected voice, Connie watched their mother closely. Her eyes widened with worry and concern. 'Are you sure it isn't dangerous? Couldn't you put it off for a few weeks?'

'That's not possible, Mama, as we'd miss the opera. But we

promise to be extra cautious. We won't be alone. The Krauss family will look after us.'

Their mother didn't look completely convinced as she held her hands together in a gesture of prayer, but her tone was a mixture of pride and anxiety. 'You are your own women and I know you will not be reckless. Stay together and keep safe.'

Even as they reassured their mother, Connie couldn't help the feeling of apprehension which now overshadowed their trip. She wondered if Dottie felt the same but to ask would bring the subject out in the open.

She stood up to clear the table, a sense of determination replacing her fear. She wouldn't be alone but would have Dottie by her side. 'We will have a wonderful time, Mama. I can't wait to get back and show you lots of beautiful pictures of the scenery.'

Travelling through Germany, sitting upright on the uncomfortable third-class train seats, nothing could dim her excitement as Connie watched the changing scenery through the window. Flying was faster but there was something about train travel which satisfied her longing for adventure, to feel close to a new place as if she were really experiencing it.

A German family was seated near them. As Connie and Dottie discussed their plans, the father, who evidently spoke English, must have overheard their conversation. He looked at them in shock.

'You cannot be serious about going to Austria now. Not two young ladies travelling alone. It is not safe. There are demonstrations, heavy police presence and lots of arrests. You should return home.'

Connie glanced at Dottie quickly before replying, 'Thank you, sir, for your concern but we have made arrangements with some friends to see the opera at the Festspielhaus in Salzburg.

We couldn't let them down now. Have you been? We heard it is a beautiful place.'

The man said something in German to his wife and, judging by her facial expression, it wasn't flattering, but Connie didn't care. They would soon be sitting listening to Mr Krauss conduct another opera. She could hardly wait.

Thankfully, the train arrived at Munich shortly afterwards and the family departed. Connie and Dottie transferred their brown travel bags to the Salzburg train and settled in for a more comfortable trip.

Connie gasped as she gazed out of the window of the train, the picturesque countryside rolling by as the wheels chugged closer to their destination, Mozart's birthplace. She loved all the composers, Mozart being one of her favourites, of course, but this time the highlight of their trip was Beethoven's *Fidelio* with their friend, Clemens, as conductor.

Dottie looked over at her and said, 'I can't believe we are here! Finally, after all these years, we are going to the Salzburg Festival. If only we could have persuaded Mother to come with us. She would have loved this scenery, the almost perfect blending of mountains and rivers. We shall have to take a lot of photographs. Oh, look at that!' She pointed to the Hohensalzburg Fortress towering over the city. 'The guidebook says it is one of the largest in Europe. Isn't it just breathtaking? Let's make it one of the first things we visit.'

The train pulled into the station with a surge of steam. They alighted onto the platform carrying their small brown suitcases, grinning at each other, their excitement bubbling over.

Connie looked around her, noticing that the other passengers appeared rather glum.

They walked along the platform, showing their tickets as they exited. When the ticket collector returned her warm smile with a tight nod, Connie's stomach dipped. She glanced at Dottie who was still smiling. Maybe it was her imagination and the man was just in a bad mood.

Their hotel was within walking distance so they set off on foot, following the directions provided by their travel agents.

Despite the warm sunshine and pretty surroundings, Connie couldn't push away a feeling of foreboding. There was a sense of uncertainty and fear in the air. People gathered in small crowds, huddling around newspapers in the public squares or sitting in the numerous coffee shops. For a few seconds, Connie worried they had made the wrong decision and that the German man was right when he'd said it wasn't safe. She tried to shake the thought off as they entered their small hotel and walked up to the polished wooden front desk.

She rang the bell.

'Excuse me, do you speak English?' she asked the hotel clerk when he appeared and took their proffered passports.

'A little.' He glanced at the paperwork. 'Fräulein Fitzwalter. Welcome to Salzburg. You have come for the opera.'

Connie nodded as the clerk handed her a pen to sign the ledger and then handed them a key before clicking his fingers to summon a porter to take their bags to their room. 'Enjoy your trip and the opera. Salzburg is a safe place. We Viennese will not bow down to Nazi scum.'

'Thank you,' Connie murmured, before following Dottie and the porter to their room. They tipped the man and, once the door was closed behind him, sank onto their beds.

'I can't believe we're here. It's such a beautiful place.' Dottie got up and walked to the window. 'I'm so excited, I don't think I could sleep.'

'Me, neither.' For a second, Connie thought about asking her sister if she had sensed an atmosphere but one look at her sparkling eyes changed her mind. The hotel clerk had seemed sure there was nothing to worry about. 'It's too early to call at the opera house. Let's do some exploring.'

Connie and Dottie roamed the beautiful lanes of Salzburg, the sound of their steps ringing off the cobblestones as they set out on their trip.

Their first stop was Hohensalzburg Fortress, high above the city.

As they made their way up the hill to the castle-like structure, Dottie's eyes grew wide with amazement. 'Connie, it's like something from a storybook!' she murmured, gazing at the turreted walls and towers.

Connie couldn't help but smile at her sister's enthusiasm. 'Can you imagine how many knights and princesses must have lived here?'

From the top of the fortress, they were able to take in the stunning view of Salzburg. The cityscape stretched out beneath them, with rust-coloured roofs and historical monuments scattered across the terrain.

Dottie let out an awed breath, overwhelmed by the sight. 'It's easy to see how Mozart could have created such masterpieces with the scenery he had right in his backyard. I can almost visualize what this area must have looked like during his time.'

Connie was just as taken with the beauty around them, but she couldn't stop herself yawning. 'Sorry, the travel seems to have caught up with me. Perhaps we should go back and see if we can find Viorica and Clemens to let them know we've arrived.'

The two sisters hurried along to the opera house, entering the foyer to find their friends deep in conversation with some other people. When Viorica saw them, she hurried over. Greetings with kisses on each cheek were exchanged.

'My dears, you finally made it here to Salzburg! Clemens will be so impressed by your dedication. How was your trip?'

'It was perfect,' Connie lied, not wanting to tell her friend about the uncomfortable train seats and disapproving German family. 'We are just glad the opera is still going ahead and we could be here for it.'

'Yes, it has been a dark time since the assassination. It is very sad, but those Nazi devils will not win. They tried to take over the government. There were demonstrations in many cities, not just Vienna; but for the most part, the police put an end to things. The show must go on. Clemens has worked so hard on it. But the opening date has been pushed to the twenty-ninth.' She looked at her friends with consternation. 'Will you be able to stay?'

Connie nodded. 'Our hotel room is booked for a week. We thought we might have a little holiday, see some sights. We took a trip up to the fortress earlier. It is so beautiful.'

'Salzburg is a wonderful city. I have reserved some good seats for you both. I'm so glad you came. But for now, you will have to excuse us as we have rehearsals. Shall you stay and watch or go and catch up on some sleep?'

Connie and Dottie exchanged a glance: sleep could wait.

Viorica escorted them to some seats in the stalls before returning to the stage. Connie could have listened to her sing scales all day long, so thrilling was the sound of her voice.

TEN

Sarah Liberman sat at the rich brown mahogany dressing table, in her Salzburg hotel room, arranging her hair.

'I prefer it when you leave it down,' her husband murmured as he bent to kiss her neck, sending shivers down her spine.

It was amazing the effect he still had on her after all these years. She smiled at him in the mirror. 'I'd shock the society matrons if I tried that.' She twisted her chestnut hair into a chignon, leaving a few loose curls to frame her oval face. Once satisfied with her hair, she took a kohl pencil to add subtle definition to her rich, deep brown eyes.

If someone were to ask, she'd admit they were her best feature.

She stood up to admire the finished result, wishing once again she was a little taller and thinner. She smoothed down the front of her dress, causing Benjamin to take her hand and kiss it.

'You will be the most beautiful woman there.'

'Thank you for bringing us to Salzburg, darling. I thought you might cancel, considering what happened.'

'Let an assassination ruin my wife's love affair with opera?' Ben joked, but she saw the troubled look in his eyes. 'It's a family tradition to come to the festival every year for your birthday. I want you to relax and enjoy it.'

She leaned up on her tiptoes to kiss him softly on the mouth in thanks. Running her fingers through his thick, brown, wavy hair, she noted the additional grey hairs at his temples.

Despite his words and his downplaying of what was happening in Germany, she knew he was worried. The short-lived civil war in February and now the assassination of their chancellor had opened his eyes: he'd started paying more attention to what Hitler was raving about.

Sarah sighed, pushing all thoughts of the Nazis from her mind. Hitler and his allies had no place in Austria.

She stepped back, running her gaze up and down Ben's suit. 'You, my darling husband, look extremely handsome tonight.' He bowed and smiled.

They were interrupted by a knock on the interconnecting bedroom door, which opened to admit their daughter, Leah.

Sarah clasped her hands in pleasure on taking in her daughter's appearance. She had inherited her height from her father, but her chestnut hair, deep brown eyes and pretty oval face could have been a mirror image of her grandmother. Sarah closed her eyes for a second as the picture of her long-dead mother filled her mind.

'Mama? What is it? Is my dress not right?'

'Darling, you are perfect. You look so grown up.'

'I am thirteen, Mama. Not a child anymore. Can I put my hair up?'

'No, sweetheart. Believe me, the boys will prefer that you wear it just like you are.' Benjamin stepped forward and kissed his daughter on the cheek.

Leah's cheeks pinked. 'Thank you, Papa. But I don't care what the boys think. I just want to see the opera, to imagine I am on that stage. I am Leonore.' Leah spun herself around as she hummed the tune.

Sarah exchanged an amused glance with her husband but neither contradicted their precious child.

'Are your brothers ready?'

'Samuel is, he's reading the paper. Daniel was but then he knocked something on his trousers, so he had to go and change. He won't be long.' Leah moved closer to her mother. 'Mama, can I wear my necklace tonight? I promise to be careful.'

'Why not? It's a special occasion, after all.'

Leah clapped in excitement. Benjamin took the necklace from Sarah's travelling jewel case and placed it around his daughter's neck, stepping back to admire the effect.

Leah put her hand up to touch the diamond sitting in the hollow of her neck. 'It's so pretty.'

'Your great-grandfather bought it, in Poland, for my grand-mother when they got married. They were very happy together. She smuggled it across the border when they came to Austria.'

'It was true love, just like Leonore and Florestan.'

Ben raised his eyes at the reference to the characters from *Fidelio* but Sarah shook her head, giving him a sweet smile. *Let our daughter have her dreams of romance.*

'A woman's first time at the opera is a magical event. Shall we go?' Sarah sprayed a little perfume and then walked into the mist of fragrance. She bit her lip, trying not to laugh as Leah followed her example, but with screwed-shut eyes and mouth twisted in a grimace.

Ben placed Sarah's fur wrap around her shoulders. 'It may get cold later. I don't want you catching a chill.'

She reached out to pat his cheek as her heart soared with love for him. Since he'd gone missing for that horrible week in February, she'd found parting from him even for a day at work difficult. She was even more grateful he'd agreed to stick to their family tradition.

* * *

Refreshed after a short nap and quick meal, Connie and Dottie, dressed in their best gowns, walked back to the opera house. They linked arms as they neared the building, seeing crowds of fellow attendees all dressed in evening wear.

Connie turned to her sister and gave her arm a squeeze. 'Thank you, Dottie. Your dressmaking skills mean we are as well-dressed as those wearing couture.'

Dottie blushed prettily. 'I probably shouldn't tell you, but I cut the pattern the wrong way around. That bow should be on your left, not your right.'

Connie glanced at her chest. 'Nobody will care. I'm so excited. This is just fabulous, isn't it?'

The crowd milled around them, their faces filled with anticipation, eyes sparkling with excitement. The grand, ornate building was busier than ever; nobody would think the country had been on the brink of chaos just weeks before.

They could hear several different languages in the murmured conversations surrounding them as they walked into the auditorium. Connie spotted an attractive family taking their seats in a box to their right, the father and who she assumed to be his two sons standing back to allow the mother and daughter to take their seats first. The young girl looked to be about thirteen and wore a stunning diamond around her neck, the stone shimmering under the overhead lights. Connie smiled as the child, no doubt trying to be ladylike, couldn't resist jumping up and down and pointing out something to the well-dressed woman at her side. The distinguished-looking man leaned in to whisper something to the young girl who, looking embarrassed, her head moving from side to side, took a seat.

'Connie, sit down. It's about to start.'

The orchestra warmed up their instruments and then the lights went down. Connie grabbed Dottie's hand. This was it.

To their surprise, the orchestra opened with Beethoven's 'Funeral March'. Connie's eyes filled with tears at the waves of emotion she felt from the incredible music the musicians played. Their harmonious sounds echoed off the vaulted ceilings and, judging by the number of tear-filled eyes in the guests around her, everyone was similarly moved. For a few seconds it seemed as if the music was lamenting a change, a foreboding of worse events to come.

Then, just as Connie felt her emotions had been thoroughly wrangled, Clemens raised his baton once more and, with a swift movement, *Fidelio* the opera began.

Connie gasped, swept instantly away by the music and the acting. It didn't matter that she didn't understand a word: the music and singing told her the whole story. She wept and smiled as the main character, Leonore, disguised as a young man, Fidelio, found work in the prison in which her adored husband was being held.

Dottie grabbed her hand as the tenor, playing Florestan, dreamed of freedom, seeing his Leonore as an angel coming to rescue him.

At the end, Leonore was given the honour of freeing the prisoners and liberating her husband. As the chorus reverberated through the theatre, Connie couldn't help but feel there was a message that freedom and justice would always prevail.

Thunderous applause greeted the conclusion of the music as the audience rose to their feet for a standing ovation. Connie clapped till her hands stung, tears flowing down her cheeks.

'I'm so glad we came. This was magnificent. The best performance ever!' Dottie gave her a hug. 'I think the message that tyranny must be stopped spoke to the audience even more than usual after what happened to Mr Dollfuss.'

Connie and Dottie followed a select group of people to the after-show party.

'Wasn't Clemens on top form? He's just incredible,'

Connie was saying to her sister – just as the young girl she had seen earlier, now speaking animatedly, walked straight into her.

'Excuse me.' Connie automatically apologized.

The girl said something in German but seemed to realize that Connie couldn't understand her. She spoke slowly: 'I'm so sorry. I wasn't looking where I was going.' The girl stepped back, and, as she did so, her shoe became caught in her dress and she would have fallen but for the steadying hand of the woman Connie assumed was her mother.

'Please forgive my daughter. It is her first time at the opera, and she is overexcited.' The woman's English was heavily accented.

'She didn't hurt me, but thank you.' Connie glanced at the girl with a smile. 'Did you enjoy it?'

'It was superb. I cried and I laughed and... oh, I don't know how to find the English words to explain how lovely it was!'

Connie nodded her agreement. 'I'm English and I struggle to find the words too. Clemens, I mean Mr Krauss, is so talented.'

'You have come from England for the performance?' the young girl asked, her eyes wide with curiosity.

'Yes, my sister and I love opera. Mr Krauss and his wife kindly invited us to Salzburg. It is out first time here. Your country is very beautiful.'

The girl turned to her mother. 'Oh, Mama, could we go to England to see the opera? Please say yes and then we could see the palace and maybe even meet the king and queen. Do you know them?' she asked Connie and Dottie, breathlessly.

'Leah, darling, please calm down.' The man Connie had seen earlier had come over while his daughter was speaking. His voice was as musical as that of a singer's. He clicked his heels and bowed. 'Please allow me to make some introductions. This rather excitable young lady is my daughter, Leah. This is my beautiful wife, Sarah, and my name is Benjamin Liberman. We are from Vienna.'

Connie smiled and bowed her head in greeting. 'My name is Constance Fitzwalter and this is my sister, Dorothea. We live in London. How do you do?'

'Ah! I see you have already met. Sarah, darling, you look so beautiful, you look younger every time I see you!' Clemens had rushed over to them, and now leaned in and kissed the blushing woman on each cheek. 'Connie and Dottie, was it worth your trip? Did you enjoy it?' Clemens asked, as he leaned in to kiss each of them as well.

Flustered at both his kiss and the use of their pet names, Connie couldn't find her tongue and a quick glance at her stunned sister showed she would be of no help.

'Clemens, are you flirting with our guests?' Viorica smiled with amusement as she came to the rescue. 'Sarah, these are the sisters I told you about. They travel all over to go to the opera; they even went to America to see...'

Leah almost jumped. 'America! You went there. Was it fantastic?'

'Leah Liberman, remember your manners.' Her father rebuked her gently.

'I apologize. I'm just so excited. Tonight was the best night of my life.'

Clemens Krauss held out his arm to Leah. 'Let me find you a drink and you can tell me how amazing I was.' Leah took his arm and together they walked in the direction of the bar.

'She is growing into a beauty.' Viorica turned back to Leah's parents. 'Come and find some drinks. I must go and mingle, but I will be back.'

They watched Viorica greet her adoring fans for a few seconds before Connie broke the silence. 'You are very lucky to have such a fantastic festival right on your doorstep.'

Sarah's face grew animated. 'Ben brought me here for the

first festival back in 1920 and we have been coming here annu-
ally since. At first, it wasn't just opera but also plays and
recitals.'

'How fascinating. But tell me, do you prefer the opera or
miss the old days?' Connie leaned in closer to hear Sarah's
response as the crowd around them grew.

'The opera. There is no contest. I just adore the music and
the storytelling. It takes my breath away every time. In 1927,
Strauss conducted *Der Rosenkavalier* for the first time here. I
was in tears laughing, along with the whole audience. Even Ben
found it amusing, although he wouldn't admit it.' Sarah sent her
husband a loving glance. 'It cemented the festival's reputation
for excellence.' She smiled self-consciously. 'I'm sorry, I could
talk forever. Tell me about America. Did you really go just to
see an opera?'

'Not just any opera, but the great Bernardi herself. It was
worth it. We'd go back tomorrow if we could, wouldn't we,
Dottie?'

'Absolutely. Have you ever been to America, Sarah?'

Sarah shook her head as Leah piped up: 'We will go one
day, Mama, promise?'

'You'll have to ask your father about that, Leah.'

ELEVEN

Later in the evening, Viorica appeared again, this time with a woman dressed in an exquisite burgundy coloured gown, her bobbed white hair curled around an expressive rather than pretty face. Her make-up was subtle, as was the pearl jewellery adorning her neck and ears.

'Connie, you must meet a friend of mine. Edith Mayer, meet Constance Fitzwalter and her sister, Dorothea. Ladies, Edith will be in London early next year. Could you look after her while she is there?'

Connie saw Edith's neck muscles tense, her hands trembling slightly as she clutched her bag. In contrast to Sarah's warmth, this woman was more reserved and, if Connie was correct, rather anxious. Connie strove to put her at ease, saying warmly, 'Of course we can. We would be delighted.'

Viorica gave her a grateful look before turning to her friend. 'See, Edith, I told you everything would be fine. These wonderful ladies are my friends and will now be your friends too. Nothing will happen to you.'

Connie wasn't sure what Edith thought could happen in London. She presumably wouldn't be walking the streets alone at night, so why was she so worried? As Edith was now deep in conversation with Sarah and Ben, Connie turned to ask Viorica, but her friend had moved away from their group.

Then Edith laughed at something Sarah said, a lovely infectious sound that made everyone around them smile. Connie saw Viorica's friend had relaxed, her smile wide as her hands moved rapidly, painting a picture for whatever story she was telling Sarah.

Viorica reappeared. 'Edith, come and meet Victor, a tenor I met in Cologne. He's heard all about you.' Edith gave them a small wave as Viorica marched her in the direction of a small, pensive-looking man standing slightly apart from the crowd.

Connie couldn't help but wonder why the woman had been nervous meeting her and Dottie. If anything, they were the ones who looked out of place, surrounded by all the silk dresses, diamonds and other finery.

'Will you return to Austria for more opera?' Sarah's voice broke into her thoughts.

'We would love to visit Vienna. Not just for the opera but to also see the Belvedere and other sights. Clemens said it is one of the most beautiful cities in the world.'

'It is but perhaps I'm biased – I grew up there and we live there still. You must come and visit us if you do make the trip. Ben and I love going to the opera.'

'You have a lovely family.' Connie looked toward Leah sitting between her two brothers.

'Thank you. Samuel, my eldest, is fifteen, very studious like his father. Daniel, he's twelve, always in trouble. Of course, we probably spoil him. At least, that is what Samuel says.'

Connie smiled. 'They look very well behaved to me. I can't say I've seen many children their age at the opera in England. It tends to attract an older crowd.'

'Ben and I usually come to Salzburg every year to the opera alone. But this year...' Sarah hesitated, as if unsure whether to explain. Connie leaned in closer. 'I'm not sure people living outside Austria heard but earlier this year, we had a lot of trouble. Fighting broke out in Vienna and elsewhere in our country. My husband was stuck at the hospital and we, the children and I, were alone and well, it was a difficult time. Now I don't like to be separated from them.' Sarah picked a thread from her dress. 'You probably think I'm being a silly old woman.'

Connie shook her head. 'I'm not a mother but Mama prefers to have her family around her too. Your children look like they enjoyed themselves and that's all that matters, isn't it?'

Sarah looked over at her brood with pride. 'You are very easy to speak to. Are you the lady who tells the stories?'

Connie hid a grin at Sarah's way of asking if she was the author in the family. 'No, I wouldn't have the imagination for that. Dottie is the writer. She is the romantic in our family.' Connie glanced in her sister's direction.

Dottie must have sensed her gaze as she looked up from her chat with Clemens to wave over at Connie before returning to her conversation.

'I work in a government office. I'm lucky as my boss is very understanding about my love of opera. He allows me to come in early so I can leave early on certain evenings so we can get to Covent Garden to queue for the best seats. Have you been to London?'

Sarah shook her head. 'Like my daughter, I would love to see it. Maybe someday. Are you staying in Salzburg for long?'

'A few days. We thought we might travel to Vienna but Viorica said now might not be the time.'

Sarah nodded in agreement. 'I think that might be wise. You may see some things that don't show my country in its best light. Maybe if you could return in September, we would meet again at another opera, when the seasons starts.'

'I'd like that. I'm sure Dottie would too.'

Ben and a sleepy-looking Leah came over to join them. 'I'm

sorry to interrupt but the children are getting restless. I think it is time we went back to the hotel. Please excuse us, Miss Fitzwalter.' He smiled at his daughter as Leah tried to hide a yawn.

'Connie, please. It was lovely to meet you all.'

'Do you want to come and see the gardens with Mama and me tomorrow? It is so pretty and you can tell me if it looks like Hyde Park in London? Please?' Leah's enthusiasm made Connie laugh. Dottie returned to her side just in time to hear Leah's question.

'Connie and I planned to do some sightseeing but we wouldn't want to intrude on your family plans.'

'You wouldn't be intruding at all. Ben is taking the boys fishing. Leah and I would welcome the company.'

'Please say yes, then I can practise my English.' Leah's imploring face was hard to resist.

Connie glanced at Dottie for confirmation and her sister nodded. 'We'd love to. Thank you.'

'We can meet you at the café you passed on the way here. Would ten be too early?'

'Perfect. We look forward to it. Thank you.'

* * *

The aroma of freshly baked goods wafted through the air, a melange of butter and sugar and flour that made Connie's stomach grumble. Leah waved to them from a table near the window, looking younger than she had done the night before.

Sarah smiled as they approached the table. 'Good morning. I hope you didn't feel you had to come with us this morning. Leah can be very persuasive.' She clasped her daughter's shoulder.

'We're happy to join you. The smell of the pastries is

making me hungry.' Connie smiled at Leah. 'Will you help me order?'

Leah nodded but seemed to have lost her voice. Connie and Dottie took their seats at the table.

When the selection of food arrived, Connie savoured the taste of delicate Austrian pastries, sweet and flaky on her tongue. She sipped her hot chocolate, listening as Leah peppered Dottie with questions about her stories.

Dottie always seemed most at ease when talking about her work and, though she was shy when it came to her recent success as an author, she was happy describing her latest idea and the characters who were as real to her, Connie knew, as their own friends and family.

Once they'd eaten, they took a walk through the Mirabell Gardens, the lush flowers and sparkling fountains reminding Connie of Hyde Park. Although the weather was better.

All too soon it was time to leave for London. Connie and Sarah had exchanged addresses with promises to write. Ben and Samuel accompanied them to the train station, Samuel insisting on carrying their travelling bags.

'Thank you very much, Mr Liberman.' Connie smiled as the young man blushed. 'Thank you for your hospitality, Ben.'

Ben bowed and kissed their hands. She loved his formal manners.

'It was a delight meeting you, ladies. My Sarah is very excited about her plans to visit you in London next year. I hope you come back to Austria soon.'

The train whistle announced their departure, and the two women quickly got into their carriage. Connie wiped a tear from her eye as she waved out the window before settling back in her seat. 'I think this week was even better than our American trip, Dottie.'

'It was wonderful.' Dottie took out a pencil and some paper, making some quick notes.

'What are you doing?'

'I just had the best idea for a story.'

Connie leaned back in her seat. Once Dottie started scribbling, she'd be occupied for hours.

TWELVE

LONDON, MARCH 1935

It was a Saturday afternoon, and Connie hurried to the café near Victoria Station where she'd arranged to meet Edith, Viorica and Clemens' friend. She was late, having had to stay back to finishing typing a memo her boss considered urgent. To Connie it had seemed minor and silly, certainly not worth keeping her back late on a Saturday.

She walked past the café window, spotting Edith sitting at a table alone at the back, staring into her cup, her shoulders slumped as if she were trying to become invisible. She had seemed anxious in Salzburg but now the poor woman looked terrified.

As she entered the café, a waitress came toward her asking if she needed a table. 'Thank you, but my friend is already here, waiting for me.'

Connie made her way past a couple of tables where some couples were having lunch. A couple of ladies – office clerks judging by their tweed skirt suits – smiled as she walked by.

Edith had chosen a table in the relatively darkest corner of the café. She stumbled a little, standing up too quickly as Connie waved.

'I'm so sorry, I was caught up at work. It's lovely to see you here in London,' Connie babbled, as she was inclined to do when nervous. 'You don't mind if I call you Edith, do you? Please call me Connie.'

Edith held out her hand just as Connie leaned in to kiss her on each cheek, as she had learned from Clemens was the way Germans greeted each other. The attempt to use each other's greeting style broke the ice, and they smiled.

The waitress came over. Connie ordered a selection of sandwiches and a pot of tea. Edith declined more coffee.

'Dottie will be along shortly. Were you waiting long?'

Edith shook her head.

Dottie arrived just as the waitress returned with the food. 'How are you finding London, Edith? Good, I'm starving. I thought you would have finished eating.' She took her seat, helping herself to some sandwiches.

'I only just arrived. I got caught at the office. I'm afraid Edith was sitting here waiting for me for over thirty minutes.'

'It is no problem. I have a free day today.'

Connie hesitated for a fraction of a second but then decided if she were the one in a strange country and obviously so uncomfortable, she would want someone to be her friend.

'Edith, you seem very nervous. I know we don't know each other that well but we have very good friends in common. So please, if there is something wrong, can you tell us? We will try to help.'

Edith gripped her handbag tighter.

Dottie added, 'Has something happened? Did someone try to steal your bag? I've heard of purse-snatchers targeting tourists but never experienced it. Do you need us to call a policeman?'

The woman paled even more, if that was possible.

Dottie changed seats to sit beside Edith. 'We are your friends. Pretend we have known each other since Clemens conducted his first opera here in London. Were you there?'

Edith nodded.

'We were too. We were probably sitting a few rows apart. I can still feel the music – it spoke to me just as surely as if someone were explaining each note. He is truly gifted, and he brings the best out in all the performers, don't you think?'

'Yes, he is very talented.' Edith's fingers loosened slightly on her bag.

'I don't think our theatres do him justice. His talents lie in the bigger venues, like the Metropolitan in New York or your beautiful opera house in Salzburg. There he really came into his own.'

Connie watched as Dottie put the woman at ease, chatting about their friends. She admired her sister's restraint, as the curiosity over what was making Edith so nervous was almost killing Connie.

'You and your sister have been very kind to me, Dottie.'

'It was our pleasure. You are so very talented and we both love music.'

'I am also Jewish.'

Connie waited for Edith to continue talking, but she seemed to be waiting for something. Connie looked to Dottie for an explanation, but her sister wore an equally bemused expression.

Perhaps seeing their confusion, Edith continued speaking. She held Connie's gaze. 'You are not bothered by this?'

'The fact you are Jewish? No, of course not,' Connie replied. As Edith continued to look at her, she added, 'Should we be?'

'Maybe I am too familiar with the German people. There are many who would prefer to die than to take tea with a Jewish woman. Or man. Or child.'

Dottie spoke up. 'There are some British people who hold similar opinions, but the vast majority take people for who they are, not what they believe.'

'It was once that way in Germany. Or at least so it seemed.'
Edith's eyes filled with tears.

Connie shifted uncomfortably in her seat. She glanced
around, but nobody seemed to be looking. Dottie handed Edith
her handkerchief, giving the woman a couple of seconds to
regain her composure.

Connie tried to choose her words with care, although diplo-
macy was not her strong point. This woman may be Jewish, but
she was also German, and Connie didn't want to insult her.
'Those people are silly. Here in England, we don't care what
religion you are. You can go anywhere, sit anywhere, and talk to
anyone.' That wasn't completely true: there had been some
horrible editorials in the *Daily Mail* recently but Lord Rother-
mere didn't represent all English men. 'Well, within reason. As
a woman, there are certain places that are prohibited. Like the
men's clubs. But that is for all women, regardless of race, creed
or religious beliefs.'

The woman eyed Connie, her expression still sad yet also
wistful. She nodded. 'At one time it was the same in Germany.
In fact, many Jewish people fled persecution in Russia and elsewhere and moved to Germany because it was considered safe.
Safe? Can you imagine we, the Jews, once thought that?' Edith's
voice shook almost as much as her hands. 'Now people disappear, and nobody will tell you where they have gone. To ask is
too dangerous – it can bring attention on you.'

Connie blinked back tears. Since their return from Salzburg, Stephen on his regular trips back to London, had told her
in more detail about how bad things had become in Germany,
and she had to admit even her natural positivity was wavering,
her hopes decimated by the reality. They'd felt the increase in
tension and a feeling of anxiety in the air the last time they
visited Germany. But this was different. To see a woman obviously scared out of her mind for her family, to personally know
people who had disappeared, she just couldn't imagine how she

would deal with it. What if it were Dottie or Mama who suddenly, through no fault of their own, became pariahs? No wonder Edith was so upset.

Connie wanted to reach out and comfort Edith but what could she say? She saw by the miserable expression on Dottie's face that her sister felt just as inadequate.

Edith misinterpreted their silence.

'I apologize. It is clear from your expressions you cannot know what life is really like now in Germany. Not just for the Jews, but for anyone who doesn't behave like the leaders of the party suggest they should. Of course, their rules do not apply within their own circles. For example, Hitler prefers the women of Germany not to smoke or wear make-up. But the wives of the Nazi elite smoke, drink like fish, and shop at all the best shops in Paris. They are not seen outside without their perfect make-up, well, apart from a few die-hard Hitler enthusiasts like Gerda Bormann.' Edith took a deep breath. 'But my friends, of course, are imprisoned for more shocking offences. That of being born Jewish.'

Dottie borrowed Connie's hanky to dab her eyes as Connie listened in horror to the stories Edith told her. It confirmed everything Stephen had hinted at – and as Edith had experienced the abuse in person, it was so much more impactful. And just when she had thought she had heard the worst, the next story would surpass it. She brushed tears from her eyes but didn't stop Edith from talking.

The waitress appeared to remove the remains of their lunch, but Dottie waved her away with an apologetic smile.

Sensing their new friend needed to get these stories off her chest and feeling more than a little guilty for thinking before that the woman was of unsound mind, Connie sat quietly forcing herself to listen. The horror the lady in front of her had already experienced made Connie angry. She felt helpless and frustrated. Why wasn't anyone doing anything to help? Why didn't the government stop Hitler and his cronies? What were they waiting for? Stephen's face came to mind. Was this what had him so worried? Was he safe? She wished he would move back to London.

'I am sorry, Miss Fitzwalter – I mean, Connie. And to you too, Dottie. I shouldn't have unburdened myself to you but there is nobody to talk to. Sometimes I think I am going crazy. I cannot believe what is happening. It is impossible for you to believe it. There are no notices here. The cafés and hotels are open to all. I can sit anywhere, with anyone.'

'Of course you can, Edith.' Dottie squeezed the woman's hand. 'I believe it will stay that way. You being Jewish is no different to me being Protestant. Who or what you believe in doesn't make you less human, does it?'

'I wish others shared your opinion but there are whispers your royal family feels the same as Hitler. The prince who will become your king has a lot of interesting friends.'

Connie rolled her eyes. She knew she shouldn't. She'd heard the same rumours as Edith. Edward would one day be king and as such, he deserved her full loyalty and respect yet... how could he behave as he did? Gadding about without, it seemed, a thought for his own people who were struggling, never mind those in Europe.

'He does, but he is not king yet. People say Mrs Simpson likes Mr Hitler and his friends as the Nazis are the only people who admire her.' Her attempt at a joke fell rather flat. 'I am sure he isn't aware of what you and your people have been going through. There has been nothing of this in the papers.'

'The real news is suppressed. Even in Germany. It is dangerous for people to tell the truth. Those who do disappear, even if they are not Jewish. When the Nazis first came to power, they arrested thousands of people. Not the Jews – at least, not at first. They were more concerned with those who had opposed them, and the communists. Those social democrat members who had been particularly vocal in their disdain for Nazi policies. But they also used their new powers to settle old scores. Those who joined the Nazi party learned the laws didn't apply to them. They could have anyone arrested on trumped-up charges. People are scared. They have reason to be. I have many friends who have disappeared, never to return.'

Connie took Edith's hand in hers. 'Please tell us how we can help you. What do you need?'

Dottie put her hand on Edith's arm. 'Let me order some fresh tea. A problem shared is always easier to solve with a cup of tea in your hand.' She waved to the waitress, who came and cleared the table, not hiding her obvious curiosity. 'Could we please have fresh tea and some of those delicious-looking cakes as well? Thank you.'

They waited in silence until the waitress returned with the tea and cakes and only when they were once more alone did Edith speak.

'I have a daughter. Her name is Else. She is seventeen and a music student. She is very talented and so beautiful.' Edith's eyes glittered with unshed tears, and her voice trembled before getting stronger.

Dottie complimented her: 'She must take after her mother.'

Edith smiled through her tears. She wiped her eyes with a hanky before folding it and replacing it in her pocket. 'Up until recently, she was a university student, but the new laws prohibit that. What will come next? She would be safer in England.'

Connie waited but when Edith remained silent, asked, 'So why don't you bring her here?'

Edith picked up a teaspoon and used it to stir her tea, concentrating on the task as if it were the most difficult thing on earth. 'It is not that easy. The immigration rules are very strict, and it is very difficult to get visas. We can come on holiday, but to stay is a problem. For an adult, it is almost impossible. For a child, it is a little easier but only...' Edith glanced at Connie before looking back at the teaspoon now sitting in the teacup. 'No, it is too much. I cannot ask this of you.'

Connie leaned in closer. 'Ask us what? Let us decide if it is too much or not.'

Edith looked at her. 'My daughter could come to live in Britain if she had a British guardian. That person would be responsible for her while she lived here.'

That didn't sound like a burden. Connie heard herself agree almost without thinking about it. 'I can be her guardian,' she replied, just as Dottie said the same.

'No, you cannot. It would be too much.'

'Why? Because we are women? Does the guardian have to be male?' Connie protested.

Edith's gentle smile calmed Connie's ire. 'No, not that. They do not care if you are a man or woman, but you must have enough money to provide for a child. We... we have a little but the Nazis make it very difficult for Jews to take money out of Germany. Forgive me for putting you on the spot.'

'You haven't. We offered.' Dottie looked over at Connie. 'You might be a more suitable candidate.'

Edith looked confused.

'What Dottie means is that some people do not believe authors can earn a steady income. But I work for the Civil Service, and you can't get more secure than that. I may not get paid much, but I have a steady job. Our government isn't going to disappear. Else can come to live with us at our home. Mama won't mind.' Under the table, Connie crossed her fingers. She had no idea what her mother would think. For now, they had to convince Edith her child would be safe.

Dottie spoke confidently, as if everything had already been arranged. 'Else can come and continue her studies at the university here. We will find a way. You must find out more about how she can transfer to the university program here, and we will speak to Mama. We'll meet again tomorrow at the Lyons'

Corner House at Marble Arch – it's near your hotel – for tea. Mama loves going there.'

Edith's eyes filled once more. Connie took a bite of cake, not tasting it but wanting to do something while giving Edith time to collect herself.

'You will really do this? For me? For a stranger?'

'Edith, you are not a stranger.' Dottie patted her arm. 'You are a friend of the Krauss family, and that makes us friends too. Now, dry your eyes. Your daughter will come here to live and, I promise you, your husband and your sons will come too. We will find a way. There is always a way around things if you look hard enough.' She glanced over at Connie. 'When we knew we wanted to go to America to see Elana Bernardi sing, we had no idea how we were going to find the money to pay for it. Did we, Connie?'

'We didn't have any idea, but it didn't matter. We knew we wanted to go. Dottie sewed our clothes– she isn't just a fabulous writer but is a wonderful seamstress too. We walked instead of taking buses or tubes, ate brown rolls instead of white, didn't have lunches like this and in less than two years, we had the money and we went. We are quite determined women when we set our mind to things. You are too. You wouldn't be the director of the Salzburg festival if you weren't. We can do this. Together.'

Edith surprised them by first throwing her arms around Dottie and hugging her and then by standing to do the same to Connie.

Connie cringed a little, inwardly, feeling the eyes of the café customers on them: outward expressions of affection in public weren't something one did in London.

Outside the café, the women confirmed their arrangements to meet again the next day and saw Edith safely into a cab.

'Can you imagine living in fear like that, Connie? I some-times wonder what the world is coming to.' Dottie linked her arm with Connie's as they walked home.

'There must be something we can do to help, apart from just giving her daughter a home. What about your contacts in the newspapers? Perhaps you could ask a reporter to write a story about Edith and her people?' Connie quickened her step.

'Do you think that could help? We could highlight the need for sponsors, and perhaps some people would offer a place in their homes to other students like Else.'

'That's a good idea. I'll make enquiries.' Dottie gave her a warm smile. 'I already feel slightly less helpless than I did when listening to Edith's story.'

Connie squeezed her sister's arm. 'Me, too. I'm so glad we don't live over there. I couldn't bear it if anything were to happen to you or Mama. And I wish Stephen would come home and take a position in London.'

'Are you coming down with a fever? You're flushed.' Dottie reached out to touch Connie's forehead.

'I'm fine, no need to worry,' Connie said with a smile, soft-ening her tone.

She didn't want Dottie to suspect that her feelings for Stephen were evolving. Was it worry for him due to his being in Germany, or something else entirely?

THIRTEEN

Later that evening, Mama asked for a fire to be lit in the small sitting room. It was easier to heat than the larger drawing room and, given they weren't entertaining, it was perfect for the family.

Connie and Dottie exchanged several glances as Mama, enveloped in a soft shawl she'd crocheted herself, pushed the embroidery needle back and forth rhythmically through the fabric she was working on.

Connie hesitated, not wanting to ruin the pleasant evening, her heart pounding against her chest. It wasn't that she didn't believe their mother would help, but she hated causing her distress by exposing her to the evil happening in another country. 'Mama, we need to speak to you.' Connie's voice trembled with nerves.

Mama glanced at her, tiredness mixed with curiosity in her eyes, before returning her concentration to her sewing. 'Are you going travelling again, darling? You're only just back.'

'No, Mama, not for a while. We would like to invite a friend to stay with us.'

Mama's fingers stilled momentarily, a faint line of concern etched across her forehead. 'A friend? Who?'

'Else Mayer.'

'Do I know her? The name is not familiar.' Mama looked as confused as she sounded.

'She is both German and Jewish. She wishes to study at the university here in London. She is seventeen and was at university in Berlin, but has since lost her place. Through no fault of her own, Mama. She is an extremely talented young lady.'

Mama resumed her sewing, but Connie noticed the slight tremor in her hands. 'If she's that good, why did they throw her out of university?'

Dottie, with hands clasped so tightly together that her knuckles whitened, interjected: 'The Nazis have prohibited Jews from taking state professional examinations and limited their attendance at university.'

A moment of profound silence enveloped the room, broken only by the ticking of the antique clock, as their mama stared at her daughters, her mouth tight with shock.

'Else cannot stay with family as she has none in Britain,' continued Connie. 'She cannot stay in Germany as the Nazis... well, they are making life very difficult for the Jews.'

'Constance, darling, why us?' Mama's voice, softer now, held a quiver that sent shivers down Connie's spine.

'She has nobody else, Mama. The Germans are doing lots of horrible things to the Jews. We do not want to frighten you with the details, but some of the things we have been told—'

Mama put her sewing to one side, switching her attention to her daughter. 'I admit to being concerned. We know nothing of this girl or her family. Are you sure what her mother said is the truth?'

Connie nodded. 'You can ask Edith tomorrow. When you see the anguish on her face, the anxiety in her eyes, you will know she speaks the truth. I wish Stephen were here. I believe he would tell you he shares concerns for the future of the Jewish people under the rule of Hitler and his cronies.'

As Dottie moved closer to take their mother's hand, the faint scent of her rosewater cologne wafted towards Connie, a familiar and comforting fragrance amidst the tense atmosphere. 'Mama, forget about Else being Jewish or the fact we don't know her or her family. We know a child is in trouble. We have the means to help her. Wouldn't Papa have wanted us to help where we could? He always said we should share what we had with others less well-off than ourselves.'

Mama looked grave for a couple of seconds, biting her lip. Connie exchanged a look with Dottie, wondering if Mama would break down in tears. But she didn't.

'Please tell this woman that her child would be more than welcome,' Mama whispered, her voice barely audible yet imbued with a quiet strength. 'We must do our best to look after this young girl. She will probably be terrified to leave everyone she holds dear behind and come to a foreign land. Does she speak English?'

'I believe so, Mama.'

'That will make life a little easier for her.' Mama patted Dottie's hand before releasing it. She stood up. 'Now, if you don't mind, I think I will retire to bed. Goodnight, girls.'

'Good night, Mama, and thank you. We love you.'

'I love you too, girls. Thank God I am not in the same position as your friend. I don't think I would bear to send my children to a stranger, even if it were for your safety.'

Connie watched her mama walk out of the room, her back straight as a ramrod, although her heart must have been breaking for any family to be put in such a position.

The next day, Mama joined Dottie and Connie as they met Edith at the Lyons' Corner House. A young waitress, looking

very smart in her black dress with the double row of pearl
buttons sewn with red cotton, a starched cap with a big, red 'L'
embroidered in the centre, and a pristine, white, square apron
worn at dropped waist level, smiled at them as she led them to
the table.

Mama ordered tea and sandwiches for everyone, along with
a selection of cakes.

Connie tried to help Edith feel more relaxed. 'They call the
waitresses "Nippies" as they move so quickly. Did you see her
taking our order without having to write it down? I'd forget as
soon as I got to the counter.'

Edith smiled but her eyes remained cloudy with worry.

'Edith, please relax. Mama has agreed to our plan.'

'You did?' The German woman was amazed they were still
willing to help.

'My daughters were right to tell you we would help you,
Edith. My husband, God rest him, would have done as much as
possible. He had connections in the government – they would
have helped too.'

'Not everyone shares your views, Mrs Fitzwalter, but thank
you for your kindness. It will be a blessing to know Else is out of
harm's way. She is such a beautiful girl.' Edith's voice shook as it
dropped to a whisper. 'I dread to think of what those animals
would do to her.'

Mama came into her own as she moved to sit beside Edith
and put her hand on her arm. 'I would do anything for my
daughters, too. It's the mother in us. Now your daughter will
be taken care of. Tell me, how soon can she travel? My girls
have flown to Cologne – is that far from where you live? Or
maybe it would be better to get a train and then the boat from
Holland?'

Connie watched her mother in admiration. She was taking
charge of the travel arrangements like she did this every day.

'I think flying would be better. We live in Frankfurt, so can get to Cologne by train. I wouldn't want Else to travel alone on the boat.'

'Tell me, Edith, about the rest of your family. Connie mentioned you have sons. What are your plans to get them out? And you and your husband? We must make a plan. We can take care of Else, but it would be better for her if your whole family were to move over here. Don't you agree?'

Filled with pride, Connie sat back and watched her mother coax and persuade Edith to trust that all would be well.

By the time tea and cakes had arrived, she had promised Mama she would come back with her family.

Later that evening, when her mother kissed them goodnight, Connie gave her an extra hug.

'Mama, I'm so proud of you. I'm lucky to have you as my mother.'

'No, my darling girls. I'm the lucky one. Don't stay up too late. Goodnight.'

Three weeks later, Connie went to Croydon Airport to meet Else. Her heart broke for the terrified-looking young woman walking alone through the terminal. She waved and called her by her name. 'Else! It is so wonderful to meet you in person. How was your flight? Did you have any issues leaving?' She took the young girl's bag. It was surprisingly light, given she had emigrated.

'No. Mama packed my bags very carefully. We are restricted in what we are allowed to take out.' Else's English wasn't as good as her mother's but she could make herself understood.

They returned home by train to London, and then took the underground. As they walked the last few minutes home,

Connie noticed the young girl looking around her with wide, grave eyes.

Else hesitated as they neared the house. 'Miss Fitzwalter, can you take me straight to my room. I… I do not wish to embarrass myself or your mother with my tears. I cannot face other people now. You understand?'

Connie's heart twisted for the poor girl. 'Of course. You can meet my mother and sister tomorrow.'

The girl's shoulders shuddered with suppressed emotion. 'Thank you. I do not wish to seem ungrateful. I just…' Else took out a hanky and blew her nose.

'We understand.' Connie choked out the words while trying to keep back a sob of her own. She turned to open the front door. Instead of leading the girl into the sitting room, she showed Else to her room. 'I hope you will be very happy here with us. I know you are probably feeling scared and lonely. I promise you the same thing I promised your mother: we will do everything we can to help your family, your parents and your brothers come to London. It will take time, so be brave.' She wanted to hug the girl but sensed it may break her resolve. Instead she squeezed her arm gently. 'My mother is a wonderful listener. She is also a little lonely, as she misses my father very much. Let her be your friend. It will help you both.'

'Thank you, Miss Fitzwalter.'

'Connie. And you are very welcome. I hope you sleep.' Connie pulled the door to the room shut behind her.

Later that night, she heard Elsa crying and then again, every night for the next week.

But Mama worked her magic and gradually the young woman blossomed. She seemed to be enjoying her new position at the music academy.

. . .

One evening, some weeks later, Else asked to speak to them. 'I hope you don't think I'm ungrateful. I can't thank you all enough for what you did for me and what you are doing for my family. But a friend at university has asked me to come and stay with her at her parents' home. They are Jewish and they attend synagogue and observe Sabbath.'

Else almost stuttered in her haste to get the words out. She had obviously rehearsed her speech several times.

Connie glanced at Mama and saw a quick flash of hurt in her eyes. Her mother had got used to spoiling the young girl. But she put her feelings aside as she said, 'Else, that's wonderful news. You have been the best houseguest anyone could ask for, but it is part of growing up to stand on your own two feet. So long as your parents are happy with your new living arrangements, we are too.'

'Thank you. You are the kindest person I know.' The young girl nearly knocked Mama over as she rushed to give her a hug.

FOURTEEN
LONDON, AUGUST 1935

'Miss Fitzwalter, there is a gentlemen downstairs waiting to see you. You know we don't encourage callers to the office.'

Sitting at her desk, Connie looked up from her filing. 'A gentleman? To see me?'

'A Mr Armstrong. I told him not to make a habit of it.' Miss Fowler adjusted her glasses, looking at Connie over their steel rims. 'He said he's in London on official embassy business and very stuck for time. You can leave as soon as you are ready.'

'Thank you, Miss Fowler.' Stephen must have really turned on the charm to make Miss Fowler allow her to leave on time.

Connie put the balance of the filing back in the tray, put the cover on her typewriter and tidied away her pencils. Miss Fowler was a stickler for tidy desks.

She took her coat and hat from the coat stand. 'Goodnight, Miss Fowler. I'll be off.'

Miss Fowler nodded but didn't look up. Connie walked as fast as decorum would allow. She hadn't seen Stephen in what seemed like months but when she got to the bottom of the stairs, she hesitated when she spotted him sitting in the reception area.

He was staring at a newspaper, frowning, but his eyes

weren't moving so he didn't seem to be reading. The more she watched, she realized he was deep in thought and, judging by his facial expression, not thinking about good things.

'Hello, there. Fancy meeting you here.' She forced a note of joviality into her voice as she approached him, rather than express her concern over the dark circles under his eyes and the slight shake of his hands.

Stephen coloured as he rose to his feet and leaned in to kiss her on the cheek. 'You look wonderful as usual, Connie. I was in the area and wondered if you might fancy a bite to eat. I hate eating alone.'

Connie smiled as she put her arm through his. 'Would you like to come home and eat with us? Mama won't mind. She is out at her bridge club this evening, but I'm sure Cook left plenty of food.'

'Tonight I thought you might prefer to eat out. My treat?'

Connie's stomach flipped a little, wishing she had taken some time to go to the ladies' and touch up her lipstick. She dismissed those thoughts. This was Stephen, a friend of the family. He wasn't asking her out.

'I'd love to. Did you have somewhere in mind?'

'Yes, a rather nice Italian place a friend told me about. I haven't eaten there yet, but he promises it's wonderful.'

'Oh, good, I love Italian food. The meals we had in Verona were almost as good as the opera. And the gelato? I could be tempted to return for that alone – but don't tell Dottie.'

'Listen to you, the well-seasoned traveller. I can't keep up with you two these days. Vienna, Italy, Amsterdam, Germany... where next?'

Her heart fluttered in response to his teasing smile; she couldn't meet his gaze for fear he might read something into her reaction.

This was *Stephen*, for goodness' sake.

'Mama has got used to us announcing we will be in Europe

for a few days. She doesn't worry so much, although she is glad when we get back to London. I wish she would come with us, but she's a home bird.'

Although he chatted as they walked, Connie sensed Stephen was holding back, but she didn't want to tackle a deep conversation while they negotiated their route through the crowded streets. Everyone was in a rush to get home.

They almost walked past the restaurant, it was so small. The smell of garlic greeted them as soon as they pushed open the door. Stephen's stomach grumbled nosily. 'Forgive me, we were stuck in meetings all day.'

The maître d' showed them to a small table by the window. It afforded them privacy without being too intimate, given the view of the pedestrians outside.

Connie let Stephen choose the wine as she looked at the menu. 'What is *ossobuco?*' She stumbled over the pronunciation.

'Braised veal.'

Connie scrunched up her face. 'Can you pick something for me?'

'Are you sure you trust me to do that? I could order frogs' legs...?'

She loved he was teasing her like he always did, but somehow it felt forced, as if he wasn't really himself. 'I know enough to know that's French food.'

The waiter reappeared and as they discussed the menu, Connie got a chance to study Stephen unobserved, noting the new lines that had appeared around his eyes, the strain lines around his lips.

Stephen ordered for them in crisp Italian, to the delight of the waiter.

When the wine arrived and the waiter poured, he raised a glass, his gaze locking on hers. 'To friendship and frog-leg-free dinners.'

Connie laughed. Taking a sip of the delicious wine she set the glass on the table. 'You look tired, Stephen. You need a holiday.'

'I don't have time for holidays.' He gave a tight smile and looked at her for a moment before saying, 'Connie, how serious were you about wanting to help the Jews?'

Her fingers played with the delicate wine glass stem. 'You know about that?'

'Yes, I heard about Else and how her parents and brothers will be joining her shortly. I wondered if you were still keen on helping, or if you'd had enough.'

'Stephen, how could you ask me that?'

Nearby diners looking at them made her aware her voice had risen; she dropped her voice.

'There are people at risk, their very lives on the line. I want to do everything I can, and so does Dottie, but we are not sure how. Neither of us have any real skills.' She looked at him intently. 'You have something on your mind, don't you?'

'Yes.'

'Well?'

He glanced up. The waiter had arrived with their meals. He put a plate in front of her, saying in heavily accented English: 'Be careful, signora, the plate is very hot.'

'Thank you, it looks delicious.'

'No frogs were involved in making this dish.' The waiter grinned as she realized he had heard Stephen teasing her.

'Thank you on behalf of all frogs.' She picked up her fork and took a dainty taste of the chicken. Flavours exploded on her tongue. 'This is delicious, thank you.'

The waiter nodded before he topped up their wine glasses. 'Enjoy your meal. Please call if you need anything else.'

A few minutes passed in silence as they both made short work of their meals. Connie hadn't realized how hungry she was.

'This food is heavenly. Your friend was right.'

'He usually is. At least when it comes to food.'

Connie saw the strained look reappear on his face. Pushing her plate to one side, she leaned in a little. 'Stephen, talk to me.'

'I am not sure it is right for me to ask you to do this. It could be very dangerous.' He paused, then looked at her. 'Never mind "could" – it *is* very dangerous.'

'Stephen, what do you do for the Foreign Office exactly?'

'I work in the embassy in Berlin. That's all you need to know about that. My work for our government is separate from what I am asking you to consider doing.'

She clasped her fingers together, resting them on the white linen tablecloth. 'You help Jewish people, don't you? I know you're involved, so there is no point in denying it.'

Stephen looked around him before whispering to her: 'Yes, but that must stay between us. The last thing I need is to be recalled from service right now, when I am needed most. I only told you, Connie, as I trust you implicitly. You cannot tell anyone else.'

'I have to tell Dottie – we don't keep secrets.'

'Okay, but don't tell your mother. It's not that I don't trust her, it's just safer for all of us. The Nazis aren't just in Germany. They have plenty of friends over here. They have agents too. People have disappeared. Always assume you are being watched, so never be careless.'

Connie was glad she had clasped her hands together: he might not see them shaking. 'Stephen, you're scaring me now. What do you want us to do?'

'I want you to continue doing what you have always done. I want you to go to the opera in Frankfurt, Cologne, Berlin, Vienna – and everywhere else we can help people.'

Go to the opera? What could be so dangerous about doing that? 'What do you need me to do? I mean, nobody gets in trouble for going to the opera.'

'As you know from speaking to Edith, there are various rules in place to hinder the Jews from entering Britain. Only those who can self-finance their stay using money held in British Banks, or have people willing to act as financial guarantors can make their way to safety.'

'Yes, I know. We are acting as guarantors for Edith's family.'

Connie blushed, not wanting to talk about money, it being considered vulgar; but there was little point in letting anyone think they could afford to sponsor others. 'I am not sure our resources could stretch to include others.'

'No, that's not what I meant. Some Jewish people have money and other means of support, but it is still in Germany. The Nazis have imposed strict rules over what they can take with them. They have to pay taxes and other charges so, basically, they can leave with nothing but the clothes on their backs. All jewellery, cash, property, etc., are vulnerable to confiscation, either officially or unofficially. When Jews and other so-called undesirables' – at Connie's wince, Stephen softened his tone – 'that's the Nazis' term, not mine, obviously... when they travel, they are searched and if found with any assets, the best that can happen is that these assets are confiscated. The worst... well, that's getting more and more serious by the day. Either way, it is too big a risk.'

Connie's heart pounded, her churning stomach making her wish she hadn't eaten. The injustice tore at her heart strings, her sense of fairness.

'How can I help?'

Stephen leaned in closer, moving a wine glass out of his way to take her hand. 'You and Dottie can travel freely. You are neither Jewish nor wanted by the Gestapo. You have British passports and are thus protected to some degree. You can smuggle the money and jewellery out.'

'You want us to become smugglers?' Connie couldn't keep the excitement out of her voice. This sort of thing only happened to the people in her sister's books. 'When do we start?'

Stephen's grip on her hand tightened, the sternness in his gaze imploring her to grasp the gravity of the situation. 'Connie, this isn't a game. It's serious and dangerous. The Nazis are not the type to mess with. Your passport can only offer limited protection and the embassy will hesitate to get involved if it is proven you are guilty of whatever charges the Germans decide to bring, should you ever be caught. So, you must be careful.'

'Of course. I won't do anything stupid and, anyway, if I tried, Dottie wouldn't let me.' Her attempt at lightness fell flat as Stephen's expression remained solemn and unconvinced. She glanced around at the other diners, the women smiling gaily as their companions leaned in to whisper sweet nothings in their ear. Her gaze travelled back to Stephen, noting his tight jaw, the serious expression on his face. Was that apprehension in his eyes? Did he regret asking her? She tried to ignore the hint of fear at the base of her spine. To distract herself, she asked more questions. If she was going to get Dottie into something dangerous, they had to know the full story.

'But I don't understand. What use is it to people in Germany if we have their jewellery here?'

Stephen loosened his grip on her hand but didn't release it. His fingers rubbed the top of her hand as he explained: 'Assets can be sold here in Britain, the money lodged in bank accounts opened in the names of the owners. They can then apply for visas on the basis they have bank accounts and funds in Britain.'

She pulled her hand away, pretending she needed some water whereas in reality his touch was distracting her. 'That is clever. I will do it. So will Dottie.'

'You have to ask her.'

'No, I don't. I know my sister. She wants to help as much as I do.'

Stephen took a sip of wine as the waiter came over to

remove their plates, asking them if they required anything else. When Stephen glanced at her, Connie smiled at the young man and asked if he could bring coffee in a few minutes. Once he was out of earshot, Stephen spoke. 'You will also take money out of Britain to Germany. This will be used to buy food and other necessities, and will be used as bribes, if required.'

'Bribes?' she squeaked rather loudly, before looking around to see if she had attracted anyone's attention. That sounded like something that really *could* land them in trouble with the authorities.

Stephen coughed and took a drink of water. 'Sometimes it is possible to rescue those already in the concentration camps if the commandant is willing to take a bribe.'

A chill ran up her spine, and Connie shivered. 'What *are* these concentration camps? Edith mentioned them, but when I asked her about them, she got too upset to speak.'

'They are like large, open-air prisons, but the only thing the occupants are guilty of is being Jewish or something else offensive to the Nazis. They have put priests and other religious folk into them for speaking out against their policies. Jehovah Witnesses and homosexuals are also targets.'

Putting both hands on the table, she leaned in closer to him, trying to stay calm despite the outrage flooding her body. 'But you cannot just lock people up! That's insane. You have to have a trial and a judge, and they must be found guilty of a crime. How can you be guilty of something that arose from the circumstances of your birth?'

Stephen picked up her glass, encouraging her to take a sip, the expression in his eyes warning her to remember they were in a public restaurant. Connie took a small drink before replacing the glass on the table. She forced herself to smile, to try to convince him she had her feelings under control once more.

'Nobody cares about law and order, at least not those in power. The Nazis are in charge and God help anyone that gets in their way.' Stephen took a large gulp of wine. 'There are various charities who will help. There are also several wealthy individuals willing to help – both Jews and gentiles. Don't worry about where it comes from. We will sort that side of things out.'

Curiosity made her ask: 'Who is *we*?'

A shadow passed over Stephen's face, but he held her gaze. 'I can't tell you that, Connie. You just need to trust me.'

Of course she trusted him. Next to Dottie and Mama, this man was her family. She nibbled at her lip, but he remained silent.

'What if I cannot contact you, when we're in Germany?'

'I've told my boss, Frank Foley, about you. If you ever need anything and cannot find me, go to Frank. He will help you. Just be careful. Don't mention this to anyone – especially his name. In his position, he can't be seen to be doing anything other than his job.'

FIFTEEN

LONDON, OCTOBER 1935

Their mother was used to them travelling in Europe now, but after meeting Edith and helping her whole family to move to Britain, she was less comfortable with them going to Germany than before.

'You girls be careful on your trip. Remember you might not agree with what is happening in Germany but you are guests in that country and should remain neutral. It is not our place to judge other people. I want you back here in the house by Monday at the latest. Don't have me read anything in the papers.'

'Don't worry about us, Mama.' Connie smiled at her mother. 'We are going to see Stephen.' At the dubious look on her mother's face, she leaned in and kissed her on the cheek. 'We will be home before you know it.'

Connie didn't add that if they were to disappear or get into trouble, the last place her mother would find out about them would be the newspapers.

. . .

The sisters took a train to Harwich, a boat from there to Holland and from there another train to Berlin.

Alighting at the station, they were both delighted to see Stephen waiting to escort them to their hotel. 'Thank you both for coming to celebrate my birthday. It would be a jolly poor show if I had to blow out the candles alone.'

Stephen's forced jovial tone didn't help their nerves and Connie felt like everyone was staring at them as they made their way through the busy train station and to the streets outside.

Stephen hailed a cab. They got in but before she could ask any questions, he kept up a continuous stream of conversation asking about mutual friends and acquaintances until the cab drew up outside their hotel. He paid, and got out first to hold the door for them.

'Don't say a word about anything,' he whispered as the two women alighted.

They followed him into the hotel listening as he spoke fluent German, passing over their passports and showing them where to sign the register. Then he dispensed with the need for a porter and escorted them to their room.

'Let's just drop your bags here and go for a walk before lunch. I'm sure you would like to stretch your legs.'

By this point, Connie was ready to hit him, she was so tired after their long journey. The last thing she wanted to do was go for a walk. Why was he behaving so oddly? She had so many questions to ask, but he ushered them out of the room and back downstairs and out of the hotel.

As they reached the open space of a small park nearby, he checked their surroundings, waiting for a couple to pass them before he said, 'Well done. We have to be very careful. Anyone could be an informant. Do not discuss anything in your room, at least nothing that you wouldn't want printed on the front sheet of a newspaper.'

'Stephen, really. Why would anyone want to write about us?' Dottie protested.

'He means we can't talk about the real reason we're here. Isn't that right?'

Stephen nodded in agreement. 'I know a couple of the newspaper people and they claim all the hotel rooms are bugged. They may be paranoid but it's better to be careful. I can't risk anything happening to you. I can't tell you how many sleepless nights I've had since I came up with this whole idea. Maybe you ladies should just enjoy a few carefree days in Berlin and go back home. I can think of other ways to help.'

Connie frowned. 'No, Stephen. Since I last saw you, Edith has shared more of her story with us; how her neighbours and people she thought were her friends have turned against her. She told us about her children's teachers disappearing overnight. Other friends have been released from camps and they won't talk about what happened to them. But it's obvious from their appearance something did, as they have shaved heads, lost a lot of weight and some have lost teeth.' Connie glanced at Dottie and, seeing a look of determination on her sister's face, she turned back to Stephen. 'We must do everything we can. So, what is the plan?'

She glowed with the look of approval he gave her before he said, 'First, I will take you to the embassy so you can meet my boss and a contact we may use in the future. Then, tonight, I will take you to visit some friends of mine. They are holding a party. There you will meet some people who want to get money out of the country. They will tell you their stories. Every word is true, no matter how outlandish they may sound.'

Connie gritted her teeth as some young men in uniform walked past them. She had so much she wanted to say, so many questions she wanted to ask, but she knew she had to be careful and try to be patient – for Stephen's sake, as well as theirs.

Stephen waited until the men were out of sight before

saying, 'For now, unless you would actually enjoy a walk, go back to your hotel and get some sleep. I suggest having something light to eat sent to your room. I will collect you at six for dinner and then take you to meet my friends.'

'Perfect.' Connie hid a yawn behind her hand. She and Dottie hadn't got much sleep over the last few nights, not that they would admit to being nervous.

They returned to the hotel studiously ignoring anyone who seemed to give them a second look.

Stephen collected them at six that evening. 'Don't say anything in the car – the driver may not only be working for us.'

Connie and Dottie exchanged a glance but didn't protest as Stephen walked them outside and a black car drove up. The driver got out and bowed before holding the doors open for them to take a seat.

'It's a pity you left your bag on the train, Miss Fitzwalter.' Stephen looked at Connie. 'But an emergency passport can be arranged.'

Connie played along. 'Thank you. That will be a relief.'

As they drove to the embassy, Stephen pointed out various landmarks on the way. They spotted queues of people standing outside the embassy first. Dottie opened her mouth but at a nudge from Connie closed it again.

They waited until they had exited the car and the driver had safely driven away before speaking. 'Stephen, who are all those people? Why are they lining up like that?'

'There is no room inside, so they have to wait their turn outside to speak to someone about a visa.'

Dottie stared at him before whispering, 'All these people want to leave?'

'This is only the tip of the iceberg. All the embassies are

experiencing the same. Tom is working flat out, hence why he wasn't able to join us this evening.'

They followed Stephen into the building, watching as he politely navigated his way through the queues. Connie had to fight back tears as she looked at all the desperate faces standing, waiting their turn.

Eventually Stephen led them to an empty office. 'Take a seat and I'll go and find Frank.'

Stephen returned with a shorter, older man wearing glasses.

'Good evening, Misses Fitzwalter. I am delighted to put a face to names I keep hearing about, especially in relation to being opera fanatics.'

'We are ardent opera fans, Mr Foley.' Connie shook his hand before he turned to shake Dottie's.

'Yes, Miss Fitzwalter, but it is your other activities that brought you to my attention. Stephen told me you volunteered to help. I wanted to commend you on your bravery. Both of you. Unofficially, of course. Officially, all I know is you love opera.'

A knock at the door interrupted them, and a young man in his late twenties stuck his head around the door. 'Frank, you busy? Oh, excuse me.' The man coloured as he spotted Connie and Dottie.

'Elias, come in. These two ladies are Stephen's friends from London. They have come to help.'

The debonair young man didn't shake their hands but kissed both twice on each cheek. Dottie giggled.

'You are both angels. Now, excuse me, I must dash. New show at the club. Frank, I left those items in your office. Stephen, be a dear and call into the bar. I have some friends who are dying to meet the most handsome man in the embassy.'

Stephen blushed but didn't get a chance to protest as the man left.

'He's always late – he'll meet himself coming back some-day.' Frank looked to the door before looking back to them.

'Now, excuse me, ladies – I have another meeting to go to. Thank you again. If you ever need my help, you know where to find me but, as Stephen said, this is very much my unofficial business so not a word to anyone.'

Stephen followed Frank out of the room but returned after a couple of seconds. 'Let's go to dinner. I'm starving.'

Connie wanted to ask more but sensed it wasn't the time.

After an uncomfortable dinner in a restaurant where every man seemed to be in uniform, Stephen escorted them to a beautiful house in Charlottenburg.

'This is Mr Levy and his business partner, Mr Auerbach.'

The men greeted Connie and Dottie with nervous smiles, glancing behind them as if they expected the ladies to have appeared with a Nazi escort. The taller of the two, a distinguished-looking man in his early forties, his salt-and-pepper hair neatly trimmed, stepped forward. 'I'm Moritz Auerbach, and this' – he gestured to a woman standing shyly to his side – 'is my wife, Judith.' He nodded to the other man. 'Jacob is her brother-in-law.' Welcome to my home. Please come in. Have some coffee and some pastries.'

Mrs Auerbach didn't raise her eyes from the ground as she took their coats and gestured to the sitting room.

'My wife is very glad you honoured us with your company. She apologizes for not being able to speak English.'

Connie smiled at the woman. 'I wish I spoke some German. Thank you for your hospitality.'

The sitting room was exquisitely decorated with silk wallpaper, and beautiful art works hanging on each wall. On one side of the room was a large wooden bookcase, packed full of books but, as her gaze roamed the shelves, Connie noticed gaps, as if some books had been removed and not replaced.

Mrs Auerbach poured the coffee from a silver coffee pot

into pretty bone-china cups. Her hands shook slightly as she handed them each a cup after they took a seat on the sofa. The men remained standing, whispering to each other in German.

Connie glanced at Stephen, who gave her a reassuring smile.

Mr Auerbach offered them a cigarette before he lit up. 'Mr Armstrong – I mean Stephen – said you are willing to help us find new homes in your country.'

Connie smiled. 'Yes. But I'm afraid we don't have any influence with the immigration authorities. I understand there are other ways we may be able to help?'

Mr Auerbach took a seat. 'If I may speak frankly, it is relatively easy to emigrate if one has money to invest in the other country. The issue we face is getting that money out of Germany. We cannot go to the banks as our accounts have been aryanized.'

Connie glanced at Stephen.

Stephen leant forward and explained: 'The Nazis have assumed control of the banks and have marked certain accounts, those known to belong to Jews. Mr Auerbach and other people in his position are unable to access the money held in the bank.'

'But it's your money—?' Connie protested.

'Yes, it is, but that's not something the Nazis are worried about. They know I can't protest or, at least, not too loudly, as then I may just go *poof*.' Mr Auerbach made a sign of someone disappearing, causing his wife to let out a sob. 'I shouldn't joke like that. There is nothing funny about our situation.'

'So you can't send money to Britain or America through the normal channels,' Connie summarized, feeling sorry for Mrs Auerbach's visible tension.

'No. But I took precautions some years ago, and I moved some of my money into something easier to transport.' He pulled a small velvet bag from his pocket and handed it to Connie.

It was heavier than it looked.

'Go on, open it.'

She looked inside, gasping as several small stones twinkled back as the light hit them.

'Diamonds!'

'Yes. Of the highest clarity and colour. I wondered if you could take these back to Britain with you? Maybe in your inside pocket. As a British citizen, you would not be subject to a search at the border crossing.'

Connie didn't know what to say; her voice having trouble getting past the lump in her mouth. It was surreal having coffee and pastries in this man's beautiful home, knowing that his future and that of his family depended on a stranger getting a bag of stones, albeit beautiful diamonds, over the border.

'I am willing to pay you for your trouble.'

Mr Auerbach's hastily added assurance swamped her in guilt.

'Mr Auerbach, that won't be necessary. My sister and I feel very privileged you trust us. We are happy to help but feel dreadful it has come to this. You must be very worried.'

He ran a hand through his hair, his fingers stained yellow from nicotine. 'I worry more for my children and my wife. She has heard so many horrible stories. Has seen her friends leave the country either by choice or they disappear in the night. The lucky ones get to France, Italy, Belgium or, better still, America and Britain. The others... they are not so fortunate. We have been lucky so far. We are quite a well-known family so I think that may offer some protection. Like Mr Israel, the owner of the famous department store, I have been arrested several times but not mistreated. But... I think things will get worse.' He took off his glasses and looked at the sisters. 'I have friends, good friends who are still part of the government.'

'You have friends in the Third Reich?'

The man smiled. 'Yes, not all party members are Nazis.

Some are good Germans who believe that by joining the party and being part of the government, they may be able to curb the worst of Hitler's plans. They have told me to leave. The sooner the better. Stephen has tried to help me with the paperwork for my children, my wife, my mother and some other family members. The wheels move slowly even when you have good friends.' Mr Auerbach glanced at Stephen before looking back at Connie. 'If you agree to take the bag to London, I have a friend there who will be able to sell some of the stones and put the money in a bank account. Then I can prove I have sufficient resources to emigrate.'

'We will take the bag, Mr Auerbach, and do our best to get it to London.' Connie waited as he translated what she had said for his wife. The poor woman put her head in her hands and sobbed, the strain of the evening proving too much for her. Connie moved to her side. 'I am so sorry you are all going through this, but I promise we will do whatever we can to help you.'

Mr Auerbach nodded his thanks. 'My friend, David Cohen, owns a jewellers' in Hatton Gardens. He is expecting a parcel, or at least he should be if he has received any of the letters I wrote. I used a code so they wouldn't alert our Gestapo friends.'

Connie couldn't help but be impressed. It seemed the man had thought of everything.

Mr Levy, however, his skin pallid, a hunted look in his eyes hinting at terrors he had endured, sat at the table, lighting one cigarette from the other, and remained silent the entire evening.

When they left and Dottie and Connie were making their way back to the hotel alone with Stephen, Connie asked about him: 'Why didn't he join in the conversation?'

'Jacob Levy, a finer man you couldn't meet, is Mrs Auerbach's widowed brother-in-law. He was married to her sister, who died in childbirth years ago. He was recently released from Dachau, a concentration camp, where he'd been imprisoned on trumped-up charges of being a communist. He's been told he has six weeks to leave the country, or they will rearrest him.'

Connie put a hand to her mouth. 'Stephen, that's barbaric.'

'It is. Moritz has done his best to get Jacob to leave but he refuses to go anywhere until we get papers for his mother and sister. He's afraid if he leaves, they will make his family pay. But don't worry about Jacob. His case is in good hands.'

That was all Stephen would say and Connie didn't press him. She didn't want to hear any more. Dottie wiped a tear from her eye but stayed quiet, not having said a word all evening.

When they got back to their hotel room, Dottie undressed and then got into bed, turning to face the wall. Only then did Connie hear her sister's sobbing. She couldn't console her: there were no words that could make any of this better.

The next morning, Connie resisted the urge to throw their clothes into their suitcase and rush back to Britain. But they had to maintain their cover, to act normally and continue with their planned trip to the opera and return home the following day; otherwise, questions might be asked.

Stephen picked them up from their hotel and escorted them to the opera house. 'Smile. You look like you are heading into the lions' den,' Stephen whispered as yet another grinning Nazi accompanied by a fawning woman walked past on their way to their seats.

'I want to feed them all to the lions,' Connie retorted, her words dripping with frustration and anger, but, deep down, she knew Stephen was right. They had no choice but to keep up appearances. Her jaw throbbed with the effort of gritting her teeth as she forced a strained nod or smile at anyone who happened to glance their way.

For the first time in her life, the music didn't provide the usual distraction. Her mind was consumed by worries. Could they really smuggle the diamonds past the ever-watchful border guards? What if they were subjected to a search? The mere thought sent shivers down her spine. If those precious jewels were discovered, the guards could arrest them, and their daring plan would unravel. Alternatively, the guards could choose to keep the gems for themselves, leaving the Auerbach and Levy families without a glimmer of hope for escape.

Connie let out a weary sigh, the weight of their predicament pressing down on her shoulders. Beside her, Stephen remained silent but reached to take her hand, giving it a reassuring squeeze. It was his way of silently conveying his unwavering belief in their ability to overcome the odds.

Their trip home was fraught. It started as the sisters made their way to the hotel's reception desk to check out. The clerk seemed to take forever to complete the simple task. Connie's heart was racing, as she expected a hand to land on her shoulder any minute. She kept wiping her hands on her skirt, and saw Dottie gnawing at her lip. The diamonds, secured in a false pocket Dottie had sewn into her bra the previous night, weighed heavily against her skin.

They walked in silence to the station, the bright sky doing nothing to lift their sprits. At the train station, they produced their tickets but the man just waved them through. Connie glanced at Dottie, who gave her a wobbly smile. They stood on the platform to wait for the train.

'Excuse me, fräuleins.'

The clipped German accent from behind her sent an icy dart of fear through Connie. She forced her feet to stay steady as she turned to look at the man who'd addressed them. To her relief he appeared to be a fellow traveller.

'Please take my seat.' He waved to a bench behind them. 'Lovely ladies like yourselves shouldn't be standing.' The man clicked his heels and walked away before they could even thank him.

Not that Connie could speak: she could barely breathe.

'I thought that was it.'

Although Dottie had whispered, Connie felt the whole station had heard her. She remained silent, the hands of the station clock seemingly stuck in the same position.

The train arrived on time and they took their seats. A German woman with an unfortunate-smelling sandwich sat opposite them, making Connie feel nauseous. Dottie took out her embroidery while Connie closed her eyes, wishing she could sleep and wake up in Britain. One of the diamonds was poking into her but she couldn't adjust its position.

Then the train stopped. Border control.

The guards came on the train, working their way through the carriage. Connie glanced down at her chest, checking that the diamonds weren't showing under her clothes. Dottie's needle seemed suspended in mid-air.

The men's guttural voices drew nearer. They questioned one couple at length, reducing the woman to tears, but when they came to Connie and Dottie, they barely looked at them once they saw their British passports.

Connie couldn't stop the relieved sigh when the train once more started moving and they passed across the border. The woman with the sausage gave her a funny look but she didn't care. They had passed the danger point.

Once they reached London, by mutual agreement they headed straight to the jewellers in Hatton Gardens, where they handed over the bag to a bemused but pleased Mr Cohen. 'I didn't expect ladies who look like ordinary British women to be this brave.'

'Your friend is the brave one, Mr Cohen. Have a good day.'

As they walked back home, Dottie looked at Connie. 'I hope our country never ends up like Germany. I couldn't bear it.'

'That will never happen, Dottie. Never.' Connie pressed her lips together, pushing her shoulders back and walking taller. Maybe, just maybe, their actions would let people come to Britain and enjoy their freedom. Their trip had been scary yet it was exhilarating, helping those who needed it. 'We have to go back again and again. We can bring out more diamonds or money.' Despite her confident words, she couldn't totally dismiss a frisson at fear at what could happen if the Nazis learned about their smuggling.

'Are you scared, Connie?'

'A little. But I'm more terrified that we won't be able to go back often enough to help those who need us. So long as Hitler is in charge, things can only get worse for Mr Auerbach and people like him. We can't go back to our normal lives and pretend there is nothing we can do.' She lifted her chin, defiance radiating from her eyes. 'I'm going to learn German so we can talk to people without relying on an interpreter. We must stand up to the Nazis, we simply must.'

SIXTEEN

FLORENCE, APRIL 1936

Connie woke up to the sound of bells and for a second thought she was dreaming. But no, this was real. Pushing back the covers, she ran to look out of the window. 'Look, Dottie! Florence is just as pretty as the pictures in the guidebook. The long journey by night train was worth it – just look at that view.'

Yawning, Dottie got up to stand beside her sister. 'It is very pretty and peaceful-looking, yes.'

Mellow sunlight reflected off flat roofs of pink tile that stood over whitewashed buildings with green shutters. Connie pinched herself: just yesterday she had been typing memos in the office looking out at the rain-soaked grimy streets of London.

Dottie returned to the bed, stretching out. 'What time are we meeting our friends?'

'At four, outside the opera house. We have some time for sightseeing. Where do you fancy going first?' Her sister stayed silent. 'Are you still feeling ill after the flight? It was rather bumpy.'

Dottie shook her head, not looking up, her fingers playing with the bedcovers. 'I feel a bit guilty.'

Shocked, Connie sat down on her bed. 'Why?'

'We're here to have fun. Just to see the opera and enjoy meeting up with our friends. Not to smuggle jewellery, money or fur coats.'

'Good job – we'd stand out a bit wearing fur in this heat.' Connie's attempt at making her sister laugh fell flat.

Dottie's chin dipped to her chest, her blue eyes watering as she tried to speak. 'We...' – her voice cracked and she took a deep breath before continuing – 'we should be at home working on paperwork trying to get visas, or in Germany helping people, like Stephen asked us to. People like Mr Levy and Mr Auerbach. We don't even know if they are safe.'

Connie pushed her own worries about the men they'd tried to help aside. In the last six months, they had completed six more trips to Germany, two to Berlin and four to Munich. By flying from Croydon to Cologne, and from there travelling by night train to Munich, they could leave London on a Friday evening and be in Munich for breakfast time. There they had stayed with Clemens and Viorica and smuggled back necklaces, rings and fur coats owned by his and Edith's mutual friends. Edith arranged for the disposal of the items and lodged the money in bank accounts thus enabling her friends to flee.

As they hadn't met the owners of the jewellery, those visits hadn't had the same emotional impact as meeting Jacob and Moritz.

Connie took her sister's hand. 'Dottie, Stephen asked us to behave like we normally do. And as opera lovers, we should be visiting other places to see the opera. What better cover than to have a short visit to somewhere different? It is only a long weekend.'

Dottie didn't look convinced, so Connie tried another tactic. 'We shall take some pictures while we're here. That way if anyone were to ask why we are visiting Berlin or Munich so often, we have proof we follow the opera – wherever it leads us.' Connie gave Dottie's hand a squeeze. 'We need a little break for ourselves, somewhere we don't have to walk around looking over our shoulders. And we should celebrate your new book. I can't believe *The Daily Sun* nominated *Call and I'll Come* the most romantic book of the month! I'm so proud of you.'

Dottie shrugged. 'It isn't the most literary paper in the world.'

'Who cares? Their readers love your books, and your sales will soar. Now, are you getting dressed or do I have to explore Florence alone?'

* * *

Dottie rubbed the side of her neck as she sat down in the sitting room, only to stand up again and walk over to the window, moving the curtains to look outside. She stood there for a couple of seconds before she turned back into the room.

'Dorothea, darling, you are making me quite dizzy. You haven't been yourself since you returned from Florence. Whatever is the matter?' Mama glanced at Connie, but she raised her eyebrows: she had no idea what was wrong, either.

'I want to buy a flat.' Dottie sat down after her announcement, leaving her mother and Connie staring at her.

'Why, darling? Aren't you happy living here?'

'Yes, Mama. Of course I am. It's not for me. I want to buy it to house some of our visitors from Germany. You know how difficult it is getting the immigration paperwork completed, and one of the issues we face is the fact that we don't always have an address where the applicant could live. So I thought if I bought a two-bedroom flat, we could use that. What do you think?'

Connie pressed her palms lightly against her cheeks, trying not to let her emotions get the better of her. She took a deep breath, filled with pride at her sister – both with her success as an author but also her generosity of spirit.

'Can you afford it?' Mama asked.

'Yes. The book sales have taken off recently and apart from funding our trips, which we manage very carefully, I've been saving more than spending.' Dottie glanced at Connie, a guilty look on her face. 'I know we spoke about travelling the world, going to the opera wherever the whim takes us, but I think this is a better use of the money. I'm sorry to disappoint you.'

Connie moved to her sister and pulled her to her feet to give her a hug, before staring into her blue eyes now sparkling with tears. 'You could never do that. I think you are the most generous person there is. You could do anything with that money, but instead you are using it to help others. I love you.'

Mama sniffed. 'Where is my handkerchief? My word, Dorothea, I'm so proud of your kind heart. Have you somewhere in mind?'

Dottie grinned and nodded. 'Would you like to come and see it? I have spoken to the estate agents and they can show us around this afternoon. I haven't put in an offer. But unofficially, she told me, the family want a quick sale.'

The flat wasn't far away but they caught a cab for their mother's sake. It pulled up outside a relatively small block of flats.

'Our one would be on the ground floor.'

The agent had yet to arrive so they walked around the grounds of the property.

'The garden needs a bit of work – just some pruning and weeding. The grass needs cutting too. But otherwise, it is in good shape.'

They walked up to the flat that was for sale but the grimy windows made looking inside impossible.

A car drove up and parked at the kerb. A young man who looked like he should still be at school climbed out. He approached them, shaking hands with each of them. 'My name is Gregory Foxton of Foxton, Bailey and Butler. This is a wonderful opportunity and the property is bound to be sold quickly. Especially as the asking price is so reasonable. The nearest tube station is five minutes that way.' He pointed. 'And the nearest bus stop is right opposite.' He glanced at Dottie. 'There are a number of good local schools nearby.'

Connie hid a grin as Dottie blushed.

Mama took charge. 'My daughter is considering the purchase as an investment, young man. Could you please open the door and let us look inside?'

Mr Foxton turned the key in the wood door and pushed it open, the hinges creaking, allowing a musty smell to escape.

'God Lord.' Mama put her handkerchief to her nose. 'Did something die in here?'

The agent pretended not to hear, immediately settling into his sales talk. 'As you can see, it is a much larger property than one would expect from the outside. As we enter, this door, here, leads to one bedroom, while the door ahead leads into the sitting room. That door over there' – he pointed to a closed door – 'is the master bedroom. Opposite is the water closet and separate bathroom, and just down there is the kitchen. I suggest we start with the sitting room.'

He led the way. The hallway walls were decorated with old, worn-out wallpaper, faded from what must have been bold colours and patterns in years past. The floorboards groaned beneath their feet as they walked down the hall, into the sitting room.

'Do you mind if I open a window?' Connie asked, but didn't wait for an answer. She walked over to the window and pushed it open, allowing some much needed fresh air in. Faded curtains swayed softly in the breeze and the only sound was raindrops pattering against the windows.

She turned and surveyed the room. A dirty fireplace, its grate covered in paper and other rubbish. There were some dusty, framed photographs on the mantelpiece. Connie studied them, noting the proud smiles of a Great War soldier. She wondered if he had made it home. An old sofa with a floral pattern was the focal point of the room, accompanied by two mismatched armchairs with moth-eaten cushions. The table was made of oak, and showed signs of usage, but looked sturdy and reliable. A small shelf of books, and a cabinet missing one of its doors was the only other piece of furniture.

'As you can see, it has a lot of potential,' Geoffrey said, appearing to be sincere.

Connie couldn't answer but Mama stepped into the breach. 'I like the high ceilings, but that wallpaper has to go.'

Connie admired her optimism.

'Let's look at the kitchen next. As you will see, it is another relatively large space.'

They followed Geoffrey through to the kitchen. The white tiles had aged and turned a dull yellow, and the metal sink was tarnished with rust. Wall cabinets, decorated with delicate ceramic knobs, were scuffed and cracked. Worn linoleum covered the floor. A small wooden table with a tattered checked tablecloth was placed at the middle of the room, accompanied by mismatched chairs.

'Of course, it needs a little work.' Geoffrey barely looked at the room, staring instead at his shoes.

'Looks like a family once lived here and got a lot of use out of this room.' Mama rubbed the window glass with her white hanky, which quickly turned black. 'I like kitchens that look out to the garden.' Mama turned to the gas stove. 'I think you might need to replace that. It looks old and in need of repair. It might be dangerous.'

'The property is being sold as is.' As Mama raised her eyebrows, Geoffrey turned a little red around his shirt collar. 'What I mean is that replacement of any items would be up to the buyer. Shall we have a look at the bedrooms?

They exited the kitchen back to the main hallway. From there Geoffrey opened a door leading into a large double bedroom. A wrought-iron-framed double bedstead with a floral quilt was pushed up against one wall which may have once been painted in cream. It was now stained yellow – like most of the property.

Connie whispered to Dottie. 'I feel like I'm intruding. Don't you?'

Dottie nodded as Mama walked over to the window, moving the delicate lace curtain to one side. 'This is a nice view of the park.'

The next door led to a smaller room, with a single bed and wardrobe. In contrast to the other rooms, this one looked as if it had been preserved in time. The bed had been stripped down to the metal frame, while the wardrobe doors hung open revealing empty hangers. The wooden chest of drawers' only adornment was a layer of dust, and a framed picture of a child.

'I think the soldier in the picture on the mantelpiece never came home,' Connie whispered, as she stared at the photo.

Geoffrey indicated the last two closed doors. Dottie opened them and quickly closed them again. 'The toilet and bathroom.' Judging by the look on her face, they were in worse state than the rest of the property.

'Would you like to see the other rooms again?' Geoffrey asked. 'Or are you prepared to put in an offer?'

'Let's go back outside,' Mama suggested. Connie couldn't have agreed more readily and they left via the front door. As Geoffrey locked the door behind him, he turned with an expectant look on his face.

'Young man, why don't you go and sit in your car for a couple of minutes and allow us some privacy?'

He hesitated, as if unsure how to respond.

'Go on now.' Mama encouraged him with a smile.

Geoffrey nodded and turned, a defeated slump to his shoulders all too evident as he walked down the short garden path to the street.

'Well, what do you think?' Dottie asked.

Connie could hear a note of excitement in her voice, which was matched by her wide eyes.

'I think it has a lot of potential, darling.' Mama walked back a little bit towards the road, to get a better view of the whole property. 'Your neighbours keep a lovely house – the windows are clean and their front door has been recently painted. They take pride in their properties around here. And at one point, the people who owned that flat did too, but it seems to have fallen into a state of disrepair. Is it owned by an older person?'

Dottie nodded. 'An old man whose wife died last year. There's no family apart from a nephew or cousin. Do you think I should buy it, Mama?'

'I think we should go home and discuss it. Don't appear too interested or you will find it difficult to negotiate a good price.' Mama looked thoughtful. 'I shouldn't speculate, but I'd say that the family who are benefiting from the sale didn't visit the owner when they were in residence. There is a feeling of sadness in that house. Did you feel it?'

'Yes, Mama.'

'Go and put the young man out of his misery. Tell him you need time to consider your options and you will contact the office in the next day or so.'

Later, as they sat in their sitting room, they discussed the purchase opposite a roaring fire, enjoying a cup of tea.

'I think you should buy it, darling. There is nothing wrong inside that a good clean and some new furniture won't solve. I would suggest you get someone to clear the house for you, remove all the old furniture. It shows signs of woodworm and the materials – the curtains, cushions and whatnot – have been attacked by moths. I'd replace the carpets and linoleum, as well as that stove, and you need a new kitchen sink. A plumber can sort out the bathroom for you too.' Mama took a sip of her tea. 'Speak to Cook or Millie. They are bound to know some good cleaners and a reputable decorator. I think you should consider buying three single beds so the double room could be shared. Just in case you need to provide accommodation for a group of friends, rather than a married couple.'

'Mama, you think of everything.' Connie smiled at their mother.

'Do you think I'm being extravagant, Mama?' Dottie placed her teacup on the table in front of her.

'Extravagant? Not at all. I am so proud of everything you have achieved through your writing.' Mama brushed a tear from her eye. 'I can't tell you how proud I am of both of you.'

Connie accompanied her sister to the estate agents where they negotiated a good price. Cook knew plenty of tradesmen and the property was soon transformed. Dottie took Mama shopping for curtains, carpets and the other furnishings required. Only when the renovations had been completed was Connie allowed to see it.

'Dottie! I can't believe this is the same place we visited a couple of months ago! It looks wonderful. It's so light and airy. It feels different too.' Connie went from room to room, leaving the sitting room to last. When she saw the framed photographs above the fireplace, she turned to Dottie for an explanation.

'The person we bought it from didn't want anything from

the property. He didn't even ask about family mementos.' Dottie's lip curled. 'I couldn't just throw this out. That young man served our country. I thought I would get a new frame and leave him looking over the place. I think he would approve of the new use of his home, don't you?'

Connie nodded, smiling, as she looked at the young man in the frame. 'Most definitely.'

SEVENTEEN
VIENNA, AUGUST 1936

Connie hugged Sarah, thankful to see her dear friend again. Since meeting in Salzburg two years previously, they had become warm friends via their lengthy letters. 'Thank you again for inviting us to your incredible home, Sarah.'

Sarah's smile lit up her brown eyes. 'I'm so glad you could come. You two seem to be travelling all the time these days. I'm getting quite jealous of how often you get to go to the opera.'

A twinge of guilt made Connie feel uncomfortable. She'd promised Stephen not to tell anyone the real reason for all their trips and that included even dear friends like the Libermans.

'Don't look so worried, I'm teasing you. Sit down and relax. I must check on the food.' Sarah disappeared through to the kitchen.

Connie gazed around the exquisite dining room. It was lit by a stunning crystal chandelier in the centre of the high ceiling, its light warming the silk-wall-papered walls that were adorned at intervals by fine tapestries and paintings. She didn't pretend to know a Van Gogh from a Renoir, but Connie assumed these were all valuable pieces.

She and Dottie were seated at a long, mahogany table. It

was draped with an exquisite white lace cloth, and stretched the length of the room. The table was covered with an array of mouth-watering dishes, fragrant aromas of garlic, spices, and other spices wafting from the food. Connie placed a hand on her stomach self-consciously, in the hope it wouldn't grumble and embarrass her in front of the other guests at the table.

In addition to the Liberman family, Sarah's father, Isaac, was also present. Clemens and Viorica made up the other guests, and Samuel had invited two friends, boys called Gunter and Kurt.

They seemed a little over-awed at the spread of food, but Connie watched as Sarah's natural charm soon had the young boys relaxing, their faces breaking into large smiles. Leah, wearing her exquisite diamond necklace, cast furtive glances at one of the boys, her cheeks pinking. Connie hid a smile, recognizing the girl's first crush. The boy, Gunter, was very handsome with his blond hair and blue eyes, but he wasn't Jewish. Was that important to Sarah and Ben? Daniel, Leah's younger brother, also looked at the boys with adoring eyes. Connie sensed he was desperate to grow up and be considered part of Samuel's group. But, judging by the way Samuel ruffled his hair in passing, it would be a while before that happened.

Dottie was seated opposite her and looked radiant in her latest creation, the blue satin almost matching her eye colour exactly and setting off her blonde hair. Another *Mabs Fashion* pattern, but one could be forgiven for thinking her sister had purchased the dress in Paris. Dottie could be a poster child for Hitler's Aryan race.

Connie couldn't help comparing the life Sarah's family enjoyed with those the Jews of Germany were experiencing. She had wondered if she should ask Ben and Sarah if they considered moving but why would they swap this lifestyle for one of misery in Britain. Ben wouldn't be able to practice as a doctor unless he re-qualified, something she'd found out when trying to arrange the paperwork for German professionals in similar positions. She wasn't sure what assets the couple had. And this was Austria not Germany.

Ben tapped the top of his glass with his fork, interrupting Connie's train of thought and causing the conversation around the table to stop. 'Ladies and gentlemen, my family and dear friends, on this blessed day, we gather to celebrate tradition, love and the bond that unites us – our love of opera.' The adults all laughed. 'Thank you all for joining us, especially Connie and Dottie for making the trip from London.' Ben raised his glass. 'To family and friendship.'

The room filled with the sound of clinking glasses, and the feast began. Connie had never tasted some of the delicacies placed before her but she was determined to give everything a try. She enjoyed almost everything on the menu, but her stomach churned at the taste of the gefilte fish, the consistency of the cold dish reminding her of school dinners. Leah caught her reaction and smiled, whispering, 'I don't like it either. It tastes a little better when served slightly warm, but Grandpapa likes it cold.'

Connie delicately pushed the rest of the fish aside and was very thankful when the maid removed her plate in preparation for the next dish. 'Your English has come on so well, Leah. You should be proud of yourself.'

Leah's eyes glowed at the praise. 'Mama insisted we all take lessons. She said it would be important for our trip to London to see the palace and Covent Garden. She made it a rule we must speak English when we come together as a family for meals. Even Grandpapa has improved.' Leah blushed a little. 'I heard you practising your German with Mama. Why do you learn it? French is much more musical.'

Not wanting to lie but unable to tell the whole truth, Connie said, 'I wanted to impress my friends. It's not fair they all have to learn English if I don't try to learn their language.'

Dottie finished her soup and turned towards her hostess. 'Sarah, this chicken soup is just divine. Mama would love the recipe – could you write it out for me?'

Sarah's face lit up with pleasure. 'Of course, Dottie. Our cook is especially talented. Her matzo-ball soup is known for miles.'

Ben shook his head. 'My Sarah is very humble, she makes one that tastes just as nice.'

As the meal progressed the hum of conversation continued, with Connie catching snatches. Clemens and Ben were discussing opera while Viorica and Dottie were chatting about the Prince of Wales and his latest romantic exploits. Isaac talked quietly with his grandson while Leah divided her time between keeping Connie company and staring at Gunter.

Connie was amused to catch the young boy sending several admiring glances in Leah's direction. As the conversation flowed around her, Connie couldn't help but wonder what was happening over the border in Germany. Had Mr Auerbach and his family managed to get to Britain?

Once the meal was over the children retired, leaving the adults to chat in the equally sumptuous sitting room. Sarah played a couple of pieces on the piano with Ben standing by her side, turning the pages.

'Your daughter is an accomplished player, Mr Borgor,' Clemens said to Isaac, as he watched Sarah playing.

'She is.'

Connie caught an undercurrent between the two men. She looked up to find Dottie raising her eyebrows at her, her sister having sensed the same.

Sarah came to sit beside them, just as the conversation turned political.

'I think some actions and commentary have been misunderstood, Isaac.'

'You would say that, given you now work for them.'

Sarah paled. 'Papa. Clemens is a very dear friend as well as a guest.'

Connie held her breath. She couldn't believe Clemens supported the Nazis. Those same people who had Mrs Auerbach too frightened to open her front door; her brother-in-law chain-smoking and unable to speak, wondering how he could protect his family and emigrate from the country of his birth. She may not condone Isaac's manners – political conversations were best not discussed on such occasions – but she couldn't fault his disgust with the Nazi regime. But this was Clemens, the man whose wife had introduced them to Edith. Clemens and Viorica were the reason Edith's family was now safe in London.

'It's alright, Sarah. Your father is entitled to his opinion.' Clemens turned to address Isaac 'Yes, I did take the position of conductor at the Berlin State Opera after Kleiber resigned.'

'He didn't just discard the job, like a woman discards a dress!' Isaac's voice was rising. 'He took a stand. He resigned in protest over the Nazis declaring Schoenberg's work to be degenerate. He is not even Jewish, but simply worked with Schoenberg! The Nazis deem the work of all Jewish artists degenerate. Maybe if more Germans were as brave as Kleiber, my people wouldn't be in the position they are.'

Connie saw Sarah's entreating glance at her husband, but Ben leaned in as if to hear Clemens response. Connie shifted in her seat – she didn't want her friends to fall out.

Isaac stroked his beard, his expression more challenging, 'Are you a Nazi, Mr Krauss?'

'Papa!' Sarah's hand flew to her chest. 'Clemens, Viorica, I apologize. I don't know what has come over my father.'

But everyone ignored Sarah's apology, their eyes glued to Clemens.

'No, I haven't joined the party and do not share their opinions.' The room seemed to release a collective gasp only to hear him say: 'I have corresponded with Hitler and other members of his government.'

Connie clenched her hands, keeping her mouth shut. How could a man she liked as much as Clemens be in league with the Nazis?

Isaac stood up. 'My apologies, everyone, but I seem to have a touch of indigestion. I will take my leave. Miss Constance and Miss Dorothea, it was a pleasure to meet you.' Isaac turned to Viorica. 'It is always a pleasure to see you. You look as elegant and youthful as always.'

Isaac walked to the door, pointedly ignoring Clemens. Sarah and Ben stood but didn't stop him. Connie glanced at Dottie before they both stood up. 'We should be going too. Thank you for a superb meal and marvellous hospitality.'

'Please sit down.' Clemens looked at Connie. 'I have to explain something, and you might as well hear what I have to say before you judge me.' He didn't raise his voice but something in his tone made the sisters retake their seats. 'Whether we like it or not, the Third Reich, as they call themselves, is the government of Germany now. It doesn't pay to make enemies of the leaders of the state you live in.'

Connie risked a glance at Ben. His face was flushed, his hands clasped tightly together.

'I do not believe in their policies or their nonsense about superior races. But I must earn a living. Both my wife and I live for the opera. We also believe we can protect our Jewish friends by keeping the regime happy.' He paused. '"Happy" isn't the correct word but being in contact with Hitler, developing contacts in his government... it allows me access to several potentially useful people. I expect that to continue.' Clemens stood up and faced Sarah. 'Thank you so much for your wonderful hospitality. I consider you and Ben some of my closest friends and I hope you can find a way to trust that I am doing what I feel is best. For all of us.' He turned to his wife. 'Viorica, we should leave.'

Sarah went to stand but Ben put a hand on her arm. He stood instead and held out his hand to Clemens. 'You are my friend. Friends can discuss anything and agree to disagree. I don't pretend to understand your actions, but I do trust you. Now, please, let's put this unpleasantness behind us. Viorica, would you sing for us?'

Viorica sent a look at her husband, and he nodded.

Viorica had given a wonderful performance, Connie and Dottie agreed as they headed back to their hotel, but even her beautiful voice hadn't rescued the evening.

Dottie said, 'I feel sorry for Clemens and Viorica, especially her. They are both so consumed by opera it makes sense they want to continue in their chosen roles, don't you think?'

Connie wasn't sure what to think about that. 'I feel sorry for Sarah. She went to all that trouble for us and look at how it ended. I hope we can all still be friends, don't you?'

EIGHTEEN

The next morning, Connie and Dottie received a note from Viorica asking them to meet at the small park near their hotel.

The sun was shining, the birds singing in the trees, yet Viorica sat on a bench looking totally miserable, her face pale and drawn, as if she hadn't slept all night. She must have heard their footsteps as, before Connie could call out, she looked up, a wary expression in her eyes, the tentative smile on her lips fading quickly. 'I wasn't sure you would come.'

Her words and expression pierced Connie's heart. How could they make their friend feel so bad? She leaned in to kiss her friend on each cheek. 'Of course we would. You are our dear friend.'

'And Clemens?'

Connie squirmed under Viorica's direct gaze as she and Dottie sat down. Dottie was no help either, remaining silent. But Connie knew Dottie was as perturbed by the conversation the night before as she was.

'He is trying to do what is best for everyone.'

Connie tried to keep her voice down. 'How is working with those people best for anyone? You specifically asked us to help

Edith and her family. You know we helped them to escape.'
Connie's eyes narrowed as she held Viorica's gaze, desperate to
understand and be understood. 'They aren't an isolated case –
it's the same all over Germany. Jewish men are leaving their
homes, in some cases their *families*, for good reason. How can
you agree with Clemens becoming a Nazi or even being friends
with them?' Connie tapped her foot, trying to get her anger
under control.

Viorica opened her purse and took out a hanky, wiping her
eyes delicately. 'I know all about it. I speak to my friends, fellow
vocalists, conductors, orchestra members. But Clemens believes
– *we* believe – that this is the best way. By working with the
Nazis, we can help to preserve jobs. Provide people with a way
to travel without too much scrutiny. To form connections with
those, like you, in other countries who are in positions to help
them.'

Connie studied her friend's face before she asked: 'Is that
the only reason he is working with the Nazis? It can hardly hurt
his career.'

Viorica coloured and looked away, staring at the beautiful
view of the River Danube. Connie sensed her mind was in
turmoil. Viorica sniffed and put her hanky back in the purse. 'I
can't expect you to understand. Of course, he wants a career. At
heart he is a performer, and he needs the adoration of the
public.'

Connie sat back, feeling deflated. But then Viorica, eyes
blazing, delivered her parting shot. 'My husband is a human
being, living at a time of great treachery. Would it be better for
him to throw everything away and retire to Switzerland? He
would not be tainted by the Nazis then. But how would that
help him save our friends?'

* * *

Connie and Dottie returned to London in poor spirits, both heartsick at the rift in their friendship with Clemens and Viorica. They had been due to see them the following week when the couple performed in London, but now Connie was unsure if they should go at all.

'My dear girls, whatever is the matter? You are both wandering the house like you lost your entire family overnight. I'm worried.' Mama looked from one to the other as they sat in the sitting room after another, rather silent, dinner.

Connie knew she couldn't hide the truth from her mother. 'Our trip to Vienna ended up in a horrible row. We found out something awful about our friends and we can't come to terms with it, Mama.'

Dottie wiped her eyes with a hanky as Connie explained what had happened after the dinner party.

Mama listened intently and stayed silent for a few seconds after Connie had finished. Then she asked, 'What good would it do for your Mr Krauss to leave Germany? Would that change anything in the country? Do you think Hitler's allies would reconsider their treatment of Mr Auerbach, Mr Levy or any of the other men they have targeted?'

Connie shook her head.

'Have you asked Edith how she feels about Mr Krauss? She is presumably aware of his position given her own role in music?'

'No, Mama, we haven't discussed it with anyone. We just... how can anyone bear to be seen to be a supporter of that regime?'

'How can they help those affected by the regime if they leave? I don't know your Mr Krauss but I do know Edith and her delightful family. A family that may not be living here if it were not for the intervention of Mrs Krauss.' Mama gave Connie the look she used to use when she caught her sneaking biscuits upstairs. 'How many times have I told you not to judge other people until you have taken a walk in their shoes? It sounds to me like Mr Krauss is trying his best to help those in need, while protecting his income and his wife.'

Tears stung Connie's eyes as her mother's mild telling-off struck home.

Dottie sighed. 'I think we should go to Covent Garden and make our apologies in person, Connie, don't you?'

Connie nodded.

Mama stood and put her hand on Connie's cheek. 'My darling daughter, life is never seen in black and white but in myriad colours.'

The following Thursday, Dottie met Connie after work and together they made their way to Covent Garden. The opera was wonderful as always. Afterwards, they went round to the back-stage door. How would Viorica react? Connie knew her friend had been hurt by their reaction to Clemens' comments, but would she forgive them?

Her anxiety disappeared at the smile on Viorica's face when she spotted them. 'My dear Connie and Dottie, you came! I wasn't sure you would.'

'We wanted to apologize,' Connie began.

'No apology needed. I'm so glad you are here. Clemens will be too. Come to dinner with us. Our treat.'

NINETEEN

Several weeks later, a letter arrived at their home. Connie
opened it, reading it out loud to her mother and Dottie. "'My
dear Misses Fitzwalters, thank you for what you did for my
family. We would like to invite you to a special dinner this
Tuesday if you are free. This is the address. Please do come,
yours gratefully, Moritz Auerbach.'"

Connie and Dottie's eyes met. They'd done it. Mr Auerbach had got out of Berlin. They hugged each other and their
bemused mother. Connie wondered if Stephen knew they'd got
out. He would have helped them with the official paperwork,
but could Mr Auerbach have made contact with him from
Britain? Probably not. She would write in code to tell him. He'd
be thrilled, just as they were.

A warm feeling flowed through her: the trials of their trip
had been worth it.

'Why is this man inviting both of you to dinner at his
home?' Mama's gaze shifted from Dottie to Connie, a flicker of
suspicion evident in her eyes.

Connie didn't want to lie but she didn't want to worry their
mother. Dottie stayed silent, staring at the letter in her hand.

'Mr Auerbach is a friend of Stephen's. He had a package he wanted to send to a friend in London, but it was too valuable to risk posting so he asked us to bring it back from Berlin for him.' Connie met her mother's gaze, holding steady until her mother looked away.

'Where is he staying?'

'Finchley Road. Will you come with us, Mama? Please.'

'Yes, but what will I wear? I don't think I have ever been to a Jewish dinner party before.' Mama rubbed the side of her face distractedly.

'Wear the lovely blue dress Stephen likes. Or whatever you would feel good in if he was taking us to dinner. You will look lovely whatever you wear, Mama.'

Connie turned to Dottie. 'I'll have to work, so I'll meet you at the tube station.'

The weekend passed quickly. Tuesday evening came about very soon. Connie picked up some flowers and some chocolates after work. Had Mrs Auerbach got out too, or was it just her husband? No, he wouldn't have invited them to a house for dinner if he was alone. That wouldn't be right. But Mama would be there as a chaperone. Her thoughts flitted from one topic to another as she walked to Charing Cross tube station, down the steps to the underground and headed to Finchley Road.

Some Orthodox Jews joined her carriage, dressed in black hats and long black coats, with white shirts and black trousers. They had beards and the distinctive long, curly *payots*. She saw a couple of people in the carriage give the Jewish men dirty looks but nobody said anything to them.

Connie clenched her jaw, her face flushing in anger. Did those people have any idea of the way these men were being persecuted in Germany? Would they care if they did?

She pushed those thoughts from her mind as the tube pulled into Finchley Road. Alighting from the carriage, she walked up to the steps to find the correct exit at which to meet her sister and mother. They were waiting just inside the entrance due to rain.

'We picked up some cakes at that shop over there. It's owned by a Jewish man and his wife. They helped us pick out similar cakes to those they eat in Berlin.' Mama held the bag open for Connie's inspection, its delicious smell making her mouth water.

They decided to get a taxi to the address, not wanting to arrive wet.

When they pulled up alongside a large building, Connie paid the driver as Dottie helped their mother out of the back of the car. The door to the house opened and Connie recognized Mr Auerbach as he rushed out holding an umbrella.

'They said it rained a lot in London, but nobody said it was every day.' He smiled in greeting as he held the umbrella over them. They bundled into the house, laughing as they discarded their coats.

Dottie introduced their mother. 'Mama, this man is a very good friend of Stephen's. His name is Mr Auerbach.'

'Moritz, please, and it is my pleasure to meet you Mrs Fitzwalter. Your daughters helped save my life. Please come inside. There are people who wish to meet you.'

He pushed the door open and, waiting inside with a small crowd, was Mrs Auerbach, almost unrecognisable from the distraught woman they had met in Berlin. Her eyes glowed as she stood with her hand on a young man's shoulder. Another boy stood at her shoulder.

'You met my wife, Judith. And these are our sons, Solomon and Chaim.'

'Thank you,' Judith Auerbach said, in heavily accented English.

Before Connie could react, she spotted another man. 'Mr Levy! You made it.'

He moved forward and kissed her on each cheek. Then he bowed to her mother. 'You have the bravest daughters. You should be very proud.' Connie saw her mother shoot her a glance, her eyes warm with understanding. He beckoned to another woman to come forward. 'This is my *mutti*, I mean mother. Mrs Aaron Levy and my sister, Naomi. We are all here this evening thanks largely to your girls.'

Connie could barely see through her own tears as her mother nodded at his thanks. 'I am very glad you all could travel. But couldn't you have brought some sunshine too?'

David Cohen, the man Connie and Dottie had met at Hatton Gardens, carried a tray full of champagne glasses into the room. 'Jacob, can you pass these out for me, please? We should celebrate in style.'

When everyone held a glass, Moritz Auerbach held his up. 'According to our religious text, the Talmud – it is similar to your Bible, Mrs Fitzwalter – if you save a life, you save the world. Your daughters, Constance and Dorothea, have saved all of our lives. We raise our glasses in recognition of their bravery and give thanks.' He held the glass higher. 'To Constance and Dorothea.'

The chorus rang out. Connie saw her mother with tears in her eyes, her face lit up with pride. She couldn't help but wonder how many other families like the Auerbachs and the Levys were, right that minute, going through a form of hell back in Berlin and other German cities.

Her eyes caught those of her sister, and Dottie came over to stand beside her. 'We will go back. We'll go again and again,' Dottie whispered, and Connie nodded.

They would go back as many times as they could.

TWENTY

A week later, as they finished dinner, Connie gave Dottie a pointed look. It was time to tell their mother about the plans they'd hatched for their next adventure.

'Mama,' Dottie began, 'we've had an idea about how to help more people, but we need your help.'

Their mother glanced up, a bewildered look on her face as she set her knife and fork on her empty plate. 'Of course. What do you have in mind? Why do you look so nervous?'

Dottie pushed her hair back from her forehead. 'You might not consider it quite... *ethical.*'

Interest and concern sparked in their mother's eyes, but there was no sign of condemnation. 'Dorothea, just get to the point.'

Dottie pulled her chair closer to the table. 'For our next trip to Berlin, I think we should take a group to see the opera. Rather like Cook's travel agency does, but we'd organize it ourselves. Clemens can help with the tickets, and we know the correct hotels. Stephen would help pick some suitable restaurants. Connie, you could buy the train and boat tickets.'

'And how would you find people interested in travelling?

Surely you don't intend putting an advert in the newspaper? You might attract all sorts! I don't want my two daughters putting themselves in jeopardy.'

Connie didn't dare look at her sister. If their mother knew half of what they were already doing on their trips, she wouldn't sleep at night. 'I thought you could help us with that, Mama. You know a lot of people and, in the nicest possible way, you are quite formidable when you want to be. The group would be very well behaved.'

'You want me to come along?'

Connie waited to see what her sister would say. It wasn't a bad idea. Their mother might even enjoy seeing an opera, but she couldn't help a spike of anxiety at the thought of taking her into Germany. Berlin wasn't the same as it had been. There was an underlying hint of tension and uncertainty in the streets, caused in no small part by the presence of so many uniformed men.

'Mama, we'd love you to, but you would find it too exhausting. We're looking to attract a younger crowd. But if this goes well, we might do another trip. To Florence, perhaps. You would love the scenery and the sunshine.'

Mama nodded. 'Yes, I think I'd prefer to wait for Italy. When you spoke about the beautiful lake in Verona and all the historical sites to be enjoyed, I confess I may have been a little jealous.' She stood up. 'Why don't we go into the sitting room, and you can tell me more about your plan? I don't see how taking a group of tourists to Germany can help rescue more people.'

Connie trailed after her mother and Dottie, trying to find the words to convey the purpose of their trip without scaring their mother. She waited for her to take a seat, picking up her embroidery as she did so. Dottie took the seat on the couch next to their mother, leaving Connie to sit in the chair opposite them.

'As Dottie said, we want to help more people. If we take a

group of ten people, they would pay for the trip with travellers' cheques. But we wouldn't have to cash them.'

Their mother looked confused but remained silent.

'Instead, we'd use the money from a group of Jewish people to pay for everything in Germany. Then, when we return, we'd bank the travellers' cheques into accounts in the names of the Jewish people looking to escape Germany.'

'Why go to all that trouble? Can't they just lodge their own money into a bank account?'

Connie shook her head, taking a second to formulate her response. Her mother's innocent question made her realize how much she and Dottie had learned over the last few months by travelling to Germany and meeting those who had suffered, hearing in their own words how intolerable life had become. 'The Nazi government prohibits them from taking money out of the country. They have implemented so many taxes on these poor people, including an emigration tax of twenty-five per cent of all their assets. Sometimes the families are made to pay this, even if they aren't leaving Germany.'

'So by taking a group of people with you, you make it possible to get more money out of the country.' Their mother nodded to herself, seeing the clever idea behind the plan. 'But what if you get caught?'

'Doing what? Going to an opera? Now that Hitler has offered a twenty-five-year peace pact, people have returned to their normal lives. People are taking trips abroad. Thomas Cook offers nine days in the Rhineland for ten guineas. We'd do something similar.' Connie purposefully made it sound simple when it was anything but.

Her mother pierced her with a look. 'Constance, I didn't come down with the last shower. There is more to what you are telling me.'

Connie tried to contradict her, but at another look fell silent.

Margaret lit up a cigarette, taking a deep puff before saying, 'I will help you. I am good at organizing things – the parties I used to organize for your father gave me plenty of practice.' She thought for a moment. 'You will need a couple of older gentlemen just to keep everyone in line. I know three or four suitable candidates, from church. Now, when are you going, and how much will it cost? We have to put together the package before you speak to any potential travellers.'

Dottie clapped her hands. 'Mama, I knew you could do it!' She shared a look of triumph with Connie. 'But now I must get back to work. My editor has sold my next story. The proceeds will be enough to sponsor another person.'

Connie stood up as well, and dropped a kiss on her mother's cheek. 'I'll write to Stephen to let him know of our arrival.'

'You're becoming very close, aren't you?'

Connie's cheeks heated, and she couldn't meet her mother's eyes. She wasn't sure what was happening between her and Stephen, if anything. She missed him dreadfully. When they did meet, her stomach did somersaults, yet nothing had actually changed between them. Stephen never gave her any clue as to his feelings, continuing to treat her like a younger sister.

Yet, the looks she sometimes caught him giving her seemed to suggest he felt the same as she did.

True to her word, Mama took charge of everything, including interviewing all potential travellers, dismissing a couple of them as too immature. Their group, consisting of ten individuals, gathered at the Liverpool Street train station in London.

While these travellers had some awareness of the situation in Germany, with Cook's and other reputable companies organizing similar trips, nobody believed it could be perilous. All held British passports and were not on the Nazis' target list. Connie was confident that, given their connections in the opera world, they could provide a superior holiday experience. Yet a nagging voice in her head questioned her conscience: Were they putting the others at increased risk by travelling with them? It was one thing for her and Dottie to face danger, but involving those unaware of potential perils weighed heavily on her.

But as the group's excitement mounted, so did Connie's. She pushed aside her anxieties, convinced that the Nazis wouldn't risk a diplomatic incident by targeting a group of tourists. Hitler wanted to project an image of magnanimity and success, and showcasing the wonders of Germany to tourists served his narrative of full employment and happy citizens.

Catching the gaze of one of the travellers, Connie offered him a reassuring smile before addressing the group.

'Thank you all for placing your trust in us. I'm certain we'll have a wonderful time,' she declared, eliciting cheers from the group as they boarded the train, making them resemble a bunch of excitable children embarking on a school trip.

From London they took the train to the coast, a boat to Holland and then another train, bound for Berlin.

Conversation ceased for a few seconds when the train pulled to a halt at the station at the border between Holland and Germany; the passengers looking around, trying to work out why they had stopped.

'Do they check our passports here?' George Hastings, a thirty-something member of their group, asked.

'I believe so,' Dottie replied, her tone dismissive, as if there were nothing untoward about their trip. Connie didn't dare look at her sister, for fear she would give away the real purpose of this expedition. Then she thought of Stephen's coded reply about how much their mutual friends were anticipating her arrival and the dinner they would share, reminding her there were lives at stake. She couldn't lose her nerve now.

It was Dottie's small gasp of surprise that alerted her. Connie inhaled sharply, trying to settle her stomach as two men dressed in long leather coats entered their carriage. She turned the pages of her novel, trying to pretend she was engrossed in the book, but kept an eye on them under the cover of her lashes.

'What element of the trip are you most looking forward to, Miss Constance?'

Startled at Mr Bentley's voice, she glanced at the tall, lean man in his early forties. He met her gaze with a look of under-standing. He'd clearly picked up on her being nervous, although she hoped he didn't suspect the true purpose of their trip.

'The opera, although I am also looking forward to catching up with our friends. What about you, Mr Bentley?'

'I enjoy the opera too, of course. I'm quite looking forward to seeing how Berlin has changed since I last visited back in the early 1920s. I was a young man then and rather enjoyed the freedoms offered by the Weimar Republic.' Mr Bentley smiled at her, his eyes sparkling with a hint of mischief. He adjusted the glasses on his nose. 'Did your mother tell you I worked with your father for a time? He was a lovely man, a proper gentle-man. Did he share your love of opera?'

The conversation distracted her from the Gestapo agents, who barely glanced in their direction as they proceeded through the carriage.

When the train door shut behind them and their journey recommenced, Mr Bentley leaned in a little closer, whispering, 'Perhaps I can offer you my assistance on this trip, Miss Constance? I am happy to help in whatever way you find appro-priate.' A glance of understanding passed between them before Mr Bentley turned to engage another traveller in conversation.

The arrival at Berlin station and their progression to the hotel passed without incident, the group dispersing to their respective rooms. Connie and Dottie feigned tiredness, but when they were sure the coast was clear, they left the hotel and hastened to their pre-arranged meeting with Stephen. He'd selected the Tiergarten, not just because it was full of tourists, but also because by being out in the open, they wouldn't be overheard.

Connie's heart raced with anticipation; it had been weeks since she'd last seen Stephen. As they walked along the gravel paths lined with meticulously tended flowerbeds, she tried to push aside the longing that she was meeting him alone.

Dottie chatted away, oblivious to the turmoil inside Connie's head.

Connie spotted him first, striding towards them, his eyes lit up with warmth. Was it her imagination, or did they linger on her for a fraction before he greeted both of them?

'How lovely you both look. Did you have a safe trip?' He fell into step alongside them, his hand accidentally brushing hers, sending a jolt of electricity through her. 'I've missed you.'

Although his comment was directed at both of them, for a moment his eyes held Connie's.

Dottie slipped her arm through his. 'We miss you too. Mother sends her love and a reminder to make sure you are eating properly. You are, according to her, too thin.'

Stephen laughed, then his expression turned more serious as they reached a deserted stretch of path.

'Are you ready to meet our friends?' He spoke in a low tone, his eyes darting around.

'Yes, tomorrow evening we have the opera. Then the group has plans to have dinner together, but we made an excuse that we were catching up with old friends.'

'Good.' Stephen nodded.

'What is it? You aren't usually this nervous. Is there something wrong?' Connie put her hand on his arm. 'Be honest.'

'Is there anyone in your party that you would trust? I think it would be less suspicious if someone else were to accompany you? I could be mistaken, but I think I was followed earlier.'

Terror filled Connie as his words brought home just how

many risks he was taking. 'Just give us the address and we can go there.'

'Not alone. Not in that part of town – that would look too suspicious. Maybe there is someone at the office...'

Connie found herself saying, 'Mr Bentley will come with us. He worked with Father, and Mother likes him. He was very kind when the Gestapo visited our train carriage.'

Stephen turned white. 'The Gestapo?'

'Don't worry, they didn't even give us a second look. I was just nervous.'

Stephen rubbed his chin, clearly troubled. 'It's not ideal but better than nothing. You are to go to a club – there is a small group of men who have some items they need to be moved. They will also give you a list of names of those funding your trip, so you can open the bank accounts and deposit the money. But be careful. The owner, Elias Katz, is your contact – do you remember him from your last visit to our office, when you met Mr Foley? Elias knows almost as much as I do about your activities. He is completely trustworthy and his... background makes him more suitable for our clandestine activities than you or me.'

Dottie spoke up: 'Never mind us. What do you mean you think you were followed? Are you in danger? Why don't you come back to Britain with us?'

'Don't fuss, Dottie.' Stephen adjusted his tone. 'Mr Foley warned all the embassy staff that they may come under suspicion. He told us to watch out for those who take just a little bit too much interest in our comings and goings. I led the poor fellow on a merry dance. He must think I'm besotted with shopping. I went into every shop until I managed to lose him.'

Dottie looked around, making Stephen smile. 'Don't worry. I wouldn't have come here to meet you if he was still following me.' But his expression turned serious. 'But I don't want to take any risks, not when we would be caught in a compromising position. Elias is not the usual friend of an embassy official or his opera-loving relatives.'

The opera was sensational and they had an enjoyable dinner afterwards, hosted by Clemens. But Connie's thoughts kept going back to Stephen. Was he safe? Would the Gestapo honour his British passport, or could he disappear?

'A real feather in your cap, Miss Constance, arranging all this for us. Any tours you book in the future will be sure to sell out fast.'

Connie took a sip of her wine. 'Thank you, Mr Bentley. You are very kind.' She picked up her napkin to dab her lips, also using it to wipe her clammy hands. 'Would you like to take a stroll around the garden? The waiter assured me they were worth seeing. Dottie will look after the group.'

He nodded and stood up. 'I'd be honoured.' Offering her his arm, he walked her out of the restaurant and out into the gardens, keeping up banal chatter until they were safely out of earshot.

'I assume your intention wasn't to take advantage of me, Miss Constance.'

She should have been shocked, but instead his comment made her laugh as he pretended to be offended.

'Call me Connie, please. I wanted to ask you whether you meant what you said on the train. That you would be willing to help.'

'Absolutely.'

'How did you guess we weren't just here to see the opera?'

'I believe you are the opera fanatic you are purported to be, but no opera enthusiast would have had that reaction to the Gestapo. But it wasn't just that. Margaret may have hinted something. She asked me to look out for both of you.'

More than a little relieved she hadn't completely blown her own cover, Connie said, 'Dear Mama, she does worry.'

'She also knows I don't pose a risk to her daughters.' At Connie's inquiring look, he explained: 'My tastes lie in other directions.'

Connie wasn't sure how to respond to that, but he continued: 'We share a common enemy Miss Cons—forgive me, Connie. He has made it very clear what he will do to men like me. If I can do something to help two beautiful, brave sisters while at the same time sticking it in Hitler's eye, just tell me how. But perhaps you could take my arm and let me escort you around the gardens? Standing here like this without me kissing you makes us rather conspicuous, don't you think?'

She took his arm with a smile. 'You are a very kind man, Mr Bentley.'

'Henry, please. Now, what are your plans for me?'

Connie told him about the meeting the following evening. He laughed when she mentioned the name of the club where they were to meet.

'What's so funny?'

'I can understand why your friend didn't want you going there unaccompanied. If it is the same as it was back in the twenties, it isn't the type of place a young lady would visit alone.'

'Oh.' What had made Stephen choose a place like that? Connie flushed at the direction of her thoughts.

'Your friends must have felt it was the safest place to meet.'

It was disconcerting how easily he read her mind, but then she supposed he was more experienced than she was at hiding who he was in real life. She felt a pang of sympathy for him. 'Will it look odd if we're seen there?'

'It might be safer if you arrived alone. A couple may be visiting to' – he coughed – 'explore certain tastes, if you get my

meaning. Your sister, while charming, appears rather too innocent to be involved in that scene.'

Connie didn't pretend to fully understand what he was
talking about, but there was no way she would put Dottie at
more risk. Her face turned scarlet. 'I don't know what I've done
to give you the...'

'Connie, you have done nothing. Your behaviour is impec-
cable. But your sister has a more... fragile bearing? Perhaps it's
the artist in her?'

Connie smiled. 'She *is* very innocent. Even now, after
everything we've heard, witnessed even, she looks for the best in
people. I'll convince her to stay behind. Tell her she needs to
look after our other guests.'

Dottie wasn't happy with the new plan but she gave in,
eventually.

Connie was surprised when she returned to the hotel to find
a box from a couture shop on her bed. She opened it, gasping
when she saw an emerald-green satin *concoction* – it was far too
sophisticated to call it a dress.

'Connie! Is there more than you told me between you and
Mr Bentley?' Dottie ran her hand over the satin fabric. 'Try it
on, although if Mama saw you in something like this, she'd lock
you up and throw away the key.'

Connie couldn't agree more. Still, part of her was excited to
try on the dress even if it wasn't entirely suitable.

The dress clung in all the right places, the colour accentuating her green eyes.

'You look incredible, like that lady we saw at Tom's party in
New York. The satin clings like a second skin. How does it
feel?'

'Liberating and scary. What do I look like?'

Dottie giggled. 'Not like a heroine in my type of books. It is rather risqué, isn't it?'

Connie turned this way and that, examining her appearance. She'd never worn a strapless gown before. Her arms felt bare. Part of her wished Stephen could see her. She wondered what his reaction would be. Shock or approval?

A knock on the door startled both of them.

'I'll go.' Dottie walked over to the door while Connie darted into the bathroom.

'Connie, come out. It's Mr Bentley.'

Taking a deep breath, Connie stepped out of the bathroom. Henry clapped when he saw her. 'You look magnificent! You will blend in perfectly.'

'The women at this place wear these types of clothes...?'

'They wear a lot less. This is sophisticated and the latest fashion. You look incredible. Well, you will if you stop looking like you've stolen it. Hold your head up high and own it.'

'I thought the idea was not to attract attention. To be secretive about our work.'

'It's easier to hide in plain sight. If you turned up at the club wearing one of your opera outfits, everyone – not just those trained to pay attention – would suspect you. I'll call for you at 9 p.m.' With a bow, he turned and walked out of the room, closing the door behind him.

'I don't know where Mama found him, but he isn't her usual sort of friend, is he?' Dottie glanced at Connie, stretching over to tuck her hair behind her ear. 'You do look magnificent.'

The club proved to be everything Henry had hinted at – and more. Connie struggled not to let her mouth slip open at some of the sights they saw on entering the place. She copied Henry's approach, appearing totally unfazed by the scantily clad couples embracing around them. She spotted their contact when they reached the bar.

'Darling, you look incredible! Welcome to the wild side.' Elias kissed her on both cheeks before turning to Henry to do the same. Taking Connie's arm he whispered, 'I like your friend.' In a louder voice, he said, 'Let's find a bottle of the best champagne and a room. Follow me.'

Connie was glad of Henry's supporting arm around her waist. She'd never been to a nightclub before and she was fairly sure it wasn't an experience she was eager to repeat. Thankfully, as soon as Elias closed the door to the private room behind him, he dropped the act.

'Great costume. Well done. Stephen not with you?'

Connie shook her head. 'He thought he was being followed so he suggested he stay behind. Mr Bentley is a friend of my mother's and an expert on nightclubs.' Connie flashed Henry a smile. Turning her attention back to Elias, she asked, 'Where are the men?'

'They aren't here. They're too nervous – Zev and Reuben had telephone calls warning them not to return home. They are our priority. We must get them out.'

'What do you mean "not return home"? Where will they live?'

'Connie, things have worsened. These men are well known and wealthy. Not a good combination when you are Jewish in Hitler's Germany. We have some good contacts in the police, who warned them they were going to be picked up and put in a camp. So, for now, they are staying with some friends. They gave me these.' Elias reached under the cushion on a nearby banquette, pulling out two bags. The first was full of money; the second contained jewellery, including two fancy gentlemen's watches.

'There is enough there to cover the hotel and restaurant bills. I know a check would be better, but it is too risky.' Elias reached into his pocket, taking out a piece of paper that he put into Henry's hand, along with the bags. 'I used the code Stephen gave me for the list of the men for whom you will open bank accounts with the money you raise. It is imperative the Gestapo doesn't find any trace of this information. It would only lead them straight to these men and their families. As I said, Zev and Reuben are the priorities.'

Elias lit a cigarette, his hands shaking as he offered one to Henry.

'What about you, Elias? Are you going to get out?'

Elias looked surprised at Henry's question. 'Me? No, not yet at least. I'm needed here.'

'I wouldn't leave it too long. Britain may not appreciate men like us, but at least they don't murder us.'

Shame engulfed Connie at Henry's remark: she hadn't even thought of the risks that Elias, both homosexual and Jewish, was taking.

'Henry is right, Elias. I'm going to add your name to the list.'

Elias took a deep drag on his cigarette. 'You can't do that, Connie. I don't have a penny to my name. All my money went into this place, and it's not like I can sell it now. I'll take my chances.'

Before Connie could argue, they heard whistles and shouting. Elias groaned and ground his cigarette out under his shoe. 'Quick! It may just be a police raid, but you need to leave. Out this way.'

Elias led the way through a labyrinth of passages, through what looked like an old kitchen to a bookcase. He took out a book and reached inside. The bookcase swung open. 'Go quickly. It's a tunnel that leads to a respectable hotel, just over the road. They won't say anything.'

'Come with us,' Henry insisted.

Temptation vied with duty in Elias's eyes before he blew them a kiss. He stepped back. 'Someone needs to put the bookcase back in place. I'll be fine. Go. Be safe. Connie, thank you. For everything.'

Before she could answer the bookcase wall closed. Tears in her eyes, Connie turned on her heel, stumbling, causing Henry to catch her. He pulled her upright and, holding her elbow in a firm grip, escorted her through the secret passageway and out of a door, into a silent corridor of the hotel.

Connie's heart was pounding with fear, but nobody looked twice at them, as Elias had said.

When they reached the street, Henry stepped outside, scanning their surroundings before he motioned for Connie to follow. Behind them, they heard shouts of protest and some shots rang out.

Connie faltered but Henry pushed her forward. 'You can't do anything for him now. We need to get back to our hotel.'

Dottie met them in the hotel reception. 'Thank God you're back. I've had a bad feeling all evening.'

Connie didn't look at Henry. 'Everything was fine. It was an eye-opener of an evening but Henry was very gallant. I'm exhausted now, though, so please excuse me. I need my bed.'

Henry walked them to their room, coming inside to hand over the cash and jewellery. He kept the watches. 'Makes sense if I wear one and carry one in my luggage. What would you be doing with men's watches?'

Once again, Connie was glad their mother had insisted he'd accompanied them. He was so cool under pressure.

Dottie opened her mouth to ask questions, but Connie turned away. Thankfully her sister took the hint. 'You go to bed. I'll write the coded list into my story notebook. Don't worry, I will burn the original.'

Connie only let the tears fall once she was sure Dottie was

fast asleep. She couldn't close her eyes as she pictured Elias's face. *Please God, keep him safe.*

They dressed carefully the next morning, having divided the jewellery and cash between them, and headed to breakfast and then to the station. Henry kept up a conversation with Dottie the whole time, for which Connie was grateful. She couldn't talk, couldn't even think. She was desperate to get an update from Stephen on whether Elias was safe, but it was far too risky for her to try to make contact.

She had thought he might be at the train station to wave them off, but there was no sign of him. She hoped that didn't mean he was in trouble. Her eyes darted around the station, but nobody seemed to be taking any notice of their group who were in high spirits, talking about the opera and other highlights of their trip. Her heart raced, speeding up as the train pulled into the station. About an hour into the journey, the compartment door opened. The tension in the air escalated, it was as if all the oxygen disappeared leaving it difficult for her to breathe. She kept her gaze focused on the book on her lap. When asked for her papers, she didn't lift her head as she passed them over. If they looked in her eyes, they may see her fear but more likely her anger. It was men like these who had shot at Elias and his friends last night. She didn't sag with relief when they returned her papers and made their way through the compartment. The conversation around her grew lively once more as the train chugged on but she didn't think she would breathe easily until they were back on British soil.

When they arrived home, Mama handed Connie a telegram. 'It doesn't make a bit of sense. Not to me, at least.'

Sorry couldn't make party. Had business meeting in Munich.
Very last minute. See you soon. Stephen.

Connie held the telegram to her chest. He was safe. Thank God.

'How was your trip?' Mama asked, as they sat drinking tea in the sitting room. 'Did your group enjoy it?'

'Very much, Mama. Your friend, Mr Bentley, proved extremely useful, didn't he Connie?'

Connie nodded.

Dottie gave her a funny look before addressing their mother once more. 'We must go to the bank tomorrow, Mama, and open these accounts. I have the names and addresses, and then Stephen will be able to get the visas issued. If luck is on our side, the men will be in Britain before the end of the summer.'

'How wonderful. I'm so proud of you both.' Mama smiled at Dottie but cast a worried look at Connie.

Connie knew she should say something to ease her mother's concerns, but she didn't have it in her to lie. Not again. 'Excuse me, but I have rather a bad headache. I think I shall have an early night.' She made her excuses and escaped to her room.

Dottie wasn't long in following, knocking on her door and then coming over to sit on the bed beside her. 'Connie, we are in this together. I know something happened and you are trying to protect me. But you can't bottle up your feelings.'

Connie pushed her hair back from her face and turned to her sister. 'I think this weekend showed me just how important it is that we continue this work. There are so many who need help. We must do all we can.'

'Of course, we will. Now, get some sleep – you do look rather done in.'

TWENTY-ONE

LONDON, MAY 1937

Connie settled herself on the sofa, while Dottie turned on the wireless to tune into the live coverage of the coronation. A small portrait of the new king and queen adorned the sitting-room mantelpiece. Mama had purchased a few pieces of patriotic bunting and some flags to mark the occasion.

'I think he will be a good king, don't you?' Mama asked no one in particular. 'He married a good woman. Elizabeth is a well-brought-up English lady with an inbred sense of duty. Those girls of hers are a credit to any mother, like mine are to me.'

'Mama, you can't compare us to the future queen of England.'

'Why not?' Mama's reply was almost drowned out by the cheers coming from the radio, as well as the streets outside. 'Shush! I want to listen.'

They listened as the radio announcer brought them from their sitting room right to the heart of the abbey, detailing the arrival of other royalty, dignitaries and illustrious guests from around the world.

'It is a momentous day in the history of our great nation.'

The BBC announcer continued, not quite hiding his own excitement. 'The stage is set for the crowning of our new sovereign, King George VI.'

Connie closed her eyes, leaning back in her chair as she let the sounds coming from the wireless wash over her. She could imagine the pomp and ceremony of the occasion, the women in wonderful dresses wearing dazzling jewels, the men in their formal robes.

The crowds of people outside the cathedral and throughout the streets of the capital roared their approval at certain points in the ceremony. At others, not a sound could be heard, especially when the archbishop of Canterbury anointed the new king.

The crowds outside erupted and Connie couldn't help but jump to her feet clapping, wishing she was outside Buckingham Palace and watching the royal family on the balcony when they made their appearance. But Mama hadn't wanted to sleep on the streets overnight, and Connie and Dottie couldn't very well have left her to listen to this auspicious occasion alone.

The next day, at work, all conversation was about the new king and queen.

Enjoying a sandwich with her friends in the work canteen, Connie couldn't believe her eyes when she read the paper.

'It says here that Goering actually flew to London!' one of the girls said, as she read over Connie's shoulder. 'He landed in Croydon airport as he thought he might be able to get into Westminster Abbey. Even Hitler didn't try that. Imagine having such a high opinion of yourself...!'

Connie wished she had the words to convey what Goering and his Nazis friends were doing in Germany, and what little respect they showed for normal conventions, such as freedom to practise your religion or live in peace. But the conversation moved on to who had the best gowns or the most spectacular jewellery so she remained quiet.

When Connie got home that night, she cut out pictures of the king and queen from the paper. She also cut out pictures of Princess Elizabeth and Princess Margaret.

Dottie came into the room, her eyes widening when she saw the newspapers spread over the table. 'What are you doing?'

'I thought Leah might like to have some pictures of the coronation. You know how she loves our royal family.'

'What a lovely thing to do. I can't wait to go back to Vienna in October. Clemens promised to keep us some good seats. We will be able to see Sarah and her family then. Give them my love when you write, won't you?' Dottie picked up a picture. 'When do you think we'll go to Germany again?'

'I don't know but soon, I'm thinking. Clemens invited us to go in September but Stephen wrote to say he is coming to London the first week of June so he might need us to go back sooner. We can ask him what the latest news is then, I suppose.'

TWENTY-TWO

BERLIN, SEPTEMBER 1937

Connie patted her bag as she looked out of the plane window.

'What do you have in there?' Dottie asked, frowning at her. 'You keep patting your bag.'

Connie smiled before putting her hand into the bag. She produced the pictures they had taken in New York with various opera singers. 'I thought it would be useful to have these – proof we are true opera lovers.'

'We are. So why would we need to prove it?' Dottie was looking perplexed.

Connie shrugged. Her sister was right, they weren't pretending, but she felt better having the pictures in her bag. They had made several trips now and it seemed to her as if the border agents were starting to pay more attention to them. At least this was purely a social visit.

'What do we do when we arrive?' Dottie asked.

'Ernst, Clemens' nephew, sent a note to say he would meet us at the station.' Connie bit the inside of her lip. 'I can't help feeling something is wrong. Why else would he want to meet us?' She looked out of the window as they started their descent into Berlin.

· · ·

It was Connie who first spotted Ernst waiting at the station, smoking a cigarette, his eyes fixed on the floor as if he were in deep thought.

Ernst ground out his cigarette, his smile not quite reaching his blue eyes. 'Miss Connie and Miss Dottie, you made it. How was your trip?'

'Fine, thank you, Ernst. Are you alone, or is your lovely wife-to-be with you?' Connie's unease grew as he kept glancing around.

Ernst's ears turned pink. 'Sonja decided to stay at home today. She is helping her mother with the dresses for the wedding. I cannot see them. It is bad luck.'

'That it is. You will be married in less than six weeks. Is that so long to wait?'

Dottie was only teasing, but Connie saw her question caused Ernst to tense up. Her sense something was wrong increased, but the station was not the place to discuss these things.

'Ernst, can you carry our cases to the hotel for us? We are exhausted.'

'Of course, Miss Connie.' He answered with a smile. 'What did you expect me to do? Leave you here to walk?'

Connie laughed as she imagined he wanted, but she gave him a quick wink in recognition of the grateful look he had sent her. She was right: he did want to talk. They had to be careful, though.

'If you ladies are not too tired, I thought we might take a walk and try some hot chocolate. You haven't tried the best until you try that which is on offer at Herr Bauer's café. He makes the best chocolate in Europe.'

'We must try some. Dottie loves chocolate in any form. I prefer coffee.'

'Not in Berlin, Miss Connie. I do not think our coffee is quite what you are accustomed to.'

Connie didn't care what the coffee tasted like. She wanted to know what Ernst had to say, but she kept her impatience under control. He knew what he was doing. He must not trust the hotel if he wanted them to go walking.

They reached the hotel without any issues and checked in at reception as Ernst carried their bags to their room for them. The hotel staff would have done it, but it gave Ernst a reason to accompany them.

He gave their room a quick once-over pointing out things to Connie and Dottie as if they had never travelled before. She was about to remind him of the extent of their travels when she realized he was checking for listening devices. Sure enough, there was one beside the bed, hidden in the lampshade. He pointed it out while chatting about the area, but didn't remove it.

He also pointed at the phone to remind them it was likely bugged too, but nobody made mention of it. They talked gaily about the upcoming opera and their need for hot chocolate.

Only once they were out in the open again, walking to the café, did Ernst drop the act.

'Sonja's father has disappeared. We think he is in Dachau, but we cannot be sure.'

Connie and Dottie exchanged a glance. Edith had told them about Dachau but, even in London, she had only whispered, as if by talking about it in a normal voice would make the horrible place seem more real.

'Why? What did he do?' Dottie asked.

'Nothing. He is a doctor with a fine reputation. Maybe they were scared he would talk the people into revolting or some-thing. It doesn't matter what they thought. They don't have to prove anything. They came in the middle of the night and took him away. Sonja's sister tried to stop them, and she ended up with a broken nose for her trouble.'

Dottie gasped aloud. Connie reached for her sister. 'We are so sorry, Ernst.'

'Miss Connie, what is my country coming to?'

'Don't worry, Ernst. We must be able to do something. Do you know anyone who could help us get him released?'

'I have heard of some people, but others say it is too dangerous to bring attention to the family. People rarely come back from the camps now. There are awful stories about beatings and men being forced to... I can't continue.'

Connie grasped Dottie's arm, seeing her sister was as white as a sheet – probably a mirror image of herself, given how her stomach had clenched painfully at the look in his eyes.

'Oh, I am so sorry.' Ernst looked stricken. 'I forget you are two ladies who do not live here.'

'We are not made of porcelain, Ernst. We won't break. We asked you to be honest with us. Is it safe to talk in this café you are taking us to?' Connie forced her voice to sound confident and normal, ignoring her instinct to grab Dottie and run to the nearest train station to go back to London.

'Yes, the owner is a friend. He is not Jewish, but unless they check my papers, they do not believe I am, either. My blond hair and blue eyes do not fit with their image of what a Jew should look like.'

Connie hated his bitter tone, but she knew they were only partially aware of the trials this lovely young man had been subjected to.

'Ernst, are you and Sonja going to come to Britain? We can help you.'

'Not yet, Miss Connie. But we want to try to get Sonja's parents out. At least, that was the plan before her father got arrested. Now her mother won't go anywhere. She says she will wait here until her husband comes back.'

'Oh, the poor woman. She must be distraught. Can Clemens do anything?'

'He has tried some contacts. I have some friends in the Zionist organizations. They may be able to help.'

'I have a friend too. I will get in touch with him and see whether he can help,' Connie added.

'Who?' Dottie asked, but Connie just smiled. As much as she liked Ernst, she wasn't going to break her promise to Stephen. His name wouldn't be mentioned, not by her.

The hot chocolate was amazing. They tried to relax and enjoy it, but it was difficult. Berlin had changed since their last visit. Now young men in Hitler Youth uniforms – brown shirts, black shorts and the horrible red and white swastika on their arm – strutted around like they owned the place. They seemed to be everywhere. Some Berliners were acting as normal, but a lot of people wore strained expressions.

Connie spotted the brownshirts approaching an orthodox Jew who was simply walking down the street, minding his own business. They stopped him and asked him several questions, all the while pushing him and pulling at his hair and beard. She gasped as she watched one of the uniformed men take a knife from his pocket and slice off the long curls at the side of the man's face, and toss his hat to the ground. When he bent to pick up the hat, at their command, they kicked him, and he fell to the ground. They walked off laughing. Nobody went to his aid.

Connie instinctively stood up, but Ernst grabbed her arm and pulled her back down into her seat. 'It is better you do not draw attention to yourself. Your work is too important to many to put it at risk for one man. His friends will come and take him away when it is safer.'

They sat for a few more moments in tense silence, but Connie had had enough. She glanced at her sister.

Dottie obviously felt the same. With tears running down her face she said, 'I am sorry Ernst, but I must go. I have some writing to do today before we go out this evening.'

'Yes, of course.' He leaned towards Dottie and lowered his voice. 'Be careful in the hotel. As I suspected, your room is bugged, but the rumours are that this is happening to all foreigners, so do not be afraid. It doesn't mean the Gestapo are after you.'

She gave him a tight smile. 'That's good to hear. Now, are you coming to the opera tonight?'

'No, it is not possible for me to attend, but we will meet tomorrow at my uncle's home. He is having a rather big party. Plenty of people want to meet you or renew old acquaintances. Now, I had best call you a cab to take you back to the hotel.'

'Thank you, Ernst, but it is not necessary.' Connie smiled at the young man. 'We'll walk back. I know the way and I wish to speak to Dottie in private.'

Ernst clicked his heels in a very German way and bid them good day. As soon as he was gone, Connie took her sister's arm and together they walked back towards the hotel.

'You are going to contact Stephen, aren't you?'

'Yes, Dottie. I need to ask him about Sonja's father. But I will invite him to the opera. He is our adoptive cousin, after all, and it would look strange if we didn't call him while we're staying here, don't you think?'

'I think you should be writing spy novels. Your talents are wasted in the Civil Service.'

Connie didn't agree. She usually moaned about her work but after the excitement of this trip so far, she found she was missing her dull job a little.

A discreet knock on the door announced Stephen's arrival. He had been delighted to hear from them and accepted their invitation while making one of his own. He offered to take them out for an early dinner prior to the opera.

Connie rushed to the door, her heart fluttering with anticipation. She opened it to find Stephen standing there, looking dashing in his black dinner jacket and glistening white shirt. He greeted them with a warm smile and a bouquet of fresh flowers, a thoughtful gesture that elicited delighted gasps from both Connie and Dottie.

'Stephen, you shouldn't have,' Connie exclaimed, taking the bouquet from him and inhaling the fragrance of the blooms.

'Only the best for my favourite cousins,' Stephen replied with a wink, and they all shared a moment of laughter.

Dottie had insisted on packing their good dresses and Connie was glad she had listened to her sister. She enjoyed dressing up on occasion, and the effort was worth it when she saw Stephen's eyes widen with appreciation.

Stephen took them to a small but smart restaurant. It was a bit disquieting on entering to find all the tables appeared to be occupied by those in uniform.

Connie glanced at him.

'Where better to hide than in the open?' he murmured as he leaned in, as if to kiss her cheek.

She smiled but inside her heart leapt and her pulse raced. Maybe he was right. At least here the tables wouldn't be bugged.

Stephen raised his voice as he said, 'This is one of the finest restaurants in Berlin. Have whatever you like from the menu, but I would recommend the house special. It is always excellent.'

Connie forced herself to ignore their surroundings and joined in with his playful banter.

'Come here a lot, do you, cousin darling? And poor Mama is

worried you will starve to death.' She smiled and shook her head.

His eyes twinkled and for a second, he looked like the young man who used to sit by their fire back in London – before he had prematurely aged and his hazel eyes had taken on a haunted expression. How she wished she could remove some of the weight from his shoulders.

'Your mama doesn't need to worry about me. Everywhere I go people try to feed me. I must look like a hungry orphan.'

They ordered the house special and allowed Stephen to choose a wine for them. Just as they were about to drink, a bottle of champagne arrived at their table. The waiter placed it in front of Connie.

'We didn't order this, there must be some mistake.' Connie glanced at the waiter before examining the label. She knew enough about champagne to recognize both the vintage and the value.

'No mistake, fräulein. The compliments of General Von Fritsch. He asked me to bring it to you. Said such pretty ladies should have the best to drink.'

Connie's hand recoiled from the bottle, and her first impulse was to send the bottle back. But she was learning and quickly hid her reaction, certain the general was watching.

Connie looked uncertainly at Stephen, but he gave her a nod. She smiled her thanks in the direction of the general, who acknowledged her with a smile of his own.

To her horror, he stood and began to approach their table. The sweat ran down Connie's back: surely he wouldn't insist on sharing the champagne?

'Good evening, ladies. I trust I am not imposing?'

Stephen dropped his linen on the table and stood up. 'No, of course not, General Von Fritsch.'

'Mr Armstrong, of course, I remember you. What are you doing in the company of such beautiful ladies?'

'Allow me to introduce my adopted cousins, Miss Dorothea Fitzwalter and her sister, Miss Constance.'

The general clicked his heels at Dorothea but he took Constance's hand in his and kissed it. It took all her willpower not to pull her arm away from him. Instead, she smiled graciously, inwardly thanking her mother for sending her to finishing classes all those years ago.

'I hope you enjoy the champagne, Miss Fitzwalter. Perhaps later you would give me the honour of a dance?'

'I would love to, but we are leaving to attend the opera. An early dinner, if you will.'

'The opera. What are you going to see? Like our esteemed führer, I too am an opera fan. I love *La Traviata*. I am also partial to Mozart's *Fidelio* but, of course, the master of the art is the great Wagner. Have you seen *Die Meistersinger von Nürnberg*? I was honoured to be among the guests when it was performed back in 1933 to mark the founding of our Third Reich.'

Connie tried hard to concentrate on his words and not her breathing, which was becoming shallower. How could a man who represented such evil like opera? Yet Hitler did, as did the general in front of her. She'd love to tell him her real opinion of Hitler and his masterpiece of Nuremberg, but instead she stayed silent. Sometimes silence spoke volumes, and perhaps he wouldn't be deaf.

She held his stare, pursing her lips, refusing to break the silence.

'Well, maybe next time I see you we can share a drink, and you can give me the highlights of your evening.'

'That would be lovely, thank you.' She couldn't quite hide the sarcasm in her voice.

His nostrils flared slightly but otherwise he pretended not to notice.

'Now, excuse me and let me allow you to have your dinner. I wouldn't want you to attend the opera hungry on my account.'

He kissed her hand again and walked away.

Stephan leaned in as if to pick up his napkin. 'Close your mouth, dear Connie. You look like you're about to be hit by a train.'

'I can't believe he likes opera, and he behaved like a gentleman. I expected everyone in their uniform to be an ignorant thug,' she hissed back, conscious she didn't want her words to be overheard.

Stephen gave a weary smile. 'And therein lies part of the problem. The most dangerous are the ones like you have just met. They are intelligent, well-brought-up, well-educated men who just happen to be murdering devils. They are more dangerous than your ordinary thugs, who most can recognize for exactly what they are: blood-thirsty hooligans. Those thugs wouldn't get far in any society but the sort you met, you could easily see dining in Westminster, being entertained by the important decision-makers. As your father used to say, "You can never trust a wolf in sheep's clothing."'

'Oh, Stephen, what a mess. It seemed so much simpler at home in Britain. Now it is just horrid.' Dottie stood up and excused herself as she went to the ladies' room.

Connie was tempted to follow and check on her, but she wouldn't have long alone with Stephen to ask him about Sonja's father.

'Stephen, we need your help. There is someone in Dachau we need to rescue.'

Stephen's eyes darted around the room as he hissed at her: 'Connie, keep your voice down! You can't start talking about places like that with these people around you.'

His rebuke stung but she wasn't going to be deterred. She lowered her voice even further. 'Sorry, but it's important. Sonja is supposed to be getting married. Her parents were waiting for her wedding and then were going to move to Britain. Now her father has disappeared and her mother refuses to leave without him. What can we do?'

'Nothing. You have to persuade the woman to leave as soon as possible. For now, they are only locking up the men. Soon that will change.' He picked up his cutlery and attacked his plate.

'But can't you do something?' She regretted asking as soon as she looked into his eyes. All traces of humour were gone. She knew she was looking into the eyes of someone who had seen too much already. 'Stephen, I'm sorry. I know you have important work to do. I shouldn't burden you.'

He dropped his cutlery and took her hand. 'It is I who should apologize, dear Connie. You have such a tender heart. You cannot know that we have one hundred, maybe two hundred enquiries, right now, just like Sonja's father. They have all disappeared and we do not know if they are living or dead. In some cases, the dead are better off. The men who run these places are no better than animals. Oh, Connie. I don't know what I can do.'

She hated adding to his burden, but the image of Ernst and Sonja came to her mind. The couple were so in love and needed to be together. She had to try.

'Can you at least try to find out if he is still alive?'

He nodded, before turning his attention to Dottie as she returned to the table, her eyes red but her face otherwise composed.

Stephen smiled at her as she retook her seat. 'How is the writing going? I believe I am in the presence of one of the most famous Mills and Boon authors around.'

'Oh, Stephen, stop teasing. I am not famous.' Dottie blushed prettily.

'Maybe not yet, but you are on your way.'

'We had better eat up or we will be late,' Connie said. She

held up her glass and the other two raised theirs. 'To success,' she said.

'Success,' they echoed.

The opera, *Carmen*, was wonderful, as was the after-show party although Connie's thoughts kept returning to Sonja's father. Connie watched from the side of the floor as Dottie danced with one partner after another. Connie was asked numerous times but preferred to people-watch. She saw Stephen taking Ernst aside and having a long conversation with him. She hoped he would have good news. Sonja was a lovely girl and while Connie had never met her parents, she assumed they were just as pleasant.

She found herself staring at a man in uniform. He wasn't in the same uniform as the general had worn in the restaurant.

'Would you like to dance?'

Connie was appalled to be broken from her reverie by the man she had just been staring at. Before she could answer, he held out his hand. Surprising herself, she took it and let him lead her to the floor.

They danced in silence for a while and then he asked her how she had enjoyed the opera. 'Is it true you came all the way from England to watch this performance?'

'Yes. I know people will think we are odd, but my sister and I are such devotees we would travel anywhere to see a favourite opera.'

'So I heard.'

Connie couldn't stop a shiver going down her back. She sensed this man wasn't exactly what he seemed. Was he German secret service? Did he suspect them of doing something other than merely visiting? She was relieved when the dance was over but, to her horror, he continued to hold her.

'It was lovely to make your acquaintance, Miss Constance Fitzwalter of Hanover Square. Perhaps we will meet again.'

'Quite possibly, given our mutual interest in opera. Thank you for the dance. I wish to return to my sister.' He bowed as she walked away. She could feel his eyes boring into her back. Gritting her teeth, she continued to walk, pretending she had to balance a book on her head. Anything to stop her body showing how scared his behaviour had made her.

'I think it's time to leave,' Stephen said, as he came toward her.

'You saw.'

'Yes. Let me go and get Dottie, then we can take our coats and go. Mr Krauss won't mind. He will understand.'

Connie didn't argue. She couldn't. Her mind was reeling, possibly with shock. She looked at her hands: they wouldn't stop shaking. She clutched her evening bag tighter, sensing his eyes on her again. But she wasn't going to behave like a frightened rabbit. She stood straighter and looked him in the eyes.

He nodded, as if appreciating her message.

She turned away from him and walked towards Stephen and Dottie.

'You look like one of Mama's linen sheets, Connie. What's wrong?'

'Nothing. I'm just tired.'

Stephen turned to Dottie and said quietly, 'Connie was dancing with a member of the *Abwehr*. The German secret service.'

Dottie paled before looking behind her. 'Oh, no. Does he know about our work?'

'No, of course not. How could he? I'm just being paranoid.' But Connie knew she wasn't. She hadn't told him her name or what part of London she lived in. Someone at the party could have told him the former, but the latter wasn't public knowledge. Was he giving her a hint they were watching her, or was he testing her? She had no idea, but neither thought was particularly attractive.

Stephen took their arms and began steering them towards the cloakroom, speaking in a low but insistent voice. 'I don't think you should try to do anything on this trip. Just go home as if it was the opera that attracted you to visit at this time. Then if they do decide to ask you anything, you won't be lying.'

Stephen's autocratic tone didn't sit well with Connie and it was Dottie who answered, although she waited until they were outside on the street.

'I am not going to behave like a scared little mouse just because someone asked Connie to dance. We have a job to do and we must do it. Sonja's father and countless others depend on us. Isn't that right, Connie?' Dottie turned her piercing blue eyes fully on her sister.

Connie nodded, but avoided her sister's gaze. She couldn't tell Dottie the truth, she didn't want to scare her. She couldn't quell the urge to protect her. Funny how people believed she was the stronger sister. Dottie was the quieter one, but she had pure steel running through her veins at times. She was also the selfless one. All the money she was earning now was going straight to their work to help the Jews. Gone were her sister's dreams of buying furs and first-class travel passes. Yet she hadn't complained. Not once.

As previous director of the Berlin State Opera, Clemens had a house made available for his use while in Berlin. The next day they went there to meet him and Ernst. A servant led them into a large drawing room where Sonja joined them for a little while, but the girl's red eyes and white face told them where her thoughts lay. Connie wanted to hug the girl tight and tell her everything would be fine, but she couldn't do that. She was in no position to make promises.

Ernst left to take Sonja back to her mother while Clemens fixed them a drink. 'Poor dear girl. She is so worried, and her mother isn't helping.' Clemens took a sip of his drink. 'She keeps screaming and crying, saying there is something we can do. I am afraid if she brings too much attention to her family, they will come back for all of them.'

'I thought the Nazis weren't taking women and children.'

'They aren't. Not yet. But it is only a matter of time.'

'Last night, at your party, a German officer asked me to dance. He gave me the feeling he knew me.'

'Ah, yes. Herr Hoffman.'

'You know him?'

'Yes, my dear. There are some uniformed officers who are decent Germans. I believe he is one of them.'

'Does he know what you are doing? Why we are really here?'

'Does he know? I cannot answer that for sure. Does he suspect? Probably. We have known each other for many years. I haven't told him anything. It would not be fair to put him in a dangerous position. Not now, at least.'

Connie didn't understand his reasoning. Surely they needed all the help they could get.

'Why? If you trust him, maybe he could help us?'

'We are not in danger. I would prefer to use my contacts like him when the need arises. For now, we are only bending the rules a little. Now, please come and meet some new investors.'

'Investors?' Connie's voice came out in a squeak.

'Sure, they are investors.' Clemens eyes twinkled. 'They are going to give you money to invest in Britain. Every banker knows that diversity is the key to good economical returns. Don't they?'

Despite the seriousness of the situation, Connie laughed. Dottie looked confused.

'Dottie, let's go and see what items we need to bank for these people.'

The Jewish men had a surprise waiting for them: instead of simple jewellery, fur coats or currency notes, they had glorious diamond necklaces, brooches and gold bars.

Connie's stomach turned over. How on earth would they get these magnificent jewels past the eyes of the border guards?

Her fingers quivered as she reached out to touch a particularly fine necklace, the diamonds meticulously arranged to resemble rain droplets. She picked it up, surprised at the weight. Her eyes met those of one of the men. 'Is this yours?'

'My mother's and her mother's before that. We can trace it back several hundred years.'

Connie caressed the necklace. It wasn't just a thing of beauty but testament to a family's love for one another. She could see a mother passing such a treasure to a beloved daughter, or granddaughter. It seemed wrong to take it or any of the other amazing pieces.

Dottie picked up an intricately designed brooch made up of deep red rubies and cornflower-blue sapphires. The stones glowed, and the diamond surround almost seemed to move with a life of its own. 'Isn't this the most beautiful piece?' Dottie glanced up, and Connie watched her sister closely as she came to a similar realization. 'These aren't just stunning adornments but a history of your lives. Each piece has a story to tell, and only your family members know that story. How can you bear to part with them?'

A man in his sixties, a slight stoop to his shoulders, wire-rimmed glasses perched on his nose, answered. 'They may tell the stories of our people, but those families will be no more if we cannot get the family members out of Germany. Hitler has made no secret of his plans. These' – the man waved his hand over the assortment of jewels – 'are a stepping-stone to freedom.

Our ancestors would prefer they give us benefit than end up decorating the neck of some Nazi *frau*.'

'I wish you didn't have to sell them. It's so unfair,' Dottie exclaimed, reaching out a finger to touch another piece but stopping short. 'They are magnificent. They look just like the jewellery the leading lady was wearing last night at the opera.'

'My wife would wish it so, certainly.' Clemens smiled. 'I can only afford paste.'

Connie didn't comment. She was still looking at the pieces.

'You think they are too valuable, or too bulky, to be smuggled past the border guards?' Clemens asked.

Connie grinned in response to Clemens's question. 'I did, but then my brilliant sister solved my problem.'

'I did?' Dottie exchanged confused glances with Clemens.

'Yes. If we wear these pieces on top of our usual clothes, the border guards will believe they are costume pieces and not the real thing. After all, how could people like us afford real diamonds as large as these?'

Clemens nodded his head up and down vigorously. '*Ja, ja*. This could work.'

'But if we don't fool the guards, they will confiscate these pieces. Your investors are aware of this?' Connie felt obliged to point out the obvious downfall to her strategy. She didn't speculate as to what might happen to herself and her sister.

'Yes, they are, and it's a risk they are willing to take. They want to get their families out, and this is the only option available.'

The man with the glasses came toward Connie. He took her hands in his and murmured something. She had the impression he was praying but couldn't understand what he was saying. She waited till he was finished before looking to Clemens for an explanation.

'Mr Stein has offered you his thanks and blessings. He said

you are very brave ladies for helping his people in this way. May God look after you both.'

Connie nodded in acknowledgement to the older man.

'And you, as well.'

He smiled sadly. As if he knew his future. Connie responded with a smile, although her tears weren't far from falling. She wasn't brave. She was going home to a free country where she could practise any faith she liked without fear. These men were the courageous ones.

She and Dottie waited while Clemens drew up records of each piece of jewellery and gave them details of the names to go on each bank account. They agreed the gold bars would have to be smuggled out via a different route, they could never explain how they happened to have them in their bags if they were stopped and searched.

As ever, it was imperative the names didn't fall into Nazi hands. Connie and Dottie had decided that Dottie could work the names into her manuscripts and plots for her books.

After the men had left, Connie turned to Clemens. 'We must go now too, our train leaves in a few hours. Dottie, let's put the jewellery in our bags for now. We can put it on when we get changed into our travelling clothes.'

'Goodbye, Clemens, stay safe and we will see you soon,' Dottie said, before kissing the man on both cheeks.

They returned to the hotel without incident. The manger was charming, especially when they told him they would be coming back in a few weeks.

Dottie spoke on their behalf: 'Mr Krauss has suggested a number of operas he feels we would enjoy. He is going to secure the tickets for us.'

'How wonderful, Fräulein Fitzwalter I will make sure your favourite room will be available.'

They headed up to their room to change and pick their bags, then checked out and took a cab to the train station.

As Connie had suspected, the border guards didn't give them a second glance, despite their diamond jewellery. They obviously believed the items to be cheap paste. Still, her breathing only settled into a more comfortable rate once they were out of Germany. Despite it being a beautiful country in the past, the current atmosphere of fear and apprehension had taken its toll. They were both exhausted, and slept most of the way home.

Connie went to work as usual the next day, while Dottie and their mama took the jewels to David Cohen in Hatton Gardens to be sold. They used the proceeds to open bank accounts in the name of their investors, enabling them to meet the requirement that the refugees would be financially independent and therefore acceptable to immigration.

Connie sat at her desk, staring at the paperwork in front of her. For once she was grateful for her boring job and so-called mundane life. She could walk where she wanted, have lunch with her friends and live in peace at home with her family without looking over her shoulder or flinching every time there was a knock on the door. She had so much to be grateful for. Even Miss Fowler's stern gaze couldn't dampen her spirits.

With a smile, she picked up the first piece of correspondence.

TWENTY-THREE

LONDON, OCTOBER 1937

One evening, Connie came home to find Stephen sitting with her mother. She was thrilled to see him, having been frustrated by his recent letters. He had explained he couldn't talk openly for fear the mail was intercepted by the German authorities, and she understood he couldn't use the diplomatic bag for ordinary correspondence, but still it tried her patience when she wanted real information and not platitudes.

'Stephen, I didn't know you were due back in London. How marvellous to see you!' Connie greeted him warmly, her eyes noticing his gaunt appearance.

'Doesn't he look dreadful, Constance? I've been telling him he needs to put in for a transfer – Germany doesn't suit him at all. Do you not like the food, Stephen? You are nothing but a bag of bones.'

'Mama.' Connie agreed, but it was rude to say so. She guessed Stephen was working too hard, not only at his actual job but at the additional work of helping those in need.

'I'm fine, Aunt Margaret. Berlin is a wonderful city with so much to offer, and I am guilty of burning the candle at both ends. I need someone to keep me in check.'

'A wife?'

Stephen choked on his drink, spluttering as Connie grabbed a napkin and handed it to him.

'You aren't getting any younger, dear, and they like married men in the foreign postings. At least that's what I've heard. It could do wonders for your career.' Mama stood up. 'Please excuse me. I arranged to play a hand of bridge and I can't let my ladies down. Stephen, feel free to stay in your old room.'

'Thank you, Aunt Margaret. Enjoy your game.'

'Enjoyment has nothing to do with it. I have to win, or I will never live it down.' Mama sailed out of the room, leaving Connie and Stephen laughing.

'She is incorrigible as soon as a deck of cards appears. Doesn't matter what the game is, she has to win.' Amused, Connie took her mother's seat. 'She's right, though.'

'About me needing a wife?'

Connie was aware that he'd glanced at her but she didn't meet his eyes. 'No, about you losing too much weight. How are things in Berlin?'

'Busier than ever. But I do have good news. Sonja's father was released and he and his wife are currently in France awaiting papers to come here. They need somewhere to stay. I wondered if Dottie's flat was vacant?'

She wanted to hug him but settled for a smile. 'That's wonderful news. The current tenant is moving up north, so we'll get it cleaned up and ready for them. What of Ernst and Sonja? Are they still getting married?'

'They went ahead with the ceremony. They will be next out. Maybe they can share the flat. It's not ideal."

'But better than the alternative.'

They sat in silence for a while before Connie prompted him with 'That's not the reason behind your visit, is it?'

He leaned forwards, his eyes locking with hers, the intensity of his expression shaking Connie, but she looked at him and held his gaze. 'I have a very special case I need help with. Is there any chance you and Dottie could travel to Berlin the weekend after next?'

She nodded. 'Why is this case so special? I mean, they are all special – but why this one?'

He hesitated.

'Tell me... you know you can trust me.'

'This man is one of the bravest men I know. I admire him greatly. He is very much at risk, but he has refused to leave.'

'Until now?'

'Now he has no choice. You will have to go to the London office to collect his paperwork. Mr Foley cannot issue it from Berlin – too many eyes on this case.' He took a second before adding, 'You may find the paperwork difficult to obtain There are some who would prefer he never makes it to Britain.'

Thrilled with the good news about Ernst's family, Dottie volunteered to go to the Foreign Office for the paperwork as Connie had to work. But sitting at her desk in the office, she couldn't concentrate. Stephen's hints that this next case was more delicate than the others were intriguing. What had he meant by saying there were too many eyes on this case?

With a muttered oath, Connie gave up all pretence of working. She had a few days' leave due to her. Her boss moaned about her giving more notice in future but he signed the form.

The next morning, deep in thought about her last conversation with Stephen, Connie didn't notice Dottie come into the room until she touched her on the arm.

'Are you nervous about going back to Berlin, Connie?'

'Yes, a little bit.' She paused, and then looked at her sister. 'I think it's time we stayed at the Adlon.'

Dottie's mouth fell open. 'But that is where all the high-profile Nazis stay. We'll be surrounded by them!'

'Exactly! Where better to hide than in plain sight? They won't suspect a thing. You could even speak to Goebbels about turning one of your books into a movie. I hear he's the expert in that field.'

'Oh, Connie, don't tease me. I shall be so nervous, surrounded by those madmen.'

'No, you won't. You have Mama's blood running through your veins. Now, let's choose some outfits.'

Glad of the distraction, Connie opened her wardrobe, inspecting its offerings. As Dottie pulled out different outfits, Connie asked her about her trip to the Foreign Office.

Dottie sat heavily on the bed. 'I came back empty-handed. They claimed they didn't have a file for Mr Siegal or his wife, Valerie.'

Connie turned to face Dottie, not bothering to hide her shock. 'But they must have. Stephen checked it himself.'

Dottie fiddled with the zip on a skirt, not looking at her. 'Why couldn't he issue the paperwork from Berlin?'

Connie didn't know the answer to that. 'Dottie, there's no point in us going to Berlin without that file. We need the paper-work, otherwise the Germans won't let them leave.'

Dottie threw the blouse to one side and hopped up from the bed. 'Don't you think I know that? I tried and they refused to give it to me. They said the file was missing.'

A knot of guilt formed in Connie's chest. Why was she getting aggravated with her sister, who had no doubt tried her best? 'Sorry, I didn't mean to take out my frustration on you. I just... well, blast it, anyway! I am going to get that file if it kills me.'

Putting on her most fetching hat and coat, Connie glanced at her reflection. She added some tasteful make-up and a hint of lipstick. A small pair of diamond paste earrings completed her look.

Dottie passed the scent bottle from hand to hand. 'Will you be long? You need to calm down before you get there, as you won't gain anything in that mood. Remember what Mother says: "It is easier to catch flies with honey—"'

'—"than with vinegar." I know. But I will stay all day if I have to. Tell Mother not to worry.' Connie kissed her sister on the cheek before picking up her handbag and heading out of the door.

She took a bus to the Foreign Office and went up to the third floor. Taking a deep breath, she pushed open the heavy wooden doors and walked down to the high counter, where she spotted Mr Murray. She groaned inwardly. Having dealt with him on numerous previous occasions, she knew him to be the most inefficient employee in the whole Civil Service... but it wouldn't serve her to let him know that.

'Good morning, Mr Murray. My sister was here yesterday to collect Mr Siegal's paperwork. We are travelling to Berlin and wish to deliver the paperwork in person.'

'I am sorry, Miss Fitzwalter, but the file has been mislaid.' He turned away in dismissal, but Connie wasn't finished.

She pretended to misunderstand, even though she knew 'mislaid' was a euphemism for 'you are never getting the paperwork'.

'I am a very patient woman. I am sure it will turn up. I will just wait. I brought a book to keep me company.' Connie smiled at the official and, sitting down, took out her book as if to read.

His eyes narrowed. 'But, Miss Fitzwalter, you... well, you can't sit here. It just isn't possible.'

'Why not? You have provided seats. I don't need refreshments. Now, please don't let me keep you. It will serve both of us if you concentrate on finding the file I need. Thank you so much.'

Connie opened her book, only then realizing it was upside down. But the man hadn't noticed. He was standing staring at her as if he wished she would disappear, his lips pressed into a white slash.

Then he turned and walked back into his office.

An hour passed and then another.

Eventually, Connie heard his footsteps but only glanced up when he addressed her.

'Miss Fitzwalter, how long do you intend to sit outside my office?' A vein in his forehead throbbed.

She used her sweetest voice, thinking of honey. 'Not long, Mr Murray.'

'Good.'

'I will leave as soon as you find the file.'

She could have sworn she heard him curse under his breath, but she didn't show any sign of hearing him. She simply continued to read. But her mind was churning. How long could she wait? Would he have her arrested? Had she committed a crime? She didn't know, and frankly didn't care. Stephen had said these people were particularly vulnerable. She wasn't going anywhere until the file was found.

Her bottom had turned numb, yet she remained seated. It couldn't take much longer, surely? As if summoned by her thoughts, Mr Murray appeared.

'Miss Fitzwalter, thank you so much for your patience.' His clipped tone told her his true feelings. 'The file has now been found and will be processed in due course.'

'Lovely, thank you. I will wait.' Connie refused to look away from his face, noting his pallor together with the angry expression in his eyes.

'But... you can't. It will take days.'

'Oh, I am sure a man of your obvious capabilities can get the file processed in an hour or two. I don't mind waiting. It's a very good book.' Connie smiled her sweetest smile at the range of emotions crossing Mr. Murray's face. 'I'll be sure to mention to my godfather, Lord Stanley, how helpful you have been.'

Murray's face became so red at the mention of the one of the most senior civil servants in the land, she was briefly afraid he might have a heart attack, but he recovered his composure and strode back to his office.

Connie hid a smile, guessing the file would be quickly forthcoming. She was right. Murray soon appeared with the paperwork in hand, almost throwing it at her but catching himself at the last second.

'I trust your friends will enjoy their stay in Great Britain.'

She ignored his irritable tone. 'They certainly will. They know our country is run by people like you. Good afternoon, Mr Murray, and thank you.'

He didn't respond but glowered at her. She could feel his eyes on her until the heavy doors shut behind her, but she didn't care. She had the paperwork and that was all that mattered. She only hoped they would be in time.

TWENTY-FOUR

Ten days later, Connie and Dottie set off for Berlin, this time travelling with five young men, all in their early twenties, who wanted to 'do their bit to put down Hitler', as they described it. Connie was slightly dubious of their real intentions: the last thing they needed was British men making a nuisance of themselves, but Dottie reassured her everything would be fine.

'Mother knows their parents and she has spoken to these young men personally. They have assured her they will be on their best behaviour, and are looking forward to going home laden with cash, watches and gold wedding rings. I rather think they are more frightened of Mother than Hitler and his friends.'

Connie hoped her sister was right, but then Dottie always looked on the bright side.

When they arrived and met him at the station, Stephen looked better than he had done two weeks previously. He still looked tired but the black circles under his eyes weren't as pronounced.

'Thank goodness you brought some friends. We have large

numbers of people wishing to use your services. Seems your reputation has preceded you.'

'Does that mean we should be more careful?'

'Yes, of course. But don't do anything different to what you usually do. You know I'm very fond of both of you but as far as the police are concerned, you are two rather eccentric ladies. They find you rather amusing, if I am honest.'

Connie knew she should be glad they weren't under suspicion, but the fact the police thought they were eccentric wasn't very flattering.

Stephen held her gaze. 'Don't look like that, Connie. You would be a lot more worried if they were fawning over you like they do over Unity.'

Connie wanted to spit like an annoyed cat at the mention of Unity Mitford, the English woman who praised Hitler at every opportunity – almost as often as she was seen fawning over him. Her elder sister, Diana, had divorced her first husband, one of the Guinness family, to marry a despicable man, Oswald Mosley the fascist. They'd even chosen Goebbels' mansion in Germany as the location of the wedding, with Hitler as a guest of honour.

'Don't mention that woman's name in the same sentence as mine. She is a disgrace. Should it come to war and the borders close, please make sure she is left behind with the Germans, will you?'

Stephen just smiled. She could see his eyes darting around as they ambled along, making the short walk to their hotel. So, the police probably weren't as uninterested as he was making out. She glanced at her sister, but Dottie appeared oblivious. She was chatting gleefully with one of the young men who had accompanied them.

'I can't wait to see your reaction to *Tristan Und Isolde*.' Stephen smiled. 'I suppose I should be grateful the Nazis still allow us operas. We have tickets for tomorrow night.'

Once at the Adlon they stood in a short line at the reception desk. It took a while for everyone to obtain their room key.

'I'll wait for you at the bar,' Stephen said, after walking them to the stairs. 'Take your time. I have the paper for entertainment.'

Connie smiled at his joke – he'd told her plenty of times that the German papers published complete rubbish. The world could be falling down around them but you wouldn't read anything about it in the newspapers.

Rested and refreshed, Connie and Dottie joined the other travellers downstairs.

Stephen was sitting alone at one table.

'You go and speak to Stephen. I'll check on the boys.' Dottie was gone before Connie could say anything.

As she approached the table she was aware of Stephen looking at her, the admiration in his eyes making her glad she had good news for him. He rose and held out her seat so she could sit down, his hands resting on the back of her chair for seconds longer than necessary, his fingers brushing the skin of her neck. *Was that on purpose or an accident?* She pushed the thought from her mind. They had a job to do. She stayed silent while he ordered her a gin and tonic from the passing waiter.

She leaned in close. 'I got the paperwork for our mutual friend. Do you fancy a late drink at your club?'

'No, we can't go there anymore. Too many prying eyes. We'll go to the embassy. Don't bring the boys with you. Just you and Dottie.'

Connie nodded and then began talking in a louder voice about all the new building works around Berlin. She didn't know who might be paying attention to their conversation, but they would be bored to tears before she let slip any interesting titbits.

. . .

Despite the late hour the embassy wasn't empty, although the queues of people who were usually found outside had disappeared. It was probably too dangerous to be on the streets after dark. The sisters could see lights on in offices.

Stephen escorted them up the stairs, leaving them sitting in an office while he went to fetch his boss.

'Connie, do you think we will get Stephen in trouble?'

'No, I don't think so. Mr Foley knows us, after all.'

As she spoke Stephen returned to them, looking troubled. Connie took a deep breath. Mr Foley had aged, being thinner and greyer than they had last met.

'How lovely to see you both.' Connie and Dottie laughed as the man put them at their ease. Did this man know the impact he had on so many people? Their Jewish friends in London spoke about him as if he were a saint. He issued visas whenever he could, circumventing the rules when there was a real threat to life. Tonight he looked very tired and distracted. She sensed caring for those who were being persecuted was taking a huge toll on him.

'You do a wonderful job here, Mr Foley.'

'Thank you, we try. But there is often little we can do. Our hands are held in so many ways. The Nazis say they want the Jews to leave, yet they make it impossible. They change their minds about conditions for exit visas, they give temporary visas only to lock up the individuals until the visa expires. Please excuse me. It has been a difficult day.'

Dottie laid her hand on the man's arm. 'If you would forgive me for being so bold, Mr Foley, I think you should go home to your wife and take the weekend to rest. Everything will still be here on Monday, but at least you will have more energy to deal with your trials.'

'I think I might take your advice, Miss Fitzwalter. You have a very caring heart.'

Connie smiled at him. 'My sister has a heart of gold. I echo her suggestion. Our friends need you, Mr Foley, and you must look after yourself. And please do call us Connie and Dottie. I feel as if we are all friends.'

'That we are, Connie. Dottie. Stephen, I shall leave you to your guests. Good night, ladies, and again, if ever you need my services, officially or otherwise, please do call on me.'

They watched him in silence as he walked away.

'Poor man looks like he's carrying the weight of the world on his shoulders.'

'He is.' Stephen sighed. 'You should see his desk and the rest of his office. He works such long hours his wife has commented she should move in so she can claim to have a husband. Don't misunderstand me. She is supportive of his work, but she is worried about him. We all are. But he refuses to rest. Not while so many are in danger.'

Connie wanted to ask him to look in the mirror. The dark rings around his eyes may have been lighter, but he was exhibiting other signs of strain. His nails were non-existent and he'd lost more weight. Being so thin didn't suit him. He needed a haircut.

When he looked up, he caught her staring at him. Electricity danced between them before he coughed and said, 'Thank goodness you got the paperwork for Mr Siegal and his wife. The man refused to leave without her, even though she begged him to.'

Connie couldn't find her voice, leaving Dottie to say, 'Mother would feel the same if Father was still alive. Will they come with us on Monday?'

'Yes, but you cannot wait until Monday. You need to leave tomorrow morning. Frank had a tip off he needs to leave as soon as possible.'

'But what of our plans to see *Tristan Und...*?' Dottie began, but Connie put her hand on her sister's arm.

'Stephen knows best, Dottie, darling. Where do we meet Mr Siegal?'

Stephen stared at a point over her shoulder rather than meet her look. 'He won't meet with you until you get to the border. Go the café Ernst took you to. The Siegal's will follow you to the station.'

'But how shall we know him?' Connie asked. 'Why won't he meet us?' Dottie asked, simultaneously.

'He is very old-fashioned. He believes women should be sheltered and cannot bear the notion anything could happen to you both because of him. This way, if something goes wrong, you will not be implicated.'

Dottie gripped Connie's arm so tightly it hurt but she didn't mind, as the pain helped her deal with the sudden spurt of fear gripping her. This was different to their usual rescues. She sensed Stephen knew more than he was telling. It was why he was acting so strangely – he was worried about them.

She needed to ease his burden. Speaking confidently, she said, 'We will do what you say, Stephen. Can you use the men we brought with us? They are trustworthy. Mother vouches for them.'

They exchanged a knowing look. Her mother had become expert at selecting people to accompany them on their trips in the last few months, so it meant a lot for someone to have gained her approval.

'Absolutely. I will speak to them myself, and arrange to have dinner with them and a few friends. These friends are very keen to invest back home in Blighty.'

Connie exchanged a grin with her sister. Despite the dangers, they both agreed every penny they got out of Germany would help save a life. It was imperative as much wealth as possible could be extracted.

Dottie excused herself to go to the bathroom leaving Connie alone with Stephen. He glanced around before discreetly handing her a note. 'Memorise that name and phone number and then destroy it.'

'Who is Mr Blanchard?' Connie whispered, keeping her eyes peeled for her sister's return.

'Someone who can help Mr. Siegal if you run into problems in England. There are some who believe he should be refused asylum. If he gets stopped at the border, insist they ring that number and ask for Blanchard. The people who can help will then take over.'

'This is why you want us to travel with the Siegals.'

Stephen glanced in the direction of the ladies. 'If he is caught before you arrive in England do not interfere. I mean it, Connie. There is nothing you can do. At least not until he is on British soil.' Stephen cleared his throat. 'Tell me, is everything ready for Ernst and his in-laws at your flat, Dottie?'

'They'll love it despite being a little cramped. It's such a lovely little place. Mother has been very involved since the beginning, making it a comfortable home for those guests who needed a place to stay for visa requirements. I wish we could add more flats but...' Dottie shrugged.

Connie pushed the piece of paper into her pocket, half listening to her sister, her mind processing what Stephen had said and more what he hadn't. What type of man was Mr. Siegal if there were those in Britain who would try to stop his entry?

'You are so generous, ladies – not just with your time, but with your finances as well. Please be careful you don't over-stretch yourselves.'

'We won't, Stephen. Tell us about the situation here. It's getting worse, isn't it?

'Yes, Dottie. Much worse. More people are disappearing. Our hands are tied up in red tape.'

Stephen glanced around him and then nodded, meeting Connie's gaze for one intense moment, but his eyes told her not to say anything more. Even in the British embassy the Nazis could have ears.

Connie changed the subject. 'It is a good job we didn't unpack. What shall we tell the boys?'

'About you leaving early? Perhaps one of you could be ill? You know, with...'

Stephen's blushes were soon matched by her own. She couldn't look at her sister.

'Right-oh. We will see you in the morning. I assume you will collect us.'

'Not tomorrow. I am to lead the Gestapo on a wild goose chase.' At Connie's sharp intake of breath, he smiled. 'I will see you in London soon. Sleep well, darlings, and the best of British.'

Connie and Dottie studied the photograph of the couple they were to help the next day and then, on Stephen's instructions, they burned it. Dottie took a bath and Connie used the time to memorise the phone number before shredding the note.

Connie couldn't sleep and could tell by Dottie's restlessness her sister was awake too. 'Shall we pray?'

'Yes, Connie, I think we need all the help we can get.'

The two of them held hands as they asked for God's help with the rescue. Then they turned over and both fell asleep from exhaustion.

TWENTY-FIVE

Early the next morning, they were packed and signing out. Telling the hotel staff one of them was ill and implying it was a female matter was one of the most embarrassing things either of them had ever done.

'I don't think I will stop blushing until I get to England. Why did you have to tell him it was me?'

'Because, darling Dottie, you are so attractive when you blush. Pink is a good colour on you.'

Dottie gave her sister a look but then they laughed. Nervous energy was wonderful.

They reached the pre-agreed café without incident, and even had time to sit and have a last coffee. Dottie spotted the couple approaching before Connie did and signalled with her little finger.

They paid their bill and, picking up their sole suitcase, walked the rest of the way to the train station. Despite the temptation to look behind them, they didn't. They smiled and flirted with the border guards and then took their seats, all the time praying the couple would be allowed to proceed unmolested.

The train journey was the same yet different to previous

times. The atmosphere was filled with tension. None of the other travellers seemed to want to engage in conversation or make eye contact with anyone.

Connie spotted two Gestapo agents, with their trademark long leather coats and trilby hats, making their way toward them. She gripped her hands in her lap but continued speaking to Dottie about opera. The men passed by. They weren't interested in them. Not today. But why were they on the train?

Connie knew Dottie was wondering the same thing – she could tell by the look in her sister's eyes – but they couldn't discuss it. They conversed a little more about the operas they wanted to see on their next trip. Dottie took out her embroidery and began to work. Connie wished fervently she had a gift for sewing or knitting. Anything to occupy her hands, which kept shaking.

She stared out of the window, but if Dottie had asked her what she saw, she wouldn't have been able to answer.

Finally, they reached the border, slowing down into a station. This was the moment of truth. Everyone was asked to produce their papers again. The man checking their passports seemed to take his time but didn't say anything. Dottie let out a sigh of relief when he passed by, but Connie wondered whether their 'parcel' was undergoing the same scrutiny.

Then, from the carriage up ahead, they heard shots. Dottie grasped her hand so tightly, it was painful, but Connie didn't complain.

Chaos erupted around them as a man bolted from the train. Through the window, Connie had a clear view of him. He appeared younger than she was, and Connie found herself silently pleading for his safety, even though the odds seemed stacked against him. More shots rang through the air, one after the other, and the man collapsed to the ground. Despite his desperate attempts to crawl onwards, he couldn't escape his grim fate. SS guards swiftly intervened, dragging him away.

'Oh, Connie, the poor man,' Dottie whispered through her tears. 'Thank God he wasn't killed.'

Connie held her sister close as she wept, unable to share her belief that the man might have preferred death to captivity. It was monstrous. She questioned why they were subjecting themselves to this ordeal, especially Dottie, who was easily distressed.

Her sister, probably conscious of causing a scene, moved away and delicately wiped her eyes with her hanky. Connie tried to control her shaking hands by gripping them tightly together in her lap, and silently swore to herself that this had to be their last time doing this.

The train moved off quickly. Connie glanced back at the platform but didn't see any sign of the couple. She sent up a prayer of thanks, hoping it meant they were still on board. She wanted to walk through the train to check but she knew it was best for everyone if she remained seated until the train crossed into Holland.

The seconds ticked by, each second like a minute, a minute an hour. Dottie remained silent but stared at the same place on her embroidery the entire time without moving her needle.

A whistle blew and the announcement came that they had passed into Holland.

Connie let out her breath in relief. At least now everyone still on the train was safe. Now they could relax.

She must have dozed off as it seemed like only minutes later, the train slowed again as they approached the last stop. Dottie put her sewing away as Connie reached for their small suitcase.

'Allow me, please.'

The gentleman opposite raised his hat and took the suitcase down for her. He set it by her side.

'Thank you.' Connie picked up the suitcase as he smiled but she didn't linger to engage him in conversation. She was too anxious to check on the Siegals.

Dottie got off the train first, with Connie following. They couldn't see anything in the crowds and waited until the platform cleared a little.

Dottie nudged Connie's side. 'There they are. Do you see them?'

Connie smiled as the couple walked toward them, their own smiles not quite hiding the look of strain on their faces.

'Good afternoon.' The man raised his hat. 'My name is Idor Siegal, and this is my wife, Valerie.'

'So nice to meet you both.' Connie shook their hands. 'We were concerned about you.'

'Nothing to worry about. Our *German* paperwork was in order. We shall find our cabins now and, when we we're in England, we will talk more, yes?'

Was it her imagination or had he put an emphasis on German? Did that mean he was anticipating problems in Britain? Connie recited the phone number in her head. She wanted to know everything now, but the man was right to be cautious. They may be out of Germany, but they were still in Europe. Better to wait until they were safe in London.

They travelled in silence to the boat, where the Siegals disappeared to their cabin. Connie and Dottie did the same, but sleep proved elusive.

The next morning, the Hook Continental arrived in Liverpool Street station. The bells of London churches pealed, alerting the faithful that services were about to start. Connie wrapped her arms around herself as they stood in the Customs line, very thankful to be back on British shores but her nerves were shredded wondering if she would have to intervene and call on *Mr Blanchard*. People went about their business as normal, no sinister uniforms in sight. She saw the Customs officials challenge some travellers over their paperwork, but nobody shot at anyone. The Siegals' passed through and this time, the Siegals' smiles were wider, their relief apparent.

'Please let us accompany you to your hotel. We can find some breakfast there,' Connie suggested. The couple agreed and, together, they hailed a taxi and drove from the station to the small hotel.

The couple's room wasn't yet available and the desk clerk apologized profusely. 'Please go into the dining room and have breakfast. By the time you finish, your room will be ready.'

Connie led the way. Mr Siegal held his wife's chair, seating her first before taking his own seat. A waiter did the same for Connie and Dottie. They ordered a large pot of tea. Mr Siegal opted for coffee.

Mrs Siegal dabbed her eyes with a hanky as she thanked Connie and Dottie for saving them. Mr Siegal took his wife's hand in his, caressing it as he spoke. 'We are so thankful to you both – we gather it was your determination that unearthed our paperwork! And of course to your contacts in Berlin. My dear wife has put up with so much over the years. She was pressurized to divorce me but she refused. For reasons I don't fully understand.' The man's loving look at his wife caught Connie's throat.

'Don't be silly, Idor. We took our vows in the eyes of God and that little man wasn't going to make me do anything.' Valerie's firm tone brooked no argument.

'We were glad to help, weren't we, Connie?' Dottie said.

The waiter appeared with their food order then, interrupting the conversation.

When they each had eaten a little, Connie's curiosity got

the better of her. 'I thought if you were married to a non-Jewish person, you got more protection. From the Nazis, I mean. Did I get that wrong?'

Mr Siegal's eyes gleamed. 'Some do. The men more than the women.'

'I don't understand, I'm afraid.'

Connie was glad Dottie spoke up, as she didn't follow either.

'The number of Aryan men in mixed marriages seeking divorce is higher than that of women. It seems women are more willing to take on the Nazis. As you two have proved.'

Dottie blushed as Connie replied, 'We only did what anyone else would do.'

'That is not true, my dear, as we know all too well. But to answer your question properly – I'm not only Jewish, but I have also been involved in the anti-Nazi resistance since before Hitler came to power. They have been after me for some time. They nearly got me too, but for some brave friends of yours. There was some risk that your border officials may bar my entry despite my papers. Had that been the case, Stephen assured me he had a contact that would help but I've no idea who that would have been.'

Connie pretended to study the lace tablecloth, not wanting to catch anyone's eye for fear Mr Siegal guessed Stephen had told her.

The man took his wife's hand once more. 'I – we – can't thank you enough.'

Valerie spoke up. 'There was an enormous price on his head, and had he been caught he was worried he would have betrayed you all, given the beatings, the—well, you know... That is why he insisted on not meeting you or travelling near you on the train.'

'Did you know the young man they shot?' Dottie asked quietly.

Valerie shook her head, her expression reflecting the sombre reality of the situation. 'The train conductor murmured something about false papers, so I assume he was a young man of my husband's flock trying to flee for his life. I only hope he died before he left the station.'

Dottie exhaled audibly. Connie decided to steer the conversation in a different direction. 'Thank you very much for your consideration, Mr Siegal, but we would have travelled with you even if we had known your full story.'

'I know that, my dear, but you are much younger than we are. You and your lovely sister have lives to live.'

In that moment, Connie and Dottie exchanged a meaningful glance, confirming their shared determination to continue their work. Connie knew her sister understood the risks, just as she did, but they would persist in helping those they could for as long as they were able or needed.

TWENTY-SIX

VIENNA, MARCH 1938

'Papa, Papa!' Daniel burst through the doors of their apartment, causing Ben and Sarah to come running at their younger son's shouts.

Sarah held her chest as she surveyed her child's dishevelled appearance, taking in his flushed cheeks and wide, shining eyes. 'Are you hurt?' She reached out a hand, but Daniel ignored her, moving to his father's side.

'They're here, Papa! In Vienna! The Germans! I saw them.'

Sarah folded onto a chair in the hall, her legs unable to carry her. Her precious son had been near the soldiers.

'The schoolmaster sent us home, told us it was safer. We were on the trolley car when we heard shouting – chanting, really. It was an anti-Nazi demonstration. Some of the other boys and I got off the car and joined in. They were shouting, "Red-white-red till we are dead!"'

'Daniel!'

'Sarah, let him finish. What happened then, son?'

'We headed towards the opera house but then we saw them – the Germans.' Daniel's eyes turned stormy. 'The Austrian police were there too.'

'That's good, isn't it? They can arrest those people.'

'No, Mama. They were there to protect them. Most of the policemen wore swastika armbands. They came charging towards us, so we ran, faster than I ever ran before.'

Ignoring the fact her son was now fifteen and taller than she was, Sarah stood and pulled him into her arms. Then she slapped his face. 'Don't you ever do that again, do you hear me? You could have been injured, or worse...'

'Sorry, Mama.' Daniel's hazel eyes filled with hurt as his hand caressed his cheek.

'Sarah, he's home and safe. Daniel, run upstairs and fetch your grandfather. Ask him to come down here, please.' Daniel turned on his heel as Ben walked into the sitting room and turned on the wireless. Sarah followed her husband.

The voice of Kurt Von Schuschnigg, the Austrian chancellor took over the room. 'Austrian men and women, the president of the republic of Austria has asked me to communicate to the Austrian people that we will not put up any resistance to violence.' Sarah leaned against the nearest wall as dizziness threatened to consume her. The Austrians weren't going to even try to stop Hitler. She listened as he continued. 'I have resigned as Austrian chancellor and am asking both the military and civilian population to refrain from any form of resistance in the event of a German invasion.'

Ben switched the announcement off as Sarah's father walked in, Daniel by his side. Sarah caught the look the men exchanged; it turned her stomach. She clenched her hands so tight, her nails cut into the palms of her hand. What would happen now? To her children, her husband, father, their home and family?

Ben broke the silence. 'Isaac, it is best we do not go out tonight.'

Sarah looked at her father, a small part of her hoping he would insist on attending the synagogue. She couldn't remember the last time he had missed Friday night prayers. If he said he was going, life as she knew it would remain the same.

Isaac nodded, rubbing one eye with his hand but not before Sarah spotted a tear. Her father never cried. He seemed to have aged right in front of her eyes, his normal straight posture now hunched as he took a seat on the sofa.

Questions bubbled up in her mind but the phone ringing interrupted them. Sarah bit her finger as Ben answered. They could only hear his side of the conversation, but she knew by his pallor, the strain around his mouth, that he didn't like what he was hearing.

After what seemed like an eternity, he put the phone down. He walked to the window and stared out. She moved to go to him, but her father shook his head. She watched her husband's back until he turned to face them.

'That was a friend of mine from England. A doctor. We met a few times at conferences in Switzerland.'

He spoke so slowly, Sarah wanted to shout at him to get to the point.

'He said it's time for us to leave. To get out of Austria. He suggested we drive to the frontier tonight.'

Sarah wanted to do just that, but her father butted in. 'That's preposterous. How can we pack up our lives and leave that quickly? You have patients relying on you. Sarah needs time to pack up the house and I... I have the business to see to. You and I fought in the war, Benjamin! We are Austrians. They will not make me leave my home. My country.'

Ben and Sarah shared a pained look, but then Ben gave a silent nod and she understood. It was too much for her father to contemplate right then. They wouldn't leave that night.

But when?

. . .

The next few days were the worst Sarah had ever experienced. There were countless telephone calls, each story worse than the previous one. People who tried to flee were shot dead in their cars; their families, even those who had remained behind, arrested. Their maid didn't show up to work, so Sarah had to venture outside. Daniel insisted on coming with her, complaining he was bored stuck in the apartment.

They walked past the park where the benches now displayed signs saying Jews were forbidden to sit on them. She felt eyes boring into her as they walked: some passers-by frowned at them, and a couple used language she'd never heard before. She gripped Daniel's arm tightly.

Everybody she saw wore a swastika badge.

'Mama, maybe we should buy a badge?' Daniel whispered to her, as they walked to the last store. 'See? They sell them on all the street corners. We don't have to buy large ones.'

Sarah glanced at the display of badges for sale. Some were very large while others were quite small.

'They say that even anti-Nazis wear them, but they buy the smallest ones.'

'Daniel, that is to prevent them being mistaken for Jews. We are prohibited from wearing them, not that I would put that horrible sign anywhere near my person.'

Her son wilted at her put-down. Immediately contrite, she tucked her arm into his and walked at a brisk pace back to their apartment, ignoring everyone around them. Her heart didn't go back to its normal rhythm until they were back at their building.

'Frau Liberman, a moment please.'

Sarah jumped at the voice coming from behind her. She turned to see the caretaker, a large Nazi flag in his hand. Sarah stared at the sinister red and white decoration; it looked like an enormous spider dying in a pool of blood. She couldn't stop the shudder running through her.

'Please, don't be frightened. I mean no harm.' The caretaker, Herr Bentall, whispered as he looked to his left and right furtively. 'You must take this and hang it from your balcony.'

'Never!'

The man grew more agitated. 'Frau Liberman, you must. They said we all have to. If you don't, they will know immediately which apartment to target.' The man's eyes fell to his shoes. 'It would be safer for you and the children.'

Sarah's eyes locked on the small Nazi pin on his coat. He held out the flag once more.

She shook her head, shrinking back from the evil she imagined flowed from the flag. 'I can't bear to touch it.'

'Would you like me to come and hang it for you?'

Sarah nodded, and led the way upstairs. It took her ages to open the door of the apartment as her hands were shaking so badly.

'Allow me.' Herr Bentall gently took the keys and opened the door, standing back to let her and Daniel walk in ahead of him. He made his way to the balcony and hung the offensive flag.

Once it was fitted correctly, he turned to face her. 'I can't put into words how sorry I am that it has come to this. You and Herr Liberman, the children, your father, have all been very good to me and my family. The things they say about Jews, they don't apply to families like yours. I... I am ashamed to be Austrian today.' He bent his head, hurried to the front door and was gone before she could find her voice to thank him.

The flag didn't last long, Isaac almost ripping it to shreds when he pulled it down. 'We will not bow down to them. Never.' He glowered at Sarah.

Daniel made to move, but Sarah caught his hand, signalling to him to stay silent. Her father was overwhelmed by everything that was happening. They heard steps outside before Ben entered the apartment, slamming the door behind him.

He stormed into the room. 'They have implemented the Nuremberg Laws, effective immediately.'

Sarah caught the look her husband and father exchanged. 'What does that mean?'

'We are no longer Austrian citizens. They will take the businesses away unless they are transferred into the name of a so-called Aryan.'

Sarah clasped her hands together tightly. 'The children?'

'We must make plans to get them out. You too, Sarah.'

Sarah forced her feet into the carpet, trying to steady her nerves. 'I'm not leaving without you.' She looked from her husband to her father and back again. 'Either of you.'

A triumphant Hitler standing in his car, giving a fixed Nazi salute, rode through the streets that were lined with crowds of cheering people. Some threw flowers, many cried tears of joy, all welcoming the streams of military vehicles, motorcycles and goose-stepping troops who accompanied him.

Isaac turned off the wireless at the first words of his speech. 'I heard over three hundred thousand people flocked to see him. To listen to his lies, his promises of jobs and freedom. What sort of life does he offer? None to us Jews, that much is clear. But those people who cheer for him now, do they not understand he isn't interested in anything but full loyalty to him? Above all else – your family, your god, your life—?'

Sarah poured him a drink. 'Papa, think of your blood pressure.'

He muttered something but she didn't get a chance to ask him to repeat it. Thunderous sounds were suddenly overhead. Samuel rushed to the windows, shouting out that the skies were full of German planes.

'The trains are full of their troops, the prisons have been opened and the once illegal Nazis released. And still they come.' Isaac stood up. 'I need to be alone.' He headed for the door.

As Isaac left, Ben came home from the hospital, a hard look on his face.

'What is it?'

'The Nazis have set up soup kitchens all over the city. They are feeding the grateful citizens and taking pictures to put in the papers. All this to prove to the world that they are welcome here.'

'They don't need to prove that. The flowers people threw at Hitler, the crowds cheering him as he drove into our city was enough proof.' Samuel's disdainful tone would have earned him a reprimand before, but Ben ignored it.

'They have laid on a whole load of events: exhibitions, special events, even official visits. We had one at the hospital, but all Jewish staff had to remain out of sight. Members of the Hitler Youth, boys younger than my own sons, told me to "disappear".'

Sarah reached out to touch his arm, to offer some consolation, but he shrugged her off. 'I suppose I should be grateful that's all they did. Those same boys are responsible for some resisters being intimidated and arrested – those they bother to arrest and don't just murder outright.'

'Ben, please. The children...'

'The children need to be aware of what is happening in our city. Just yesterday, Frau Cohen and Frau Silverman told me they had to pay a weekly cash payment to their janitor. The man responsible for cleaning the floors in their apartment building.'

'But why?'

'He said he would report them for anti-Nazi activities. Two old ladies. What harm could they do to him?'

Sarah paled. She didn't want to hear any more but Ben wasn't finished.

'There is no such thing as law and order any more. At least not for Jews.'

'Ben, you have friends in the police. All those men you helped with their medical problems after the war. When they couldn't afford to pay. They will help us.'

'Will they?' Ben strode over to the drinks cabinet, poured a whisky and downed it in one. Then he poured another. 'The Gestapo, SS, even those police friends of mine, now have the power to arrest any *unliebsame*.'

'Who?'

'A disliked person. Rich, poor, young, old, Jew or Christian. Vienna will turn into a society of turncoats and weasels. Old grudges will be settled. I never thought I would live to see my country turn out like this.'

For a split second, Sarah felt like laughing. What had Ben expected, given the actions of the Austrians they thought they had known? The same people had thrown flowers at Hitler and his cronies when they arrived and not bullets like they should have. But it was pointless thinking that way. Now they needed to concentrate on getting out of Austria, whether Papa agreed or not. Her family didn't have a future there, not anymore.

Sarah turned off the radio after the announcement ninety-nine per cent of the Austrian people had voted for the *Anschluss*. Austria was now a German province, the Ostmark. *Was anyone surprised given the vote had not been anonymous, the voters subject to abuse from Nazis if they were brave enough to dissent.*

Hearing frantic knocking on her front door, Sarah met her son's eyes. Samuel stood up but she shook her head. 'I'll go.' She clamped down the fear in her chest and hurried to open it.

A woman she barely recognized almost fell in, supporting the weight of Leah.

'Leah, what happened? Are you hurt? Tell me.' Sarah moved to her daughter's side. 'Samuel, come and help me.'

Leah opened her mouth to speak but nothing came out, her eyes wide with terror in her pale face. She stared at Sarah as if she didn't recognize her.

Sarah put out her hand to touch her child's face: it was frozen. 'Leah, darling, tell me. Please.'

'Mama.' Leah crumpled into tears and would have fallen but for the woman holding her. Sarah put her arms around her daughter, her eyes meeting those of the woman. Leah's sobs broke the silence. Samuel stood, his face losing all colour.

'I found her on the street. They made her get on her hands and knees and wash the pavement.' The woman wrung her hands. 'I tried to stop them, but nobody would listen to me. I fetched a policeman, but he only laughed and then he said he'd lock me up if I tried anything. I couldn't stop them. I waited until they left and then I helped her home. I'm so sorry. I...' Tears fell down the woman's face as she put her face in her hands and sobbed.

'Come in, please. I'm Sarah Liberman. I know your face but not your name.'

'Hedwig Berger. I used to come to your father's shop to look at all the pretty things he had. I couldn't afford them, but he never stopped me from looking. He is a lovely man. I... I feel so ashamed of what is happening.'

'Come in and sit down please, fräulein.'

'No, please, look after your daughter. I hope she will be alright.' The woman turned to leave.

'Samuel, please go and put the water on. I'm sure Fräulein Berger could do with a hot drink for the shock.'

'I don't need anything. I will leave you be.'

Sarah was torn between the need to see to her daughter and the wish to thank the woman. 'I'd really like it if you could wait. If you have time, that is?'

Fräulein Berger shook her head. 'I'd like to come back tomorrow to see how she is. But for now, your child needs you.'

Sarah gave the other woman a grateful look. 'Please, do come back. Please. Thank you for bringing her home.'

The stranger nodded and left.

Sarah led Leah to the bedroom. 'Would you like to have a bath?'

'Yes, Mama, although I don't think I will ever feel clean again.'

A chill flew down Sarah's spine as she ran her eyes over her child. 'What did those animals do to you?'

Leah blushed scarlet. 'Mama, it was horrible. They... they...'

Sarah wanted to pull her daughter into her arms and remove all memory of the events of the last few hours. But instinct told her not to move. To let her child speak.

'They spat at me, Mama, made me kneel on the ground and scrub it with a toothbrush. A group of them. Kurt and Gunter were there! Kurt kicked an old man and Gunter... he turned his back when he saw me. I know he knew it was me. I saw it in his eyes before he turned away. How could he do that, Mama? After all the time he spent here with Samuel. I thought... I thought he liked me.'

Rage filled Sarah. She wanted to catch Gunter and slap him hard. 'Let me run you a bath.'

She walked to the bathroom and while the water was running, she let her tears fall unchecked. Why would anyone want to hurt her precious Leah? The child was kindness personified.

Taking a few deep breaths to calm herself, she returned to the bedroom. 'The water is ready now, darling. Let me help you.'

'I can undress.' Leah's voice trembled but she stood straighter. 'Fräulein Berger was so kind. Everyone else just laughed, joined in or walked on by. I think those who walked by were the worst.'

Sarah bit back her tears as she hugged Leah again, and then left her to have her bath. 'Leave the clothes on the floor. I'll burn them.'

She found Samuel pacing the kitchen floor, his hands turned into fists. 'What did they do to her? Did they...?' He wouldn't meet Sarah's eyes.

'No. She wasn't harmed in that way, at least. They spat on her and humiliated her.' Sarah ached to go back to her daughter but Leah needed some privacy. Instead, she took out the chopping board and some vegetables to prepare the evening meal. She pulled a sharp knife from the knife block.

'Did she know who they were?'

Sarah hated lies but there was little to gain from telling her son Leah had recognized two of them. She chopped rapidly, trying to work off some of her rage, focusing on the board in front of her rather than having to look at her son. 'I didn't ask.' That at least was a partial truth.

'I want to kill them, Mama. All of them. Why would they do that to her? To anyone. What sort of man does that?'

Sarah finished the vegetables, wishing she had an answer. How did she explain to her son how neighbours, friends, even family, could turn on other people just because someone decided that person was a lower being due to their heritage?

She set the vegetables on a low heat, then busied herself making some coffee, thankful they had the real thing. She added sugar to all three cups. 'Drink this and stay here. I don't want you leaving the apartment. It is pointless going looking for trouble. Do you hear me?'

'Yes, Mama.'

'Good. I need to check on Leah.' Sarah wished Ben was home, but he was working double shifts at the hospital. She didn't want to risk sending Samuel out for him. And where was Daniel? Why hadn't he come home?

The telephone rang and she heard Samuel speaking softly in the hall but she couldn't make out the words. She waited for him to finish. He called out: 'Daniel is staying at his friend's house. He said Mr Goldman thought it was safer.'

Sarah knew it probably was, but she couldn't help wanting all her children by her side, to make sure they were safe. But how could she keep them that way in a world that had turned into something she couldn't recognize?

TWENTY-EIGHT

The next morning, a gentle knock on the door announced their visitor. She opened it to find Fräulein Berger, shifting from one foot to the other, looking distinctly uncomfortable.

'Thank you for coming. I hoped you would.'

The woman gave her a little smile. 'How is Leah?'

'Better, thank you,' Sarah lied. There was little point in telling the woman Leah had crawled into her bed in the middle of the night and couldn't sleep, couldn't close her eyes as she relived her ordeal. 'Please, come in. The water is hot so coffee will only take a minute. Let me take your coat.'

She hung up the woman's coat on the coat rack and led the way into the sitting room, before leaving to hurry back to the kitchen to put the water on to boil for coffee. She made two cups, one from real beans for her visitor and an *ersatz* one for herself. She added some sugar to the tray and two pastries, before carrying it into the lounge.

Fräulein Berger stood near the mantelpiece looking at the photographs. She jumped hearing Sarah come in. 'You have a lovely family.'

'Thank you. Please sit down and make yourself comfortable.'

Berger looked around self-consciously. As if she thought she might dirty the couch, she sat on the very edge. Sarah noticed her red, chapped hands, taking in the cheap cotton dress, the polished but well-worn shoes, the battered handbag. But none of that meant anything to her.

'Leah will be fine. I can't thank you enough for bringing her home, Fräulein Berger. She's strong. She will recover.'

'Those animals.' Fräulein Berger set her cup down, her shaking hands making the china rattle. 'That's an insult to animals. You should have seen them. They made some pregnant women run around in circles until the poor creatures collapsed. Nobody was safe from them. They beat a Rabbi with their truncheons. I've never seen anything like it. And nobody did *any*thing.' Her breathing grew laboured as the words flowed out.

'You did.'

Fräulein Berger eyes shone with tears. 'I didn't do enough.'

Sarah moved to sit beside her and took the woman's hands in hers. 'You treated my child with kindness. You could have walked away but instead you risked your safety, your reputation...'

The woman looked uncomfortable. 'My reputation?'

'It won't be easy for you if people think you sympathise with the Jews.'

'Oh. I thought you meant something else.' The woman coloured. 'I don't care what people think. I can't afford to worry about that, not since my father got injured at work. Mother died and we had no money, so I had to work. At whatever jobs I could find.'

Up close, Sarah realized the woman was younger than she first appeared. She guessed she was only twenty.

'Life hasn't been kind to you, has it?' At the small shake of her head, Sarah continued. 'I hope that changes. You deserve more.' Sarah coughed, trying to clear the lump of sadness in her throat. She continued. 'Leah's father hasn't come home yet.'

Fräulein Berger paled, causing Sarah to explain: 'He's working at the hospital. He will be home this evening. I'm sure he would like to give you something as a thank-you.'

The woman recoiled in horror. 'I don't expect to get paid.'

Mortified, Sarah apologized. 'Please, don't be offended! I'm sorry. I don't know what to say. The thing is, Fräulei—'

'My name is Hedwig.'

'Hedwig, Leah recognized two of the boys who attacked her. They are, I mean were, friends with my sons. They used to come and visit so often I wondered if I should ask them to move in.'

Hedwig smiled at Sarah's attempt to joke.

'These boys took our hospitality and repaid it by treating our daughter like that. I just wanted to do something nice for you. If I had all the money in the world, I couldn't pay you enough for what you did.'

Hedwig picked at a loose thread on her skirt. 'May I take the pastry home for my father? He has a sweet tooth and we... well, we don't get to buy pastries very often.'

Sarah acted instinctively. She put her arms around Hedwig and hugged her.

The young woman broke down in tears, telling Sarah all she had to do to keep them afloat. The years had been difficult, almost impossible.

When the woman had dried her eyes she drank her coffee, slowly savouring every sip. 'I think that times being difficult has helped Hitler and his supporters. People believe that he has created new jobs, that he has made Germany better, and they hope he will do the same for Austria.' Hedwig lifted her head but she couldn't meet Sarah's eyes. 'For a time, I thought he might help people like me and my father.' Then her gaze hardened. 'But I'd rather starve than be party to what happened yesterday. What they are doing is wrong. I thought those stories in Germany were just lies. But after seeing what they did, out in the open, in broad daylight...? Well, I could believe anything now. And I won't stand by and be silent about it.'

Sarah reached for Hedwig's hand again, feeling a wave of maternal protectiveness flow through her body.

'Hedwig, your words and how you feel are something to be proud of, but you must be careful. You are young and have your whole life ahead of you. Don't make your feelings too obvious.'

At the mutinous look on the girl's face, Sarah was reminded of her own children. 'I don't mean you have to join in, but you must be careful. Those men who attacked Leah won't care you aren't Jewish. They take pleasure in doing what they want.'

'But I can't just pretend nothing is happening.'

'I'm not saying that you should. Just be clever about it. There must be ways you can help without putting a target on your head.'

Hedwig continued to look at her, causing Sarah to shrug. 'I don't have the answers now, but they will come. Maybe what happened yesterday is just a reaction to the *Anschluss* and things will settle down. In the meantime, please allow me to give you something.' Sarah hesitated, not wanting to offend the young woman. 'I was given a new handbag for my birthday last year but it's not my style: it would suit a younger woman. Would you like it? Perhaps a scarf too, to help ward off the chill of the wind?'

Sarah coaxed the younger woman into taking the leather handbag, two silk scarves, a pair of gloves and a rich woollen coat. 'Now at least you will be warm.'

Hedwig's smile would have lit up the opera house. She put on her new coat, scarf and the gloves, and picked up the bag, glancing at her reflection in the overmantel mirror as she did so. Sarah watched as the young woman put her hair behind her ears, an incredulous expression on her face as if she didn't recognize the young lady staring back at her.

Sarah left her and went to the kitchen, where she packed up a parcel of food, adding the rest of the pastries. Then she returned to the sitting room. Sarah leaned in and kissed Hedwig on each cheek. 'Please take these to your father and thank him for bringing up such a wonderful young woman. I will be very proud if my Leah turns out to be like you.'

Taking the pastries from Sarah, Hedwig gave her her address. 'If I can help, please call on me. Thank you again for everything.'

'No, Hedwig, thank you.'

TWENTY-NINE
LONDON, MAY 1938

Connie sat at her desk, watching the second hand on the clock tick by. Her official lunch break was in five minutes but there would be trouble if she left early, even if she had completed all her allotted work already. She'd never lived for her job: it was mundane but relatively easy, and overall the boss was flexible when it came to taking time off to go travelling to operas. She knew he thought her a boring spinster who had nothing better to do but live in a world of fantasy. A view shared by many she worked with. If only they knew what she and Dottie had really been doing for the last few years. They made fun of Dottie writing love stories – one of the nicest comments being what would a dried-up old spinster know of real love – but those stories saved lives.

Every penny Dottie earned went towards saving lives.

Connie picked up her brown paper bag containing a sandwich and an apple and walked down to the canteen. Some of her colleagues were sitting at a large table, the surface pockmarked with cigarette burns and other stains. Connie pulled up a seat, exchanging a smile with Jane and Helen, two of the girls who also worked in her section.

Hilda, another colleague but one Connie couldn't warm to, no matter how hard she tried, looked up from the newspaper she was reading. 'Have you seen these adverts? I got the paper to find a new place to live in the classified ads section, and all there is begging ads like this one.'

'What are you talking about? How can you beg in a newspaper?' Jane asked, before taking a bite of her sandwich.

Hilda took the cigarette out of her mouth, setting it down on an overflowing ashtray. Then, putting on what she probably thought was a good Austrian accent, she read out one ad after the other.

'"Three modest sisters, 11, 13 and 15, half orphans, pray to be accepted as foster children by kind family."' Hilda glanced up. 'As if anyone would want to adopt three children, foreigners at that. Oh, this one is even better.' Hilda took a drag of her cigarette before she read out loud, again using a bad accent: '"Will someone foster the beloved only child of a Jewish lawyer? Please write to Dr Karl Lumberg."'

'*Stop* it.' Connie couldn't contain her fury. 'How dare you make fun of these people? Have you any idea how desperate they must be to put an advert in a foreign paper? A lawyer, sending his only child to a stranger?'

'Don't tell me how to behave!' Hilda looked outraged. 'Who do you think you are? I'm not the one putting my children in a newspaper. Probably desperate to get rid of them. You know what those people are like.'

Connie's cheeks flushed as rage overwhelmed her. This woman had no idea how bad things were in Europe. The newspapers, while not covering every injustice, had outlined some of what was happening in Nazi-occupied territories. *What those people were like?* Ordinary innocent people were being terrorized! Connie clenched her fists, wishing she could enlighten her colleague. Tell her some of the reasons why families were so desperate they had to resort to advertising their children. But she didn't want to have to face questions about her regular opera trips. As Stephen said, Nazis lived everywhere not just in Germany. The air around her seemed to crackle as she stood up. 'What do you mean by "those people"? They are the same as you and I.'

Hilda ground out her cigarette. 'You and me, we got nothing in common. You are a bitter old woman. Me, I got the whole world ahead of me. I got better things to be doing than arguing with you over some stupid stuff.'

'It's you and *I*, not you and *me*, you uneducated little madam.' Connie would have said more but for Jane pulling her sleeve.

'Connie, sit down. She isn't worth it.'

Connie realized everyone in the canteen was staring at her. She sat back down as Hilda marched out of the room.

Trembling with fury still, Connie picked up the paper. She could barely read the text. Ad after ad.

URGENT. WHO WILL HELP VERY PLEASANT, TWIN BOYS AGED 21 TO GET OUT OF CONCENTRATION CAMP BY OFFERING TRAINEE POSITIONS. STRONG, HARD WORKERS. FROM GOOD JEWISH FAMILY.

JEWISH TAILOR (49), THIRTY YEARS EXPERIENCE IN OWN BUSINESS, SEEKS ANY POSITION IN CLOTHING URGENTLY – FACTORY, SALES, CLEANER. NO JOB TOO SMALL. CURRENTLY IN CONCENTRATION CAMP. HAS SIX YOUNG DEPENDENT PRIVATELY EDUCATED CHILDREN ALSO TRYING TO PLACE. HELP PLEASE.

FATHER IN CONCENTRATION CAMP. HAS THREE BOYS 7 – 15 AND ONE GIRL AGED 13. HAVE TO LEAVE GERMANY. IS ANYBODY WILLING TO HELP.

Young Viennese woman, aged 16, willing to work as cook or housekeeper. Not Aryan. Will consider any location in Britain. Write please to Vienna.

'I never saw you lose your temper like that before. You feeling alright?' Jane asked.

Helen returned to the table with a cup of tea. She placed it in front of Connie. 'I put some sugar in it for you. You get that down you and forget about that selfish witch, Hilda. She's a nasty piece of work and she'll get what's coming to her.'

'Thank you, Helen and you too, Jane. Mother would kill me if she saw how I acted. I made a show of myself, didn't I? I'll be the talk of the office.'

Helen took the newspaper and folded it closed. 'Don't worry about it. That lot will find someone else to talk about tomorrow. Now, tell us about Dottie's new book. When will it be out? My mother is her biggest fan. She has that copy you got signed for me sitting pride of place on the bookcase. She shows it off to everyone – well, not the vicar, of course. She doesn't think he would appreciate romance books, even if they are as tasteful as your Dottie's.'

Connie joined in the conversation, knowing her friends were trying to help, but her mind kept going to the newspaper. Things must be awful in Vienna for people to place adverts like that.

She hadn't had a reply to the last letter she'd sent to Sarah. How bad had things got for her friend?

THIRTY

VIENNA, MAY 1938

Sarah pushed her hair back from her forehead as she contemplated the form in front of her. Issued by the Vienna Jewish Community Welfare Department – Immigration Office, it was supposed to make emigrating easier. She doubted whether that was true. The two-page form required her to complete details of their names, occupations, income, family members, their preferred destination to emigrate to and any relationships with people abroad.

The only people she knew in England were refugees like Edith and of course the Fitzwalter sisters. If only she could ask Connie and Dottie for help, but her friends weren't rich and probably couldn't afford to be sponsors. Ben had some cousins in America.

She tapped her pen against the wooden desk in Ben's study, looking at the part where she had to fill in relationships. She studied the notes she had taken when she'd collected the form. The clerk had suggested she apply to the American embassy, they were slightly less overwhelmed than the British embassy but warned her she would still have to face long queues. Emigrants would have to pay emigration taxes, atonement fees and payments to the Emigration Fund, on top of the costs of the steamer tickets and visas. Where would all the money come from? She had a couple of pieces of jewellery, but there wasn't anywhere in Vienna she could sell them without having to pay over some of their value to the Nazis.

She read through the form again. What if she made a mistake and it stopped them leaving? What if they couldn't leave together? She threw the pen down in frustration. This wasn't a decision she could make on her own – she had to discuss it with Ben and her father.

Sarah glanced at the clock for the umpteenth time. Her father was due for dinner but hadn't yet appeared. Ben was at the hospital, but the children were ready to eat.

Going into the kitchen, she checked the temperature of the oven, not wanting the apple strudel she was baking to burn, before taking off her apron as she heard something in the corridor outside.

Opening the door of her apartment, she heard her father's footsteps shuffling up the steps to his apartment. 'Papa, have you forgotten dinner? Papa?'

There was no answer.

Checking her pocket for the key, she closed the door behind her and followed her father to his apartment. The door had been left open. She pushed it open and walked in, calling his name.

'Papa, answer me! You're scaring me.'

Her father sat at the dining table, his head in his hands, his body rocking back and forth.

'Is it Ben? What? Tell me!' she screamed, but he still didn't react. She pushed herself to walk to his side, putting an arm on his shoulders. Only then did she notice his dishevelled appearance. His coat was dirty and stinking, but the state of his beard made her cry. He'd had a full beard for as long as she could remember. The children used to tease him about his long whiskers when they were little. Now it looked like someone had attacked him with a pair of blunt scissors.

She put her arms around him, pulling him to her chest as if he were Daniel or Leah. 'Papa, I'm sorry.' His muffled sobs made her cry, but she held fast to him, supporting him as best she could.

A noise behind her alerted her to the presence of her children: Samuel standing to one side, Daniel and Leah clinging to one another. All three had ashen faces, but Samuel's expression was one of anger.

'Go back downstairs, please, children. I will be down in a minute. Leah, turn off the oven for me, please. You can go ahead and eat if you wish.'

'We're not hungry,' Samuel protested, just as Leah whispered, 'What's wrong with Grandpa?'

'Do as you are told,' Sarah retorted, but immediately censored her tone. 'Please. Go on now. I will be there shortly.'

Leah led Daniel out of the door, with Samuel hesitating until they left. 'Shall I go to the hospital and fetch Papa?'

'No, I don't want you on the street.' His eyes flared, a mutinous look on his face. She reached out to touch his cheek. 'Thank you. Look after your sister and brother.'

She felt her father shudder against her before he pushed her away. Samuel glanced at his grandfather before turning and walking out of the room. She heard the apartment door click behind him.

'Go to your children, Sarah. Leave me be.'

'No, Papa. They will be fine. Let me help you.'

She poured him a brandy before heading into the kitchen to boil some water. Once hot, she filled a bowl, added a teaspoon of salt to help clean out the small wounds on his face. She fetched a clean flannel and towel from the bathroom, before returning to find him still seated at the table, his drink untouched.

'Wash your face, Papa. The water is hot but not burning and I put some salt in it. It will sting but I don't want those cuts to get infected. When Ben gets home, he can take a proper look at you.'

'Thank you for looking after me, daughter, but your place is with your children now. Go and feed them.'

Sarah hesitated, wanting to know what happened, but something in his eyes told her to leave. She bent down to kiss his head. 'I love you, Papa. I will bring you a plate later.'

He didn't reply. She left him staring at the water.

Walking back down the stairs, Sarah heard the front door to their apartment building close. Heart thumping, she hurried down the last few steps, wanting to get inside her home.

'Sarah.'

Her heart soared at the sound of her husband's voice. 'Ben, Thank God.'

'Is your father home?'

'Yes, but he is in a dreadful state. Something happened and he isn't talking. He told me to leave him.'

'The children?'

'Are all fine. A little upset but not hurt. Why are you home?'

He opened the door to their apartment and pulling her inside, closed it behind him.

'Herr Weber, an old patient, came to the hospital. He saw what happened and thought I should be here. He said some men came into the shop and accused Isaac of something. They dragged him outside and then, in front of a baying crowd, they cut off his beard with scissors. Is that true?'

Sarah nodded. 'They cut his face. I think they may have hit him as well. His clothes were all dirty. He was crying. I have never seen my father cry. It was horrible.'

Ben embraced her, holding her in a firm hug for a few seconds. 'I'll go and check on him.'

She nodded, wiping her face with her hands. 'I'll try to salvage dinner. Not that I'm hungry, but the children probably are.'

He kissed her on the forehead. 'I love you.'

The children were sitting together in silence, the table set for dinner. They looked up as she walked into the room.

'How's Grandpa?' Daniel asked.

'Your father is home, and he went to check on him. I'm sure he will feel better in no time. You must be hungry. Leah, help me please.'

Leah stood but instead of moving towards the kitchen, she whispered, 'Mama, what happened to his beard?' Leah's eyes looked too big for her face.

Sarah swallowed. 'Some men cut it off.'

'But why?'

'Who knows why people act the way they do?'

'Because they hate us, that's why,' Samuel responded, his voice harsh.

Sarah dished up dinner, but the food sat untouched on their plates as the four of them sat at the table waiting. When they heard the front door open, all four stood up but sat back down when Ben appeared on his own.

'You didn't have to wait for me. The food will be cold.'

'How is he?' asked Leah.

Ben walked to his daughter's side. 'Grandpa will be just fine. He has a couple of bruises and doesn't feel like eating so he sent his apologies. He is resting now, but you can go and see him tomorrow.'

Sarah moved towards the kitchen. 'I left yours in the warmer. I just hope it hasn't dried out.'

'Thank you, darling, but I'm not hungry. I have a couple of calls to make. I will be in my study.'

She watched her husband walk to his study, shoulders slumped.

The children retook their seats, but they didn't have any appetite either.

Instead of her usual lecture about wasting food, Sarah told them they were excused. Leah offered to help her clear up, but she wanted to do it alone. Having something to do might help her get her mind off the look on her father's face.

Once the kitchen was clean, Sarah boiled some water and made some coffee. She quietly pushed the study door open to find Ben hunched over, his brow creased as he studied some papers scattered across his desk.

'Thank you, darling.' He barely glanced up as she placed the cup beside him.

'How is he? Really?' She leaned against the desk, crossing her arms, trying to hide her apprehension.

Ben rubbed his forehead, then looked up with a strained attempt at a smile. 'Physically, it's like I told the children. A few bruises, a couple of cracked ribs. Nothing too serious.'

Sarah's hand flew to her mouth.

'Sorry, that sounded callous. I meant, it could have been worse. Much worse.' Ben stood up, his chair scraping against the wooden floor, and he took her hand in his. 'I'm not worried about his physical injuries but' – he paused, his grip tightening – 'he's lost the store. It's now the property of the German Reich.'

'They just took it? Can they do that?' Her voice trembled.

'They can do anything they want.' Ben sighed, his shoulders drooping in defeat.

'Poor Papa. He loved that place.'

'He's devastated, but knows he is lucky they didn't arrest him and ship him off somewhere.' Ben's gaze met hers, his cheeks flushed with emotion. 'We know so many who have disappeared.' His voice softened, filled with regret. 'When I think of how I dismissed your concerns for your cousin's husband... I was a pompous idiot.'

'Ben, don't.' It was pointless going over a conversation they had had several years previously.

'I was. Helga wrote to you with her fears for Paul, and I didn't want to believe anyone could be arrested for simply being Jewish. I was stupid. Forgive me?' His eyes searched hers, seeking forgiveness.

She leaned in to give him a kiss, her lips barely brushing his. 'There is nothing to forgive. What will happen now? Will Papa be a target? Or will they be satisfied with his store?'

'I telephoned some of my contacts; some didn't take my call.' Ben turned to look out of the window. 'But a couple of the policemen I helped over the years suggested Isaac keep a low profile, maybe stay home for now.'

Sarah clenched her fists, her knuckles whitening as she tried to suppress her anger, recalling the countless times Ben had selflessly tended to policemen and their families, often without any payment during the periods of high inflation when cash was worthless. 'He can't live in hiding forever.'

Sarah couldn't stop thinking of her father, alone in his apartment. A few hours passed before she decided to check on him. She walked up the stairs, clenching and unclenching her hands.

Using her key, she let herself into his apartment. 'Papa, it's only me. I brought you some dinner. In case you are hungry.'

Silence greeted her. She wanted to turn and run back down the stairs, but she couldn't. Straightening her spine, she walked through the hall into the dining room. She left the plate of food on the table.

The heavy brocade curtains had been pulled closed, blocking natural light. As her eyes adjusted to the darkness, she made out the figure of her father slumped in his favourite reading chair.

'Papa.'

More silence. A chill crept up her spine as she forced herself to walk to him. 'Papa, please answer me. I'm worried about you.'

After several seconds, Isaac jumped as if he'd just noticed her presence. 'Sarah?'

She knelt by his chair, taking his hand in hers. 'You scared me, Papa. When you didn't answer, when I found you sitting here in the darkness. I thought your heart may have given up.'

He looked up, the disgust in his eyes piercing through her. 'You mean you thought I took my own life. They stole my store, my dignity – but they will not force me to sin. The Talmud prohibits suicide, Sarah.'

She didn't mind him scolding her; it meant he had not given up.

Her father turned on the small reading lap on the table to his side. 'My heart hurts for my adoptive country. When I came here after the pogroms of my youth, I thought it would be safe. But now I am in fear for my family. I'm an old man. I've lived a long and happy life.' His eyes flitted to the painting of Sarah's mother on the wall. 'I married a wonderful woman who gave me a most cherished daughter. I'm glad your mother isn't alive to see this day.' He swiped a finger across his cheek as a tear escaped.

'Papa,' Sarah croaked, her throat clogged with tears.

'I love you, my child. I want you to promise me to get out. By whatever means necessary.'

'I'm not going anywhere. Not without you.'

He put his hand under her chin and forced her to look up at his face. 'Sarah, your duty is to your children. *They* are the future.'

THIRTY-ONE
VIENNA, JUNE 1938

Ben lay his knife and fork on his plate. 'Thank you for such a wonderful meal, Sarah. You truly spoiled us.' He lifted his glass. 'A toast to your mother, children. Happy birthday, darling.'

Sarah clinked his glass and drank a sip of water pretending it was a French sauvignon blanc, her wine of choice. If only she could imagine a time when the family didn't live in fear. Her eyes went to Leah, picking at the food on her plate. If only she knew how to help her daughter recover.

Samuel told a joke, making them laugh and then Daniel told another one. Ben gripped her hand as they exchanged a smile.

Loud knocking echoed down the hallway, interrupting their brief moment of respite, returning the room to a heightened sense of tension.

Samuel stood to go to the door but Ben spoke up. 'Children, go to your rooms and stay there. No matter what you hear, I do not want you to come out. Understood?'

'Yes, Papa.'

'Samuel, make sure they listen to me.'

Samuel nodded. Ben gripped Sarah's hands once before making his way out of the dining room and down the hall.

Sarah sat, frozen to her seat, her nails digging into the palms of her hands. The knocking intensified until she heard the door open.

'You are the Jew, Benjamin Liberman.'

'Yes.'

Sarah found her legs and forced herself to walk to the door of the dining room. Her hands flew to her mouth at the scene in front of her: a group of stern-looking men, dressed in dark uniforms making the red armband more conspicuous.

'We have orders to take you into custody. You will come with us now.'

'Why? I have done nothing wrong.'

Sarah clutched the doorframe at Ben's protest. She saw one man put his hand on the gun in his belt. A policeman she recognized stepped forward and slapped Ben hard across the face.

'Shut up, swine.'

Ben reeled backwards but remained standing. Sarah moved faster than she thought possible, launching herself down the hall, toward the group.

'My husband is a doctor, he saves lives. He's spent years treating everyone who asks, often without being paid. Please, leave him alone.'

'Step aside, Frau Liberman.'

'But...' Sarah's eyes locked with Ben's. His gaze reflected the harsh reality of their situation, yet there was an unwavering determination in them. It was as if he was trying to convey a thousand words in a single look: reassurance, love and a plea for her to stay strong. She swallowed hard before she gave him a tiny nod to show she had understood the message.

'May I take my coat?' Ben's voice didn't shake; he could have been addressing a patient. The officer nodded.

Sarah took the coat from the coat stand and handed it to him.

Ben leaned in to kiss her on the cheek. 'Don't argue, think of the boys,' he whispered.

He was right. If these men saw Samuel, they were liable to take him too. Sarah stayed quiet for the sake of her son.

As they started to lead her husband away, Sarah found her voice. 'Where are you taking him? Please tell me.'

The one policeman who had held back from the group, as if to distance himself, turned to her. 'The Metropole hotel.'

Gestapo headquarters. Sarah's legs shook but she remained upright until she closed the door. Only then did she sink to the floor.

THIRTY-TWO
VIENNA, JUNE 1938

Sarah waited until the children were in bed. Then she retrieved the phone book she had borrowed. She didn't know where her neighbour had got hold of a New York phone directory, and she didn't care.

Sarah copied out the list of addresses of all the Saul Libermans listed. Her husband's cousin had emigrated to America at the turn of the century, and he was the only person she knew in America.

She copied out and sent the same letter to all twelve Saul Libermans in the hope one would be Ben's cousin and would be able to sponsor him by providing him with a financial affidavit and other documents required by the US authorities.

A month later, Sarah hadn't managed to find the correct Saul Liberman in New York. A couple of the men she had written to had had the decency to reply, but it was to tell her there was no blood link. One, despite not being a relative, had offered to sponsor a young man, someone who could work in his shoe store. He was quite apologetic that he couldn't afford to pay a grown man's salary, but could stretch to room and board and a low wage for a young man without family commitments.

Could she send her son, Samuel, to a stranger? Before the Nazis arrived in Vienna, it would have been unthinkable. But that was then, this was now: when law and order no longer existed – at least not for a Jewish person. So far, Samuel had not been subjected to any personal violence but given what had happened to Leah and then Papa, and now with Ben's arrest, it was only a matter of time.

Sarah headed to the American embassy the next morning and took her place in the long line that stretched down the street of would-be emigrants queueing up to enquire about a visa.

Men and boys in brown uniforms taunted the crowd, throwing things at them, calling them hideous names.

'Ignore them, they couldn't spell the words they are using if they were held at gunpoint. Ignorant savages, the whole lot of them.' The old man next to her murmured as he stood at her side, protecting her from the view. 'Why are you here and not your husband?' he asked, glancing at her hand.

'My husband was taken. He is being held in the Metropole.'

The man blanched before muttering, 'I'm sorry.' He didn't ask why Ben had been taken. They both knew the answer to that.

Sarah thought her legs would give way when, finally, it was her turn to speak to someone. The clerk asked for information on all members of the family.

'Your husband was born in Kiev. That means he has Russian citizenship.'

Sarah clutched her hands together. Was that a good thing? Did the Americans like Russians better?

'Mrs Liberman, that is good news. The way the system works is we receive a quota of visas for each country so, a certain number for Germany, Austria, Russia and so on. Most people who come here trying to get to America are applying under the Austrian or German quotas. There are fewer applying under the Russian quota, so your chances of success increase. You said you have an affidavit already signed by an American citizen. Is he a relative of your husband's?'

Sarah hesitated. Should she lie? After all, they shared the same surname. She heard her father's voice in her head: *Don't let the Nazis turn you into something you aren't.*

'No, unless he is a distant cousin, as we share the same surname. My husband is not at home. He has been detained but he used to speak of a cousin called Saul Liberman who went to live in New York. I wrote to all Saul Libermans in that city and asked for an affidavit.' Something about the kindness in the clerk's eyes made her continue. 'Not everyone wrote back but this man did. He apologized, saying he couldn't afford to assume responsibility for Ben and our family, but he could take in our son. Samuel is eighteen and very tall and... conspicuous. He is a good boy, never been in trouble with anyone but...' Sarah faltered. She tried to dampen the tide of emotion threatening to engulf her.

The young man was quick to offer reassurance. 'You are doing the right thing, Mrs Liberman. America is a wonderful place to live, and your son sounds like just the type of young man who will thrive in New York. Come with me and I will help you complete the correct paperwork. Your son is also eligible to apply under the Russian quota.'

His kindness was too much after all she had been through. Sarah put her face in her hands as the tears came.

The young man whipped out his hanky; it had the initials 'CK' embroidered in blue. 'My mother keeps me well supplied.'

'She must be very proud of you.' Sarah took the hanky and wiped her eyes.

'She is like most Jewish mothers,' he whispered.

Sarah couldn't help but stare. This man was American, he didn't have to be there in Vienna yet there he was, helping others.

'Not everyone knows. I prefer to keep it that way.'

Sarah nodded. 'I won't tell a soul. Thank you.'

By the time Sarah left the building, there was no sign of the brownshirts. She walked home unmolested. Perhaps it was because she walked straighter and with a smile on her face. The young clerk had not only helped her complete the forms but also made her a cup of coffee and insisted she share his lunch. He'd made her laugh, telling her tales of his mother and her efforts to get him to marry a nice Jewish girl and settle down. His mother didn't understand his need to see the world, to do something to help. 'Mrs Liberman, I thank God every morning my mother has no understanding of the horrors you have to deal with every day. I guess I shouldn't say that, at least not to you.'

She sensed he was lonely for all he wanted to stay in Vienna to help.

'I think that is completely understandable. You want to protect her. It would be best for everyone if nobody experienced what is happening here in Austria, Germany and elsewhere. But then I wouldn't be here and would not have met you. You are a real credit to your mother, Caleb. Thank you. Not just for your help with the papers, but for treating me like a real person.'

That evening, Sarah walked into the sitting room where her children were sitting and chatting. She took a second to enjoy their interaction, taking the time to compose herself. Samuel smiled as he pulled Leah's hair after she made a joke about him being too serious. Sarah would have smiled too, but for the fact she was about to break her son's heart.

'Leah and Daniel, can you please go to bed. I need to speak to Samuel.'

The children exchanged looks but with a glance towards Sarah's face, stood up and made their way out of the room in silence.

When the door closed behind them, Samuel moved towards her, his hands jammed under his armpits, blinking rapidly. 'What is it, Mama? Papa? Have you heard something?'

'No, darling. I would tell you if I had.' She took a seat on the sofa and patted the cushion next to her. She waited for him to sit beside her before continuing: 'I went to the American embassy today. I applied for a visa.'

'For Papa?'

'For you.'

Samuel's eyes widened, his face losing all colour. 'Me? But Papa needs one the most. I can wait.'

She put her hand on his arm and squeezed. 'No, son, you can't. We don't know how much longer they will allow us to live here. They could throw us onto the street at a moment's notice. Like they did to the Friedhams and others. Why they have left us alone is anyone's guess.' She continued to hold his arm. 'Samuel, you know we love you with all our heart. I hate to ask you, but I must. I wrote to everyone I could think of after being told our best chance of escape was via the American quotas. We have no choice but to rely on strangers. I've only managed to find one person to act as a sponsor. He offered to take a young man to work in his store. Daniel is too young. Caleb, the clerk at the American embassy, said your number would come up quickly. We must be ready to buy a passenger ticket and get the exit paperwork we need from the Germans.'

Sarah could hardly breathe as she watched emotions cross her son's face: fear, excitement, guilt, terror. She leaned in to put her arm around him, drawing him to her side. 'If there was any other way, I would never let you go. But you must. I'm scared they will come for you, Samuel. I couldn't bear it if they took you.'

He pushed his brown curls away from his eyes to look directly at her. 'I'm scared too, Mama. But I can't leave you alone. Not with Papa gone, and Grandpapa needs me too.'

'I can look after your grandpapa and he, me. When you are in New York, you can help by looking up your father's cousin, the real Saul Liberman. Or maybe you will find other people who would sponsor a fine doctor like your father or a young woman like your sister. If you tell them, tell them what it is really like to live here, under this regime. The truth, not what they read in their papers or hear on their wireless.'

He pushed her away to face her, his voice trembling with emotion. 'Mama, I don't want to leave you behind.'

'You will never do that. I will go with you, in here.' She pointed to his chest. 'The same as you will always be in my heart. Someday we will be back together, the whole lot of us as a family.'

He couldn't hide his disbelief, but she pretended she didn't see it.

'Caleb, he said it will take time but not too long. For now, we need to be organized – you need to keep a bag packed, just in case. You also need to stay indoors.'

He moved as if to protest, but she held firm. 'I mean it, Samuel. I don't want you outside just in case there are more attacks on the street. You stay inside. Until we get the call when you have to go to sign the paperwork. Are you listening to me?'

'Yes, Mama.'

'You promise?'

He nodded but she held his gaze until he spoke. 'I promise.'

The weeks passed slowly. She checked with Caleb every two weeks to see if Samuel's visa had been granted but there was no news. Caleb seemed hopeful. A weekly letter from Ben would arrive and she kept writing in return. Once a month she was allowed to bring him a fresh shirt, a pair of trousers and some clean underclothes. She could collect Ben's laundry, but she wasn't allowed to see him. The guard passed her the parcel. She hated going but at least it was proof of two things: Ben was still alive and still in Vienna.

THIRTY-THREE

Connie read the morning's newspaper, although the news was only making her more depressed.

'Mama.' She coughed to clear the lump from her throat. 'Did you know that, for many people, their first realization of being Jewish came when the Nuremberg Laws were enforced?'

Her mother paused in her stitching, her hands momentarily still as she met her gaze. 'Yes, my dear,' she replied, with a sigh. 'It's a tragedy beyond words.'

'How can they do things like this? The Nazi newspaper, the *Frankfurter Volksblatt*, published the names and addresses of six thousand Jews living in Frankfurt. Some of those families had been attending church, believing they were Christians. Some of them even converted, and many were born and brought up as Catholics, only to find out they had two Jewish grandparents, which, in the eyes of the Nazis, makes them Jewish.'

Tears glistened in her mother's eyes as she placed her sewing aside, giving Connie her full attention. 'Darling,' she began, her voice filled with both sadness and anger, 'I never thought I would live to see the day when a little man who isn't even German could hoodwink an entire country into believing such a load of nonsense.'

Connie's throat tightened. 'It's unfathomable, Mama. Nobody is more deserving than anyone else. As Father used to say, we all bleed red blood and need air, food and water to stay alive. We all love our families.'

Mama reached out and took her hand, offering a comforting squeeze. 'How can those Nazis keep a straight face when their leaders strut around proclaiming the existence of a race none of them resemble?' She shook her head in disbelief. 'Under Hitler's own rules, he isn't an Aryan. He's not blond or blue-eyed.'

Connie closed the newspaper. 'How are your fundraising efforts going?'

A look of satisfaction crossed her mother's face. 'People are very generous. You know I have been invited to speak at various gatherings, from scout clubs to churches to Women's Institute meetings. Most people contribute something, whether it is a pound, shillings or a few pence. Your school friends, the two sisters... I've forgotten their names...' Her mother scratched the side of her head.

Connie prompted. 'Isabella and Sybil—?'

'Yes. Of course, how could I forget? They are two very well-brought-up young ladies.'

Connie smiled at the highest compliment her mother could attribute to her friends. They had been so supportive, visiting Dottie's flat to make new arrivals feel welcome; cleaning it when the latest rescuee had found a more permanent place-ment, in preparation for the next visitors who would use the flat as the first stop on their route to freedom.

Mama's head tilted slightly to one side, her eyes wide and glossy with admiration. 'They have been wonderful, travelling all over the country, speaking to similar groups. We are slowly driving home the message that if people want to help, it doesn't automatically mean they have to sponsor someone personally. Most can't afford that level of financial commitment. But coming together as a group, their scout troop for instance, can collectively sponsor a young man and get him out of Germany. People really have been wonderful.'

A surge of love for this amazing woman overcame Connie. She stood up and kissed her mother on the top of her head. 'You are wonderful, and I love you.'

Her mother patted her hand, pleased but a little embarrassed at the affectionate gesture. 'You aren't too bad yourself. You and your sister have made me so proud with all your efforts to help those less fortunate. Did I tell you about my visit to the Jewish Council in Devon? Reverend Calder invited me to accompany him. It was nice of him – you and Dorothea were travelling, and he knew I'd be alone for the weekend.' The 'again' was left unspoken.

Guilt tightened Connie's chest as she realized she had been so focused on helping strangers that she hadn't considered her mother being alone at home. Her mother's once vibrant auburn hair had turned completely grey, and the wrinkles on her face were more pronounced now. The worry for her daughters and the loneliness had aged her, yet she had never once complained.

Connie retook her seat. 'No. I didn't realize you had travelled so far.'

'Maybe you girls caught the travelling bug from me.' Mama smiled at her own joke. 'It was a rather interesting experience. They were expecting a man, for some reason. They directed most of their questions at Reverend Calder but he insisted they listened to me. It was rather amusing. I don't believe those gentlemen were used to taking direction from a woman.'

Connie bit her lip to stop the smile. There was no better woman than her mother to put someone back in their place but now wasn't the time to comment.

'What was most interesting was that only one of the three

men had opened his house to refugees. The other two told me they were worried about taking in Germans and stirring up resentment in the local community. It seems prejudice against the Jewish community doesn't just exist in Germany.'

'I think prejudice exists in every country, every community. I like to think it comes from a lack of understanding of each other, but who knows?' Connie sighed. 'Did you manage to change their minds?'

Her mother coloured slightly as she picked up her sewing. 'I may have suggested that they couldn't preach to others about the need for fundraising without having a foot in the race.'

Connie smiled. She could just imagine the look the men had got when her mother delivered that message. 'Good for you.'

Samuel's number finally came up.

The American embassy issued his visa, and the day they had all been dreading came. Sarah's eldest son was leaving and who knew when her family would be together again? *Maybe never.* Sarah pushed that horrible thought out of her mind as she gathered her children together. Hedwig had come to the rescue, suggesting they cook a feast for the family to eat together before Samuel's departure. She had gone to the shops and bought all the ingredients she could find from Sarah's list.

Leah, Hedwig and Sarah shared the cooking with Sarah teaching the younger woman how to make *Krautfleckerl.*

Hedwig picked up the cookbook Sarah had laid on the counter, although Sarah knew the recipes by heart. '*Wiener Küche.*' Hedwig traced the name on the cover. 'You used this a lot.'

'My mother gave it to me when I got married. She taught me how to cook from an early age, even though we had a cook and a maid who came in every day. She said all women, regardless of their station in life, should know how to make a meal for their family. She had experienced the pogroms of Poland.'

'I'm not a good cook.' Hedwig studied Sarah's hands as she chopped some garlic cloves before starting on two large onions. 'I wouldn't know where to start.'

Sarah smiled at her, handing her the knife. 'Anyone can chop onions and garlic. You finish these and I will start on the cabbage.'

The time passed quickly as they prepared the meal, Hedwig a willing student as Sarah showed her the steps. Sarah had made a *Linzer torte* and some Purim cookies the day before. It had been a long time since she had baked these herself: usually she bought them from the Jewish pastry store. But with the Nazis in Vienna, those shops no longer existed.

As they finished the dishes, Hedwig smiled. 'I'll come back tomorrow and see how it went.'

Sarah stopped what she was doing. 'You aren't going to eat with us? After all this work?'

'I'd love a little taste of it but no. This is your family time.'

Sarah tried to protest but Hedwig shook her head. 'I need to go home and check on things there. I will come back tomorrow. Thank you, Sarah, for teaching me.'

Sarah hastily put a small basket of cookies, a large slice of torte and a plate of the *Krautfleckerl* in a bag. 'Now your father can taste what you cooked. I hope he likes it.'

Hedwig leaned in to kiss Sarah's cheek. 'Thank you for being so generous to me. I never had a friend like you before.'

Hedwig held her package carefully as Leah showed her to the front door.

Sarah fought down tears as she got ready to feed her family, together for the last time. If only Ben were with them too.

Her father insisted that they leave an empty chair at the head of the table where Ben would have normally sat. 'He is with us in our thoughts.' Isaac rubbed his stomach. 'Something smells delicious. Thank you, Sarah and Leah, for your hard work.' Isaac took his seat, the boys too, and then Leah and Sarah dished up the food.

'There is no meat. Our budget didn't stretch to that,' Sarah apologized, as she placed a heaped plate in front of Samuel. He picked up a fork and tasted the cabbage dish.

'This *Krautfleckerl* is the best you ever made, Mama.'

Leah and Sarah exchanged a smile.

'What are you smiling at? I mean it. It's delicious.'

'Hedwig made it.'

'Mama helped her but, yes, she did most of the work. She'll be pleased you liked it.'

They ate and talked, swapping stories the family had heard before. When the *Krautfleckerl* had disappeared, Sarah brought out the desserts.

'Looks like someone got hungry and ate already.' Daniel joked about the missing slice of *torte*.

'I gave it to Hedwig to take home to her father. He has a sweet tooth. I hope you don't mind, Samuel.'

'Not at all, Mama. She has been very good to our family. We should have invited her to eat with us.'

'We did, but she wanted to be with her father.'

Sarah stumbled over the lie but she didn't want to voice the obvious. The fact that this was their last time to eat together. She put several cookies on a plate with the largest slice of *torte* and handed it to her eldest child.

'Mama, I'm not sure I can eat all that.'

'I'll have it. I'm starving.' Daniel reached for the plate but Sarah shook her head and placed it in front of Samuel.

She ruffled Daniel's hair before putting a slightly smaller piece of the pie and some cookies on his plate. Leah only took a small slice. Sarah met her father's eyes across the table and had to look away from the depth of understanding shining from them. He understood what it was like to say goodbye. Sarah's older brother had gone to war and never come home. Fighting for the same Austrian empire now chasing them away.

When everyone had finished eating, Sarah and Leah cleared the table as Samuel went to fetch his bags. Daniel followed him, for one last brother-to-brother chat, Sarah imagined.

'I'll miss him,' Leah whispered, as she scraped off the plates before putting them into the bowl of hot water in the sink.

'Darling, just let these soak. I'll finish them later. Go and be with your brothers.'

Sarah let the tears run down her cheeks as she tucked the precious third-class tickets into a satchel, together with all the paperwork required to cross the borders. Samuel had written to Ben, but their request to see him had been denied.

She picked up the bag from the kitchen table and returned to the sitting room, where the family had now gathered.

'How will Samuel get to America?' Daniel couldn't hide his curiosity. Sarah knew he'd miss his brother, she also knew her younger son was a little envious. He wanted to see New York.

'Samuel will take the train through Germany, to Rotterdam in Holland. From there, he will board the Holland America Line steamer. In New York, Mr Liberman will be waiting for him.'

Samuel caught her gaze for a second but then looked away. Not before she spotted the glistening tears in his eyes. He had been relieved the paperwork had come through but the reality of saying goodbye, not knowing when he would see them again, was hitting him hard.

Isaac broke the silence. 'Samuel, my grandson, you have made your parents very proud. You are an exceptional young man. Kind, considerate, steadfast, stubborn.' Isaac raised a glass. 'To your success, your future happiness. May you have a long life, full of laughter and joy, a good wife and many children.'

Samuel blushed scarlet at the mention of a family, while Sarah could barely see through her haze of tears.

Her gaze fell on each member of her family. Daniel, whose excitement was now bubbling over; Leah, a shell of her former self – the girl only spoke when spoken to and was constantly looking over her shoulder. Her beautiful hands, once so accomplished at playing piano, now had nails bitten to the quick. Sarah moved on to her father. Up until the Nazis had marched into Vienna, he was a young man in his late sixties. Overnight, he had aged and now shuffled like a man twenty years older. Losing his home, his independence, his freedom – he didn't go out in the streets anymore – had taken their toll. Now he had to say goodbye to his favourite grandchild knowing there was a chance they would never meet again.

She couldn't do this. Pushing her chair back from the table, she mumbled an excuse and made for her bedroom. Once there, she wanted to throw herself on the bed and cry until the pain went away. But her children, her father, needed her to be strong. She went to her dressing table, picking up her photograph of Ben. 'I need your strength. I can't do this alone.'

There was a knock on the door and Samuel came in. For a second, he looked just like Ben had done the first time she met him, with his thick, curly brown hair and his height. But Samuel was more serious than Ben had been at eighteen, less inclined to laughing and joking.

'Mama. Please don't be scared. When I get to America, I will find a way to get you all out of Vienna. We will be together again, I promise.'

She turned to face him, reaching out her hand for his. She held on tight, looking up so she could hold his gaze. 'Son, your father and I are so proud of the man you have grown into. Thank you for your strength, particularly these past few months. Don't make promises you can't keep, not even to yourself.' He opened his mouth but she laid a finger on his lips. 'You can't control what happens here in Vienna. Put your mind to your future. That is all I ask. That you be happy.'

'How can I be? Knowing that I ran out of here like a rat? Leaving my brother and sister, you and father. And Grandpapa.'

She led him to the bed so they could both sit – she was getting a crick in her neck staring up at him. 'Samuel, that guilt will eat you up inside. You are not responsible for any of this. We know, you know, you wouldn't be getting on that ship if you had a choice. You can't make a good life if you are constantly looking over your shoulder into the past.' She stood up and walked to her wardrobe, taking out a small box. She removed two photographs and a smaller item. She closed the box and returned it to its hiding place.

Returning to sit beside him, she handed over the photographs.

'My bar mitzvah.'

Sarah nodded. 'The whole family came for your special day. I was the proudest mother in Vienna – no, in the whole of Austria.' Then she gave him the second photograph. 'Your father and I on our wedding day.'

His finger ran over the image. 'You look so happy.'

'We were blessed with a loving marriage. I want the same for you. Don't rush into a relationship because you are lonely or missing us.' Sarah swallowed, and then produced the smaller item she had removed. She took his hand and placed a diamond and emerald ring into it.

'Mama, your engagement ring! I thought the Nazis took it.'

'Your father told me to remove it when they crossed into Vienna. He said to hide it. I had never removed it from my hand, not since the day he put it on. It was his mother's ring and although it's extremely valuable, the sentimental worth is price-less. Now, as my eldest son, it is yours. Take your time to find the right girl to wear it. Pick someone we would approve of.'

'Didn't you tell me the perfect woman hadn't been born yet and her father was dead?' Although he tried to joke, Samuel's voice trembled with emotion. He tucked the ring inside the small pocket she had sewn into the belt area of his trousers, beside a precious five US-dollar note.

'I may have been too picky. I only want the best for you, my son.' Sarah lost control and grabbed him to her, wanting to hold on to him and never let go.

A knock on the bedroom door a while later admitted her father. 'It is time.'

Sarah nodded, pushing Samuel from her so she could hold his face in her hands. 'Go with God, my son.'

He held her so close, his heart beat next to hers. She felt him trembling, and then the moment when he dug deep into his strength and straightened his spine. He stood up. 'I will see you again, Mama. I promise.'

Walking from her, he didn't look back. He clasped his grandfather's hand. 'Thank you, Grandpapa, for all your lessons – the ones I enjoyed and the others too. If I grow to be half the man you are, I will be happy.'

Sarah saw tears glistening on her father's cheeks as he hugged Samuel. She heard him whisper something but couldn't make out the words. Then she heard the door to the apartment bang.

With that, Sarah lay on her bed and cried until her tears ran dry.

A week later, Connie came home from work to find a letter with an Austrian stamp waiting for her. She ripped it open, reading the contents before she even took off her coat. Then she ran up the stairs.

'Dottie? Listen to this!'

'Connie, you gave me a fright. What's wrong? Why are you shouting? Oh... is that from Sarah?'

'She's finally written but she doesn't mention any of our letters. What if she never got them? She might not know we were worried about her and wanted her to leave Austria.'

Connie skimmed Sarah's letter again. 'She must be worried her letters are being read or censored in some way. Listen. "The children miss you and speak of our trip to Salzburg. Leah still remembers the café where we had tea and Daniel talks about the train station. Have you news of our mutual young friend? Ben is still away but we remain hopeful he will return to us soon. We have no other news for now. We hope things are progressing well in London. Do you think you will visit us soon? Your friend, Sarah."' Connie tapped the letter with her finger. 'Ben still hasn't returned to live with them, and now Samuel must have left too. Otherwise, why make a point of mentioning Leah and Daniel?'

Dottie nodded, her expression thoughtful. 'I wonder if she thinks Samuel will write to us. Is he coming to London?'

Connie shrugged. 'I wish I knew. If only we could pick up the telephone and have a real conversation. Or, even better, go and see Sarah and her family and find out what is going on.'

Dottie bit the end of her pen. 'Why can't we do just that? Hitler hasn't stopped foreign travel, has he? Vienna sounds quite grim for Sarah and her people, but we should be able to travel freely around the place. They wouldn't dare attack two British subjects, would they?'

'Dottie, that's the best idea I've heard in a long time. Tomorrow I shall go into Cook's and see how soon we can go. Now, get some writing done. You need to get that book finished or I may have to go to Vienna alone.'

Connie closed the door behind her, thinking about their plan. They couldn't just arrive at Sarah's home. That could look suspicious and cause more trouble. Much as she wanted to be in Vienna as soon as possible, it would make more sense to try to coincide their visit with an opera. But would one be available? It was coming to the end of the season. She wished she could telephone Clemens but he was away. She'd just have to wait until Cook's opened tomorrow and make enquiries then.

The morning dragged by, not helped by Connie watching the office clock until finally her lunch break arrived. Grabbing her coat, she strode out of the office and, taking a tube, was in the queue in Cook's travel agency fifteen minutes later.

'Miss Fitzwalter, how lovely to see you again. How is your sister? Has she completed another book? My wife loves her stories.' Mr Donaldson ran a hanky across his brow, serving only to make his bald patch shinier.

'I'll ask Dottie to sign a copy as soon as the new book comes out. I'll bring it here myself.'

'You are so kind. Now, how can I be of assistance?'

'We decided to celebrate the end of her novel by taking a trip to Vienna. We so love the city. I was wondering if you knew of any operas taking place there?'

'Let me have a look.' He took out a folder and leafed through it before looking up with a satisfied gleam in his eye. '*Der Trompeter von Säckingen* by Viktor Nessler. Have you seen it?'

'Not yet.' And if she had anything to do with it, she never would. A favourite of the Nazi regime, little wonder that was the one on show. 'Is it too late to book tickets?'

'It is very popular, but I can book two tickets for the Saturday evening, two weeks from now. Would that work for you?'

Two weeks. Did they really have to wait that long? But what was the alternative? Arriving in Vienna on a sightseeing trip and the first visit they made being to a Jewish family would set teeth on edge if the Nazis were making life difficult for Sarah.

'That would be lovely. Can you book our hotel too, please?'

'Of course.'

She waited as he made the necessary phone calls and totalled the bill for the trip before writing him out a cheque. 'Thank you, Mr Donaldson. We appreciate your help. Enjoy the rest of your day.'

Connie hurried down the road to the tube, noting her lunch time was almost over. As soon as she got back to her desk, she wrote up the application for some time off. She'd need the Friday, Saturday morning and Monday just be sure. Three days in total. *If only I had a job like Dottie's where nobody keeps tabs on how many days' holiday you take.*

. . .

That evening, Connie knocked on Dottie's door, hearing the *tap tap* of the typewriter keys.

'I hope you're almost finished, as we are going to Vienna,' she said, as she came into the room. 'I called into Cook's at lunch time and booked everything, including the opera tickets.'

Dottie looked up, surprised. 'What are we going to see?'

'*Der Trompeter von Säckingen* by Viktor Nessler.'

Dottie turned up her nose before Connie quickly explained: 'It's better we have a reason for visiting Vienna, in case Sarah's family is under suspicion. I have little interest in going to see *Der Trompeter* but needs must. It was the only one available, it being so late in the season. Also, I don't think we should see anyone else on this trip. We can't smuggle any jewellery or meet with anyone other than Sarah. I couldn't bear it if we made life more difficult for her. Does that make sense, or do you think I'm making too much of things?'

Dottie took the page out of the typewriter. 'I think you should follow your instinct. It hasn't failed us yet.'

Connie blew her a kiss. 'Oh, by the way, I promised a signed copy of your book to Mr Donaldson. He said it is for his wife, but I think it might be for him. You have a secret admirer.'

'Go away. I have work to do.'

Connie walked away, laughing. But she stopped when Stephen's face came to mind. Should she let him know they were going to Vienna? No, he'd only worry, and he had enough to deal with. He might also say they shouldn't go and while he had no right to tell her what to do, she didn't enjoy arguing with him. He wouldn't be able to help Sarah and her family, not when they didn't live in Germany. She'd tell him when they got back.

THIRTY-SIX

Two weeks later, their train pulled into Vienna station. Apart from the yet-again increased presence of uniformed men strutting around, the place seemed to be the same as it had been the year before. They booked into their small hotel without any issues.

'I think we should go to Sarah's home to see what the situation is. She may not feel comfortable meeting us in public.'

They had only visited Sarah's apartment once before, but they were confident they would be able to find it relatively easily.

As they walked, Dottie muttered, 'Do you think anyone realizes just how ridiculous all those flags look?' She nodded at the swastika flags draped down the front of many of the buildings. 'They make this beautiful city look as if it has been invaded by a swarm of spiders, or horrid ants.'

Connie nudged her sister to be quiet as another group of brownshirts marched past them.

'That's another thing, why do they have to march everywhere? Do they like the sound of their boots on the cobblestones? Does it make them feel important?'

Connie frowned. 'Dottie, you will get us both arrested! Will you be quiet? What's come over you?'

'I'm angry. How dare they march into this wonderful city and take it over?'

Connie took her sister's arm as they walked. 'I think you will find that many of those marchers were born here in Austria. Stephen says there were more Austrians in the Nazi party than anyone realized – when it was illegal to be a member, I mean. Back before they shot Mr Dollfuss.'

'Do you remember how annoyed we were when they did that? All I cared about was whether we would miss the opera festival. I didn't for a second think about what it might mean for our friends.'

'How could you? Back in '34 nobody would have thought anyone would be living like this.' Connie peered up at the name of the street. 'I think this might be it.'

They walked up to the double doors of the block but before they could ring a bell, a man who appeared to be a caretaker, Connie judged from the toolbox in his hand, greeted them.

'Can I help you?'

'We're friends of Mrs Sarah Liberman. Does she live here?' Connie spoke confidently in German, even though her knees had turned to jelly. What if this man had taken over Sarah's home? Wasn't that what Sonja's father had told them? That Nazis just threw Jewish people out of their homes if they took a fancy to it.

'Yes, Frau Liberman still lives here. Allow me to show you.' The man spoke softly, but they saw him looking up and down the street. He opened the main door, standing aside to let them enter, checking once more behind him before he entered and closed the door behind them. 'It doesn't pay to be too careful. Many wish Frau Liberman and her family harm.'

He walked up the stairs and then pointed to a door. 'This is her front door. Tell her I said hello.'

Then he was gone.

They stood looking at one another for a couple of seconds before knocking. It seemed to take an eternity before they heard footsteps on the other side of the door. Then it opened, but only a fraction of an inch.

'Can I help you?'

'Sarah? It's us, Connie and Dottie.'

Sarah opened the door, her eyes wide with amazement. 'It's really you! Come in! Quickly. Shut the door behind you. What are you doing here?'

'We got your letter but we didn't understand it. It worried us so we came to see you, to help...'

But Sarah continued as if Connie hadn't spoken. 'It is so good to see you.' She fired one question after the other as she hugged each of them in turn before leading them into the large sitting room.

Connie tried not to stare at the walls where paintings had once hung.

'Would you like something to eat or drink? I don't have any coffee now, but I can make you a mint tea?'

'A glass of water would be perfect. Where are the children?'

'In the bedroom, hiding. I didn't know who was at the door. Let me get them.'

Connie bit back a sob when she saw Leah and Daniel. Neither looked like the children they had met in Salzburg. Both were too thin for a start, but it was the air of despair and sadness that enveloped them that brought a tear to her eye. She saw Dottie wipe her eyes.

'How lovely to see you. My, you've grown so much, Daniel! And Leah, how beautiful you are. You look just like your mother.'

'Thank you,' Leah murmured, her voice sounding as strained as she looked.

'Leah, can you fetch some water for our guests? Daniel, ask

your grandfather to join us if he'd like to. I imagine he heard the knock at the door.'

'Yes, Mama.'

The children disappeared to do Sarah's bidding.

Connie saw her own shock at Sarah's appearance and behaviour mirrored on Dottie's face. Sarah, who'd once been so polished in her appearance, looked dishevelled, her nails bitten to the quick. She was thinner than the children.

'Sarah, please sit down and tell us what is going on. We came as soon as we got your letter. We guessed it was a message of some sort but we didn't understand.' Even the worst of their imaginings hadn't been as awful as this reality.

'You got it?'

'Yes. We were worried. Where is Ben?'

'He's a guest at the Metropole hotel.'

Connie exchanged a glance with Dottie. Why was Ben staying in a hotel when his family were starving and falling apart?

Dottie looked to Sarah for clarification, asking, 'The large hotel we passed, on the banks of the Danube?'

'The very one. They have converted it into Gestapo head-quarters.'

Gestapo. Connie felt the blood chill in her veins. What did those men want with Ben? Sarah continued in a monotone, her lack of emotion distressing. 'The basement is used as a prison, amongst other things. I don't know what to do. Nobody will let me see him. I know he's still alive as they allow me to collect his laundry.' Sarah laughed, but it was almost a maniacal sound. 'They have Kurt Von Schuschnigg, the now-deposed chancellor, and Baron de Rothschild, the head of the Austrian banking family, held there too. Rumour has it that they make those men clean the Gestapo toilets. Who would do such a thing?'

Connie choked back her tears. Falling apart would not help this family. She wanted to grab all of them and head back to the station and take the first train out of this once beautiful city that had turned into something horrific, straight from Grimms' fairy tales. But that wasn't possible. 'Sarah, we're so sorry. What can we do?'

'Nothing for Ben, but can you get the children out? Samuel is on his way to New York. To a stranger. But at least he is safe. Or at least I hope he is. He left three weeks ago, and we haven't heard a word. I'm so worried. I can't sleep or eat. I must look a sight.' Sarah ran a hand through her hair.

Dottie stared at their friend, a helpless look on her face. Connie tried to get a grip of the situation. She curbed her feelings of panic and tried to focus on being practical.

'Let's start at the beginning. But first, when is the last time you had something to eat?'

Sarah held up her hands. 'I can't eat. My stomach revolts at the smell.'

'That's not good for you. You need your strength. Have you food? Or can we take you to a restaurant?' At the crazed look on Sarah's face, Connie gathered that was a stupid suggestion. 'Can we go and find something, in a shop maybe?'

'You can't buy food and bring it here. They will follow you.' Sarah moved to the window and looked outside, biting her lip. 'Did they follow you here?'

Dottie and Connie exchanged a worried look before Connie said, 'Nobody followed us but the nice man who showed us where you lived, he checked to make sure.'

'The caretaker? Herr Bentall is a nice Nazi. He brings milk and bread sometimes. For the children.'

Connie took a step towards the door. 'I shall go and ask him to buy some food.'

'No.' At the terror in Sarah's voice, Connie froze. 'We have enough. It is better you don't bring attention to the fact you are here.' Sarah sat back down at the edge of her chair. 'It is so good to see you.'

Connie retook her seat, wondering now if they had done the right thing in coming. Had their visit placed the family at more risk?

'Nobody will tell me anything.' Sarah put her hand to her mouth. 'Sorry, I keep repeating myself, don't I? I think I'm losing my mind.'

Leah returned from the kitchen with a tray set with three glasses and a jug of water. She put it on the table, pouring a glass for each of them. But she didn't take a seat. Once she'd handed out the glasses, she disappeared in the direction of the bedroom.

'Leah isn't herself. She was attacked by some friends of the boys.'

'Attacked?' Connie clenched her hands. 'The poor girl.'

'They didn't hurt her, not really, but they scared her. It could have been much worse... there have been some horrible stories of women being taken against their will.' Sarah's cheeks flushed scarlet. 'I have to get her out of Vienna, but I don't know how.'

'Can she come to London as a student? Like Else did?'

'She hasn't finished school. They kicked all the children out in June. There are some Jewish schools, but I don't want her on the streets. She stays home with Daniel. Only I go out now. Papa, he isn't like he was.'

Nothing was like it was. Connie couldn't bear to see her friend so upset.

'Leah is seventeen now, isn't she? She could apply to come to England as a domestic.' Sarah looked incredulous, but Connie ploughed ahead. 'Of course she doesn't have any experi-ence as a domestic and probably wouldn't know how to clean a house. I know I wouldn't, but can't you pretend she does? Or maybe she could come as a governess. There are women at work – they know people with children. We don't. All our friends are single like us, but they must know someone.'

'We shall find out when we get home.' Dottie took charge. 'For now, you eat. There must be something we can do.'

Sarah hugged herself around the waist. 'I don't have any money. I spent it all on trying to get Samuel out and then what was left has gone on bribes at the prison. I... I sold some artwork. Not as many as you would think – some of the paintings walked off the walls when we had a visit from the Gestapo.'

'They were *here*?'

'Yes. They came to check on our living arrangements. They kicked Papa out of his apartment. One of their women friends now lives there. They said they would be back soon to take this one, but Papa thinks the caretaker has a friend somewhere. They haven't come back. Yet.'

'So how do you buy food?'

'We have a friend, a gentile. Hedwig brings us whatever she can spare.'

Connie opened her purse and took out the reichsmarks they had left over from the last trip to Germany. 'Do the shops take German currency? I don't remember what we used when we last visited.'

'They love everything German.'

The bitterness in Sarah's voice cut through Connie. She had to get her friend out of Vienna before the woman lost her grip on reality.

'Then give this to your friend, Hedwig. Ask her to buy what she can – maybe she can store some of it at her home. Just in case.' If the Nazis came to take the house, they were unlikely to allow Sarah to take the food. 'You must give this Hedwig our home address. Just in case you do have to move.' Connie left the money on the table and took a seat beside Sarah. She put her arm around her friend. 'We will get you all out of Vienna. I don't know how, but we will, trust us.'

Sarah turned her face into Connie's shoulder and sobbed.

Isaac shuffled into the sitting room sometime later, but

Sarah didn't move. She kept her head where it was, the tears still flowing.

Isaac nodded a greeting at the sisters. 'My daughter is lucky to have such good friends. I heard you tell her you can help her leave. Please do all you can for her and the children.'

'We will try to help you too.' Connie couldn't remember the man's surname and she'd been brought up not to use an elderly man's first name.

Isaac nodded and took a seat in the armchair. 'I got a letter a few days back. Herr Bentall brought it to me. I am being sent home in a week. To Poland, to the land I left as a boy of twelve.'

'Papa.' The anguished cry in Sarah's voice broke something inside Connie. She struggled to hold back her tears.

'Don't cry, Sarah, we both knew this was coming. I have had a long and happy life in Vienna.'

Dottie and Connie stood; Dottie spoke first. 'We shall leave you to discuss the news in private. We'll come back tomorrow. If you need us before then, call or ask someone to call to our hotel.'

Sarah shook her head. 'You shouldn't return here tomorrow, just in case someone saw you call. They won't like it: Jewish people conversing with foreigners. I'm sorry, but I can't risk upsetting them.'

Connie wanted to protest but Dottie spoke again. 'We won't come back if it makes you more anxious. But we will write and we will find a way to help. We promise you that.'

The two sisters couldn't speak as they walked back to the hotel, their arms tightly linked together, each caught up in the sorrows that had befallen their friends.

When they got to their room, Dottie took a writing pad from her bag and wrote something.

Connie paced the room.

'You're distracting me. Can't you sit down?' Dottie complained.

'We should get ready for the opera.' Connie half hoped Dottie would refuse to go. But that could be dangerous for Sarah, if the authorities were watching them.

Dottie bit the end of her pen before writing something and handing the page to Connie.

I don't want to go but we should or it will look suspicious

Connie nodded, relieved her sister was thinking the same thing. Or they were both paranoid.

'Will we have dinner here in the hotel, or a restaurant?' Connie asked, playing the part of the eager tourist.

'Here, I think. Look at the time. We'd best get moving or we will miss it.'

No such luck. But Connie stayed silent.

They couldn't concentrate on the opera, not when they were surrounded by men in uniform. Connie shuffled in her seat, counting the seconds until the final curtain and they could return to their hotel.

She got as far as the interval before she stood up, claiming loudly to have a bad headache. Dottie didn't argue and, arm in arm, they began walking back to their hotel.

'Do you think Stephen can help?'

Connie shook her head. 'Not his territory.'

Dottie nodded. 'I want to murder the next person I see in a uniform.'

Connie couldn't chide her sister; she knew exactly how she felt. They returned to their hotel in silence, getting undressed for bed.

Dottie picked up pen and paper again.

'What are you writing? Surely not notes for one of your stories?' Even her sister couldn't see anything romantic in this scenario.

Dottie put a finger to her mouth before making her way over to Connie's side and whispering: 'I'm making a list of things we need to do. We must get the address Samuel went to in America to check if he arrived. That will help to reduce Sarah's suffering. We must speak to Mama and see if she can find a friend willing to take Leah and Sarah on as domestic servants.'

Connie opened her mouth, but Dottie waved her pen in the air. 'I know they have no experience, so we need someone wealthy enough to give them a job to meet the visa requirements but not someone who needs a servant. And then there is Daniel. We need someone to sponsor him. There must be someone who will offer the poor boy a home.'

Connie kissed her head as her sister bent over her list. 'You are incredible, and I love you.'

Dottie brushed a tear from her eye. 'Making a list is easy. Finding these people in time to save Sarah and her family will be the hard part.'

The next day being a Sunday, the sisters went to church. They didn't usually bother at home but both felt the need to say a prayer. The service was packed. Connie couldn't help but look around the congregation wondering how many of those kneeling and praying were helping people like Sarah. Or were they actively hurting them? The pastor said nothing in his sermon about the actions of the Nazis. He didn't mention the mobs of people who attacked respectable old men like Isaac or children like Leah.

The service did nothing to make them feel better; if anything, they felt worse. They walked around, wanting to be able to talk in private.

'I wanted to walk up to the pulpit and shout at all those people praying in the church to wake up. To see that Jewish people are the same as we are. Just normal people. Why didn't that pastor say anything? Isn't it his job to warn people about evil?'

'I think people are scared, Connie. That man yesterday, the one Sarah calls the nice Nazi, he seemed terrified that someone might be watching him. Yet he helps Sarah in his own way. Stephen told you people were disappearing in Germany. He said the first people the Nazis took away were the communists and those who dared say anything about Hitler. It's that fear that is making people act the way they do.'

'I think that's too simplistic.' At the look of hurt in her sister's eyes, Connie immediately apologized. 'Sorry, Dottie, I didn't mean to hurt your feelings. I just think it is easy to say people have to act a certain way because if they don't, they will be taken away somewhere. That fear may account for some of it. But groups of people attacking innocents in the street, making them wash the pavements with toothbrushes, burning down synagogues and sacred scrolls, beating up women and children and all the other things they are doing... Fear doesn't make people turn into braying violent mobs.'

'So what does?'

'Hate.'

They returned to the hotel, repacked their case and made their way to the train station. They had plenty of time but preferred to spend it in the waiting room rather than walking the streets of Vienna.

Connie thought about the adverts she had seen in the *Guardian*. Who did she know who might give Leah a job as a governess? Would they be able to secure Sarah a job as a domestic? She was an excellent cook – of foreign food, yes, but maybe some people would like that. Daniel was young enough to be fostered, wasn't he?

Glancing around to make sure they were alone and therefore couldn't be overheard, she whispered, 'Dottie, we need to speak to Mr Auerbach when we get home. He and Mr Cohen have lots of contacts in the Jewish community. They may know of some people who can help Sarah and her family.'

Dottie's face lit up with enthusiasm. 'Even if they don't, they are better placed to know of ways to get the Libermans out. That's a brilliant idea.'

Connie motioned to Dottie's bag. 'Let's make a list of all the people we know with children. They may need a governess. Or they may have other friends who need one.'

Dottie took out her pen and pad and scribbled away. As her sister wrote the list, Connie glanced at the clock, hoping their train would be on time. She wanted to speak to Stephen, hear his voice on the telephone if even just to say hello. She knew he was taking risks, into something more than his official embassy role. Was he putting himself in harm's way? Was there a Gestapo list somewhere with Stephen's name on it?

Raw fear sent a chill down her spine causing her to shudder. Dottie glanced at her, but Connie burrowed her face in her scarf, pretending to be cold. She couldn't share her fears with Dottie. Putting them into words would only make them more real, and they were vivid enough already.

Sarah washed and ironed her father's shirts. Leah sewed in a missing button on his best suit. Daniel shined his shoes. They all tried to be cheerful despite the circumstances. At sunset, the start of Sabbath, Isaac led the prayers, asking God to look after their family. He would be leaving the next morning.

The children said goodbye before retreating to their bedrooms, leaving Sarah alone with her father.

'Be strong, my daughter. I'm so very proud of you.' Isaac held her close, wrapping his arms around her. She tried to hold back the tears.

A knock on the front door made them jump. 'I thought you were to go to the synagogue. Why have they come here?' Sarah couldn't stop herself shaking.

They walked into the hall and Sarah watched as her father opened the door. Two men, tall, blond and blue-eyed, dressed in *Wehrmacht* uniforms, barged inside. They looked like a picture advert for Hitler's Aryan race. Sarah clenched her teeth so hard to stop herself crying out, they almost cracked. She prayed her children would remain in their rooms.

'You are the Jew, Isaac Borgor?'

'Yes.'

One of the Germans turned to the two policemen who had accompanied them. 'You will remain at this door. Shoot anyone who tries to escape.' The policemen gave the Hitler salute.

The man returned the salute before slamming the door closed. Then he turned to Sarah.

'Make some coffee, please.'

Sarah was about to protest she didn't have any when the other man pushed a parcel of coffee into her hands. They trembled so much, she almost dropped it.

She couldn't look at her father but headed into the kitchen and put the water on to boil. She set a tray and waited. The kettle took forever but eventually it whistled. She carried the coffee and two cups to the sitting room.

Entering, she stopped in her tracks. Her father sat on a chair, the two Germans sitting on the sofa.

'I brought you some cold water. I assume you drink your coffee black?' Not that it mattered, as she didn't have any milk.

One man got up and took the tray from her hands. 'Why did you only bring two cups? The coffee is for us all.'

Sarah risked looking at his face to find him smiling. He gestured to the other man, who got up and walked in the direction of the kitchen.

'Sarah, these men are not what they seem.'

Sarah couldn't believe her ears. What did her father mean?

The second man reappeared carrying two ordinary cups. 'I couldn't find the nice ones and I didn't want to search your cupboards.'

Sarah wanted to pinch herself but the blonder of the two spoke again.

'Your father and husband saved my father's life in the first war, Frau Liberman. Some of us do not forget such things. I am here to repay the debt. We have only recently been posted to Vienna and came as soon as we found your father's name on a list. We would have come sooner but we had to make sure a few details were ironed out. Please sit down and don't be afraid. We mean you no harm.'

Sarah sat. She had little choice; her legs had turned to jelly. The man who'd spoken to her poured a cup of coffee, adding a little cold water to it before he handed it to her. Seeing her hand trembling, he placed it on the table nearest to her chair.

'Things are much worse here in Vienna than they are in Berlin. That is where we were stationed up to now. There the Jews go to see operas, theatre and shows, just not the same as the ones for true Aryans. The Jewish Council has set up their own. People are not attacked on the street, never mind being made to wash pavements. That would never happen in Berlin.'

Sarah kept a neutral expression on her face, not wanting to show him how insulting he was being. She guessed he thought he was being friendly. He spoke as if the segregation he described was reasonable.

'Here, they have gone mad. The things we have seen people do. Demanding men in top hats and women in fur coats to scrub graffiti off the walls with toothbrushes. That isn't what Hitler wants.'

Sarah wasn't inclined to argue. She took a sip of coffee, hoping he would get to the point of his visit.

'We will take your father away with us, Frau Liberman, but you have my word he will come to no harm. We will escort him to the Metropole hotel—'

Sarah's stomach churned.

'—where we will collect your husband, Benjamin. He, Isaac, and a few other men will be assisting us with our enquiries. That is what we will tell the men in charge. We have paperwork to validate our claims. We will personally escort the group to Poland.'

Sarah groaned. To lose her father was bad enough, but Ben too?

The man continued as if he hadn't heard. 'Once there, we have some contacts who will help them leave. We know your eldest son is in America. Unfortunately, our contacts do not extend that far. But we are confident we can secure passage to Britain.' The man smiled, she assumed he meant to be reassuring. 'The answer to the Jewish question is emigration. That is what our führer wants. Ideally you would travel to Palestine, but the British have not been as accommodating as one would have hoped they would. Quite why they allow the Arabs to dictate terms is beyond our comprehension.' He glanced at Sarah.

Was she expected to explain it to him? She took another sip of her drink.

He hadn't introduced himself and it didn't appear as if he was going to give her a name. He took a rather large gulp of his coffee and stood once more. 'Would it be possible for you to pack a small bag for your husband? Having been a guest at the Metropole, he will certainly need a change of clothes.'

Sarah nodded. She glanced at her father.

'May I help my daughter?'

'Of course. Just don't take long. We don't want to risk anyone coming to check why two policemen are on guard at your door.'

Sarah walked to her bedroom, her father shuffling behind her. Once he was inside the room, she closed over the door, not completely. Keeping her voice to a whisper and her eyes on the sitting room door, she asked, 'Papa, who are they? Is it a trap?'

'I don't think so, no. The young man told me his father's name and how he credits me and Benjamin with saving him. Ben could have, of course. He's a doctor after all. But I don't know what he thinks I did.' Isaac scratched his beard before shrugging. 'You should pack a case for Ben. We should take up their offer.'

'But what if this makes things worse?'

'How? Killing us quickly would be a blessing. Ben isn't coming home, at least not back to this apartment. You know that. They will ship him to a concentration camp. Someone has protected him thus far, but who knows when that protection will run out. This is a chance. Maybe our only one. We must take it. Those men didn't have to come here.'

'Yes, but you heard what they were saying, how they spoke about Hitler's plans. They aren't our friends.'

'No, but they aren't murderers, either.'

Sarah took Ben's suit from the wardrobe, a fresh shirt and underwear from his drawer and packed it into a small bag. She added a set of cufflinks and a gold lighter. If his bag wasn't searched, he might be able to use them as bribes. She took a photo of the family from her box and placed it on top of his passport before she shut the case.

'Papa, tell Ben I love him.'

'I will. We will write as soon as we can.'

Sarah gave him a hug but then, hearing the men speaking more loudly, she picked up the bag and walked back to the sitting room. 'Papa needs his stick. He can't walk too far without it these days.'

'Of course. We must be going now. Is there anything we can do for you before we go?'

'No, thank you. I'm grateful to you for your help.'

The taller and more talkative of the two men extended his right hand in the Hitler salute before colouring, having realized what he had almost done.

Sarah stood against the wall as her father walked down the hallway, escorted on either side by the uniformed men.

When the door slammed shut behind them, her whole body shook and she thought she might be sick. Would she ever hear from her father or Ben again? Or had this all been an elaborate trick, another form of torture devised to hurt her people?

THIRTY-EIGHT

LONDON, SEPTEMBER 1938

Connie met with her friends Isabella and Sybil at the Tottenham Court Road Lyons' Corner House.

'Mama is so happy with you. She keeps praising your fundraising efforts.'

Isabella, the more vivacious of the two, spoke first: 'I don't know where she gets her energy. She is always moving. And you should hear her charm the donors! She could sell snow to the Eskimos.'

Connie forced a smile of agreement.

'Connie, what's wrong? You look rather down in the dumps.'

'I'm sorry. I really am grateful for all you have done but we have a rather pressing case at the moment. One of our dearest friends is in trouble and we are struggling with how to get her family out of Vienna. There are five of them in total. Two adult males, although one may be in Poland – or at least we think he is. We need more immediate help finding places for Sarah, my friend; and her daughter, Leah, and the younger son, Daniel.'

Isabella exchanged a look with her sister. 'We can help. We've been saving and have almost enough money to sponsor another adult. Mother and Father have also agreed, finally, to offer to home a child refugee, so that takes care of two of your friends. How old is the daughter?'

'About seventeen.'

'Could she work as a governess? Does she speak any languages other than German? French might be useful?'

'Bella, give Connie a chance! You are rather throwing ideas at her.' Sybil admonished her sister gently.

'Not at all. I think you're wonderful.' Connie smiled at her friends. 'I don't know about languages but she is well educated, so should be suitable as a governess.' She glanced at the clock. 'I have to run or I'll be late back and Miss Fowler is bound to be waiting. Can we talk about this more when we meet on Saturday? You are going to the opera, aren't you?'

'Wild horses couldn't stop us. Now go and don't worry. We'll think of something for your friend's family.'

Connie returned from work later that week to find Dottie in excellent spirits.

'I thought you would never walk in that door. If it wasn't raining so much, I would have come to meet you from the bus.'

'What is it? Why are you so happy?'

'We got a telegram today. From Ben Liberman. He and Sarah's father are here in Britain.'

Connie's mind raced: relief her friends were safe fighting with confusion. 'They are? But how? Ben was in prison and Isaac, they said he had to go to Poland.'

'They both went to Poland and from there they came here. They didn't go into how it happened, but they've asked if they can call to see us on Sunday next. Maybe they have news of Sarah and the children.' Dottie hugged the letter to her chest. 'Isn't it wonderful? Sarah must be so relieved.'

Sunday couldn't come fast enough. Mama asked Cook to

bake a special cake, and Connie couldn't concentrate on work – even Dottie was hard-pressed to write. But, finally, the day arrived.

Connie kept a watch on the road as the minutes ticked past. The men were due at four but it was almost five before they heard the rusty hinge on the gate creak and then footsteps on the path. Connie had the door opened almost before they got a chance to knock.

When she saw Ben, she couldn't speak. The man in front of her bore little resemblance to the man she'd met in Austria. His once speckled brown hair was now completely white and his smile was missing two front teeth. He'd lost so much weight, his clothes hung on his frame. Isaac almost looked younger and stronger.

'Come in, please. Make yourself at home. This is my mother, Mrs Fitzwalter. And of course you know Dottie.'

Connie waited until the men were inside to close the door.

'Sorry we are so late, we took the right tube but in the wrong direction. We ended up almost at the other end of the line.' Isaac's voice sounded the same.

'Oh, that doesn't matter! It is so good to see you! Please sit down. We are dying to hear your news but first, would you like a cup of tea or coffee? Cook made a lovely fruit cake specially.'

The men took a seat while Connie excused herself to go to the kitchen to make the coffee.

Dottie joined her. 'What did they do to that poor man? Did you see his teeth? He must have been tortured.' Dottie waved a hand in front of her face. 'I can't cry. I won't cry.'

Connie handed her a hanky. 'Dearest, you are already crying.'

Dottie blew her nose as Connie made up a tray of cups, plates, the cake and finally the coffee pot. She carried it into the sitting room, leaving Dottie to bring in the tray with the teapot, milk jug and some cold water.

When they entered the room, the conversation was flowing between Mama and Isaac, but Ben looked to be exhausted from their journey. 'Forgive me. I have yet to regain my strength.'

'Ben, you look dreadful. Have you seen a doctor? Should you be in hospital? Are you taking proper care of yourself?' Dottie peppered him with questions, leaving Mama to come to the rescue.

'Dorothea, stop haranguing our guest.'

Ben gave a tired smile. 'I know it's because she cares. Your daughters have big hearts, Mrs Fitzwalter. Isaac told me how you visited my Sarah. Thank you for doing that. He said you might be able to help us get her and the children out.'

'Yes, Connie has been working on that. With friends of ours. Isabella and her sister, Sybil, would sponsor Sarah. Their mother and father will foster Daniel, and we think we have found a position as a governess for Leah. We are just finalizing the details.'

Ben swiped tears from his eyes before he leaned back in the chair. 'That's wonderful news. My family will be safe.'

'We just need some paperwork. I've written to Sarah and am awaiting her reply. We haven't had a letter in a while.' Connie didn't add how worried that had made them. Instead, she turned to Isaac. 'How did you get out? If you don't mind me asking?'

'It's a long story and somewhat unbelievable. On the day I was due to be sent to Poland, we opened the door to the apartment to be met by two *Wehrmacht* officers. They escorted me to the prison where Ben was being kept, ordered his release, and escorted us and two other men by train to the Polish border. They signed some paperwork, paid some bribes to the Polish border officials, and left us on a train to Warsaw with an address and contact details of a man known to be helpful to Jewish people. From there, our passports were stamped and here we are.'

'Why would the *Wehrmacht* help you?' Dottie asked.

'They believe in solving what they called the "Jewish prob-lem" by emigration. Ben saved the man's father in the last war. When he was posted to Vienna, and realized the gravity of our situation, he decided to help.'

Given the state of both men and the look in their eyes, Connie couldn't help but feel the trip had been more fraught than Isaac was letting on, but she decided not to question him. It wouldn't serve any purpose and would only lead to upset.

'I think your escape deserves something a little stronger than a cup of tea. Will you join me in a sherry, Mr Borger?'

'Isaac, please, Mrs Fitzwalter. And I would love to.'

Connie sat back, listening to her mother chat to Isaac as if they were old friends as Ben dozed in the chair. Dottie excused herself, claiming she had a deadline but, knowing her sister as she did, Connie guessed she needed a little cry.

THIRTY-NINE
LONDON, SEPTEMBER 1938

Her mother put her sewing to the side. 'I'm tired so I'm going up. Are you staying here tonight, Stephen? You know you are more than welcome. And maybe a good night's rest will improve your mood.'

'Mama.' Connie couldn't believe her mother was being rude to Stephen who had turned up unannounced on their doorstep.

'I'm sorry, Aunt Margaret. I shouldn't bring my work home with me. Forgive me.'

'Nothing to forgive but do get some sleep. Those bags under your eyes become more difficult to get rid of with age. Don't ask me how I know.'

Connie waited until her mother had shut the door behind her and they heard her steps on the stairs, before turning to Stephen. 'I'm so sorry. I don't know what got into her tonight. She is probably worried about Dottie.'

'Where is Dottie?'

'On a book-signing tour in Scotland. At least that is what she told Mama. In truth, I think she is scouting out more homes for our refugees.' Connie poked the fire, before Stephen stood and took the coal bucket from her.

She sat back on the sofa watching the flames catch the new coal pieces. When he remained silent, staring into the fire, she said softly, 'Tell me what is keeping you up at night.'

'There is nothing to tell.'

'Stop lying to me, Stephen. I know you are trying to protect me, but I want to know what you are hiding. I know how things are in Germany and Vienna – we saw them shoot a man when we travelled with Mr Siegal. We've heard more from Ben, Isaac and the others. I am not fragile. I worry about you. Talk to me. I can see it in your eyes. You have seen things you never thought were possible, haven't you?'

'Oh, Connie. How could I ever have thought I would be able to hide anything from you? I... I just can't bear to put what I saw into words. It was just too horrifying.'

'Have a drink, Stephen, and tell me what you want to say in your own time. You cannot keep this inside; it will destroy you.'

He took a drink before setting it to one side. 'I went to the Jewish hospital. Connie, I knew things were bad. I'd seen Jacob Levy and others who had been released from the camps. But the scale of the suffering! This was a hospital in name only. They have nothing. They are treating patients with little more than warm water. Operations are done without anaesthetics. I just...' His voice broke as he put his face in his hands.

She wanted to take him in her arms and tell him he couldn't fix everything. He was doing his best. He was only one man up against impossible odds. But she stayed silent. Nothing would make him feel better. She edged closer to him, taking his hand in hers.

'We will find a way to help. Maybe we can give the hospital some money to buy things.'

'I fear time is against us, darling Connie. There are too many people who need help. The clock is ticking, and it seems to be getting louder.'

'But Chamberlain says there will be no war.'

'Chamberlain doesn't want a war. Don't repeat this, but he knows we are not ready to take on Germany. He cannot depend on America as although Roosevelt may be keen, his government and backers aren't behind him. The generation that fought in the last war don't want another war. They would rather do anything else to avoid it.'

'Even if it means forsaking the Jewish people?'

Stephen stared into the fire. His lack of reply chilled her to the bone.

'But we can't just stand by and let Hitler march over Europe. We must do something.'

'They have reduced the quotas for emigration visas. The Arabs don't want a whole load of Jewish people arriving en masse. On some levels I can't blame them. They are worried for their own people. Emigration is virtually impossible to most so-called civilized countries. Some South American countries have opened their borders but for a fee. Honestly, Connie, I don't know what we are going to do.'

She sat down opposite him. 'Stephen, don't apologize, this is me. I think you should retire and rest. You are exhausted, both physically and emotionally. Tomorrow we will sit down and work out what we can do. There have to be ways to help those poor people, and we will find them. Now, off you go to bed.'

'Yes, ma'am.'

She smiled at his teasing, thankful he seemed a little better, but she wanted to prove they were a team. He wasn't on his own.

Connie stood and held her hand out to help him to his feet. She didn't release his hand and he didn't pull away. She stared into his eyes. 'You are not alone, and you never have to hide anything from me. I'm stronger than I look.'

He reached over to push a curl behind her ear. Her skin tingled at his touch. Would he kiss her? He leaned in but then a floorboard creaked upstairs. He dropped her hand and walked to the door.

'Stephen, when do you go back?'

'As soon as I've briefed the boss. Mr Foley begged me to get them to allow more visas, but I fear the answer I will receive.'

'I will pray for some solutions. As Mother always says, where there's a will there's a way.'

'Your mother should have been put in charge of fighting the Nazis back in '33. She could have put them back in their place or destroyed them entirely.'

Connie allowed herself a small smile. Her mother was certainly formidable, but even she might have struggled with the Austrian maniac.

FORTY

FRANKFURT, OCTOBER 1938

Connie rubbed her eyes, discreetly stretching her muscles as the train pulled into Frankfurt station. She nudged Dottie in the side, smiling as her sister opened her eyes in wonder, forgetting for a second where she was.

'I'm getting too old for this travel.' Dottie rubbed the small of her back. 'I wish we could fly straight here, rather than catching the last flight to Cologne and then the night train.'

'Perhaps someday there will be direct flights. And we should consider using a different route next time.' Connie dropped her voice to a whisper. 'We got some funny looks from the airport staff last night.'

'They recognized us. Bit hard not to given how often we have been going back and forth. But maybe we are just being paranoid.' Dottie stood to take down her small travelling bag from the overhead baggage shelves.

'Allow me.' A young man in army uniform stepped forward and lifted the case down, handing it to Dottie with a smile. 'I hope you enjoy your time in my hometown.'

Connie admired Dottie's reaction as her sister gave him a big smile.

'It's so lovely to meet a fine young man with lovely manners. Thank you. Your mother must be very proud. You speak very good English too.'

'I went to school in Oxford. I loved it and made many friends. Would you like me to carry your case off the train?'

'Thank you but we can manage. I'm sure you are eager to get home and spend your leave with your family.'

The young man nodded in thanks and walked off the train ahead of them.

'I hope he didn't hear what you said about the airport,' Dottie whispered, as they made their way off the train.

'Even if he did, he won't have known what we were talking about. Don't worry – and mind your step.' Connie stepped down from the train first, turning to take the case from Dottie so she could climb down unhindered.

Even at this early hour, the station was busy with food vendors competing with the steam locomotives. The first time they'd come to Frankfurt to visit Clemens, they'd admired the beautiful station with the large glass windows, ornate décor, high ceilings and sparkling chandeliers. But now it was as familiar as Kings Cross station in London.

They were making their way through the throngs of people towards their exit when the sight of a soldier yelling at some civilians brought them to a standstill.

'What are they doing? Where are they going?' Dottie grabbed Connie's arm and pointed to a group of people being hustled along the platform at gun point. The group consisted of individuals of all ages – men, women and children.

The other passengers walked on, pretending not to notice, or they cheered the soldiers accompanying the group. Only one or two frowned, but nobody intervened.

'I don't know. I'll ask the porter. Wait here.' Connie hurried down the platform, spotting a porter and asking him what was going on.

He gave the group a disparaging look. 'Only Jews.' He trotted on ahead of her.

Connie could only stare after him. What did he mean, *Only Jews?* She couldn't do anything but look at the terrified bunch of people being driven down the platform to a decrepit-looking train. There they were pushed on board, those who even looked as if they would protest being treated harshly, the guards using rifle butts to hit them. Blinded by tears, she made her way back to Dottie and their small bag.

'Hurry. I have to get away from here or God help me I might grab one of those guns and shoot those brutes. What do they think they are doing? They're people, not animals! And even if they were animals that treatment would be appalling.'

Dottie rubbed her arm as they walked as quickly as possible out of the station. They boarded the tram car, sitting in silence until they came to the stop near Clemens' house.

Connie couldn't imagine how Viorica felt when she opened the door to find them in tears on her doorstep.

'Connie, Dottie, what's wrong? What happened? Clemens, come quickly. Our lovely friends are upset.' Viorica hugged them before leading them into the sitting room.

Clemens strode in, concern radiating from his face. 'Was there trouble at the airport? The station? Are you hurt?'

Connie explained what they had seen at the train station. 'It was just awful. Those poor people.'

Clemens moved to the drinks cabinet and poured two small glasses of brandy, which he insisted they drink despite the early hour. 'Medicinal purposes for the shock.'

Viorica walked over to the fireplace and rang a little bell. The maid arrived. 'Gerta, some coffee for our guests.'

Connie sat on a sofa, beside Dottie, facing the couple on another. 'What is going on? I know things have been difficult, but this was a whole group of people being escorted away on a train. Where are they going?'

Clemens ran a hand through his hair. 'For the last four days and nights people from all over Germany have been gathered up and deposited along the Polish border.'

Connie inhaled sharply. 'Why? What did they do?'

'Nothing. Some were still in their nightclothes. Under the Nazis' rules, they are not German citizens but Poles, although some of them don't speak a word of Polish.'

'How can you go to bed a German and wake up Polish? That doesn't make sense.' Connie shared Dottie's confusion.

Clemens stood up and walked over to the fireplace, standing facing them, his hands clasped behind his back.

'The government has overturned all the naturalization of people made since the last war. People who sought sanctuary from pogroms in Russia and other places felt they would be safer here. And they were, for years, but then the Nazis got other ideas. They have withdrawn their German citizenship, so they revert to being Polish. In the eyes of the Nazis, anyway. Poland has a different opinion and refuses to allow those poor devils to cross the border.'

'So where are they going to live?' Connie asked, squeezing Dottie's hand. Her sister was crying silently.

Clemens coughed as his voice trembled. He took a couple of seconds before he continued. 'Viorica and I have a friend, a reporter who visited a camp. She works for one of the American newspapers. What she told us, well... it is difficult to believe.'

'No, Clemens, not so difficult now.' Viorica clasped her hands on her knees. 'A few years ago, yes, but after the indignities our Jewish friends have been subjected to, I find it hard to be surprised anymore.'

Clemens took a seat beside her once more, taking her hand in his before he looked at Connie. 'Those that survived the trip have been put into a prison camp. They shot some of the old people and the children who didn't move as fast as they wanted them to.'

Dottie covered her face with her hands. 'No, don't tell us another word. I want to go home, Connie. Right now.'

'Shush, Dottie.' Connie put her arm around her sister's shoulders, trying to comfort her. From the start of their work, Connie had sheltered her from the worst of what she'd learned from Stephen about the treatment of the Jews. Dottie had seen for herself what Sarah was enduring but it was different hearing it from someone to experiencing it first-hand.

Dottie hiccupped as she struggled to get her emotions under control. Her voice quivered as she asked, 'What do you mean a prison camp?'

Clemens shrugged but Connie knew it was an act. He was as devastated as they were. 'They have been housed in Zbazyn. It was once racing stables, and where every horse once stood, there now lives eight people. At least eight – some stalls are even more crowded.'

Dottie sat up, shrugging Connie's arm off. 'What can we do? Surely there is someone who can close the camp and order those people be returned to their homes?'

Connie wondered how her sister could still be so innocent after everything they had heard and now seen. She hoped Clemens would be gentle in his reply.

He shook his head. 'No, my dear English ladies. There is nothing that can be done for those people.'

The maid arrived with a tray of coffee and some pastries, but nobody ate.

Viorica excused herself and returned after a couple of minutes carrying two luxurious fur coats and a small box. She handed one coat each to Connie and Dottie. 'You should wear these to tonight's performance. Then nobody will ask questions when you are wearing them on your return journey.'

Dottie opened her handbag and took out a small sewing set and some labels. She handed one to Viorica. 'We have a friend who supplies some of the best shops in London. He gave us these to sew into the coats. They may help to fool the border guards. They can be removed when we get back to London so the coats can be sold.'

Viorica clapped her hands. 'What an excellent idea!' Then she picked up the small box and handed it to Connie. 'Look inside.'

Intrigued, Connie opened the box. 'Oh, gosh, is it real? Can I take it out?'

'You will need to wear it. Leaving it in the box will only invite the border guards to steal it.'

'It's exquisite, isn't it?' Connie examined the piece in her hand: a large, pear-shaped diamond, sparkling with inner fire, was surrounded by a series of smaller, round diamonds arranged in a delicate, intricately crafted pattern as if to mimic a vine.

'They look like they're lit up from inside, don't they?' Dottie reached out her hand but hesitated to touch it.

Viorica explained: 'It is a Jacobson family heirloom, believed to have been gifted to a great aunt by a czar of Russia. The family hopes you will be able to sell it and bank the proceeds to fund their emigration. Herr Jacobson and his son are in a concentration camp.'

Connie put the brooch back in the box, wishing she didn't feel like she was in the business of buying lives. 'How do we get them out of there?'

Clemens answered: 'The local officials have advised Frau Jacobson she can secure their release in return for a donation to the party. But we must wait until you can sell the brooch and we can get papers for England, as the Nazis will only give them eight weeks to leave Germany from their release date.'

'Eight weeks? That isn't enough time to get everything done! How do they expect ordinary people to navigate all their rules and regulations, which they keep changing, in that time period?' Connie fought down the feeling of nausea in her stomach. 'I don't know if we will be able to help them fast enough.'

'Connie, my dear lady. You can only do your best. It is not your fault that these animals now hold the power of life and death over our old friends and neighbours.'

Dottie wiped a tear from her eye and Viorica moved to give her a hug. 'If only other people were so caring, then we might not be in this mess.'

Embarrassed at how emotional she had been in front of her friends, Connie excused herself. 'I think the overnight trip has left me more exhausted than I realized. Please excuse me if I go to my room.'

'Of course. We will call you later for lunch.'

* * *

Connie linked arms with Dottie as they walked towards Border Control. They were both wearing the furs. Connie had attached the fabulous brooch to her jumper, not wanting to ruin the luxurious pelt. Her pulse thundered in her ears as a man dressed in a dark suit seemed to be studying them. She tried to act nonchalantly, chatting away to Dottie about the plot of her latest novel as the queue moved ahead of them but every time she looked up, his eyes were on them.

She glanced at her sister out of the corner of her eye, but Dottie seemed blissfully unaware.

The queue progressed very slowly, with a family of four going through next. Connie watched in horror as the two men, presumably father and son due to their familiar facial characteristics, were pulled to one side, with only the women being allowed to pass through. The men were roughly manhandled to a waiting car.

Then it was their turn.

The border guard asked for their passports, his eyes roving over their appearance, appearing to linger on the brooch.

Connie didn't hold his gaze but stared at a spot of paint on the wall behind them.

He was just handing them back their passports and travel tickets when the man in the suit stepped forward.

'Your papers, please.' His English was almost accent-free.

Connie handed them to him, feeling Dottie tense up.

The man scrutinized the tickets, studied their faces and then the paperwork once more.

'That is a fine piece of jewellery you are wearing, Miss Fitzwalter.'

Connie's mouth was dry. She didn't respond but continued to stare at the paint.

'Are you hard of hearing?'

Connie pierced him with a look, adopting the same response she had used to deal with school bullies. Going to an all-girls school had taught her about bullying from a young age.

'I didn't realize you asked me a question. You expressed an opinion about my brooch.'

'*Your* brooch?'

Connie pulled herself up to her full height of five foot five. 'Do you have a question, Mr...?' She held his gaze. Despite her defiance, her heart thudded under her ribcage, each beat echoing the tension ratcheting up between them.

The man's eyes widened, his nostrils flaring at her attitude. 'The border official does not remember you wearing such a beautiful piece on your way into our country.'

Connie shrugged, trying to appear as if his recollection was beneath her while trying not to choke on the arid, bitter taste of fear in the back of her throat.

The man took a step closer, reducing the distance between them to one less than would be considered polite. She restrained the urge to step back, wrinkling her nose as his sharp cologne fought for dominance over the smell of fear around them. 'You have nothing to say?'

She stood her ground. 'I am not sure what you expect me to say. I would have thought your border officials had more pressing matters to attend to than an old brooch. Border control is usually only interested in false papers.' She held his gaze again, praying he didn't see the sweat on her forehead. 'As you can see, our British passports are very much in order. Now, may we proceed? We risk missing our connection.' She clenched her stomach, forcing herself to smile at him.

'Why were you in Frankfurt? You seem to come to our country a lot.'

Growing irritated now, she lost patience and snapped: 'We travel all over the world to see opera. Your führer himself is an enthusiast. Are you?'

'All over the world?' Scepticism dripped from the words. He sneered, his eyes widening with satisfaction.

He thought he had them.

Connie swallowed a wave of fear, not wanting to acknowledge it in case it overwhelmed her. Stephen had warned her their passports only offered them limited protection. The man would expect her to behave like she had something to hide.

Attack is the best strategy here.

Connie yanked her bag open, pulling out the photographs and newspaper articles written about their meeting Elana in New York, thrusting them in his face. 'Just in case you have never been, those pictures were taken in New York.' Her sarcastic tone matched his. 'You can see the various landmarks in the background. Or read the print in the accompanying newspapers. Now, pleasurable as this conversation may be, do I need to remind you we are not German citizens but British. We are free to travel as we see fit.'

She didn't dare look at Dottie, in case she saw her own fear mirrored on her sister's face. Instead, she glared at the official, almost baiting him.

She saw the flicker of uncertainty in his expression before

he glanced at the newspapers and once more at the brooch. He almost threw their papers back at her.

'I suggest you may want to visit your opera elsewhere in future, Miss Fitzwalter.'

Incensed, Connie retorted: 'As a loyal British subject, I shall travel where I wish, but I *will* be advising the German embassy in London of our encounter this evening. Herr Brisken is a family friend, as is his boss, Herr Ribbentrop.'

She saw his face blanch before she put her arm through Dottie's elbow and marched past the man. Her breathing was coming so fast she saw lights flashing before her eyes, but she was determined he wouldn't see her fear.

Once on the train, Connie almost fell into her seat with relief.

'You were wonderful! Thank goodness you kept those photographs of America! I was so scared I felt sick. How did you do it?' Dottie whispered although their carriage was empty.

'I imagined he was Pamela Duncan and treated him accordingly.' Connie took several deep breaths to regulate her heartbeat. 'Bullies are always cowards at heart.'

At the mention of the sisters' school bully, Dottie stared at Connie for a second before she burst out laughing. 'He *did* look at bit like that awful girl. Never thought I would have to thank her for anything but cold wet sheets. She was mean and nasty, wasn't she?'

'She'd make a perfect Nazi.'

FORTY-ONE
VIENNA, NOVEMBER 1938

Someone pounded on the front door, calling her name.

Sarah opened it to find Hedwig, her eyes wild with fear, glancing over her shoulder. 'Sarah, come quickly. Bring the children. You must leave now.'

'Hedwig, come inside. What's wrong?'

'There's trouble, the mobs are attacking Jewish shops, properties, people. It's worse than before. Grab your bags. Leah, Daniel, where are you? Come on we must leave. Now.'

Sarah didn't argue. She ran to the bedroom calling to the children to grab their bags and follow her.

Hedwig helped Leah with her coat: the girl was shaking too badly to do it herself. They froze, hearing footsteps in the hall, then Herr Bentall stuck his head through the door. 'Hurry, there isn't much time. Come on now.'

He exchanged a look with Hedwig, who nodded. She put her arm around Leah. 'It will be fine, we won't let anything happen to you. Come on now, your mother and Daniel will be right behind us, with Herr Bentall.'

Sarah held tight to her son's hand as the distant sound of shattering glass, taunting and angry shouts drew nearer. Herr

Bentall locked the front door. 'It might delay them for a few minutes.'

He led them down the back stairs, past his property and out via the back door. They huddled into the walls as they walked. Both Herr Bentall and Hedwig wore swastika arm bands so they walked on the outside of the group, Hedwig's arm around Leah, holding her close. Even from behind, Sarah could see her daughter was struggling. She prayed hard that luck would be on their side, and they would reach safety.

The sounds of high-pitched screaming was punctuated by gunfire and the whoosh of flames. They passed a burning synagogue, the rabbi and a group of Jewish men were being forced to kneel and watch as the sacred scrolls burned inside. Sarah covered Daniel's eyes, but not before he saw sights she knew he would have difficulty forgetting.

On reaching a building, Hedwig put her finger to her lips. They understood they had to stay quiet. She ushered them inside, up the stairs until they reached a door. 'This is my home.' Using a key, she opened it and pushed them inside.

Herr Bentall dropped the bags and turned to leave.

Hedwig tried to stop him. 'Will you not stay here too? It could be dangerous out there.'

'No. I might be able to protect the apartment.'

Sarah moved closer to the man. 'Don't take any risks. There is nothing of value, at least nothing that is worth you losing your life or your freedom.'

The man nodded before he left, closing the door behind him.

Hedwig ushered them into the sitting room, apologizing as she did so: 'I know it's not what you are used to but at least you will be safe here.'

'Hedwig, thank you. You are putting yourself at risk to help us. What about your father? Will he not mind?'

'My daughter is very brave and strong-willed. She will do as she wishes. She always has.'

Sarah spun around, not having seen the man sitting in the shadows. 'My apologies, Herr Berger. I didn't see you there.'

'Please sit down, make yourself at home. My daughter has told me about your family, Frau Liberman, and your kindness to her. Thank you.'

'Your daughter has done more for me than I could ever do for her. She was the one who told me to keep a bag packed in case something like this should happen.' Sarah grabbed Hedwig's hand and brought it to her cheek. 'I can never thank you enough.'

Hedwig hugged her and then, embarrassed, she pointed to a seat. 'Please sit down, it might be a long night. Daniel, let me show you where you can sleep. Leah, you will have to share with your mother and me.'

Leah didn't respond. Sarah pulled her daughter down to sit beside her, wrapping her arms around her. 'You are safe, Leah. Nobody is going to hurt you. I promise.'

FORTY-TWO

LONDON, NOVEMBER 1938

Connie and Dottie listened to the wireless, tears running down their faces as the news broke of the disturbances all over Germany and Austria. They were calling it the 'night of the broken glass'. Nobody knew how many Jewish people had died. Several hundred according to some estimates, with thousands more having been rounded up and driven off to goodness knew where.

'I wish we knew how Sarah, Leah and Daniel are doing. Ben and Isaac must be going out of their mind. They've tried ringing Sarah over the last month but the phone just rings out. Their friends in Vienna who do answer haven't heard anything. Where could they be?' Dottie asked, wiping the tears from her face. 'They couldn't be dead, could they?'

Connie couldn't answer: she didn't know. And she wasn't about to lie to her sister and tell her not to worry.

'If she's alive, Sarah will find a way to contact us. We just have to hope for the best.'

Connie couldn't even mention Stephen's name. Putting her fears into words would make the danger more real. She hoped he was safe and not out on the streets, trying to be a hero.

. . .

By the following week, there was still no news of Sarah or Stephen.

Connie put the kettle on before going upstairs to change out of her office clothes. When she came back downstairs, the kettle was whistling and Dottie was flicking through the stack of envelopes on the hall table.

Connie made the tea before walking back out to see what was keeping her sister.

'Connie, listen to this. I don't know how he found our address. Maybe he knows Clemens or someone.'

'Who?'

'A boy who has written to us. From those stables in Poland that Clemens told us about. Listen: "Dear Miss Constance and Miss Dorothea, my name is Pieter, I'm a sixteen-year-old orphan and I want to go and live in America. It is the land of opportunity. I have an uncle over there who gave me papers. Can you please help me? I heard you help lots of people. Forgive my English but I didn't get to finish school. I have written my address above. Please help. I want to live. Thank you. Pieter".'

Dottie turned to her sister, her eyes wide. 'Connie, we must help him.'

Connie hated the feeling of helplessness coming over her. 'How can we? We don't have any of our own money left, and we have a list of people waiting for guarantees.'

Dottie had a determined look on her face. 'I'm going to help this boy. I will write back and tell him to have courage and that we will do everything we can to get him out.'

'But, Dottie...'

'No buts. Can you imagine how terrified the poor child must be? To be all alone without parents or a home. We are going to help him and that's the end of it.'

Dottie took the letter with her as she went upstairs but not before Connie saw tears running down her sister's cheeks. She leaned against the kitchen door. Of course she wanted to help the child, but they could only do so much and right then it seemed impossible.

Later that evening, Dottie came searching for her. 'I'm sorry I snapped. It was a combination of a lack of sleep and those horrible men and the stories we heard and...' She threw her arms up. 'Just all of it.'

Connie went over to her sister and enfolded her in a hug. 'I know. I feel the same. I want to help the boy, I just can't see how.'

'We'll find a way. Even if I have to eat bread and drink water for the next six months, I'll do it. I've written back to him to tell him we will help.'

One week later, Dottie and their mother were entertaining some guests. Connie was reading a book in the sitting room when the front doorbell rang. As Nellie had left for the evening, Connie went to answer it, and gasped as she opened the door.

He'd lost weight, but it wasn't just that making him look older. There were black bags under his eyes, and his cheek-bones, always chiselled, were now standing like angles on his face. His hand trembled as he brushed wayward strands of grey hair from his eyes.

'Stephen, thank God. Thank God. You look exhausted. Come in and sit down. What can I get you? A brandy, a cup of tea, a sandwich?'

'Connie darling, stop fussing. I'm fine. It's nothing a few nights' decent sleep won't fix.'

Biting her lip and trying not to cry, Connie led Stephen into the small sitting room, where the fire was a beacon of light and warmth. Stephen sat down heavily on the sofa. If it weren't for the smoothness of his movements and the articulation of his voice, Connie might have mistaken him for an old man.

'Mama is entertaining guests in the drawing room. I'm sure you don't want to disturb them, but perhaps...'

'This is perfect. Can you sit with me, or are you needed?'

'Of course. I'll stay,' she whispered, determined not to cry. 'Just let me rustle up some tea and sandwiches. You look half-starved.'

Connie left the room and closed the door behind her before letting her guard fall. She blinked away her tears, biting down on her hand to strangle the cry. What had happened to the poor man since she'd seen him last?

She walked past the closed drawing room door, the sounds of the gramophone mingling with the guests laughing and chatting, all enjoying a normal Friday night.

Making her way to the kitchen, Connie turned on the light, hoping Cook had left some bread and perhaps a little cake. Stephen had a sweet tooth. Boiling the kettle, warming the teapot, doing all the essential yet mundane tasks required to make the tea just as he liked it helped her to regain her composure.

Carrying a tray of sandwiches, she pushed the door open with her foot and stepped into the sitting room. Stephen was asleep in the armchair, his head lolling on the back cushion. Taking a deep breath, she smiled and said, 'My sandwiches aren't as good as Cook's but hopefully they'll do...'

Stephen suddenly sat up, his eyes wide with surprise. He took the tray from her hands and their fingers brushed briefly; a jolt of electricity shot through her. Looking up into his face, their eyes locked for what felt like an eternity before a loud laugh from down the hall broke their trance.

Blushing, Connie released her grip on the tray and stepped back, awkwardly. She wanted to say something witty or clever, but she could feel all her words melting away in the heat of

Stephen's gaze. Clearing her throat, she managed to mumble, 'If you set it down over there, I'll pour the milk.' She wanted to linger in the moment forever, but instead turned away and busied herself pouring the Earl Grey.

She handed him a cup and a plate of sandwiches before settling herself on the chair opposite his, feeling the dainty china cup in her hand. Old Country Roses, her mother's favourite tea set. Granny had collected it, piece by piece, after her marriage.

Why am I thinking of tea sets and such things now?

Connie risked looking at Stephen again. He had finished one sandwich; the rest discarded on the plate by the fire, along with his cup. His gaze lingered on the hearth, but she felt his mind was elsewhere.

'Stephen, tell me. The truth. What is it?'

He sighed. 'Connie, you have no idea. I couldn't even begin to describe the horror of the last two weeks – they're calling it *Kristallnacht*... "the night of broken glass". But that doesn't even begin... If I had the words, which I don't, I wouldn't know *where* to begin. I... I just... can't.' His voice broke.

Alarmed, Connie spotted the tears in Stephen's eyes despite his best attempts to hide them. Reacting instinctively, she put her arms around him.

He tensed for a moment before breaking down, sobbing on her shoulder.

Hearing him cry was one of the worst moments of Connie's life. A good man like Stephen couldn't stand by and let innocents be tortured and murdered. She held him until the sobs subsided, then she moved away and busied herself with the fire to allow him to compose himself.

'Sorry about that, old girl. I'm not usually one for the waterworks.'

She put her cup down on a table before moving to his side, kneeling on the floor by his seat. Taking his hands in hers, she gazed up at him. 'Whatever it is, you can tell me. You can't deal with it alone. I read the reports in the papers. It was horrible. I can't imagine what you saw. Tell me.'

'We thought there might be some trouble after the events in Paris. You know about the young man shooting the German officer?'

Connie nodded.

'Robert – Vice-Consul Smallbones – was back in London, but his mother and grandmother live with him in Berlin, and were incredible. They kept people, so many people, supplied with food but more importantly they consoled them by treating them like real people. The SS, they burned down the synagogues and Jewish businesses, buildings, everything they could. It didn't matter how old or valuable the buildings were, the ancient scrolls, holy books, everything was burned to the ground. The police stood by and did nothing. The firemen too, they only acted if there was the chance a "real" German's building or home could catch fire.'

'Oh, Stephen.'

'It's worse, Connie. They weren't happy with destroying property. The SS beat up people, shot them, threw them from windows.'

Connie gasped but he didn't seem to hear her.

'There were crowds of men, some only boys, all bound by their hated for a group of innocent people whose only crime is to be deemed Jewish. Non-Aryan. That isn't even a real race, but the truth doesn't mean anything to Hitler's followers! The stories we heard, from one person after another, I can't repeat them, I can't bear to even think about them... So many people died, or were badly injured, and that wasn't even the end. They rounded up all the men and some boys and have put them into concentration camps. Places like Dachau, Sachsenhausen...'

Stephen began struggling to get the words out, his chest heaving. His pulse trembled through his hands.

Connie gripped him tighter, afraid he would fall into madness. 'I'm here, Stephen. Tell me.'

'Inga, that's his grandmother, rang Robert in London and begged him to do something to help. We'd been working around the clock trying to get visas and passports for these people, but you know how slowly official wheels turn. There is so much paperwork and the regulations imposed by both sides... it's over-whelming. But Robert wasn't going to be deterred. He went to the Home Office and asked them what they intended to do about things. They had to do something to help the Jews leave Germany. Seems the initial concerns were about causing unem-ployment here if they opened the door.'

Connie rubbed her thumb along his hand. She knew, better than most, the attitudes towards mass immigration. She and Dottie fought every week against the miserly quotas to try to save lives.

'What happened? Did your boss find a way around the rules?' Connie prompted, when Stephen fell into a world of his own.

'Yes. It was quite ingenious, really. He used the US Immi-gration Act.'

'How?' Connie looked at him, incredulous. 'We've spoken to people on our visits to Germany and Austria and they complain about the Americans not issuing visas. They said the USA works out quotas based on two per cent of the total number of people from that particular country living in the USA in 1890. Which means they will only allow 27,000 immi-grants from Germany *each* year. That's less than a tenth of those making applications.'

Connie tried to curb her anger. It was all very well for some bureaucrat living in his nice home in the safety of the USA to come up with these figures when he'd never deal with the woman whose husband or son was languishing in a concentra-tion camp in fear for his life.

'I know, Connie. Robert knows the rules too. But what he pointed out was that Britain's immigration laws are more flexible.'

'They are?' Connie couldn't help being sarcastic. Her idea of flexibility must differ to Stephen's.

Stephen ignored her interruption. 'In an emergency they can be expanded, and if what is happening now in Germany isn't an emergency, I don't know what is. Robert asked the Home Office to provide a way for the Jews who have papers to travel to the USA but cannot go this year or next due to the quota system, to get out of Germany, and danger, now and wait for their number to come up.'

'I don't understand. Where would they go?'

For the first time, hope lit up his eyes. 'They would come here.'

'Oh, Stephen! You mean everyone who applies will be saved?'

She wanted to shove her comment back into her mouth as his face paled.

'Not everyone. But more than before. Robert met Otto Schiff from the Jewish Refugees Committee and between them, they came up with a proposal which has now been adopted by the Home Office. Under this new system, applicants who are been approved for eventual travel to the USA can apply for a British visa provided they swear not to seek employment in the United Kingdom. They must secure a guarantee from a bank or a responsible individual based here, and not become a burden on the state. That means they have to have enough money to live for up to two years.'

Connie bristled. 'I know what it means. Dottie and I have been trying to secure these guarantees for years now.'

Stephen immediately looked contrite. 'Sorry, Connie. I didn't mean to talk down to you. I'm just tired.'

'It's me being silly. What I don't understand is how this differs from the system already in place?'

'It differs in two ways. People with approved US Visas waiting for their number don't have to risk being imprisoned or worse by the Nazis. Perhaps more importantly, they also confirmed the exact paperwork required by the American consular authorities in Germany to make sure the applicant will be admitted to the USA. The new rules were sent to the Passport Control office in Berlin and to all British embassies. That alone is going to make things easier, Connie. You know how many times the forms get refused for being incorrect or incomplete, or whatever other excuse some of the staff dealing with immigration use.'

Connie did. Only too well. It seemed that anti-Semitic feelings weren't reserved just for those who'd sworn allegiance to Hitler. She'd lost count of the times staff in not only British or American embassies had refused paperwork, which everyone knew to be in order, on the flimsiest of excuses. Did these people not realize lives were on the line? Their decisions were often the cause of deaths.

Her eyes closed as she remembered Frau Oppenheimer, the lovely wife of a rabbi kicked to death outside his own synagogue. Dottie and she had travelled to Munich to the opera, and had had seats beside the lovely couple. They had told them of the threats to his life and their trips to several embassies begging for their visas to be approved. Their son and two daughters had all sworn affidavits of support, one from the USA, another from London and the third from Paris – but to no avail. A week later he was dead.

Frau Oppenheimer had dressed in her finest clothes before turning on the gas oven.

'But what of the Gestapo? They don't make it easy for people to get the German paperwork they need.'

Stephen laughed but it wasn't one of happiness. 'That's an

understatement, but Robert is fantastic, Connie. You have to meet him if he comes back to London.'

'I can see him in Frankfurt when we next go out.'

Stephen grasped her hand. 'You must not go back in Germany. It's too dangerous. I know I have said this before but this time I mean it. Things are worse than ever.'

Connie pulled her hand away, unnerved by the expression on his face and conscious she was still sitting on the floor. Wiping her hands down the side of her skirt, she picked up the cups and placed them back on the tray. 'Dottie and I must go. You know what we do, and the need for our work has increased.'

'Connie, you can't go back. I forbid it.'

She glared at him. 'Who do you think you are? You can't stop me doing anything. I'm a grown woman not a child, Stephen Armstrong.'

They stared at each other, the atmosphere charged. He was the first to look away. 'I'm sorry. You're right. I have no authority over you. But you can't stop me worrying about you. You've had the perfect cover but that won't work now – it's too risky. I can't let you take that risk. I couldn't bear it if anything happened to you.'

He cared for her. Her anger disappeared, replaced by a feeling of joy. She took a seat, wanting to reach out and hold his hand, but feeling shy for some reason.

'Tell me what your friend said to the Gestapo. Will they co-operate?'

'There is nothing a bully understands more than a threat.'

Connie didn't understand. She waited for him to elaborate. He had gone back to staring into the fire.

'Robert met the head of the local Gestapo who insisted that the Jewish men needed to get their emigration papers in order. Robert queried how they were supposed to do that when locked in a concentration camp, together with the Jewish lawyers who would ordinarily act in their place. Robert suggested that so-called Aryan lawyers might not be inclined to help. The Gestapo man laughed. He laughed!'

Connie clasped her hands together, her knuckles whitening. She hated violence but she had an urge to throttle every member of the Gestapo.

'Robert lost his temper. He doesn't do that often, but I believe he is quite fierce when he does. He shouted at the official, warning him that his refusal to help would be the subject of a telegram back to London. He insinuated it would reach the highest authority, who would then take it up with the government in Berlin.'

'They'd give the Gestapo man a promotion, surely?'

'No, Connie, they can't risk a diplomatic incident. Not now. Or at least that is what we believe, as the Gestapo man crumbled. It's worked too. Every case we have promised a visa to has been released. So far.'

'That's wonderful, Stephen! Your friend Robert is a hero.'

'He would be the first to say it's a team effort. Every single visa has to be typed and signed by him or a member of his staff. We've been working long hours trying to get everyone out.'

'That's why you look so shattered. You can't kill yourself, Stephen – you must rest. That way you can help more people.'

'The clock is ticking, Connie.' The urgency in Stephen's voice was palpable, echoing around the dimly lit sitting room. The flickering flames in the fireplace cast a warm but sombre glow, highlighting the deep lines of concern etched across his face. 'People are dying in those camps. Not dying, but being *murdered*. They are fed starvation rations, and worked to death when they're not being kicked or beaten. How can I or anyone else sleep in a warm bed when someone's life depends on me?'

Connie couldn't answer that.

He continued, his voice tinged with a mix of duty and weariness. 'I'm only here as Robert told me he would have me replaced if I didn't take the weekend off. He gave me some papers to carry. Sensitive ones. Along with an order not to return to Frankfurt until next Wednesday, at the earliest.'

'And you came to see us when you should be in your club, in bed.' Connie attempted a light tone, but it felt hollow in the dense air of the room.

'I wanted to see a friendly face.' He glanced at her, his eyes reflecting a mix of gratitude and something deeper, something he seemed eager to conceal, before abruptly turning his gaze back to the fire, his face flushing. 'To see you.'

She wanted to reach out, to take his hand, offer comfort, do something to ease his burden but she froze. What if she was misreading his signals? He meant the world to her but if he saw her purely as a friend, a confidante, she'd ruin everything. And they couldn't risk falling out now, not when lives depended on their working together.

'Stephen, you should rest. Come back tomorrow and have lunch with Mama, Dottie and me. Dottie has been so busy with her church meetings. She goes to talk to several groups during the week, raising funds or trying to find sponsors who will take in a man or a woman. Our dear friend Sarah in Vienna is missing, her children too. Nobody has heard a word from them.' Connie stood and put the guard in front of the fire. 'I'd offer you a bed here but the room you used to use is occupied by one of our temporary guests. Tovah Goldberg arrived two days ago from Berlin – he's a friend of Clemens'. Mama offered him the room just for a week until his sponsor returns from a holiday.'

Stephen stood up. 'I will return for lunch, thank you. An English meal with the people I love will do me the world of good.'

Love. He was out the door before she could react. Did he mean he loved her? She knew how she felt but the timing was wrong. She couldn't add to his stress by announcing her feelings now. She had to wait for the right time.

FORTY-THREE

VIENNA, JANUARY 1939

Sarah jumped as the apartment door banged shut, her heart racing. She huddled with Leah in the corner of the dimly lit bedroom, their faces etched with anxiety. Sarah's trembling fingers clutched Leah's hand as they listened to the escalating argument between Hedwig and her father in the next room.

As the heated exchange continued, Sarah could see the fear in Leah's eyes, her daughter's body tensing with each shouted word. As Leah's eyes welled, Sarah's fingers brushed gently through Leah's hair as she held her close, her comforting touch meant to soothe her daughter's nerves. 'Shush,' Sarah murmured softly. 'Hopefully, Hedwig will win him around. She usually does.'

Suddenly, the argument abruptly ceased and the apartment door banged shut again. Sarah, with a mixture of worry and curiosity, slowly disentangled herself from Leah's embrace. She tiptoed towards the bedroom door, her ears straining to decipher whether it was Hedwig or her father who had left.

The door swung open, and to her immense relief Hedwig walked in, though her face bore the signs of shame and distress. Sarah's heart ached for her friend.

'I'm sorry you had to hear all that,' Hedwig admitted, her voice trembling. 'My father met someone in the market this morning. This man, he hinted that he knew my father had something to hide. Papa isn't a brave man. He is scared, and this makes him say terrible things.'

Sarah nodded in understanding, realizing that their presence was indeed putting Hedwig's family in grave danger. 'Your father has been very generous letting us hide here for so long,' she acknowledged. 'But he is correct. Our presence is putting you in danger. We must go.' Inside, Sarah's heart was heavy with the knowledge that they had nothing – no money, few clothes and hardly any belongings.

Hedwig, her expression determined, leaned so that Leah would not hear and whispered, 'I have a plan, but you may not like it. We need to speak alone. Let's make breakfast for the children, and while they eat, we'll talk.'

Sarah and Leah hastily dressed while Hedwig prepared breakfast for the children. Daniel sat at the table, his eyes troubled as Hedwig served up the food. Hedwig then poured two cups of *ersatz* coffee, gesturing for Sarah to follow her into the bedroom.

Sarah paused to kiss each of her children on the head and whispered reassuring words: 'Everything will be fine. Stop worrying.'

Daniel responded, 'Mama, we aren't children anymore. Stop trying to protect us.' Sarah managed a sad smile before closing the door behind her.

Inside the bedroom, Hedwig's eyes were locked onto Sarah's, and she took a moment to gather her thoughts. 'I heard good news this morning,' she began, her voice steady now. 'There is a Dutch woman, a Frau Wijsmuller, who met with Eichmann last December.'

The mention of that name sent shivers down Sarah's spine.

'She made him agree to send six hundred children away on a train to Holland. From there, most of them went to Britain.'

'Eichmann let them leave Vienna? Alive?' Sarah couldn't hide her disbelief.

Hedwig placed her cup of coffee on the dressing table. 'Yes. This woman has come back a few times, and each time she takes more children. I spoke with a friend, and he said we can get places for Leah and Daniel on the train.'

'But they aren't children, not really,' Sarah worriedly pointed out. 'Leah is seventeen, and Daniel sixteen. Will they let them travel?'

Hedwig reassured her. 'Yes. The cut-off age is seventeen, so we can't wait. Who knows how long this woman will be able to keep doing it? There are lots of families who want their children to go, but my friend' – Hedwig blushed – 'he works for the train company. He will help us.' Hedwig's gaze remained fixed on Sarah. 'He is a good man, a kind one. I think we should trust him.'

Sarah paced the small room, torn by conflicting emotions. Could she really send her children away? But what was the alternative? To take their chances on the dangerous streets of Vienna? Every argument Hedwig had with her father eroded their safety. She couldn't bear to think of what might happen if they stayed.

'I don't know if I can do it,' Sarah admitted, her voice trembling with uncertainty. 'Or if Leah would even go. You've seen her. She can barely dress herself her hands tremble so much. She is so scared. What if something happened to her on the train? Nobody would protect her. Daniel might try, but they would...' Sarah couldn't bring herself to voice her darkest fears.

Hedwig's next words gave Sarah a glimmer of hope. 'You could travel with them, Sarah.'

Sarah's eyes widened with surprise and anticipation. Could it be true?

Hedwig's voice dropped to a hushed tone, her gaze avoiding Sarah's. 'You can accompany the train through Holland to the British port, but you can't leave the boat. You would have to return to Vienna like all the other Jewish companions. If you attempted to escape, you might be shot. But even if you achieved your freedom, there would be no more *Kindertransport* trains. The Nazis have made that clear.'

Sarah groaned. *What a choice.* She could either put her children on the train alone and pray they travelled unmolested to safety. Or she could accompany them but turn back alone, within view of safety. And if she didn't, if she choose freedom, she condemned hundreds, maybe thousands of children to living under the jackboot of Nazi terror.

'Think about it, Sarah, but we don't have much time. The next train departs in three days. Each child can take ten marks and one small bag, but no photographs or valuables.'

'They want to wipe us out – not just the living, but the dead too. To erase all memory of our existence. What harm could it do, to allow the children to take a photograph of their father? Their family? Have they no hearts?'

Hedwig didn't answer. Instead, she picked up the cups and left the room. Sarah heard her tell the children to leave their mother alone for a while.

Sarah sat on the bed, staring at her hands. What should she do? If she sent the children, her family would be scattered like ashes in the wind. But at least they would be alive. Samuel was safe in America. He'd written to a gentile friend who had passed it on to Hedwig.

Ben and her father were safe too, if the *Wehrmacht* men were to be believed. They were somewhere in Poland. And now she would send her children to Britain.

What choice did she have?

Summoning her courage, Sarah walked into the living area, finding her children sitting at the table in silence. 'Daniel, Leah, we are leaving Vienna. You must each pack a bag. But it can't contain any photographs or items of value. Leah, we will give your necklace to Hedwig.'

Leah gripped the necklace she had worn constantly under her clothes. 'But, Mama, it is all I have of Papa.'

Sarah stepped towards her daughter and took her hands. 'No, darling. Your father lives in you. In your heart. Nobody can take that away, not even the Nazis.'

'Where are we going, Mama?' Daniel asked, a hopeful expression on his face. Their incarceration in this apartment had been toughest on him. Her son, who had loved to roam the city streets, meeting his many friends, playing all kinds of sports, now didn't have even a tiny space where he could be alone. He slept on the couch or, if Herr Berger was in a bad mood, on the floor of the women's bedroom.

'To Britain.' Sarah forced some joy into her voice. 'Leah, you wanted to see the palace and Covent Garden, remember? You told Connie and Dottie. Now you shall.'

'We all will. I can hardly believe it. We will soon be free.' Leah leapt up and hugged her mother.

Sarah buried her face in her daughter's hair for fear Daniel would see her expression. She would go with them, but she wouldn't tell them under what terms.

When Connie got home from work one evening, Dottie showed her a note. 'It came today.'

Thank you, Miss Dorothea. I can live now on hope. It will keep me warm until my new papers arrive.

I thank you with all my heart.

Pieter

Connie handed the short note back to Dottie, wondering how on earth she would help her sister keep her promise.

'Don't be afraid, Connie darling, something will turn up. We will get Pieter out.'

The two sisters spoke of little else over the next weeks. There were no trips to Europe: Clemens, having been summoned to Berlin for a meeting with the regime, had suggested they keep their distance until he knew whether he was a suspect. The Nazis didn't look favourably on anyone who helped rescue Jews, and Clemens was taking a risk arranging opera tickets when he knew they were using the opera as a cover for their smuggling, never mind introducing them to the *investors*.

Worried about Stephen, Sarah and her children and now Clemens, Connie filled her time anyway she could. She went to work, using her lunch hours to file the paperwork with the visa departments to enable those whose bank accounts were now funded, to escape. From work she went to meetings organized by their mother to find sponsors. For relaxation, she wrote to Stephen every couple of days. His replies told her how much her gossipy, fun letters kept his spirits up. They never discussed anything about their work or anything too serious, knowing the regime was probably intercepting the mail.

Dottie wrote her books, getting ever increasing advances which immediately went on funding their expanding refugee family. In the evenings, she filled in the required, never-ending paperwork.

Dottie had applied to sponsor Pieter but her application was turned down due to unsteady income source. Connie had already sponsored two people, as had their mother, so that avenue was closed to them.

Mama came to their rescue, greeting Connie when she returned weary from work one day with a large smile on her face. 'Constance, I have just had a wonderful chat with a lovely rector up at St David's. He said his congregation has collected enough money to provide a guarantee of three years' hospitality for a young woman, a relative of a member of their congregation.'

'That's wonderful, Mama.'

'Let me finish, darling. It turns out that this young woman is getting married and her new husband wants to take his chances in France. So, the rector wanted to know if you knew anyone who could take her place. They really can't bear to hand back the collection. I rather think they were hoping they would get someone to spoil.'

A photo of Dottie's boy popped right into Connie's head. 'Mama, I love you.' She grabbed her mother and hugged her. 'Dottie's Polish boy. That's who needs three years, and after everything he has been though in that horrible camp on the Polish border, he needs as much spoiling as he can get. Dottie will write to him as soon as she gets back from seeing her agent and tell him to get his papers in order.'

Mama grinned. 'I shall go to the telephone box and ring the rector. He will be delighted.'

Not as much as Pieter. But Connie didn't voice her thoughts.

FORTY-FIVE

LONDON, FEBRUARY 1939

They were having dinner when there was a loud knocking at the front door. Connie put her cutlery down. 'I am sorry, Mama, I don't know why anyone would come here. I'll be right back.'

She walked quickly to open the door to three people standing on the path: two huddled together standing beside a tall, thin man with a smile she remembered.

'Henry. How wonderful to see you. I've heard great things about your work with the *Kindertransport*. Come in. Please.'

'It was Elias who got me into it. You need to blame him.'

'He wouldn't be here if you hadn't gone back to Berlin to find him.' She winked at him. 'I'm so glad you could sponsor him and bring him to London. Come on in.'

Only when the group stepped into the light cast from the hallway did Connie recognize the couple. 'Daniel, Leah! Oh my goodness.' She leaned out to look into the path. 'Where's your mother? Sarah?'

'Connie, Sarah isn't here.' Henry's soft words hit her harder than a brick. She whirled around to see Leah sobbing quietly with Daniel's arm wrapped around her shoulders, his eyes glistening with tears. 'Can we go inside? The children are cold.'

Connie froze. She couldn't help it. Where was Sarah? How had the children got to Britain?

'Connie, who is it?' Dottie's voice came from inside the house.

Connie was spurred into action. 'Come in, the fire is lit. You can leave your coats on the stand there. Go through that door to your left. I'll just fetch my mother and Dottie.'

Connie saw them into the sitting room before she returned to the dining room where her mother and Dottie stared at her. 'It's Sarah's children. But she isn't with them. I don't know why.'

Mama moved quicker than any of them. 'Those poor children.'

Connie and Dottie followed their mother into the sitting room, where the children now sat huddled together on the sofa, with Henry standing to one side.

'Henry, how wonderful to see you and thank you for bringing these precious children to our home.' She turned to the children. 'Your father and grandfather will be so happy you are here safe.' Mama reached out to embrace both the children.

'Papa? Is here? In this house?' Daniel rose.

Dottie answered, 'No, but he is in London. Connie, will you go to fetch them? If only they had a telephone. But it won't take too long on the tube, will it?'

Connie forced herself to smile reassuringly. 'No time at all.'

Henry stepped forward. 'Let me drive you. I have my car outside.'

Connie smiled gratefully. She wanted to know where Sarah was, but something stopped her asking the children. Leah had yet to speak.

'Let me fetch my coat.' Connie left the room as Dottie said she would make hot cocoa, leaving Mama to fuss over whether the children were warm enough.

Henry followed Connie and Dottie to the kitchen. Once

there, he said, 'Sarah accompanied the children from Vienna. I
don't know how she managed to get them seats on the *Kinder-*
transport – the trains they are using to ferry children out of
Nazi territory – but she did. She watched them leave the boat
and go through border control.'

Connie couldn't help it: her anger at the injustice of what
had happened to the beautiful family she had first met in Salzburg bubbled over. '*Watched* them? Why didn't she come with
them? How could she get to Britain and not be here? With them
now?'

'If she had left the boat she would have condemned
hundreds of children.'

Connie knew she was gaping at him, but his words didn't
make sense.

'The Nazis allow Jewish adults to accompany the trains, on
some routes only. But their journey is conditional on them
returning to the point of origin. If they don't, all future trains
will be cancelled. Effective immediately.'

'You mean Sarah had to sacrifice herself to save other
people's children?'

Henry nodded.

'That's barbaric.' Connie groaned. 'Poor, poor Sarah, how
will she manage without her family?' She gripped the kitchen
chair. 'We have to go to Vienna and get her out. I don't care
how, but we must.'

'You may not get that chance.' Henry lowered his voice to a
whisper. 'Rumours are that the Jewish adults are arrested as
soon as they return to the port of origin. Even as we speak, I'm
afraid your friend could be in prison, or worse.'

FORTY-SIX

LONDON, APRIL 1939

Dottie was away on one of her book promotion trips when two letters arrived.

One was from Clemens, inviting them to a dinner in Frankfurt with some special family friends. That was their code for someone who needed immediate help. Connie would have to travel alone. She pushed down a shiver of fear – she'd never turn her back on those who were in danger. Mama would probably try to stop her going but she'd have to.

She read more of the letter. He wrote to say he had been honoured with an audience with Hitler to discuss operas and had been introduced to the composer, Richard Strauss. He waxed lyrical about the Nazis – she sensed this was for the censor's benefit. Connie let out a breath. So, he hadn't been called to Berlin to be arrested, as he'd feared. There was no mention of Sarah, but perhaps he had news and would share it when they met.

The second letter that arrived was from Pieter, along with his paperwork. Having her sister's permission to open it, Connie read through her tears. His joy and relief were jumping off the page.

She grabbed her coat and hat and headed straight out to the Guarantee Department at Bloomsbury House, where the next stage of his journey would start.

Thankfully, Anna was on duty on the desk. Connie had dealt with her several times and found her to be more than accommodating, especially given the red tape surrounding these types of applications. Bloomsbury House, set up in 1938, was the headquarters of eleven aid organizations working to help refugees, but like everywhere some people were better at navigating the system than others.

'Anna, Pieter got his paperwork. I don't know how he did it given he lives in that awful place but it seems to be in order.' She passed the paperwork across to the girl and watched as Anna studied it, her face breaking into a smile.

'It's all here. How wonderful.' Anna's smile was genuine. She knew how challenging it would have been to get the papers, and knew how long Pieter had been waiting. With the rumblings that war would break out any day growing louder, time was not on their side.

'What number is his quota for the United States?'

Connie glanced at the paperwork – not that she needed to. She knew it off by heart. '16500.'

Anna paled, her mouth opening several times but not able to say a word.

'Anna, what is it? What's wrong? What did I say?'

'We had an order come down today. We cannot accept anyone with a number over 16000.' Anna rubbed her hand across her cheek as one tear followed by another rolled down her cheek.

'No. That can't be.' Connie immediately forgot how impossible she had told Dottie it would be, how they couldn't get Pieter out. They had to find a way. 'There must be something we can do. I can't write back now and tell him we can't save him – that he will die.'

She and Anna exchanged a long look. Then Anna blinked and smiled a dazzling smile. Leaning in, she shuffled through the papers in the file, handing one back to Connie. 'Take this home with you. I shall write to you on official letterhead but will date the letter three days ago and will ask you for the missing paper. That way his case will be marked as being in progress and this new rule won't apply.'

Connie resisted the urgent need to grab Anna and hug her. Instead, she discreetly squeezed her hand, recognizing she was risking her job, if not more. 'Thank you, Anna.'

The next few days dragged but the letter arrived as promised, and Connie duly returned to the office and passed over the forgotten paperwork.

'Now the case will follow the usual channels. It could take up to three months to get the visa. You will have to have patience.'

'Anna, you know I have no concept of the meaning of that word.' They both laughed. Connie almost forgot she was a lady and practically skipped out of the office, thinking of how happy Pieter would be to learn his visa was in progress.

Instead of going home, Connie decided to go to Dottie's flat to check on their new visitors: a lovely couple from Munich.

Karl was a member of Clemens' orchestra, so they had plenty to talk about, and his wife was content to just sit and listen, even if she struggled with the language. She was due to give birth in the next few months and kept telling Connie she couldn't wait for her child to be born free.

'When are you next travelling to Germany, Miss Connie?' Karl asked, as he lit up a cigarette. She noted how he had waited for his wife to go to bed before asking.

'I'm heading to Frankfurt this weekend. A friend has invited us to dinner.'

Karl shook his head. 'You take too many trips. It is not safe. For nobody.'

She stood up, not wanting to be rude but tired of the fact that everyone kept telling her not to travel. Stephen had been insistent during his visit after *Kristallnacht*, and he'd kept saying in his letters since then how he looked forward to seeing her *in London*. Mama was against her travelling too, but she had to go. A whole family depended on her getting a package out of Germany. How could she say no? And Clemens might have word of Sarah. She had to know what had happened to her friend.

'Tell Miss Dottie to take care of herself too.'

'She isn't coming with me on this trip. She must do a book signing with her publisher and can't get out of it.'

Karl blanched.

'Karl, I will be fine. I'm going to see Clemens. I'm British, so my passport will protect me. Please don't worry.'

'That is like telling me not to breathe. I started to worry in 1933 when Hitler came to power, and I will stop when he is dead.'

Connie couldn't help wishing that day would come soon.

* * *

Connie closed the front door with relief, leaning against it. She was home safe. Fingering the necklace she'd hidden under her blouse to smuggle back from Frankfurt, she couldn't help feeling sad for the family, friends of Clemens, who'd parted with it. They hoped she could sell it for enough money to secure visas to enable them to flee Germany.

Clemens had been in good spirits, although he had no news of Sarah. Despite there being no trouble at the border, she was exhausted. All she wanted was her own bed. Walking toward the stairs, she jumped when she spotted her mother waiting in the sitting room, the door open so she would see her.

'Mama, what are you doing up so late?'

'Waiting for you. I never see you these days. If you are not at work, you are travelling back and forth to Europe. You are wearing yourself out, Constance. I'm worried about you. How was your trip?'

Connie ran a hand through her hair, conscious she probably looked a sight. She'd returned from Frankfurt that morning and gone straight into work. She'd managed to convince her boss to allow her to build up time off by working through lunch and late into the evenings so she could take more Saturdays off.

'Aside from being a little tiring, the trip was not taxing. I promise. I'm fine.'

Her mother shook her head. 'No, you aren't. But if you won't listen to me, maybe you will listen to Stephen.'

She felt her cheeks flush, her heart racing a little. 'Did he write?'

'No, he sent a telegram. He will be here tomorrow evening. Don't be late home.'

He was safe. Connie sagged against the door. She'd see him for herself. But even with the excitement of seeing him, she dreaded it too. He was bound to be cross she had gone back to Germany alone. She knew he was only being protective, but she didn't have the energy to argue with him.

Connie trudged up the stairs to find Dottie waiting in her bedroom.

'Please don't lecture me as well.'

Instead Dottie gave her a hug. 'I missed you. How did you get on?'

'I saw Clemens, he sends you his love. He gave me this.' Connie put her hands up to her neck and unclasped the necklace she'd hidden going through border control. She'd worn it all day, not daring to leave it anywhere in the office. 'It weighs a ton.'

Dottie gasped as she took the necklace featuring an enormous, perfectly cut pigeon's blood ruby at its core. 'It looks like it's glowing, doesn't it? Imagine wearing something like this? Each of the rubies and diamonds surrounding the centre stone is bigger than any I've ever seen set into an engagement ring.'

'Will you be able to take it to David Cohen? Tell him Clemens said it came from the personal collection of Czar Nicholas – or maybe his wife's.' Connie took a slip of paper from her purse. 'This is the name of the owner.'

Dottie closed her hand over the note, watching her closely.

'I asked. He hasn't seen or heard from Sarah.'

Dottie's shoulders slumped. 'Where could she be? It's been two months since the children arrived. Ben is frantic. Leah won't eat and Daniel is in trouble at school again.'

'What did he do this time?'

'He poured a bucket of cold water over some local boys. He said they called his family horrible names. No doubt they did, but Isaac believes Daniel is punishing everyone for Sarah not getting off the boat. He's angry.'

Connie couldn't blame him. Didn't she feel the same? She changed the subject. 'Mama said Stephen is calling tomorrow evening. Did you know he was back in London?'

Dottie played with the necklace.

'Did you?'

'Yes. We had lunch today. He is worried about you too.'

Stung, Connie retorted, 'You do as much as I do. You would have been in Frankfurt with me if you hadn't been busy signing books. Your book sales help save people.'

'Don't snap. I know. For what it's worth I told him you would, no – *we would* continue our trips until we were forced to stop. Mama and Stephen will just have to put up with us.'

Tears filled her eyes at her sister's support. 'Thank you, Dottie. I couldn't bear it if we weren't in this together.'

The next evening, Stephen arrived on time for dinner. Mama let him in as Connie returned to her bedroom to check her appearance. As she looked in the mirror for the umpteenth time, she laughed at herself. What was she doing? Stephen had no doubt been summoned by Mama to lecture her, and she was worried about her hair?

She made her way downstairs, his deep voice sending goose pimples down her arms. She walked in to find him seated at the table. He looked tired and thin, as usual, but when he smiled, his eyes twinkled with merriment.

'You're enjoying this, aren't you?' she whispered to him, taking her seat at the table.

'Being summoned to tell you off? Maybe just a little.' He nodded at her mother. 'Even I know better than to disobey Aunt Margaret.'

Connie was tempted to stick her tongue out at him but she controlled herself. He couldn't be in London just to tell her off. The embassy must have sent him over on business.

By mutual, if unspoken agreement, the dinner conversation flowed with gossip about friends and acquaintances.

At the end of the meal, Mama stood. 'Constance, why don't you take Stephen through to the sitting room. Dorothea and I will clear up.'

'Yes, Mother.'

Connie didn't wait for the door to shut behind Stephen. 'If you've come here to talk me out of our trips aboard, you are wasting your time. I know Mama is worried and I'm sorry about that but I can't stop. I won't. Nor will Dottie. Sarah is still out there somewhere, and I have to find her. I just have to.'

Stephen held his hands up. 'I surrender.'

'You do?'

'Will you please sit down so we can talk about this like reasonable adults?'

'When people use that phrase, they tend to speak to you like a child.' Still she sat. 'Stephen, you of all people should understand. You haven't stopped helping, have you?'

He stared at her for two or three seconds. 'No. But that's different. I have good reason to be in Berlin. You don't.'

'Clemens still gives us a list of operas to see. He reserves us seats. Usually, good ones, so we don't look out of place wearing furs and jewels.'

Stephen let out an exasperated sigh. 'Will you listen to yourself? How did that boy, Pieter, know to write to Dottie? A child, a stranger, yet he knew to write to "the opera lady". Don't you think that the Gestapo – hell, any border agent, knows that you are up to something more than attending operas?'

Why did he have to use logic as an argument? She fell silent, staring into the unlit fireplace.

He moved to sit beside her, taking her hand in his. 'I couldn't bear it if something were to happen to you. I...'

She looked up and their eyes locked.

'I hope you've talked sense into her.' Mama pushed open the sitting room door as Stephen sprang away.

Connie clasped her hands in her lap to stop them from shaking.

'I tried. But your daughter is stubborn and strong-willed and... oh, to be honest, I can't blame her, Aunt Margaret. How can any of us stand by when so many need help?'

Connie stared at the floor although she wanted to send him a grateful look, but her mother wouldn't appreciate them ganging up on her.

'That's what I said to Mama when we were doing the washing-up.' Dottie closed the door behind her, before taking a seat next to Connie.

'I'm sorry, Mama. I don't want to worry you, but I can't stop now. I must follow my conscience and do what little I can.' Connie hesitated before adding, 'Clemens will be in Vienna in two weeks' time. He has reserved seats for us at the opera. I have to go and see if I can find Sarah.'

'I am going with Connie, Mama.' Dottie discreetly squeezed Connie's hand.

Connie looked at her mother. 'Can you understand?'

Her mother brushed away a tear. 'Yes, I think I can. But at least promise me you will try to be careful. All of you.'

FORTY-SEVEN

VIENNA, MAY 1939

Connie stared out the window as the train pulled into Vienna.

Dottie whispered into her ear: 'This is worse than Berlin. At least there, people pretend they are having fun.'

The people looked miserable, totally different from the way they had behaved even a year previously.

There was even a checkpoint at the station exit.

'Are they stopping people entering Vienna now? I thought they just wanted to stop those trying to leave.'

Connie wanted to tell Dottie to be quiet but she guessed it was nerves making her sister prattle on. She didn't reply but joined the queue, showing her passport when they reached the beginning of it.

The first solider handed it to a man dressed in civilian clothing.

'Why are you in Vienna?'

'To see the opera, *Salome*. We have tickets for tomorrow night's performance.' Connie kept her tone confident but relaxed. She wasn't going to be intimidated, but she didn't want to antagonize either.

He glanced at their passports again before stepping

forward. 'You have a rather distinctive colouring, Miss Fitzwalter. Red hair and green eyes. Are you Jewish?'

Connie stiffened as she tried to control her temper. 'Not as far as I know. My mother credits an Irish ancestor for my auburn hair.'

He smirked, saying something to his friends in German.

She replied, in German: 'But you do not have blond hair and blue eyes? Are you certain you are an Aryan?'

The men around him laughed, causing him to flush a deep and rather unbecoming shade of red.

Dottie took over. 'My sister's temper is legendary. It goes with the Irish colouring. Now, may we please be on our way? We are meeting Mr Krauss and I believe, his friend, Mr Fraunfeld, for dinner, and we don't wish to be late.'

Connie saw the man's eyes widen as Dottie dropped the name of one of Austria's highest-ranking Nazis.

The man thrust the passports at Dottie and glared at Connie, before turning his back on them and strutting away.

'Enjoy your visit, ladies. It is lovely to see you again.' The station master bowed, his eyes twinkling with amusement.

They walked in silence most of the way to the hotel before Dottie erupted: 'What on earth came over you? We promised Mama to be more careful! What did you say to that man? I know you insulted him but you spoke so fast, I didn't catch what you said.'

'I asked him if he was an Aryan.'

Dottie paled. 'Have you lost your mind?'

Connie didn't answer. She'd been stupid and she knew it. But being back in Austria had brought it home to her how much had changed since their first visit in 1934.

'I'm going to Sarah's apartment. I want to check for myself she isn't there. Are you coming, or going to the hotel?'

'I'm coming. You can't be left alone.'

They went to the hotel to drop off their bag and to phone

Clemens to confirm their dinner arrangements. Connie hoped Mr Fraunfeld was too busy to attend dinner. She didn't like him, nor did she like to encourage Clemens's friendship with the man.

They walked toward Sarah's apartment building but when they arrived, the janitor they'd met at their last visit hurried over to them.

'They aren't here. They left last November.'

'Yes, we know. But we wondered if you had heard where Sarah might be now?'

He looked left and right before whispering, 'She was living with a friend but she left with the children on a train. She came back alone but then she disappeared.'

Connie's knees buckled, her eyes filling with tears. She wanted to throw herself onto the pavement and scream. Dottie took out her handkerchief and blew her nose.

'I wish I had better news. I tried to help but...'

'Thank you. We should be on our way now.'

Connie forced herself to walk around the corner, keeping a firm grip on Dottie's arm. Then she hailed a taxi and gave him the address of their hotel.

Even in their room, they couldn't give in to the grief they shared for fear the room was bugged. They had to wash their faces, change and meet Clemens for dinner. To pretend everything was normal.

To their relief, Clemens cancelled the restaurant and insisted they dine at home. Alone.

'I heard what happened at the train station. The man you insulted has some high-ranking friends. You cannot return to Vienna. It is too dangerous.'

Connie had more pressing issues to worry about than a jumped-up Nazi with a wounded ego. 'Clemens, have you news of Sarah? We went to her apartment but the janitor said she had disappeared.'

He shook his head, his eyes glistening. 'I'm sorry, but I can't tell you where she is. I wish I could.' They had a little cry before he shocked them: 'Tomorrow, my friend is travelling to Berlin and asked I accompany him. I have purchased two tickets for you to accompany us.'

'But the opera?'

'You can see *Salome* anytime. My understudy is not as good as I am. My friend would like to meet you. He heard you are very charming.'

'Who is this friend?' Dottie asked, but Connie had a horrible feeling she knew the answer.

'Why, Herr Fraunfeld, of course. He heard he was supposed to be dining with you so he thought he should oblige.'

Connie's stomach churned and Clemens leaned in to take her hand. 'I shouldn't make jokes at times like this. I have explained you cannot come with us as you are due back in London.' His expression became serious. 'I mean it, my dear friends. Vienna is no longer a safe place for you to visit. This must be the last trip, and you will return as you came. You must go to the opera.'

'You don't have any jewellery or things you want us to bring out?'

'Nothing. It is too high a risk. When you get to Cologne, Viorica will meet you with a package. That little man you upset at the station doesn't have any power outside Vienna so it will be quite safe.'

Assuming we get out of Vienna... but that remark stayed in Connie's head.

They attended the opera but didn't enjoy it. It was nerve-wracking being surrounded by Nazis strutting around like they owned the world. The women on their arms weren't any better, dripping in jewellery and fine gowns, talking their way through the performance.

On their way out of the auditorium, Dottie gripped Connie's hand. She'd seen him too: the man who'd accosted them at the station. He nodded in their direction. Dottie smiled back but Connie's face was frozen.

They hailed a taxi and returned to their hotel, packed their case and lay awake all night on top of the bed.

'I keep thinking they will come through that door any second.' Dottie glanced at the door.

'This is how our friends have lived for the last few years.' Connie's voice trembled. 'I never understood it, not really. Not till this minute.'

They arrived early at the train station and sat waiting for the train, both pretending everything was normal. Connie saw Dottie's hands shaking as she adjusted her bag. She was the same, counting backwards in her head from one hundred to try to stop thinking of what could happen next.

With a surge of relief she heard the low rumble of the approaching train, then she spotted the white steam billowing from the black smokestack. She stood as the train drew nearer. Dottie glanced around again, irritating her. She wanted to tell her off for looking for trouble.

The passengers around them moved closer to the edge of the platform. The station master blew his whistle as the train screeched to a stop. Doors opened as people poured out of the train. A man held the carriage door open for them, offering to take their bag. Dottie smiled her thanks as Connie nodded in appreciation. They stepped inside. The door closed.

Why wasn't the train moving? Connie couldn't look at her sister. She closed her eyes and willed the train to roll forward.

With a lurch, it did just that. She refused to look out of the window for a last glimpse of Vienna, preferring to remember it as it had been.

The train journey took longer than usual, with several unscheduled stops along the way. Connie was tempted to think that the man from the station had arranged them to torment them.

Dottie dozed a little but Connie was too strung-out to sleep. She'd been stupid to let that man's racist remark get to her. If she did have Jewish blood, she'd be proud of the fact. How dare a man like that denigrate a whole people? How could she have let him get under her skin?

They finally reached Cologne. 'Thank goodness we are flying. I can't wait to see home.'

Connie couldn't reply. She'd spotted Viorica on the platform and she wasn't alone. She blinked rapidly but, no, she wasn't dreaming.

'Dottie, do you see her? Come on!'

Connie walked as fast as she could without knocking over other passengers.

Her gaze locked with Sarah's as they moved towards one another.

'I can't believe you're here!' Connie hugged Sarah before moving aside to let Dottie do the same.

She looked from Sarah to Viorica and back. 'How?'

Viorica's eyes sparkled. 'We must hurry. Your train was late and you can't miss the plane.' She leaned in and kissed them both on the cheek. 'Act normally. Sarah will explain all later. Her papers are in order, thanks to your friend in Berlin.'

Viorica had a car waiting to take them to the airport. She kept them entertained with tales of her singing at various venues. Connie assumed the inane chatter was for the benefit of the driver.

Although dressed beautifully, with her hair styled in the latest fashion, Sarah looked dreadful. She was far too thin for a start, but it was more than that. Her eyes lacked vitality, as if the effort of living had almost proved too much. Connie held her hand, almost too scared to grip it in case it crumbled. What had Sarah been through since she'd sent her children to Britain back in January?

Once at the airport, Viorica escorted them to border control.

She smiled as she hugged them goodbye. 'I have to say good-bye, but I prefer *au revoir*. I hope to see you all very soon.' Viorica didn't fool them with her act. They saw she was struggling to contain her tears.

Connie gave her a second hug. 'That's for Clemens. Thank you. Both of you,' she whispered. 'Tell him I was wrong to ever doubt him.'

Viorica gripped her by the shoulders. 'Be safe, my dear friend.'

With a last wave, Viorica waited as they walked through the border control.

Connie's heart beat so fast she was barely able to breathe. She couldn't look at either Sarah or Dottie.

The woman just ahead of them was pulled to one side. The border agents opened her suitcase and began throwing her things out. Connie swallowed. Then it was their turn but, to her astonishment, he barely looked twice at them.

Her breathing didn't return to normal until they were up in the air. Sarah fell asleep almost as soon as they sat down, leaving Dottie and Connie to exchange bemused glances. They couldn't ask questions, not until they had cleared Customs back in England.

Eventually, they too fell asleep.

. . .

Taking a cab from Croydon airport allowed for Sarah's most pressing question: 'How are the children? Have you heard from Samuel?'

'Samuel has written to Ben a few times. He is doing well but missing his family. He was worried sick about you, of course. The children will settle in better now you are here. They need their mother.'

Sarah nodded but stayed silent for the rest of the trip, gazing out of the window at the passing scenery.

Connie sensed she hadn't felt safe to speak in the cab. It would take her friend time to get used to being free. And, given her pallor, she doubted that Sarah's mind was on the journey. What horrors had her friend gone through since they had last seen her?

It was only once they got home to their house and Sarah had had some tea that she was able to tell them the whole story.

'Clemens rescued me. I believe Hedwig got word to him that I had taken the children on the *Kindertransport*. They, the SS, were waiting for me and the other Jewish volunteers when we arrived back in Vienna. Someone said Eichmann was annoyed that the Dutch lady had out manoeuvred him. He made some deal with her expecting her to fail but she didn't. Anyway, we were to pay the price. They marched us down to the Metropole where we were thrown into cells. Days passed without any food or water, but they didn't touch us. We were lucky.'

Connie didn't interrupt.

'Then a man came in and called my name. He actually apologized for having incarcerated me. They gave me some clean clothes and a hot shower and drove me to the opera house. Clemens was waiting there. He'd used his contacts, just as he said he would that time with Papa. He worked with your friend Stephen to get me the right papers, and here I am.'

'Clemens didn't give us a hint when we saw him in Vienna!'

Dottie clasped her hands to her chest. 'When he said we had to collect a package, I assumed it was jewellery, as usual.'

'Were you disappointed?' Sarah joked, and Connie grinned with delight at this sign of life in her friend.

A knock on the front door interrupted them. Mama went to answer and came back with a broad smile on her face. 'Sarah, you have some visitors. Constance, Dorothea, come and help me in the kitchen.'

Connie saw Sarah's face light up as her father, husband and two children crowded into the sitting room. Henry gave them a wave before he headed to the kitchen.

Dottie and Connie followed, closing the door to give the family some privacy.

Mama put the kettle on, looking very pleased with herself. 'I went down to the telephone box and telephoned Henry and asked him to collect Sarah's family.'

'Thank you, Henry.' Connie gave him a kiss on the cheek. 'You always seem to come to the rescue.'

Mama pulled them into a hug in the kitchen. 'I don't think I have ever been prouder of the two of you than at this moment.'

FORTY-EIGHT

LONDON, SEPTEMBER 1939

Since Germany's invasion of Poland the previous week, which had left Britain gripped by rumour and speculation, Connie hadn't felt like she had taken a single breath. She couldn't eat or sleep worrying about Stephen, Mr Foley, Clemens and Viorica, and all their other friends. She had gone to work, but couldn't speak to her colleagues, who all seemed to have heard one story after another, each wilder than the previous one.

Finally, the news came that the prime minister would address the nation. Connie, Dottie and their mother sat in the sitting room glued to the wireless waiting for the announcement.

'This is London. You will now hear a statement by the prime minister.'

Connie bit her lip, glancing at Dottie, who stared at the wireless. Time seemed to stand still as they stared at the box.

'I am speaking to you from the cabinet room of 10 Downing Street. This morning the British ambassador in Berlin handed the German government a final note stating that unless we heard from them by 11 o'clock that they were prepared at once to withdraw their troops from Poland, a state of war would exist between us. I have to tell you now, that no such undertaking has been received and, consequently, this country is at war with Germany.'

Connie sat in stunned silence as their mother switched off the wireless. Despite the news being expected, it was still a shock. The sword had dropped. War had been declared and all borders were closed.

Mama let out a sob. 'After all we lost in the last war, the war to end all wars. We learned nothing. Nothing!'

Connie rose to give her mother a hug, but Mama turned away and walked out of the room. Connie sensed she needed a few minutes alone.

Dottie wiped her face with her hanky. 'Connie, I can't believe it. What about all those we didn't rescue? What will happen to them now?'

Connie had no answer. *What about Stephen? Where is he?* They hadn't heard from him in days, and now this.

The next morning a telegram arrived. Dottie ripped the envelope open. 'It's from Henry. The last ship with rescued children will arrive on Thursday the fourteenth. We must meet it in case Pieter got out. Will you come with me, Connie?'

'Yes, of course.'

The sun split the skies on a bright September day as the boat carrying the last of the children rescued from Europe arrived.

Connie grabbed Dottie's hand and held on tight as they watched 200 children, ranging in age from less than six months old to youths of seventeen, making their way slowly down the gangway. Some carried little bundles of clothes, others a teddy or a doll. None spoke English, and all stared around them with big eyes.

Dottie kept glancing at the tattered photograph in her hand, comparing the children to the image. Connie brushed her tears away and when her hanky became too wet to be useful, she furtively used her coat sleeve.

Then, suddenly, Dottie was pulling on her arm: 'Connie, look, there he is! Pieter! Over here! We're here.' Dottie abandoned all pretence of behaving in a ladylike manner and began screaming his name at the top of her lungs.

People turned but when they saw the young boy waving back, a huge grin on his face, they broke into smiles and started clapping. The crowd parted, allowing Connie and Dottie to run towards the young man racing to them.

The boy grinned and spoke breathlessly: 'I was the last person to get on the boat. Something went wrong and I was sure they were going to leave me behind but then I remembered your promise. You said you would get me out and you did. Thank you.' He hugged Dottie and then Connie and then Dottie again.

An exasperated Customs official came running over, waving his clipboard. 'Oi, you! Come back here. You must go through the proper channels. Can't just have you running off the boat like that! Come back here.'

Pieter waved at him. 'I'm coming.' Then he turned back to Connie and Dottie. 'I won't be long. Sorry for keeping you waiting.'

They smiled as he ran in the direction of the pompous official. They could wait all night now they knew he was safe. He was free.

Connie stayed watching as the newly arrived refugees moved through Customs. Where was Stephen? She'd know if something had happened, if he was... No, she wasn't going to think like that.

Where was he? Surely, he had got out in time. Frank Foley would have seen to it. He couldn't have let Stephen fall into the hands of the Nazis. Not now, when all hope of a rescue was gone.

And then she saw him. His face was lined with exhaustion, his eyes... haunted by visions she could only begin to imagine. She forced her feet to move forward, as close as she was allowed. She waited, watching as he scanned the crowd, his face growing in disappointment. Then his gaze caught hers and he stopped moving so suddenly the man behind him walked straight into him. She saw Stephen mumble an apology and move towards her without releasing her gaze. He didn't break eye contact until he was standing right in front of her.

'You're here. I rather hoped you would be but I...' He crushed her to him, and his kisses rained all over her face. She sensed his longing, his desperation, his fear and his sense of failure.

She pulled away and took his dear face in her hands, looking up at him. 'You saved as many as you could. Nobody could have done more.'

She murmured the words over and over, trying to convince him as he held her close as they walked away from the ship. With a last look in the direction from where he had come, she heard him say, 'May God help them now.'

Shuddering at his tone, she held his arm tight as they made their way to the exit. There they met up with Dottie and Pieter, and together the four of them headed to the station to take the train back to the sanctuary of Hanover Square. There Connie would ensure Stephen rested and relaxed for the weekend. Only then would she think about what the war would mean for him. Would he have to leave her again to go and fight? She glanced at his dear face, noting that grey hair was now more prevalent than chestnut, his suit hanging on his frame – the toll his work had taken. She clasped his hand, never wanting to let go. Connie wanted to keep him safe and out of harm's way forever.

EPILOGUE

NEW YORK, 1960

Connie gasped as the plane started its descent into New York airport. 'How different it is to come in by air. Remember our first visit here, when dear Tom met us off the boat?'

Dottie nodded, wiping a tear from her eye. 'He was a good man. It's hard to believe it has been almost twenty years since he died.'

Stephen leaned in, offering his hanky. 'He died a hero, fighting to the last for those desperate to escape the Nazis.'

The three of them fell silent and Connie knew they were each remembering all their friends who hadn't survived the war.

Stephen's cough broke the silence. 'How does it feel, Miss Bestselling Author, to be interviewed on the *Twilight Talks* show?'

Dottie blushed. 'I can think of several authors who are better suited. I still can't understand why Mr Hammond wants to interview me, of all people.'

Connie exchanged a smile with Stephen. Despite having written almost one hundred novels, Dottie still refused to believe in her own success.

* * *

Standing in the wings of the TV studio, Connie and Dottie waited nervously for the host, Mr Hammond, to call them to join him on stage.

'Why do they want me to sit with you? I haven't written anything,' Connie whispered to Dottie.

Connie's nose tickled from the heavy make-up applied by the studio assistant, who had remarked on never seeing such pale skin before.

Dottie waved a piece of paper like a fan. It was hot in the studio. 'I've no idea but I'm glad they insisted. I'd hate to be going through this alone. Did you see his picture? He looks like a movie star.' Dottie bit her lip. 'What on earth will they ask me?'

'Where you get the inspiration for your stories? How do you come up with the different plots? I suppose. Didn't they give your publisher a list?'

'If they did, he didn't share it with me. He just smiled and told me it would be fine. Connie, what if I stutter and can't find the words. I mean...'

'Ladies, you are on.' A young man appeared to escort them to meet Mr Hammond.

Charlie Hammond was even better looking in the flesh, with warm brown eyes, a clean-shaven face, and dark hair with a hint of silver at the temples adding to his distinguished presence. Connie could see why his show was so popular. His smooth baritone voice should have helped their nerves but instead the butterflies in Connie's stomach exploded – she could only imagine what her sister was feeling. They heard the audience clapping. She peered out into the faces hoping to see Stephen's reassuring smile, but the glare of the lights in her face blinded her.

Dottie took the seat by Mr Hammond's side, with Connie sitting on Dottie's other side.

'Good evening, ladies. Thank you for travelling all the way from London. Let me introduce you to our audience. Miss Dorothea Fitzwalter, you're the author of several best-selling Mills and Boon romance novels. The lady sitting next to you is your sister, Mrs Constance Armstrong.'

Connie nodded. Why was he introducing her?

'I'd like to congratulate you on your success, Miss Dorothea, as a writer, but that isn't the reason we invited you on the show tonight.'

Connie and Dottie exchanged a bewildered glance.

'The real reason is to reunite you with some very special people.' Mr Hammond stood up and headed towards the front row of the audience. 'In fact, there are several people here who have waited many years to renew their acquaintance in person. Could we ask those people to please stand up.'

The audience seemed stunned into silence as rows of people seated toward the front of the studio stood up.

Connie squinted into the lights, and as they were dimmed she began to make out the faces of those in the front rows. She covered her mouth with her hands as she recognized Sarah Liberman, her hand on the shoulder of a young man who looked like Daniel had all those years ago in Salzburg.

She turned to Dottie, who gasped, tears running down her cheeks, as she pointed at another lady. 'Connie, look, it's Else and her mother. What are they doing here? Who are all those people?'

Dottie's words were captured by the microphone above her head, causing Mr. Hammond to turn his attention back to his guests. He returned to sit by them.

'Connie and Dottie, if I may call you by the names your friends use, these are the people you saved from the Nazis. Yes, ladies and gentlemen of the audience, we have these two special sisters to thank for the lives of the majority of the guests in our audience. From the years 1934 to 1939, the Fitzwalter sisters were responsible for the direct rescue of twenty-nine men and women, but in reality the numbers they rescued are much more. Isn't that the case, Mr Levy? Perhaps you could join us and explain how the sisters were instrumental in saving your family? Please welcome Mr Jacob Levy to the stage.'

The audience clapped as a man in a wheelchair was wheeled up to the host by a young woman.

'Mr Levy?'

The old man smiled and said, 'My name is Jacob Levy and I too owe my life to these wonderful ladies. This is my grand-daughter. Her name is Constance Dorothea Levy.'

Connie and Dottie stood up to kiss Jacob's cheek and to greet his grandchild. They hadn't see any of the family since they had emigrated to America in the late 1940s.

The audience clapped and then Mr. Hammond asked them to retake their seats.

'Please tell us your story, Mr. Levy.'

'Jacob, please.' Jacob held a hanky in his hand and briefly wiped his eyes as he smiled at Connie and Dottie before turning his attention to the host. 'I was arrested by the Nazis for being Jewish and spent time in Dachau concentration camp.' The audience gasped before falling silent. Jacob's voice trembled as he outlined the harsh treatment the prisoners were subjected to. 'I can't speak of some things on television but imagine the most awful things you can do to another human being. It was much worse. I thought I would die, but one day they released me. I still don't know why, but they gave me eight weeks to leave Germany.'

Mr Hammond leaned in closer. 'But you had a mother and sister and wouldn't leave without them, is that correct?'

Jacob nodded. 'I was worried they would be taken and murdered in my place. I was resigned to my fate until I met these two ladies. Their friend, Stephen, brought them to my brother-in-law's home.'

'Yes – Stephen Armstrong, who went on to marry Connie, correct?' Mr Hammond directed the question at Connie, who could only nod in reply. Her throat had closed over with emotion. 'Mr Armstrong is in the audience, I believe. Can you please stand.'

Connie spotted Stephen as he stood to the clapping, but sat down again just as quickly.

'He's very shy.' Charlie Hammond laughed before turning his attention back to Jacob. 'Tell us what happened.'

'Moritz, my brother-in-law, had anticipated trouble and had the foresight to convert some of our assets into diamonds. These he gave to the ladies to smuggle out of Germany. A bag of diamonds. They agreed and refused all payment. If they had been caught smuggling the stones, they could have been arrested or even shot. They didn't hesitate, but took these diamonds to London to a jeweller who gave them cash. This cash was used to open bank accounts in my family's name and thus allowed us to escape via a British visa. There are thirty members of my extended family now alive thanks to these women. They saved my mother, my sister, Moritz, Judith his wife and their sons. We were also able to use the monies from the diamonds to fund the escape of another cousin and his family from Holland, just before the Nazis marched over the border. We all owe these ladies our lives.'

Connie couldn't believe her ears. After all he had suffered and his bravery in putting off his escape to save his family, she had to protest. Tears choked her voice as she said, 'We didn't do anything, Jacob. Carrying the diamonds was easy.'

'But that isn't true, is it, Connie?' Mr Hammond wasn't looking at her but at his audience. 'I believe you were stopped and questioned by a rather nasty Gestapo agent over a brooch? From what I've heard, you gave him a very public dressing

down. Maybe he should have known red-haired women are
fiery.'

Connie blushed as the audience clapped once more. Jacob
blew them kisses before his granddaughter wheeled him back to
his seat in the audience.

'Now, we have a guest whom you haven't met in person. Let
me introduce Miss Carla Neven.'

Connie didn't know who the woman was and glanced at her
sister; judging by the curious look in Dottie's eyes, she didn't
either. They waited as a dark-haired, brown-eyed woman in her
mid-twenties walked toward them. 'Carla was also rescued by
the sisters, but this is the first time the three of you have met,
isn't it?'

Carla nodded. 'I only found out recently the role you
played in our rescue. My mother had been turned down for a
visa due to ill health. She'd had arthritis, which meant the
British refused her a worker's visa in early 1939. My father had
already died in Buchenwald. My mother said she had decided
to take her own life rather than wait for the same fate. She was
all alone. Somehow, she contacted you wonderful ladies. You
found someone to sponsor my mother, an elderly couple who
lived in Scotland." Carla's voice trembled, tears filling her eyes.
'Her name was Sophia Linden.'

Dottie stood up and gave the woman a hug. 'I remember
your mother, a very elegant lady with a soft voice. But I don't
remember her having children.' Dottie glanced at Connie, but
she shook her head. Dottie took Carla's hand, holding her gaze.
'It wasn't us who saved her, it was Beverly and Reginald
Kingston. Such a lovely couple. I named a character in one of
my books after their son, who died in the first war.'

Carla held on to Dottie's hand and Connie moved seats so
Dottie could sit down beside her. Carla continued. 'Beverley
and Reg told us what you did. They said they didn't have the
full amount they needed to sponsor someone of my mother's

age. They said you paid money into their bank account right through the war. You see, you did save her life and mine too. My mother was pregnant with me – she didn't know it at the time. She thought she was barren after twenty years of marriage. She was forty-two when you rescued her and four months pregnant. I am here today because of you.' Carla leaned in to kiss both of them on the cheek. 'I have asked Yad Vashem to honour both of you.'

Carla returned to her place in the audience. Mr Hammond looked at his notes, allowing the audience to stop clapping and settle down.

'There are many of your friends in the audience and I'm sure you are looking forward to catching up with them. We have arranged a party afterwards for you to do just that. In the meantime, can you tell me a little bit more of your story?'

Connie and Dottie exchanged a glance and Dottie nodded, encouraging Connie to answer. 'We did very little, Mr Hammond. As you heard, wonderful people like the Kingstons offered their homes and sponsorship to people like Carla's mother. Others in Germany, such as our friends, Clemens Krauss, and his wife, Viorica, introduced us to people who needed help. Clemens gave us details of operas to attend – that was our cover, you see. We'd travel to see the opera and return with jewellery, money, gold and fur coats. Clemens gave us tickets a lot of the time to give us an excuse for our travels. Without them, and others including my husband, we couldn't have done what we did.'

The audience clapped as Charlie Hammond said, 'You are so modest.' He waited for the clapping to die down before asking, 'How did you pick those you saved? I mean, there were millions who needed help. Why these people? Was it because they were Jewish?'

'You don't ask a drowning man his religion, you just jump in and save him,' Dottie responded, before blushing and putting a hand over her mouth. 'I apologize. What I mean is that all we needed to know was the individual was in danger. If we could help, we did. Often all we could offer was an understanding ear or a shoulder to cry on. They were desperate times. So many...' Dottie couldn't continue, using her hanky to rub her eyes.

Connie took her hand, swallowing hard. 'What my sister means is for every person we helped, there were plenty more in need. And there were many heroic members of staff such as Mr Frank Foley in the British Embassy in Berlin, Mr Sawbones and, of course, our dear friend Tom who died in the war. He worked in the American Embassy in Berlin and helped too.'

'It must have been heartbreaking to speak to people and not be able to help them. Can you give us an example?'

Connie looked into his eyes. One example out of so many. Her brain went blank for a couple of seconds.

Charlie Hammond prompted: 'You seemed to concentrate on older people. I mean, not children, like those rescued by the *Kindertransport.*'

'Yes, we helped anyone we could, of course, but there were organizations better equipped to get children out in large numbers. We grew up in a loving family and couldn't bear to think of being separated from our mother or vice versa, so we tried to make sure all family members got out. It was more difficult to arrange visas for those over eighteen.'

'I see.' He glanced at his notes again. 'Does any particular case cause you sleepless nights?'

Connie bristled, but she knew he wasn't being unkind. He was asking the questions the audience wanted answers to, and he had his television ratings to consider. She glanced at Dottie but her sister pursed her lips.

'I remember one family Clemens introduced us to. A lovely lady married to a Jewish man. Often men in mixed marriages were safe but Chaim came to the attention of the authorities and ended up in Buchenwald. He was released and we met him in the hospital. I thought he was going to die, his condition was terrible. The doctors couldn't believe he had survived so long, especially as he was being treated in the Jewish hospital where they had no supplies. No drugs and only a skeleton staff of doctors and nurses, many who chose to stay despite having a way out.' Connie closed her eyes, the images of the broken man's body in her head. Dottie gripped her hand and the support allowed Connie to continue. 'Chaim and Gertie had three children: two boys and a little girl. Gertie was beside herself, as you can imagine. She begged us to take the boys with us, but she wanted to keep her youngest with her. We tried everything we could, but we couldn't get those children out. I can still see them now. The four of them huddled by Chaim's bed. The little girl had the bluest eyes I ever saw. We tried to find out what happened to them but the chaos... the camps...' Connie gulped, wiping tears from her eyes.

Mr Hammond handed her a box of tissues, before taking a couple for himself. He brushed his eyes before he looked at his notes once more. Connie saw him swallowing hard a few times. The audience broke their silence and rose to their feet, clapping as if they sensed the trio needed a minute to recover.

'Thank you, ladies and gentlemen.' Charlie Hammond stood and moved towards the audience. 'I have one more special guest this evening. Annalise, can you stand up, please?'

A blonde-haired young woman in her early thirties, dressed like Jacqueline Kennedy, stood up and made her way to the stage. She held hands with an older man, who brushed his eyes with his handkerchief.

Mr Hammond shook hands with the man and kissed Annalise on the cheek. Then he stepped back so the audience could see Connie and Dottie.

Connie glanced at her sister but she was staring at the couple.

'I'm the little girl you spoke about, Miss Constance. This is my brother, Rudi.'

Connie gasped as Dottie's hand flew to her mouth.

'You survived.'

'Yes, thanks to you and our very resourceful mother. Papa too. You gave some money to some friends who took us into their house in Frankfurt. They hid us for the entire war. Even when the bombs fell, nothing happened to that house, although the area around it was flattened. God was watching over us. He wanted us to live. Papa saw the fall of the Nazis. He shook hands with the British and Americans who rescued us. He died at the end of 1945. Mama couldn't live in Germany anymore, so she took us to America. She is still alive but in a nursing facility. Our elder brother, Ansel, joined the American forces and died in Korea. Mama couldn't remember your names or how to find you – when she found out Clemens Krauss had met Hitler and Goering and knew many Nazis, she refused to have anything to do with him. Not even to ask him who you were.'

'Mr Krauss was a Nazi?' Mr Hammond turned to face the sisters, his voice loud in a now stunned studio.

Connie opened her mouth to speak, but before she could answer Sarah Liberman stood up. 'I am alive today because of Clemens Krauss, his wife and these wonderful women. Clemens used his Nazi contacts to save people like me and people like your mother and father.' Sarah aimed that remark at Annalise. 'He could very well have introduced Connie and Dottie to the people who sheltered your family. He is one of my heroes.'

The audience muttered but then Stephen stood up. 'And mine.'

A few more of the survivors stood and claimed the same.

Dottie spoke up. 'I think Clemens is a perfect example of all human beings. He made some mistakes, made choices perhaps we don't agree with, but he used those connections to save lives.

It took a man or woman of courage to take a stand against the Nazis. For that reason, he is our hero too.' Dottie walked over to Annalise and pulled her into a hug. 'I can't tell you how happy you being here tonight has made us.'

The audience jumped to their feet, a thundering applause filling the studio. Mr Hammond gave up all pretence of not crying, tears running down his cheeks as he nodded to his assistant, and soon a recording of Viorica singing with Clemens as conductor filled the studio.

Connie gulped, closing her eyes, seeing her dear friends as they had been at that first meeting in the 1930s, in Covent Garden.

Mr Hammond thanked the sisters for being on the show and wrapped up, saying goodnight to the audience at home, the cameras turned off, and the studio lights came on.

Connie and Dottie stood up and their friends came forward, all talking at once. For a moment Connie laughed with joy, and her gaze locked with her husband's as he moved towards her. She felt Dottie squeeze her hand tight.

Connie closed her eyes briefly, seeing the faces of all those who they had tried to help – all those who had died despite their attempts to save them – before turning to concentrate on the survivors, their friends and family.

A LETTER FROM THE AUTHOR

Dear Reader,

Huge thanks for reading *A Song of Courage*. I hope you were hooked on Connie and Dottie's journey. If you want to join other readers in hearing about my new releases and bonus content, you can sign up for my newsletter.

www.stormpublishing.co/rachel-wesson

If you enjoyed this book and could spare a few moments to leave a review that would be hugely appreciated. Even a short review can make all the difference in encouraging a reader to discover my books for the first time. Thank you so much!

This is a work of fiction but like many other similar works, it is based on real people. The real-life story of Ida Cook and her sister, Louise, inspired this story, as did the real-life story of Mr Foley – often called the English Schindler. They are all recognized by Yad Vashem for their bravery.

I have changed the timing of certain events, not major historical items such as changing the date of the war or battles etc., but of minor things to meet the needs of the story. For example, the English ladies went to the USA in 1926 for the first time to see Amelita Galli-Curci and not in 1934 to see Elana Bernardi (a fictional character) as in this story. They met her and her husband, Homer, and were treated like royalty by the couple. It is true that their first trip abroad was to America.

They took three weeks holiday and three weeks unpaid leave. Ida became a very successful novelist, writing for Mills & Boon under the name Mary Burchell. She contributed so much to the world of romance, also helping to found and become president of the Romantic Novelists Association, thus helping authors like me.

The characters of Sarah and her family are not based on real people as such. But having read Ida's autobiography, *Safe Passage* (originally published in 1950 as *We Followed Our Stars*), I was inspired by the stories of the people they saved.

The story of the boy Pieter in my book is based on real life although it reads like fiction. A young boy did manage to get a letter to Ida and Louise, although nobody knows how he found out their address.

The story of the children surviving in the house in Frankfurt is also based on a true story. That house did remain unscathed despite the intensive bombing of that city.

Other books have been written about these incredible women but I wanted to tell a story as, I believe, by fictionalizing events you reach a wider audience. And in my mind, the more people who know about these sisters and other heroes like Frank Foley, Robert Smallbones and the like, the better. Especially now, when the world is in turmoil, we need to hear how those who went before sought to shine a light in the darkness.

The romance in my story is fictional. Both sisters remained life-long spinsters. Their parents were alive during the war, supportive of their efforts and they had brothers who served with the forces.

The Cooks were interviewed on *This Is Your Life* by Eamonn Andrews in the UK in 1956. Just like in my story, they assumed they were being interviewed due to Ida's writing but it was their heroic behaviour that warranted the program. They didn't appear on US television, as far as I'm aware.

Clemens Krauss did liaise with Hitler and was promoted

when other conductors were removed either due to being Jewish or for protesting about decisions made by the regime. There are also rumours he tried to join the Nazi party. But whatever the truth of that, he never supported Hitler's racial policies. He did use his position to protect Jewish people, and was instrumental in helping many survive, not least those he introduced to the Cook sisters. There was sufficient proof of these actions after the war for Krauss to satisfy the Allies he was not a Nazi.

Most people have heard of Nicholas Winton in relation to the *Kindertransport* trains. Mrs Wijsmuller-Meijer is well known in Holland for her work in saving the lives of the most vulnerable. She did meet Eichmann in Vienna in December 1938. He was in charge of emigration and she persuaded him to allow her to take 600 children to safety. He is purported to have told people she was crazy, setting her up to fail by giving her a couple of days to arrange everything. Yet she managed it. The journey took over thirty hours. Of the children, 500 went to Britain with 100 staying in Holland. Mrs Wijsmuller continued organizing trains until war broke out. She kept working to save Jewish and other victims of the Nazis and was arrested by the Gestapo. She was eventually released and went on working during the war to save everyone she could including fifty Jewish children transported to Theresiendstadt (all survived due to her claims they were not Jewish but children of mixed parentage) and Allied soldiers in the hands of the Germans. She died in 1978.

As in the story, Jewish companions were allowed to travel on some of the trains, their role to soothe the children. But they knew their travel was conditional on their returning with the train to Nazi-occupied territory. They all kept their word, despite knowing or at the very least suspecting the fate that lay in shop for them. Mass extermination had yet to start on indus-trial scale but even by as early as 1938, most Jewish people knew life under the Nazis meant, at best, incarceration for an undefined period.

Robert Smallbones is credited with saving about 48,000 lives but I struggled to find more information on him, which is a real shame. The part he plays in this fiction work is based on what information was available.

Tom, although a fictional character, represents many individuals who worked in American embassies and endeavoured to aid those persecuted by the Nazis. Unfortunately, their efforts often resulted in demotion rather than recognition and advancement. During the 1930s, America, Britain and other democratic nations were grappling with the Great Depression. There was a prevalent belief that immigrants would worsen economic conditions, leading to job losses and increased financial strain. Government departments also harboured the misguided notion that Jewish refugees would propagate communism, a belief stemming from the aftermath of the Russian Revolution.

Readers often ask me why I write the books I do. I love history – not a bit obvious, I know, lol. But to read a history book takes a certain amount of fortitude. Or perhaps, as my children say, only nerds read history. By combining historical events with a fictional twist, I hope to interest more people in the past.

To quote Edmund Burke: 'People will not look forward to posterity, who never look backward to their ancestors.'

 x.com/wessonwrites

ACKNOWLEDGEMENTS

I would like to thank you, the reader, who read my books and write such complimentary reviews. You are the reason I do the job I love and for that, I'm beyond grateful. I try to answer every message and comment you make, so please do get in touch. Thank you.

There's a saying that it takes a village to raise a child. Similarly, writing a book is rarely the sole effort of the author. My incredible editor, Vicky Blunden, is a master at transforming my thoughts into a fully realized story. The copy editors and proofreaders at Storm diligently refine my prose, turning what once gave my school English teacher nightmares into polished writing.

To Oliver, thank you for your understanding and kindness and for having me at Storm.

The team at Storm, including the other Storm authors are so supportive and wonderful to work with. I can't be more grateful for their efforts, especially during the last few months which have been tough, for personal reasons.

I'd also like to acknowledge my family. My father who instilled my love of reading – he reads real history books, lol. My two sisters who not only read my books but tell me what parts they loved or not, as the case may be.

I want to give thanks to my husband who keeps me sane and our incredible three children. You are my world.

PS: Gracie, our border collie, just barked to make sure she is included too.